The Machine Lord

To Shelley

Calvin Ball

CJ Hobbes

C.J Hobbes

1

About the Author:

C.J Hobbes has been writing his entire life, and he really enjoys it. He has been filling empty notebooks with hand written stories since the moment he learned how to write. He went to Shelley High School where he wrote a short story and helped publish a book called "The Tale Hunters". Born in 1996, and married in 2016 to his loving wife Miranda, his biggest goal is to simply have people love his writing. He currently lives in Idaho, and he greatly appreciates everyone who reads his stories.

This book is dedicated to:

Ronald Miles

Jessica Harrison

And my best friend Nate Osburn

Special thanks to:

My beautiful wife Miranda for believing in me

My Grandmother Eudora Miles for her time

Dennis and Dorothy Croft

Jonathan and Kara Boll

Dave and Chris Hailey

Chris and Emily King

Kris Kingsolver

Angel Neil

Wynn Johnson

Everyone who believed in me

All my friends and family

All of those who enjoy my writing

1: The Machine Lord

In order to become a lord, you have to meet one of three requirements. You have to have a large estate, a large collective group of loyal servants, or you have to have massive amounts of money. In the city of Wellington, where I live; I have two of those, I have a large Estate, and a decent amount of followers. So I am considered a lord in today's modern society.

My "estate" is an old robotics facility. A massive empty maze of a building full of lifeless machines and rusting robotic parts. Since the facility is hundreds of years old, I am still focusing on repairs in some parts of the building. Some parts of the building don't have a roof. It's old, its walls made of concrete and cinder block. A rusting ten foot chain link fence with spiraling barbed wire along the top wraps all around the parking lot and the property.

It was my castle, my estate. It was too big for one person. Since I lived there alone, I had a lot to do: walls to fix, pests to exterminate, and followers to repair.

I am the only human to live on the estate. The followers I speak of are all machines. Old machines that I had repaired or created in the eight years that I have lived here. I have over seventeen machines around the estate, all repaired or constructed entirely by me. I love working with technology, I love tinkering, and I love the sight of sparks flying from a torch or grinder.

One of my greatest passions was watching a robot come to life. It was like reviving a rusty old skeleton from the grave, and years have gone by so I'm getting better and better at it. I get a rush from watching a robot's eyes light up, because of the hard work I did reconnecting the optical sensors to a working power core.

It rained a lot here, and was usually cold. It never snowed, and every once in while we would get warm sunny days. According to the old maps I found while digging around, I was in what used to be part of Oregon or Washington, I wasn't sure.

It was fun to learn about the past, when everyone had access to water and electricity. When The United States was a flourishing economy, when the culture was entirely different, before mankind was nearly annihilated and forced to start over with whatever they could. All anyone knew was that mankind's downfall had to do with something called the Darkness.

Nobody can quite remember what the Darkness was, a disease, an army, or maybe a nuclear war. . . It's all just rumors. I hope someday while I'm learning about the old world I'll stumble across some clues as to what the darkness was. Either way it doesn't sound very fun. It destroyed everything, forcing mankind to start over, repairing old buildings and banding together to survive.

They went from tribes, to villages, and now there are towns, organized territories and even militaries across the New United States. I am in the Western Territory, alone on my estate with my machines though that is the way I like it. I live fifteen minutes away from Wellington, a descent town ruled by five lords.

There was Jazz Wellington, a greedy and selfish man that I was glad I never met. He was Lord of the biggest domain in Wellington. The second biggest domain belonged to Lord Ella Lovewind, who was a sweet older woman who ruled her domain with her husband. Third was Alysha Collinder who I didn't know much about, and after that was Lord Nathan Osburn who was my distant friend that visited every couple months to check on me.

5

Technically I was the fifth Lord in the town, but I rejected everything that came my way. I liked isolation, but inside me felt empty. Isolation was beginning to sound less and less appealing, but I did not know how to undo my past rejections. I was beginning to want connection with other people, and I was trying to muster the courage to go to town. Though the thought of all the crowds of a city sounded terrifying, I still felt like I wanted human companionship every once in a while.

It was a Monday morning, and I was repairing a section of the robotics shop roof. We were laying out rusting steel trusses across cracked concrete covered in moss and dirt, and locking the heavy beams in place with mixed concrete. I was working hard in the morning sun with three of my laboring machines, two of which were old service drones I had repaired from the estate.

The third, Buster was a slow calculating and absolutely massive robot designed for heavy lifting and slow labor. He held the trusses in place down below extending his metal arms upward, while 6 and 7, two of my service or labor drones helped me meld it into place. We were patching holes to keep the constant rain from dripping into this part of the facility.

They could talk, but their vocabulary was very limited to the words they had learned from me, the socially awkward guy who lived with a bunch of robots. I ran away when I was twelve, tired of my parents and their constant bickering, choosing a life of isolated back breaking physical work instead.

Mandy, my pride and joy. One of my favorite and most sophisticated creations was an old customized maid unit with maroon plastic casings over sanded down metal. I worked hard on that specific unit, and was well rewarded with a nearly human machine capable of understanding emotions and humor. I had spent several months building on an old frame before she finally came to life.

6

"Zander, my Lord," she said with her robotic voice. I was still unable to perfect their voice box recalibrations yet, "I have two messages for you, sir," she nodded crawling onto the tall roof from the old rickety metal ladder. I turned unable to see her for a moment because my long hair was thrashing in the wind. My body was sore from moving the heavy metal beams around.

"What is it Mandy?" I asked wiping sweat from my brow and I leaned back from my work. I moved my long hair out of my face so I could see her clearly. She had two soft glowing white eyes and the motor in her neck made it always sound like she was humming.

"Lord Osburn is here to see you my lord," she did a little curtsey, "Also the weather equipment has stated that it is going to rain soon. You should return to working inside to avoid getting cold and sick."

I wiped concrete off my hands with a slightly irritated groan, "Dang, I thought I would have more time to work this morning."

"Six, seven," I turned to them across the roof, "continue working please. Mandy please collect the robots that are not waterproof and get them inside. I want them cleaning up the old great big assembly line room."

"Will do, sir," she nodded, "Shall I invite Lord Osburn into the lobby?"

"No," I shook my head and slid across the concrete roof to the ladder, "I'll go talk to him through the fence gate. As I usually do to any visitors."

I stepped down the old metal ladder, and I headed through the clean uncut grass into the front yard of the estate. It took me almost a year to clean up around the front. Piles of old cars and robots everywhere, some of them rusted together. Now they all lay in the scrap yard in the back, and the front was carefully maintained by Mandy as she planted flowers, raked and mowed the lawn.

Lord Nathan Osburn was a tall muscular man with a gentle approach and a soft hearted demeanor. He wore a pair of thick glasses that fogged up when it was raining heavily and he was the only Lord I got along with. The others made fun of me for what little I had, but not Nathan. He always came with information, and insisted that he would get me to talk to other people like any friend would.

"Hey sexy beast, what is your intention?" I bowed with a smile and a wink. We usually called each other that in a playful manner. It started the first day he approached my estate, and called himself sexy in comparing himself to my robots which made me laugh. He was good at making me laugh.

He bowed in return with a smile, "You know it. How are you, Zander?"

Lord Osburn's horse drawn carriage was a fine looking well-built carriage with powerful healthy looking horses. The carriage's shocks were solid, metal, and up to date. It was hard to find working cars or motors in today's society.

"I'm okay," I nodded, "What brings you to my neck of the woods?" I asked curiously and began to unlock the gate to let him in cautiously.

"Well, actually a couple reasons," He sighed, "Things are really stirring up. There's a lot of rumors going around the town. Some of them about you."

"Really?" I asked curiously as I swung the gate open, "Come in."

"I haven't seen you in six months," he shook his head and stepped through the gate. His servants stayed behind with his carriage, "I have so many things to talk to you about Zander, and first of all, tomorrow is market day. I strongly encourage you to come to buy or sell. Come meet people, Zander. You never know what good can come from making friends with humans."

I laughed and said nothing as we followed the cracked cement path to the lobby doors which were technically my front doors to my living room. Nathan followed and looked distressed, "I'm serious, Zander, I will even come pick you up tomorrow morning. You and I are alike, bullied by the other lords because they have more power than us. If we stick together we can stand up to them. Surely you have something around here you could sell off, that would be worth money to someone else."

"I'm sure I would, Nathan," I thought for a moment before I continued talking, "But that's a lot of people. There would be so much noise, so many people bickering and fighting in one area, I would not be able to hear myself think."

"I understand you do not like crowds," he changed his tone to tease me flippantly, "or other human beings for that matter. I'm amazed you let me into your estate today, let alone talk to me. Some of the town folk think you're a cyborg, or a robot, in fact some of the people in town absolutely think you are simply a frightening legend. You've become a ghost story the children tell each other, "The robot man on the hill"," he laughed, "Seriously have you trapped and murdered any small groups of children lately?" He laughed and gave a playful shrug.

I shook my head, "No, of course not, I'm an introvert not a monster."

"Well there you go, case solved," he nodded as we approached the front entrance to my estate, and I swung open the old wooden doors and held it open for him to come in.

9

"Do you ever get lonely out here?" Nathan asked, "Do you ever wish you had companionship? A sweet heart maybe, a wife. You know, it's an honor to be the wife of a lord. You could easily obtain a beautiful wife."

"Obtain is a cold word," I said flatly, "Maybe I wish to fall in love."

"Then keep being isolated in this old building. The robots will slowly grow more attractive," he winked and I smiled, "I get it, Nathan."

"Please," he raised a hand, "call me Nate. We're friends."

"So what other news do you have for me?" I asked. I motioned for him to sit down and we both seated ourselves facing each other in my bare wooden chairs. He wore a comfortable dark hand stitched suit and a metal necklace hung around his neck that dangled when he leaned forward to talk.

"The townsfolk found a book in a rusting old safe. It was a handwritten soldier's journal, back from when the war against the darkness was happening. It is a detailed description of what the darkness is. Little did we know, there was actually a safe zone here where our town used to be, and it was overrun by the Darkness. The soldier was a guard here, and he explains everything very well, the battle, what he saw and what he heard," Nate said, "It's terrifying. We found out we did not win the war against the Darkness. We lost, which means the darkness is still here in the world. I guess according to the soldier's journal it's an army of demons."

A chill ran down my spine, and I shivered as I spoke, "Really? An army of demons?"

"Yeah, sounds ridiculous," Nate sighed, "But I guess I just it's another rumor to add to the mess."

"Well, is that what you came to tell me?" I asked thoughtfully.

"I thought you would want to know about that," he shrugged, "Anyway, I will be back here with my army and I will drag you to market day tomorrow if I have to... speaking of army do you have any military force, Zander? What if another Lord were to attack you. Lord Wellington is getting pretty greedy. I've heard word he plans on attacking two other lords. There's only five lords around here, and you are one of them."

"I never asked to be a lord," I said plainly, "I fixed a building to live in, and I built some robots. I deserve no title."

"Neither did I, but you have the biggest estate out of all of us. Your house is the biggest, and Lord Wellington is really wanting what you have," Nate motioned to the estate behind me, "He's been gathering up weapons, old assault rifles, forging swords and armor... I believe you should come with me tomorrow, to build a reputation, and gather resources in case he attacks you. I could lend men to your aid, but then I would be open for attack myself. Either way, I want to show the town you exist. I want to show them that you are not a monster or a robot. I beg of you Zander come to the market day tomorrow, and I swear that I will never ask a thing of you again."

My eyes narrowed. He *really* wanted me to go to this stupid Market Day. I had never seen him beg like this before.

"If you mention you have electricity, I bet the whole town would switch lords, and come build houses around yours. If that happened you'd control the whole town with your electricity. Not even Wellington has electricity," Nate took a deep breath, "but it is a double edged sword. If everyone finds out, they may try to take it by force."

Lord Osburn cleared his throat and smiled at me, "Either way, you need to interact with other people more. You really do, even just accepting a human butler or maid to your estate. A real flesh and blood person to boss around that is not a robot."

2: The Machine Lord's Allies

"Come with me this evening," Nate leaned forward, "Stay on my estate. I have great cooks, and I will treat you as an honored guest. We could play some old faded board and card games. We could even make up the rules as we go along, because the cards are so old and faded we can't read them! We just have to bend the rules so I win every time, of course," He winked and we both laughed.

He then grew serious for a moment, "Pack your bags. Come with me this evening, and I'll bring you back once the festival has ended."

"You are serious?" I cocked an eyebrow.

Mandy entered the room, "I have gathered the other machines. They are doing as you said Zander. Hello, Lord Osburn," She turned to him and bowed.

"How are you Mandy?" Nate asked and did a half hearted bow.

"I am great," she nodded, her voice smiling, "Thank you for asking! No one ever cares about the robot!"

I turned to Mandy with a confused look and she corrected herself, "Except my lord, Zander, of course."

Lately I had been craving human company, so I shrugged with a why the heck not attitude, "I guess I could use the break. A little vacation. Mandy, pack me a bag please and prepare to leave. We are going to stay at Nate's estate this evening. Then we'll go to market day tomorrow."

"Excellent!" Nate rose up quickly and shouted motioning his hands to me, "I will make this worth it for you! I will, my friend!"

I shrugged, "There's going to be a lot of people, I doubt you could do that."

"Just you watch," his eyes narrowed intensely, "This could benefit us both."

An hour later, Mandy and I were riding in Nathan's carriage. The ride was incredibly smooth down the gravel roads towards the city. Mandy was more interested than myself as Nate talked about the Lord's from other towns coming to trade here in our "little town" of Wellington. It was founded by Lord Wellington's grandfather years ago.

The city of Wellington has been steadily growing as people move in, and as people have children over the years. It was a big growing town now, even though we jokingly called it a small town. We had quite a flourishing comfortable city, home to thousands of people.

The Lords were like the local government, helping the people in their domain in return for a tax, or a trading system. I was only considered a lord, because Lord Osburn had told many people throughout the city that I had a big estate and working robots.

There was lots of poor happy people, and as we entered Osburn's domain they all waved at the carriage from the side of the road, and Lord Osburn waved back smiling. There were so many houses, some freshly built, and some repaired from years ago. There was so many colors, smells, and so many people it was making me uncomfortable even though I was safely hiding in a comfortably cushioned carriage.

Nate had a tall stone wall around his estate, and two guards in hand forged armor with assault rifles in their hands standing at the gates. As we arrived the two guards opened the heavy metal gate for the carriage to enter onto the gravel driveway to his home.

His estate was a large two story well decorated home. I got excited like a child when I discovered he had a room with a fish pond full of colorful fish.

He had multiple maids and servants who happily and efficiently collected our things at the doors. I guess they were going to set up a room for me and took my heavy bag. With years of hard work I had built up quite a bit of strength and it was amusing to watch two grown men in suits work together to drag my luggage up the spiral staircase.

Some of them were young, some of them were old, but they all were as equally relaxed and happy. They behaved like they truly enjoyed getting bossed around by Osburn and it amused me. They almost seemed like robots themselves even though they had hearts instead of processors.

They all called me Lord Zander or honored guest, and did whatever I asked them just like my robots. I was not very demanding I simply asked for a glass of clean water and started small talk. They were loyal servants, and when I asked them, "Why do you serve like this?" They all responded with the same thing, "Because Lord Osburn takes good care of me."

Mandy never left my side, and she loyally obeyed as they did.

They were so sweet and loyal, and I began to grow jealous of my friend Nathan. Secretly I began to want a human maid. I wanted that human presence in my life like I once had, but I had no idea how or who to approach if I wanted a maid.

He set his cooks to work and gathered his servants to play a game of volleyball in his backyard. Which was a well-groomed series of fresh thick lawns and flower gardens, and he forced Mandy and I to play. I'm not going to lie, I was having a lot of fun, not to mention that my incredibly accurate robot gave me a massive defensive advantage. I had not laughed that much in a long time, roughing up my elbows and knees diving to hit the old volleyball in the soft grass.

They all stared in amazement at Mandy, and I could tell Nathan began to want a robot as she began to help with evening chores, quickly, accurately, and steadily. She made the other servants look bad, but none of them took it to heart. Some laughed and tried to challenge her at cleaning or dishes. They tried to see who could wash more in a shorter amount of time.

Nate and I grew closer that night. A true friendship blossomed, and I knew he had baited me. He wanted to influence me to socialize more. This small amount was fine, but the fact that there would be thousands of people the next day terrified me. There was a delicious meal of roasted chicken and mashed potatoes with thick chicken gravy. It was the best meal I had ever had. I will admit that Mandy was a terrible cook because she could not taste, and there was no cook books left in the world. Though more were being created as recipes surfaced.

I went to bed that night with a happy heart and a full stomach, but with unnerved terror for the next day. I hated crowds, all the loud noise, and the bickering and shouting.

The next morning one of Nate's pretty maids gently woke me by opening the bedroom window, "Good morning, Lord Zander. My Lord asked me to inform you that you need to get ready to go. He also had me make you some new clothes, so you 'don't look like a homeless man anymore'." She set the clothes on the foot of the bed as I lazily sat up. She was a young pretty girl with small focused blue eyes and red hair.

"Where is Mandy?" I asked as I sat stretching on the comfortable mattress not wanting to get out of the bed.

"My lord has asked her to help with preparing the carriage by loading the goods he is bringing to sell at market day," she bowed, "I apologize, my lord did not think you would be upset if he asked her help."

I shrugged, "No it's fine. I'm just making sure she's okay."

"Of course she is. My lord has great security," she smiled, "Anyway, My lord is leaving soon. He expects you to join him before he leaves. Shall I prepare breakfast for you? We are celebrating market day by having cereal this morning."

"Wow, cereal," I blinked, "I've heard cereal is fantastic, but hard to make."

"It's true," She smiled, "you have to make the dough, cut it out by hand, and carefully bake it at high temperatures for short periods of time."

"Yes my lord, and the faster you get to the table, the more cereal you can have before you guys go," the red haired woman smiled, "Please take care now."

She handed me a hairbrush, and headed out of the room. I eagerly headed for the dining room to try cereal. It was a good combination, fresh milk from a cow, and baked corn based sugary squares. It was delicious, and they refilled my bowl four times for me. The cooks always responded with smiles and kind demeanors as they refilled my bowl for me.

Then I headed for the carriage in the hand stitched pants and the shirt. The leather jacket was a comfortable new luxury as well. They were comfortable clothes, and I nearly looked like a new person in the jeans and the black shirt. Especially since I had been wearing the same rags for eight years.

"I feel very pampered my friend," I smiled at him as I approached the carriage hinting to the comfortable clothes, and Mandy waved after loading a box, "Good morning, Zander!"

"That's what I'm aiming for," he clapped his hands together victoriously with a facetious smile, "So I was thinking Zander," he motioned for me to enter the carriage. Mandy helped me in before she climbed in and sat beside me loyally.

He quickly scratched his chin, "oh wait, first of all, how did you sleep?"

"I have not slept that great in years," I nodded honestly. I seriously could not remember when I was this comfortable or happy. I wanted to stay there forever in pampered comfort.

"That is fantastic. Do you think we could talk *business* for a moment friend?" He asked as the carriage doors closed, and the carriage began to move. He crossed his leg over his knee leaning back in a different nice suit looking like he was thinking pretty hard, "Those clothes look a lot nicer bro, those rags you had before were ugly, and they smelled awful too..."

"What do you mean business?" I asked in suspicious thought raising an eyebrow.

"Like I said I have been thinking," he said, "Don't get me wrong, you have every right to reject my proposal and I will still always be your friend, but you see. I'm quite jealous of your electricity."

I smiled, "Oh you are?"

"Yes, and if I do all the labor, throw up some power lines running from my domain to yours, would you be willing to share it with my people and I?" He asked, "Of course I can offer you something in return, I just don't know what you want."

"Your friendship and alliance as a lord is all I could ask for in return. Could you stop by more frequently with some of that delicious food?" I asked with a smile, "However I should remind you that if I extend power to your domain, every domain will want power. I should prepare by designing a bigger self-sustaining turbine that could fuel the whole city, which may take me some time."

"I understand," he nodded, "It is your power, you may do with it as you wish of course, I only ask that you bless your friend with such a luxury. I planned on stopping by more frequently anyway regardless of if you gave me power or not. If you want, I could help you get a cook of your own. They would just have to live with you."

I looked down in serious silence and after a moment I looked at him, "I would like that a lot actually."

"Well I would *really* like electricity. By the way I have not told a soul in this city that you have it. Wellingtons been trying to get electricity, but he's not getting very far, and you just whipped together a- what did you call it, A "self-sustaining turbine" with your bare hands?" He asked, "You truly are a gifted man. There is not another electricity source until Vegas."

"I will help you with the power lines and help provide power to your domain. In return I expect help from you and your men if I am ever attacked. Also, I expect your help in obtaining a cook for my estate," I extended a hand to shake.

"That's like trading a tire for thousand racecars but you have a deal," he shrugged and shook my hand. "A cook for electricity. Seems more than fair to me, as your friend I have to insist. You must want something more than that in return, Zander."

I thought for a moment, "When word gets out that I have electricity. Will you help me protect it? How bad can Wellington really be?"

Nate laughed and mumbled under his breath, "How bad can he be?"

He turned to me, "His great grandfather founded the city, and he has the biggest domain. He thinks the city is rightfully his. Hopefully we don't bump into him. As for your second demand, protection, of course. We are already allies, if you want something, just ask."

Market Day was an entire open field full of booths where people were selling and buying, and just as I thought in horrid terror, there was people everywhere. There was so much noise it was already giving me a headache as the carriage came to a stop, and two of Nate's guards opened the carriage doors for us to exit.

Nate exited, followed by Mandy, who pulled me out by my sleeve and we stood there in the grass overlooking the massive market around us.

"So what do you think?" Nate asked admiring it all.

I just groaned and lowered my head, "that's a lot of people."

"Yes, exactly," he winked, "In that mess is your cook, or even more servants if you wanted."

"Fine then," I growled, "However I will be following you."

"Lord Osburn!" A masculine voice shouted and approached us and we turned to see a handsome man in a hand tailored violet suit, with a beautiful woman on each arm wearing very revealing low cut dresses.

"Wellington," Nate turned, "I see you came to the Market Day festival as well."

"Of course," He grinned with a laugh and he looked over at my robot and looked surprised and shocked, "A working robot! Where did you obtain that! Did you get it here?"

"No," Nate shook his head and motioned to me, "This is Lord Zander. Mandy is his personal servant and maid in his estate."

"Fantastic," he grinned and pulled an arm free and extended it to shake my hand, "Jazz Wellington. Lord of the Wellington Domain."

I shook his hand, "Zander."

He raised an eyebrow, "Are you not the Lord of a domain?"

"Not by choice," I shrugged.

"Say, do you have any of those fantastic machines for sale?" He asked, "I would love one!"

"I could probably build you one," I shrugged, "but I hate crowds, so come talk to me later when I can concentrate."

"Eh, I don't blame you," he shrugged, "It's quite crowded in my city today. Very well, I will stop by after the fair with my spoils and maybe we can work out a trade."

"Sure," I shrugged.

"So Lord Osburn," he turned to my friend, "what is your intention on this fine day?"

"I am trying to get Zander here to meet more people, so the children in town will quit turning him into a scary story," Nate laughed, "Kids say the funniest things."

"Indeed they do!" Wellington gave a brief fake smile and a fake laugh, "Well I am going back to browsing! Do have a great day!"

I shivered, "Well I'm not having very much fun. Come Mandy let's head for the estate."

"I insist, Zander. Don't you wish to pick out a chef?" Nate quickly stepped in my way with troubled look in his eyes, "It would take you an entire day to walk to your estate!"

I sighed, and Mandy turned to the crowd, "I believe this would be good for you, Zander."

"Come on," Nate grumbled, "Let's go. We won't stay very long then. We'll just introduce you around for a little bit. Then we'll get you a cook and get you out of here."

Then I suddenly caught sight of her, a lone walking girl a couple years older than me with long braided blond hair and beautiful brown eyes, walking with an umbrella in her hand. She was wearing an expensive looking black and Red Dress, a neat white bow tied in her blond hair.

She had to be one of the prettiest women I had ever seen. She made my knees tremble as she walked through the rows of booths curiously looking left and right with big brown eyes.

For a moment the crowds disappeared and all I could see was her. So on an awkward impulse I pushed passed Nate who looked after me in confusion as I weaseled through the crowd, "Zander? Where are you going?"

"Zander?" Mandy followed me as I headed towards the woman on an intercepting course.

I gently stepped in front of her and I swallowed. She was forced to stop and look at me, "Umm can I help you?"

I didn't know what to say. No words were coming out and she just gave me a pathetic look like I was a waste of time and headed to move around me.

Mandy caught up to me, "Wait, ma'am. I'm sorry it took me so long to get here. My name is Mandy, and this is my lord, Zander, the Machine Lord." She was clearly trying to repair the awkward situation I had put myself in.

"Wow! A Robot!" she looked surprised, "I did not think there was electricity this far out West."

"My power core is self-sustaining. My master merely repaired me. Isn't that so?" Mandy nudged me, "Now that I have introduced you, you may speak my lord."

I swallowed and almost flushed. She was so pretty and I just spoke, "Actually I built her... with the core, I found the core."

She smiled, "Well that's interesting." She gave a little curtsey, "It's an honor to meet you my Lord, and if it's all the same to you I'll be on my way."

"My name is Zander," I spat out, "I am the machine lord."

She smirked, "I get that. Your robot told me, though I will admit I have not heard that title before. I apologize, if you are trying to impress me your reputation betrays you."

"Where are you from miss?" Mandy asked, "Sorry, he does not socialize very much."

"I can tell," she looked impatient, "I moved here from Vegas, It was getting too crowded for me. I wanted a change of scenery so I have moved into Wellington's domain. Now, if this interrogation is through, I really should be on my way." She gave a curtsey and headed around us and I followed her with my eyes as I turned around in a dreamy haze.

"Your behavior is off," Mandy smacked me on the back of my head, "What is your deal?"

"Wasn't she pretty?" I asked Mandy with a grin.

Nate approached from behind, "Well you just kind of dove right into the crowd. Did you see something you liked?"

I froze realizing I was surrounded by thousands of people everywhere.

"Well if you were attempting to flirt you did a great job looking like you were crazy," Mandy said sarcastically, "Seriously my lord. What were you planning to do?"

Her big brown beautiful eyes flashed before my eyes. "I don't know." I lowered my head and felt inadequate from my lack of social ability and the fear of the people around me.

Many people oohed and awed at Mandy as we patrolled the fair trying to get through the crowds, until Nate led us to a booth with hanging pots and pans. Sitting in the booth was a thick built man with greasy black hair displaying a fancy knife set.

"Are you selling kitchen supplies?" Nathan asked the man curiously, "Or are you selling your skills as a chef."

"I represent an organization of great chefs, you see we have a system. We only send one chef per booth. I get your information here, then for ten thousand cents, when I get back to our elite culinary academy we send an elite chef straight to your door on a one year contract. We only serve Lords, however I can tell you are one because of your working robot, those are awfully rare."

"How about it? Ten thousand cents for a top of the line gourmet chef, straight out of the culinary academy?" He rose to his feet and was sharpening one of the displayed knives as he spoke and gave Nathan an intent look.

Nate looked to me, "Is that okay with you? There is your new chef you wanted."

"Sure," I said quickly, mostly wanting to just leave.

"Well, then one chef to the Zander estate here in Wellington," Nate dug in his neatly trimmed jacket and pulled out a bag and counted out rolls of shiny quarters to the man who nodded with gratitude, "Your new chef should arrive to the Zander estate by the end of the week."

"Great," Nate shook the hairy man's hand, "thank you!"

"I cannot believe I made such a fool of myself in front of that girl," I groaned as we walked away from the stand that made sounds like wind chimes from the dangling kitchen utensils and the odd man in the white chef's uniform that was stained.

"I can," Mandy shrugged, "I watched it happen."

"Do you think she is single?" I asked as I followed Nate through the people like a child hiding behind their parent.

"More than likely if she was walking alone," Mandy nodded obviously.

Nate turned to me with a grumpy sigh, "I'm not seeing anyone else important. Come on Zander I'll take you on home and I'll return afterwards. I'd hate to see you embarrass yourself in front of more pretty women."

"That's probably best," Mandy agreed and I shot them both a dirty look, "Get me out of here."

We switched directions heading towards Nate's carriage and moved slowly through the crowd for what felt like fifteen minutes. Suddenly as we walked Mandy nudged me, "Hey look, you feel like making the situation worse?" She motioned to the blonde woman smiling and talking to a booth owner who was selling fancy dresses.

I knew she was teasing me, but I stopped in the middle of the crowd watching her from a distance. I wanted to talk to her, I just didn't know what to say.

"I wasn't serious," Mandy gently blocked my sight, "Don't you think you've harassed her enough?"

I moved through the crowd without thinking and she looked away to roll her eyes as she noticed me approach, "Well if it isn't Zander, Lord of Machines and his faithful robot."

"I apologize for earlier," I choked out and then I cringed, "I just think you are really quite beautiful."

"Sorry, Zander," she said harshly, "but I'm into men with bravery and guts. Men willing to fight for a lady. Not men who walk up and make their robot do the talking. You must have grown a little bit of a spine for the apology, but I'm guessing a guy like you honestly doesn't know how to even swing a sword. You're not my type. Go back to fixing robots, my lord."

Nate put a hand on my shoulder, "Ouch."

"It's true. I am not very aggressive, and I spent most of my life learning how to make robots and not how to wield a sword or rifle like everyone else, but I assure you I can learn," I said quickly, "Why are you so quick to reject me?"

26

She blew her bangs out her eyes in disbelief, "You probably could not even beat me in a sword fight."

"So then come to my estate in a couple my days," I said my eyes narrowing, "If I win you have to tell me about yourself, especially your name. Deal?"

"Sure, Lord of Machines," she stood up straight from leaning against the booth counter with a humored smile.

"Prove to me you're a real man, and I'll maybe tell you my name," She smiled, "I'm going to enjoy beating you. You bet I'll come."

She walked away waving behind her, "See you then."

Nate laughed at me, "Really Zander?"

"She's a girl, how hard could it be to beat her?" I asked as we began walking through the crowd. As usual there was quite a few eyes on Mandy, and it made me exponentially more uncomfortable.

"Something feels off," Mandy said and gazed at me, "She seems very confident in her abilities."

"We'll see," I said as we began walking towards the carriages. Nate's carriage was a sight for sore eyes, and the moment it was visible I power walked straight to it and climbed in to escape the crowds.

Mandy easily kept up and climbed in beside me, but Nate was caught by a sandy blonde haired woman in a luxurious dress who laughed and began talking to him."

"Will you help me practice?" I asked Mandy, "I'll make some wooden swords when we get back."

"I doubt I have a say in the matter," she gazed at me with her soft glowing white eyes, "So I guess I'll give you the satisfaction of saying, *sure*."

"Thank you," I nodded with a humored smile, "You're a good friend."

"It's almost like I'm programmed that way," she flashed her right eye to replicate a wink.

"Even if you are a bunch of wires, you are still a good friend," I shrugged, "You are capable of making decisions."

Nate finally returned to the carriage a couple minutes later after his guards had loaded back up and we took off through the city back towards my estate.

"Who was that?" I asked him curiously, "Who was that who stopped you?"

He glanced at me, "That was Lord Alysha Collinder."

"I'll drop you off and head back to sell my goods," Nate shrugged, "It sounds like you need to swing a sword around a little."

I looked down at my callused hands, "I guess."

"So my lord," Mandy asked, "What are you trying to play at here? Are you interested in making her your wife?"

The thought of a woman that beautiful as my wife made me smile and close my eyes for a moment.

I could see myself waking up to her with a smile, breakfast in her hands, I could imagine her standing in an evening gown with her hair in a ponytail, "Good morning my love..."

"Well, if that's the fish you are trying to catch," Nate said with a smug grin, "apparently you're going to need to hone your

28

net skills. She looked pretty happy about beating you up with a sword," Nate laughed.

"Seriously though," Nate suddenly cleared his throat growing serious, "I shall start making preparations, putting up power lines, we'll run the lines through my district and then hide them by running them through the trees to your domain. That way we can keep my power source a secret for as long as possible. To attempt to avoid people coming to pester you. If word gets out every town in a three hundred mile radius will want your power."

I swallowed, "I see, then we shall try to keep this operation as low profile as possible." It was nice to think about something besides that woman for once as I scratched my chin. How was I going to design a reactor to put out that much voltage?

"Well," Nate said as we entered the edge of my domain which was nothing but forest at the Northern edge of town, "I had my servants prepare your bag ahead of time in case you wanted to go home early. It's here in the carriage, so don't stress about it. I hope you know I meant well today, by bringing you to Market Festival."

"I know Nate," I nodded, "I truly had a lovely evening last night though, that was great, I am jealous of your fantastic caretakers."

He smiled, "I don't know what I did to deserve them. However I can tell you I would march my army to rescue any of them in a heartbeat. They mean a lot to me, so I try to show them that."

"I see," I looked at Nate and I asked him, "How do I show my new cook I appreciate him or her?"

"You are a genius, you'll figure it out," He shrugged, "Also I wish to discuss your lack of military power. Seriously, at least gain some guards Zander, at least have the ability to protect your estate in case it is attacked. I don't care if it's more robots, just make sure you can protect yourself from Wellington's greed. I know he's had sights on your place for a while. He could roll up with an army and slaughter you when he comes later today."

"I forgot I invited him," I growled and looked at the carriage floor, "I hope he does not."

"I highly suggest you get some protective military power around the old fort. Put up some spikes or something," Nate gave me a playful slug in the shoulder, "Seriously. If I wanted to, I could walk in and take everything from you myself, but I prefer peace and friendship over pointless slaughter."

My chain link fence came into view along the roadside as the carriage rolled along, the horse's' hooves making clicking and crunching sounds in the gravel as they pulled the carriage.

"I thank you for everything," I said honestly to Nate, "I look forward to a future of delicious meals."

"Of course!" Nate grinned as the carriage came to a halt at the gate, "I would be interested in a robot of my own as well. Perhaps we could leave those negotiations for a different day."

"Okay," I shrugged, "I'm getting pretty good at it. I'm no expert…"

"You built Mandy. My brain hurts wondering how she works, I would call you an expert you modest guy. I like that about you. Honest, modest, and caring. In some ways I don't feel you deserve that rude woman from before."

"She wasn't rude," I argued, "She was upset that I delayed her with my awkward attempt at communication, I understand that."

"Well," Nate shrugged as his guards opened the doors, "I will see you in a couple days more than likely."

"Okay," I nodded as Mandy and I stepped out of the carriage. It felt good to be home.

I took up my bag as one of the guards dragged it to me, and he blinked in disbelief as I picked it up with one hand, "Thank you."

3: The Machine Lord's Enemies

Nate scratched his head in his neat uniform and shook his head without saying a word, and climbed onto the carriage as the other guard closed up the doors and joined him. Then they were off, the horses pulling the carriage away leaving me standing at the estate watching them ride away in a cloud of dust.

"It sounds like we have a lot to do," Mandy shrugged enthusiastically standing beside me.

"Yes, I feel I should trust him on the whole guard thing. Let's start a new project," I produced my keys to unlock the gate. I let us both in and closed and locked the gate behind us.

"I want you have Buster Search the Scrapyard for four damaged but mostly intact machines. We'll begin the construction of Nathan's new machine, as well as a prototype for a guard droid that can be easily adapted to the different kinds of robot bodies lying around the compound," I said, "That way the service drones can replicate the process to create more functioning droids. I shall call them soldier droids," I said in thought looking over the estate.

"Certainly," Mandy nodded, "I'll get right on it. Is there anything else? Shall I get one for this Wellington person as well?"

"Of course," I said, "I better try and keep friendly relations with him I suppose."

She walked away with a nod, "Very well, sir." Her plastic was shiny unlike the other machines I had created or repaired. I had worked the hardest on her, but I had an idea on how I did it. So my next creations were going to be easier since I had almost mastered the hardest concepts of all of this Robotic engineering. I might have to go back to the old robotics books I found in a safe for a quick reference once in a while, but beyond that I could probably make another Mandy.

I headed to the old robot production room on my estate. It was the biggest room in the entire facility, and took up more than two-thirds of the whole building. The walls of this room were dull, bleak and dirty because I had never put too much thought into cleaning it up. I had mostly picked through it for parts in my eight years here.

My robots were obediently sifting and sorting through the ancient contents of the room around me which were old rusting robot torsos and parts. The robots were even pulling apart the old assembly robots and conveyer belts that ran through the room. Those old robots once spun with life assembling the countless service drones that were sold here, as well as used in the facility.

The scattered service drones were hauling most of the old rusting contents out of the massive room, picking it up and hauling it out the back end of the building to the scrap yard that was the entire rear of my estate. Tucked hidden behind the massive building was a graveyard of robotic bodies and rusting parts where I could find multiple of whatever I needed at the moment if I dug deep enough.

"What are you thinking?" Mandy approached me from behind a moment later.

"This is the room where I will build the new reactor. It will fill this whole room," I said in anticipation, "That way it's indoors and protected from the weather. This room has one of the sturdiest roof structures, right?"

"Yes, sir, disregarding the ceilings you have repaired," Mandy noted.

"Mandy," I glanced around room with a melancholy sigh, my mind spinning in quiet wishful thinking.

"What is wrong my Lord?" her sweet electrical voice sounded honestly concerned.

I looked at the creeping mold, the layers of dirt on the floor, and the musty old machine skeletons wishing I had taken time to clean this room before now, "It's always cold here, and everything is so dirty... do you remember how clean Nate's Estate was? How cozy his was? Look at mine, dull boring, dirty... it reminds me of ruins more than an estate."

"Nonetheless it is yours, Sir," she shrugged, "Perhaps we could create some maid bots that have the sole purpose of cleaning up the estate and repairing it. Or perhaps you could recruit some servants by offering them housing and electricity. The old locker rooms and offices would make fantastic living quarters with a little adjustment."

"This building is too much work," I sighed, "Maybe it's too big."

"You just need more help sir," Mandy shrugged, "That's all. This old building has always been our home, we can make it better."

I tried to distract myself by pacing around the room and drawing out ideas in my mind. Mandy left my side to resume her daily duties as she always did. Soon I had motivated myself enough to head to my workshop.

When I arrived in the big dusty room, Buster had placed five well-chosen rusting robots in my workshop. He was too big to enter the building, so we built a sliding door into the wall for him a couple years ago. That way he could retrieve things from the scrap yard for me.

Buster was the easiest to fix out of all of my robots. His armor is so thick and durable that despite all of the years he sat on the decaying property it had hardly affected his inside components and machinery. All it took from me was a couple of power core re-activations and some fuse replacements. He was the strongest and most powerful addition to my team. It only took him one arm to place complete heavy robots through the wall, and they just fell down onto the concrete floor.

I pulled off one of the robots armor after grinding off the rust, and then I cut the wires and pulled everything apart. For being hundreds of years old, most of these old robots were in better shape than you would think. Their water tight plastic and metal frames acted like a mummy sarcophagus for wires protecting their internal components from the elements.

I tore out wires and grinded at rusty patches of metal my mind spinning in anxious and eager circles. I began to think about the blonde woman again, so I decided to concentrate on the soldier droid concept to help me train with a sword. I had to beat her in a fight or this was all in vain. I hated the idea of fighting a girl, especially with a sword, but at the same time I really wanted to see her again.

I wanted to make the robot I was working on smart enough to decipher the difference between friend and foe. It needed to make the correct decisions under the pressure of combat, and act accordingly to destroy threats. I had never modified an artificial intelligence this much before, but I understood them enough to feel comfortable trying.

"Lord Zander," Mandy poked her head in, "I'm sorry to interrupt you, but Lord Wellington is at the gate to speak to you."

I looked up, "Very well, I shall stop what I'm doing."

I left the keyboard of my computer and followed her. As we walked through the estate, I got an idea and I turned to Mandy, "Please, prepare service drones 3 and 4. I may allow him to pick *one* of them to take today to keep things friendly. Since I don't have anything better to offer him quite yet."

"Very well," Mandy nodded, "I will head out and grab them, and then I'll meet you at the gate, my lord."

"Thank you Mandy," I smiled at her and headed to the gate. Sure enough Lord Wellington was standing impatiently at the gate with the same women from earlier on his arms. A luxurious armored blue carriage connected to healthy well decorated horses behind him. Multiple guards were standing around the blue carriage at the ready, watching the fence line in front of them as well as the tree line behind them as though they were expecting an ambush.

He was an older man, maybe late forties or early fifties, and the two women looked dramatically younger then he was. They shiftily looked at him, and their eyes explored my estate. It almost looked like they wanted to get away from Wellington and run towards the estate to get away.

"What is your intention?" I smiled warmly and waved before I began nervously unlocking the gate.

"I am here to talk business as you invited me to earlier, what was your name again, Lord Zane?" He asked stepping through the gate as I opened it, "Also, I brought you a gift, a token of my generosity if you will."

He motioned to the guards who revealed a young woman sitting on the back of the dirty carriage. His guards tugged her down, carried her over and tossed her to my feet. She hit the grass with a painful whimper and it made me suck in my breath in disbelief. She looked to be my age or perhaps a couple years

36

younger, and she wore a green maids dress and a frilly white elegant apron.

"My name is Zander," I suddenly felt incredibly uncomfortable and irritated. Human beings were not items to just be given away. Even in today's sparse and rugged culture it was not acceptable behavior. I rushed to the girl's side to help her up. She felt fragile as she worked with me to get up.

"I heard you came in to town today to get a cook, so I thought you may need a maid. Don't worry about it, she did not meet my criteria, and I have too many maids as it is. In fact, I accidentally hired too many today at the market. So like I said, the maid is simply a gift of good faith."

All of her things were dropped behind her in the grass as she was shoved through my gate by the guard and landed at my feet. One of the things being a small razor sharp battle axe that glinted in the afternoon light.

She was dirty from riding on the back of the carriage. The dust coated her from head to toe and she began coughing harshly and spitting dust. She had an emotionless expression on her small dirty face as she gazed at her feet.

"Are you okay?" I asked her cautiously.

"Um.. Of course my lord. My name is Anna Bee Rishel, I look forward to serving you." She gave a nervous bow. She seemed very scared. I felt bad for her, the way she was thrown around like that. In her shoes I'd be upset too.

"So," Wellington slapped his hands together, "I have to ask, where did you get such a fine machine as the one I saw earlier today."

"I built it from parts laying around my estate. So I hope you will understand that it will take me some time to build one for you," I said hiding my anger. I did *not* want to accept this gift, but I did not want to send her back to Wellington's cruel hand either. It made me wonder how many other servants he had in the carriage, and how poorly he was treating them.

"I understand," he smiled, "and what would you like in return?" He asked, "Money?

"Let me think about it," I said thoughtfully and I glanced at my estate, "I have not thought about it at all, I have been looking over what I have here at the estate, and I suppose I could use more food since I'll have a cook and human servants..."

"Well," he interrupted, "Mister Zander- was it?"

I nodded, "yes, my name is *Zander*."

Mandy approached with the two rusty service drones following behind her, their motors humming and their mechanical legs making slight whining sounds with every step.

"These are service drones, I named them number three and Four. They are designed for physical labor, painting, lifting, and things like that, but they are not very good at cooking, talking, or more sensitive tasks. I wanted to give you a machine since you came all the way out here..."

He interrupted me, "You shouldn't have! *Two robots?* Two functioning robots for me?" He walked around them inspecting them, "How cool is this Natasha?" He tuned to the women on his right arm and her makeup covered cheeks, and he smacked her rear a little harshly startling her.

She forced a giggled, "*So* cool, my lord." Secretly the woman looked like she was terrified of Wellington. She looked as though if she would have said anything else there would have been consequences.

"What a swell guy!" He grabbed my hand forcefully and pulled it up to shake it. "Yet you still say you still will build me another! I have to ask, how many do you have laying around that you can just give away two like this? I truly see why they call you a lord now!"

"Well," I tried to correct him, "I can only give you one because I don't have very many actually. I brought two so that you could pick between them..." the look he was giving me as I tried to explain frightened me. It looked as though he was getting ready to give the order for his men to attack... "Since you gave me a gift though..." I choked nervously, "You can have them both."

His eyes lit up again, "Well look at that. What a generous fellow."

Man this guy was a jerk, he was terrifying. I hated him already. His men came and collected the two machines by grabbing them by the arm, even though they were willingly following the two guards. They then were loaded up in the carriage where Anna Bee was moments ago.

"So how long until I can pick up this new machine you promised me?" He asked with a smooth smile, as though moments ago he had not given me a dirty look.

"I will have to build it from scratch, it could take two or three weeks," I said, "It took me nearly a year to perfect Mandy, so it will take me some time."

"So, let's say *two weeks* then," he said it in an almost hostile tone, "When I return, you will have my robot ready, and you will know what you want in return. I'm afraid Lord Ella controls most of the food growth and creation in her domain. I could arrange a meeting for you in return. If food is what you are after, then she is who you want to talk to."

I swallowed, "Sure. I'll think about what I want."

"Very well, see you in two weeks," he nodded and headed out of my open gate with his guards. The two women never left his side carefully smiling and giggling to please him.

He hesitated before he was nearly through the gate, and turned back around his tone growing dark, "Hey there, Zane. I don't want to have to be the bad guy here and hurt anyone, so make sure that robot is completely done. If it is not done, well- I'm sure you don't want to face the consequences."

He motioned to me and then around the estate, then he turned his back to me after an intimidating glare, and headed for his carriage.

I closed the gate and locked it behind them with a frustrated groan. "What's that guy's problem?" I asked under my breath, "Consequences?" It was as though he planned on giving me nothing in return even though he spoke of something. There was no negotiation, just him pushing me around. I hated interacting with other people for that very reason.

I sighed and I watched the massive carriage turn around and head down the gravel road. Then night began to gently creep across the sky as I stood watching the cloud of vanishing dust in frustration.

"Excuse, me," the young girl did her best to brush dirt off of her hair and dress creating a small cloud of dirt around her, "You said your name is Lord Zander, right?"

I spun around startled and she looked down shyly when I looked at her, "I'm sorry, my lord. I did not mean to startle you," Anna Bee cleared her throat, and flinched like she expected me to hit her.

I had no idea what to do. I was not used to interacting with other people, let alone a girl near my age. I nodded, "Yes, my name is Zander."

"My name is Anna Bee Rishel. I wish to inform you that I graduated the North Dakota Maids academy. I hope I can be of service to you, since I am your maid. I am not the best at most things I was taught how to do..." her voice shyly trailed off as though she did not like to listen to her own voice, "But I will do my best."

When it came to interacting with other people, it felt as though she was as awkward as me. I authentically appreciated the fact that she was similar to me in that way. I looked her up and down thoughtfully, and I decided I thought she was fairly pretty. If she were to get cleaned up, I bet she would be a lot prettier.

"You came all the way from North Dakota?" I asked curiously, "That's quite a ways away."

"Yes, sir," she nodded with her quiet voice, "I entered the academy when I was very young. The rule in the orphanage was: If a young girl was not adopted by parents before the age of twelve, then they were sent to a maid academy. So when I was sixteen, I graduated from the academy. I was not as good as the other maids, so no one bought my service until today..." her voice trailed off, "I'm sorry, am I talking too much?"

4: The Machine Lord's Maid

"No," I smiled shaking my head, "Absolutely not. You can talk as much as you want here in my estate. I do not own you, Anna Bee."

"But I am your new maid, my whole purpose is to do as you say. Who else would own me?" She asked, "I am sorry if I am not good enough."

I quickly cut her off, "You seem just fine. What I meant is you can expect nothing but kindness from me, Anna Bee. I don't own a single penny, so I cannot pay you anything at all. If you want to stay and serve me, then I guess you can stay as my friend. Also you are a human, it's wrong to *own* another human being…"

"Sweetheart, he's a very kind master," Mandy interrupted me, having been standing there watching all of this. She approached the fragile looking girl cautiously, "Come on Anna Bee, let's get you cleaned up."

"Oh- Okay. I will continue my introduction later if that is okay with you, my lord," she forced out a sweet little smile and a bow towards me before she walked away, "*Thank you*, for accepting my service."

I stood there for a moment and I heard the chain link fence rattle in the distance as though something struck it. I turned my head to follow the clang and jumped, "What the…?"

It stood there its claws clutching the fence. With blood stained pink fuzzy fur with bloody rotten patches missing. With a massive wicked smile of razor sharp teeth and two uneven rabbit ears flopping down the side of its head. It stood on two legs like a man leaning against the fence as though it had tried to smash through it watching me hungrily.

It looked like a monster from my nightmares, its head cocked to the side and beady black eyes watching me from a distance. Its teeth clicked together with a bone chilling chattering sound, and its breath cut through the cool air in what looked like blood red steam. Mandy and Anna Bee turned, and it disappeared as though it broke and crumbled into ashes. Then the wind gently carried the ashes away.

At first it felt like I had hallucinated, but a worker droid approached the fence line scanning left and right, "Did anyone else hear something hit the fence?"

That had to be the most terrifying thing I had ever seen. When I closed my eyes I could see it seared into my eyelids. I wondered what it was and where it came from, or if it was even real? My mind clouded in fear as I stood frozen in place on the lawn. Had Wellington left that thing, was it a coincidence?

Anna Bee quickly returned and gathered her things. Then she ran off after Mandy who shrugged. She was half way to the estate, gazing in the direction of the clang having barely missed seeing it, "Must have been our imaginations. Weird."

I watched the fence line regaining control of my petrified body, sweeping left and right for a good ten or fifteen minutes. Then I shivered before I headed into my estate, following Mandy and Anna Bee's footsteps on the lawn.

I quickly returned to my work shop, and I sat in my comfortable chair. I found myself staring in terrified thought at the glowing computer screen, my fingers strumming the dust. The computer screen was a flat glowing hologram that was maybe three feet across shooting out of the metal projector on the dusty computer desk.

My workshop was a massive room. My desk beside my workbench in the corner opposite the door, with aisles of tools and robotic parts that I had organized and collected throughout the years. It was dirty and messy, but there was methods to my madness.

I impatiently walked through the aisles of the workshop digging and searching through the rusty parts before I returned back to my desk. I wasn't trying to find anything specific, just something to distract myself with.

"What was that?" I asked myself.

Instead of continuing work on the robot like I had planned, I grabbed a thick piece of long metal and spent the rest of the evening grinding and tempering a sturdy well balanced double edged sword. I even melted down some old plastic robot casings and used them to create a perfect plastic sheath for the newly forged sword. Immediately after completion I swung a couple practice swings to familiarize myself with weight of the blade, then I sheathed the still warm blade to belt loops of my ripped up jeans.

"My lord," Anna Bee appeared in the doorway after several hours, "I have prepared dinner for you."

"You wha..?" I turned startled by her sudden interruption, "Oh cool, thank you, Anna Bee."

I followed her down the hallway toward the old building employee lounge, which was converted into my kitchen and dining room. A very oversized dining room and kitchen to be honest. It was nothing like Nate's small organized kitchen.

"I could not find very much, but I trapped an old rabbit a couple hours ago on the estate to make you potato and Rabbit stew. I hope it is acceptable," she poured me a steaming bowl from a pot on the stove with a gentle smile, "This is incredible, my lord, I had no idea you had *electricity!*"

"You said you killed a rabbit?" I shivered and the pink monster flashed into my mind briefly, "Where?"

"Towards the edge of the scrap yard, under some metal," she sucked in her breath, "Did I do something wrong?"

"No, no," I said glancing around, "You are fine."

Mandy entered the room, "Isn't she a busy little Bee? She wanted to surprise you."

The entire room was cleaned, all my dishes cleaned and organized. The light fixture was cleaned warming the room with clear beaming light. The light covered the entire room instead of just portions of it which made me realize how messy it had been before. The table was wiped down and scrubbed thoroughly, even the table legs. The chairs were spotless, and the whole dining area felt like a totally different room.

"Did you do all of this, Anna Bee?" I asked running my finger along the large shiny plastic table top.

"Yes, my lord," she looked nervous as she brought me over the steaming bowl of stew, "Is it not good enough? I will do it again..."

Mandy turned to me, "Believe me, it's good enough..."

"It's great, Anna Bee! It's fantastic. I've never seen this room so clean!" I said cutting off Mandy and accepting the warm bowl. It was very basic, and as I tasted it the broth was kind of flavorless, but I understood that I didn't have very much food around here, especially when it came to spices.

She created something awesome with what little I had, and I had never felt more comfortable in my own dining room. I was impressed and grateful. Mandy was never as great of a cook as this new addition to my estate.

"It's amazing the academy taught you to trap and skin animals like that," Mandy commented as she moved and sat a couple chairs away from me.

"Times are tough nowadays. Food is not as abundant as it used to be, but I hope it is good enough for you, my lord," Anna Bee gave a little bow in my direction.

"Please, get a bowl and join me," I motioned to the chair across the table from me, "You tell me what you think. I think that this stew is great."

"Are you sure?" She asked, "It is not very polite for me to taste what I have prepared. That is one thing the academy has taught me, I would not want to hurt your reputation if someone learned you ate with your maid, my lord."

I burst out laughing, "Like I care what others think of me!" I nearly fell off my chair, my ribs hurting, "They really taught you that!? Oh my goodness, that is ridiculous. I'd invite Mandy too, but she is a robot." I poked a teasing shot at Mandy who glared at me.

"I-it's not ridiculous, it is to help me serve you better..." she seemed confused, and I waved at her to stop talking, "You want to serve me better? Sit down, be my friend, and enjoy this delicious stew with me. Not, Mandy though."

"I dare you to keep rubbing it in," Mandy turned and her eyes flickered, "I could malfunction and smack you *again*. I've always wondered what human food would taste like, sometimes I wish I was human."

Anna Bee smiled a sweet smile. Now that she was cleaned up you could see adorable little freckles on her cheeks. She had beautiful blue eyes, and she had long brown hair that was tied into a ponytail to keep it from falling into her cooking. She was an adorably sweet and shy looking girl, "I think you would make a great human, Mandy. You have been very nice to me since I got here, both of you have."

She poured herself a bowl and obediently sat across from me, "I thank you for your kindness towards me… You are nothing like the lords that the academy described to me… *you are… nice.*"

I gazed at her for a moment and she quickly covered her mouth, "Did I say too much, master?"

"No, no, no!" I said quickly, "You are really nice too! You will *never* be restricted to what you can say on my estate, you may freely speak, say whatever you like! I'm glad I have a new maid as fantastic as you!"

"I am beginning to feel obsolete. You do far better than I can, but then again you are a pretty girl with real eyes that can distinguish dirt from table top," Mandy shrugged.

"You'll never be obsolete Mandy," I gazed at her, "Anna Bee can't lift several hundred pounds, she is pretty though. I'll agree with you on that." I glanced over at Anna Bee, and then absent mindedly back to my stew.

She blushed sweetly and looked down stuttering, "Thank you, my lord. Thank you Madam Mandy, no one has ever t-told me that."

I shrugged, "It's true. I don't see why anyone would *not* buy your services, but I am glad they didn't," I looked at the scrubbed floor below the table, "Look at this! Spotless, sheesh I'm a lucky guy."

I loved the way she lit up when I complimented her. It was like every compliment I gave her increased her sweetness, and boosted her confidence.

"You really mean it?" She asked.

"Of course I do!" I smiled, "It would be meaningless for me to lie, because things would not get done the way I wanted them to."

"He's not wrong," Mandy glanced at me, and then she looked over at Anna Bee, "Zander is not the kind to lie. I don't think he knows how."

Anna Bee grinned and brushed through her bangs with her hands. The evenly cut hair hung down at the perfect length to hide her blue eyes if she tilted her head forward. It was like her eyes disappeared, and then she gave me a brief spirited look, "T-thank you."

"Yup," I smiled and gave her a satisfied thumbs up, "You did well!"

"I really like it here," she said after a moment, "I like that it is so serene and beautiful. I really like all the thick trees, and the cloudy sky makes the sunset look truly magical. I especially like the electricity. I have never seen a working light bulb before," she motioned to the lights above us, "You must have worked really hard to fix this place up."

I shrugged, "It's all I have, and I have nothing better to do but fix things. It gives me something to do out here all alone."

"Mandy told me that you built her, and that you fixed all the robots around here. I think that is awesome that you can do that! I wish I was smart enough to fix robots," she smiled, "You are an incredible person, my lord. I cannot express the happiness in my heart that I get to stay here with you, and serve you."

I smiled, "thanks, Anna Bee."

"My lord," she said gazing down at the floor and changed the subject, "I don't mean to trouble you..."

"What is it?" I asked raising a nervous eyebrow. The look on her face seemed as though she was going to give me awful news.

"I d-don't have a room, or a place to sleep yet..." she nervously pulled on her ponytail, "I'm sorry I don't mean to bother you..."

I blew a bunch of air between my lips feeling stupid, "Oh, I'm sorry Anna Bee. Come on we'll figure something out."

"I can do that," Mandy offered standing up, "If you want, so you can get back to work?"

"No, it is okay. Come on Anna Bee, you can have a room by mine," I motioned her to follow, and turned to Mandy, "Will you please clean up the table and load the dishes into the dishwasher?"

"Of course," Mandy bowed, "I'll get right on it.

Anna Bee and I began to head down the Hallway in awkward silence.

"I like Master Mandy," Anna Bee said as she walked behind me, "She is very nice."

I agreed, "Mandy is a good friend. She's been with me for four years now."

"She informed me you wish to learn how to sword fight. I could practice with you if you like. You made a very nice sword today," she smiled cautiously as we headed down the hallway and she motioned to the sword on my hip. I laughed at her, "I appreciate the offer Anna Bee, but I prefer to learn from a professional, not a maid. No offense."

"None taken," she said and opened her mouth like she was going to say something, but didn't. She just gazed at the offices in the hallway left and right as we walked. The old dusty wooden door frames and cobwebs of the offices were not all that appealing, but I used them as bedrooms.

I found the cleanest looking office that was closest to the kitchen. It had cracks in the walls, and there was an old musty desk with an old office chair tucked underneath it. It was pretty empty, but it looked the cleanest and the most intact. I turned to her, "This can be your room, if you want. You can pick any of them if you don't like it, and there should be another old bed in the infirmary. Hang on, I will get it for you."

"No master!" She squeaked, "I do not wish to trouble you! I can grab the bed! Thank you for the room, I love it!"

"It's no trouble Anna Bee." I smiled, "If it means that much to you go right ahead. However, please promise me you will not hesitate to ask me if you need something. You really don't have to apologize all the time. You aren't troubling me. I appreciate what you've done for me today."

"That is my job, I am your maid," she bowed, "I am glad my service is satisfactory."

"Whatever," I laughed at her, and I walked away, "I'm going to bed."

"Have a good night, my new master," she smiled, "Thank you for accepting my service today."

I liked having a maid, and I wondered how long I got to enjoy her company. It was only one sweet girl that I appreciated very much. I felt like we were going to get along great, and I was honestly glad I accepted her. She made me smile, and she made me feel comfortable.

As I lay in bed that evening, the creature at the fence still haunted me. The way its teeth clicked together hungrily, the way it stared intently at me through the fence. It felt like if there would have been no fence in the way, it would have attacked me. I could just imagine it tearing into me with its long sharp bloody claws, and the thought made me shiver

I laid in my bed for at least an hour tossing and turning until I finally fell asleep.

I awoke to a gentle hand on my shoulder, "Please, Lord Zander."

I stirred and sat up lazily, "What is it? What's wrong?" I turned to see who had awoken me, and there it was. The terrifying monster inches from me, its bloody claw on my shoulder. Blood trickled down my shirt from its claws, but I could not feel any pain. Then I heard the rattling of its razor sharp teeth, and it snapped at me. Its bloody unhinged jaw and teeth lunged at me, and I jerked my body away out of reflex.

It scared me straight awake for real this time, sitting up in a sweaty panic alone in my dark room in the middle of the night. It had only been a brief nightmare, and moments later Mandy entered the room quickly, "Are you okay? Why have you awakened so suddenly?"

I let my mind clear for a moment lying there to make sure I had really woken up this time and Anna Bee poked her head in the doorway behind Mandy concerned, her blue eyes studying me carefully.

"Yes, it was simply a bad dream," I said relieved to be in reality, "It wasn't very pleasant."

"I see," Mandy sighed, "Do you want me to stay in the room with you the rest of the evening?"

"I should be okay," I rolled over, "Thank you though." I closed my eyes and went back to sleep.

This time I had a pleasant dream. The beautiful blonde woman from the fair was my wife, and we lived together happily on the estate. Young beautiful and healthy children ran about the estate laughing and playing various games. Then I awoke the next morning to Anna Bee's gentle voice, "M-my lord I'm sorry to awake you."

I sat up dreamily trying to keep myself feeling how I felt in the dream, "What is it?"

"I went into Wellington this morning to get groceries, and when I returned Lord Osburn was here at the gate. He says he needs to speak to you, and that it is urgent," she said, "please forgive me for waking you up."

"Anna Bee, really it's fine," I spun out of my bed and quickly threw on my torn up leather jacket and shoes.

As I walked through the hall of my estate, I noticed that Anna Bee's room was cleaned spotless. Her bed neatly made with a blanket she must have brought with her. The desk was turned on its side shoved against the wall being used as an improvised clothing closet.

It looked like a completely different room, and one thing stuck out to me. Under the infirmary bed was that metal double sided battle axe. It looked like it had a sword hilt and handle towards the bottom. It was a weird looking weapon, but I shrugged without giving it a second thought and moved on down the hall.

As I walked through the lounge, it was in the process of being cleaned. A big wood burning stove was constructed near the wall, forged of concrete, stones, and metal pieces collected from around the estate. I really liked the way it looked. It had a great balance of colorful stone to sanded rusty metal. It was a fantastic modern addition to my living room that must have taken *hours* to make.

"What the?" I asked surprised, studying the fireplace confused, "Anna Bee, did you make this all by yourself?" I asked motioning to the still drying mortar and then to the firewood gathered and set beside it.

It had a hand forged door on the fireplace with sanded metal strips welded neatly to a hinge in the side. The joints squeaked when the door swung open, and I could see multiple minor flaws with it upon inspection. As I inspected it she followed me around it nervously.

"No, my lord. Master Mandy said I could enlist the help of your working robots. It was my idea though, so please be mad at me if you don't like it. It was cold, I wanted you to be more comfortable master. I am sorry I did not get your approval first..." she nervously cleared her throat and flinched again as though I was going to hit her.

"Seriously, Anna Bee," I said and spun to confront her and she tilted her head hiding her eyes behind her bangs scared, "I'm sorry!"

"*I love it*, there is no need to apologize. You must have started right after I went to bed since the concrete is nearly dry. I really like it! I'm impressed. Thank you," I smiled, and she looked back up with a relieved look, "Thank you, my lord."

I turned to head out the front door in quiet smiling thought, and she caught my sleeve, "Wait! My lord, I have something for you."

I turned to her, "You have something *else* for me? What else could you have possibly done for me in only one night?"

She stuttered, "As a lord, I noticed you did not have a flag, so after some careful thinking, I made you one while I was waiting for parts of the fireplace to dry..." She produced a white piece of fabric from under her apron shaking, "Since you were called the machine lord, I was not sure what I should do... I hope you like it..."

As I opened it up, it was a rectangular hand stitched flag. The design was a round black monochromatic black gear stitched to the center of the white flag. Black wires ran behind the gear across the length of the flag, some broken, but most of them intact. The hand stitched detail was incredible. I could clearly tell it was sewn in a hurry, but I still loved the simple design.

I loved it. I turned to her with an excited smile, "This is awesome. I love it! Please, if you would, hang it up right away. Fly it as high as you can!"

She looked relieved but still slightly scared as she forced a smile, "I was hoping you would like it my lord... I didn't know what you would want..."

"I love it," I insisted, "Please go hang it up. I would love to accept it as my flag and my symbol as a lord."

I headed out the door with an excited smile thinking about the flag and the fireplace, and she rolled up the flag tucking it carefully under her arm and stoked the crackling fire behind me.

I could see the smoke coming out a chimney that was carved out of the wall a couple feet away from the front door in the ceiling as I walked through the door onto the estate lawn. Mandy appeared shortly after from around the corner of the building, and followed me out to the gate where Nate was waiting patiently. This time he had three times the guards standing around him. This made me cautious as I approached, my heart sinking as I began to question his intentions.

"Morning Zander," he said anxiously, as I unlocked the gate. He was behaving as though he was embarrassed to be here.

"Morning Nate, what is your intention?" I asked as the gate creaked open, "Why have you brought so many guards?"

"An extra precaution if you will, some weird things have been happening," he said, "Can we talk?"

I nodded and motioned for him to enter, watching his guards suspiciously.

"Well I just..." he leaned in close to me and lowered his voice as he came through the gate his hands folded behind him "some of my maids last night reported seeing *a terrifying monster rabbit*, and I was wondering if you needed some more servants..." he whispered in my ear, "I'm afraid they could be a bit crazy, and I don't want them if they are..."

"I saw it too..." I said loudly, "Over there by the fence," I motioned, "everyone in my estate heard the clang of it hitting the fence, but I was the only one who saw it. They are not crazy. I thought maybe I was crazy, but if they saw one too..."

"Really?" he raised an eyebrow, "describe to me what you saw."

"I-I don't want to," I said, "Sorry."

"Well then," he looked skeptical, "About what time did you see this 'monster rabbit?"

"It was right after Wellington left my estate," I said, "I thought at first it was his doing."

"Well then," Nate sighed, "I'm sorry to have bothered you. Don't fret, I'll figure this out and lay this rabbit problem to rest. However if I end up hunting a "monster rabbit", can I count on your cooperation and use of your domain territory, to hunt this beast?"

"Of course," I nodded, "Knowing it has been killed would bring me comfort. It is starting to give me nightmares."

"Two more things," Nate said quickly, "First of all you have a very sweet maid. Very pretty, congratulations on the new maid. Not sure where you got her. Second of all, that is a great looking sword at your hip. I did not know you *owned* a sword, but that's a nice one," Nate smiled, effectively lightening the mood, "Sorry I bothered you this morning, but apparently I should look into this matter more. How did your meeting with Wellington go?"

"To be honest, great" I shrugged and turned back towards the estate entrance, "Because I got Anna Bee. I really like her. She does a great job. Wellington still seems like a jerk though."

"Well, please be careful. Sorry to nag but, you should get some firepower going for you. You control the electricity. You literally have the power," Nate smiled, "*I* will look into this monster bunny thing, so don't worry about it, okay? I find it hard to believe that there is a monster bunny around, but if there is I'll find it."

I remained silent, "Just be careful with yourself. Don't do anything stupid," I said, "I'm sorry to say it, but if your servants are crazy, so am I. So I'm not much help."

He folded his arms studying me for a moment, "Do you think it could be connected to the darkness?" He whispered, "The whole rumor going around about the demon army?"

"I doubt it," I sighed, "Probably a practical joke meant to scare us. We still can't cross out the fact that Wellington could have a hand in this. It could be costumes."

"Well," he shrugged, "don't forget you have a sword fight tomorrow." Nate sighed after a long awkward silence, changing the subject, "I wish I could come watch. That sounds very entertaining."

"Sure," I shrugged, "though I don't know what time she will come, or if she'll come at all, but you can come if you want." I glanced down at my feet nervously, "I honestly hope she does come."

"Well, I should get going," Nate said thoughtfully, "That's all I needed. Good luck to you. I will hopefully see you tomorrow."

Nate began heading for his carriage and waved behind him, "Make sure you at least practice sword fighting somehow."

His guards nearly covered the wagon as they let him in and then loaded up onto it. The horses took the carriage away, turning around to head back to the city.

"Monster rabbit?" Mandy asked me confused, "Why did you say nothing about this?"

"I thought for a moment I was going crazy," I said, "but the fact that I wasn't going crazy scares me even more," I watched the tree line for the monster as though I expected it to reappear. Then I turned to head for the estate.

"Anna Bee is preparing breakfast for you," Mandy nodded standing there, "I insist you eat some before you head to your work shop, where I anticipate you will spend most of your day."

5: A Single Sided Duel

"Yeah," I said glancing at Mandy, "I want to finish the soldier droid concept as quickly as possible. Things are changing really quickly around here, and I don't like it." I frowned, "I just want to be left alone, and live here on the estate. Anna Bee can stay though, she's a hard worker."

We walked through the estate doors and it began raining gently behind us as we closed the old wooden doors.

Anna Bee was in the kitchen making toast from fresh bread she had made from scratch, and she had scrambled eggs and thick slices of bacon cooked to perfection. She was placing it on a plate, and neatly setting the plate down on the table for me as I entered the lounge. The bacon was still sizzling, and everything smelled so delicious it made me drool a little.

"Please," she nervously motioned to the plate and smiled bravely, "I made you breakfast, my lord."

"Thank you," I grinned floating towards the table, "This looks delicious... by the way where did you get money to buy groceries?"

"I used my own money sir," she bowed, "I have a little bit saved up from small jobs when I was in the academy for a special occasion, and I thought getting hired for my service as a maid was a special enough occasion..."

She slid me a glass of milk that she poured from the fridge, "I am your servant. My job is to serve you."

She looked nervous as I began eating. To be honest, I felt like she always looked nervous, like I was going to flip out and attack her. She carefully watched my reactions as I ate, and she watched me carefully with everything I did.

"You have to understand, Anna Bee. I have never had a servant before. I have always cooked my own meals, and I have to tell you you're a lot better cook than me. This is delicious! I have not had *real* eggs in *years*. Your stew last night was fantastic for something you created with what little you had. You've done nothing but impress me, *why* do you always seem nervous?" I asked her curiously putting down my silverware, "You need to eat too, so sit down and join me."

"It is proper for the servant to eat on her own, when her master is no longer in the room..." she tried to explain but I cut her off, "Not *this* master... I mean I don't like the idea of *owning* someone, I'm not your master... I told you, you were more than welcome to stay as long as you want to as a guest..." I began to confuse myself and my voice trailed off.

"My purpose is to be a servant..." she said, "I am sorry that I am frustrating or upsetting you master. I was trained to be a servant. It gives me purpose, my lord. Do you not accept me as your servant? Am I not good enough?" Her blue eyes studied me worried.

I sighed and smiled at her, "Of course you are good enough. If it means that much to you, you can be my *servant*, but I should warn you that I'm changing the rules. The new rule in my estate, is that you eat with me when I ask you to," I raised an eyebrow at her, "Understood?"

She obeyed, dishing herself up a small portion and sat across from me and she looked at me hesitantly, "You also said I could say anything I want on your estate?"

"Of course," I said with a curious look, glancing at her. She neatly kept her cut up and splintered hands in her lap politely,

"Why are you so nice to me? No one else has ever been as nice to me as you..."

"Why am I-?" I asked in disbelief, "No one?"

She blinked, "I'm sorry, did I cross a line?"

"No!" I said loudly, "Anna Bee, do you not see how hard you have been working for me? Of course I am going to be nice to you!"

"But, I am your maid that is my job..." she said quickly and I rose my hand for her to quit talking snapping it up with a kind smile, "Anna Bee, I truly and honestly appreciate you. That is the *only* reason I could ever *need* to be nice to you. Please, show me your hands."

She looked confused but held up her hands as I had commanded. There was scratches, cuts from the fireplace, small painful looking metal and wood slivers that had been scratched at as though she tried to remove them, and there was even chunks of mortar under her fingernails.

I gently took her hands, and they were rough and shaking, "Anna Bee look at this. This has to be painful." I looked at her hands sympathetically.

"I-I'm sorry," she stuttered, "I did not own a pair of gloves until this morning. I made some from the rabbit hide..."

I just smiled at her, "Please take it easy. Please don't hurt yourself." I released her hands and finished my meal. Then I thanked her again as she started on a small pile of dishes, and I headed for my workshop.

The thought that the pretty blond haired girl from the market could come tomorrow scared me. How good of a sword fighter could she really be? I drew my own sword inspecting it, and swung it around my workshop before re-sheathing it. I began to continue tinkering with the damaged droid, typing adjustments and testing its A.I compatibility with the changes.

I worked on reinforcing its joints and hinges, and I added armored shoulder plates to keep bullets or swords from hitting its shoulder joints. I cleaned up the motors and re-activated the old A.I command processor by swapping out bad rusty wires for some cleaner more preserved ones.

Before I knew it Anna Bee was knocking on the door. "Dinner is ready, sir," she said, "I am sorry, I don't mean to interrupt anything."

She curiously drew closer, walking cautiously into the room, "May I ask what you are doing, my lord?"

"I'm thinking up a soldier drone concept. A concept that can be repeated and manufactured so I can turn a bunch of these old robots into soldiers," I said distracted by my busy work, "This is the first construction of a proto type. I'm just trying out an idea."

"It looks really cool, my lord. I am amazed you were capable of doing all of this work in one day. It looks like a completely different robot compared to yesterday, it even looks like it could be new," she said with a curious little spark in her eye, "It's incredible. You are truly gifted my lord."

I looked at her with a quiet look that turned to a smile, "I just learned over time. When I was twelve, I ran away from home because my parents were always yelling at each other. I found my way here to this building and I found some old books on robotics and engineering. I just read and tinkered until I made things work. Starting small... It's what I enjoy doing, I enjoy building and repairing all these old robots. It feels like I'm saving somebody when they turn on."

"That's so cool," she neatly placed her hands behind her back and did a sweeping gaze of my workshop, "If you want I could clean up in here for you. I won't throw anything away of course, but I could organize things by how they look, and I could build some more shelves for you. That way you could store more, and stay more organized."

I gazed down at the wires held in my oily hands and I looked at the dirt and dust across the floor. I looked up at the lights that were still covered in dirt and smoke residue from the old fire lit torches when I had first set up this shop to work in. The shelves were cluttered and messy, sticky with robotics oil and dust. It would be nice to have it be as spotless as she made the kitchen and the lounge.

"It would give me an excuse to work in here and watch you, I think it's fascinating to watch you piece things together and take them apart. That way I could see you every once in a while as I walk by," she said, "my lord?"

"Well, would you like to help me?" I asked curiously, "To be honest I could use an extra pair of hands."

"Oh, I'm sorry, I would not know what to do. Robotics was not a topic taught in the academy..." she looked a little sad, "I appreciate the offer though."

"So?" I shrugged, "I will teach you. You could hold things in place for me or hand me tools, and I think you are wrong on one account. They seemed to have turned *you* into a robot," I teased her playfully and poked her in the shoulder, "You need to loosen up a little."

"I am not a robot, sir," she said quickly, "What does loosen up mean? I would happily do that for you sir, is there a stain somewhere that needs *loosened*?"

"No Anna Bee, loosen up means you need to have to more fun, it means you should not be so worried all the time," I said laughing at her, "I thought I was the one with terrible human interaction."

"I enjoy serving you, sir," she looked down and her cheeks flushed gently as though she was embarrassed to say it, "I like the way you tell me I am so great."

"Well you are, Anna Bee," I smiled and I turned and stood up eagerly tossing the oily wires a side, "Now what have you made me for dinner?"

"Spaghetti and meatballs," she said, "I used some of the leftover bacon from breakfast and put it in the meatballs. It was something I learned in the academy that I enjoyed. I hope you like it, my lord."

Anna Bee led me to the kitchen through the hallway and the lounge. She had an elegant stride and she always had her hands neatly behind her back unless she was holding something.

Mandy entered through the front door with an old rusting hand cart full of firewood that she parked beside the fireplace. She began to start a fire, fueling the flames with air and making it even more comfortable and warm in my estate. "Hello Zander," She waved at me as we walked by and I waved back.

I sat at my table with a dumb smile on my face. Everything was clean, everything felt homey. I deeply and sincerely appreciated everything this new maid did. The whole room smelled delicious and she had a cute little smile on her face as she served me.

"How long does a maid service last?" I asked her curiously as she put steaming homemade noodles onto a plate, and then poured sauce on, "a couple years? a couple months?"

"It depends on the contract, my lord," she said cautiously setting down the pot of sauce, "Why do you ask?" She went back to looking worried again, "Am I doing something wrong?" She stood there with a straight back, her hands behind her back at the table edge.

"No, I just want to know how long I get to enjoy your presence here," I said picking up the preset fork she had set for me.

"My contract is two years long my lord," she said watching me, and I nearly dropped my fork, "Really?"

"Yes my lord," she said, "Usually they are one year contracts. Mine was increased to two years because no one was buying my service. It was so they could get rid of me longer since I brought the academy no income..."

"What happens when the two years is up?" I asked, "Can I renew?"

"Yes my lord, the renewing cost is ten thousand cents, for another two years," she said, "If it is not paid to the academy then I am supposed to return to the academy and wait for someone else to purchase my service... but I am not as good as the other maids, and I am... *weird*."

I leaned back and I asked, "You're *supposed* to? So you could chose not to?"

"It would be breaking the code of maid conduct taught to me in the academy. The academy owns me, they taught me everything I know," she said, "I do like it here a lot more though. However, I'm sure when the time comes you will be tired of me just like everyone else my lord."

I stared at her curiously for a moment, "Why would I ever get tired of a sweet girl like you?"

She shrugged blushing, "Because I am weird, and I am not as good as the other maids."

I shrugged, "Whatever Anna Bee." I spun the soft noodles onto my fork and took a bite, "What did you say this was called? I think I can remember this from when I was little."

"Spaghetti and meatballs," she suddenly looked shocked, "My lord," she spun and picked up a pan full of little seasoned balls of meat, "I forgot the meatballs!"

She quickly came and placed the meatballs on my plate, "I apologize for my mistake…"

Mandy approached and sat at the end of the table to my left staring at me, "Can I have some? Oh wait, I'm a robot." Her voice was teasing and jocular, and she turned to Anna Bee, "How are you Anna Bee?"

"I am good ma'am," Anna Bee smiled.

I just laughed at Mandy, "Mandy, I'm sorry if I hurt your feelings… Wait a minute… you're a robot."

Mandy just stared at me for a moment, "I don't really have a comeback yet. I will tell you that I organized some good candidates for your soldier project when you finish. I have been cleaning them up, and I have been sorting the scrap yard like I usually do every day."

"Thank you, Mandy," I grinned and she shrugged, "Your welcome, Zander."

"Anna Bee, don't forget you have to sit and eat with me," I turned to her and I motioned to the chair across from me.

Anna Bee obeyed and she looked a little weary as she sat down. She looked tired, her eyes wanting to close, her body looked sore from the way she held it.

"Anna Bee," I said, "I want you to get a lot of sleep tonight. Tomorrow you will help me in my workshop, and you seem tired. So, I need you to be wide awake if you are going to be helping me tomorrow. That is an order." I shivered as I said it. I did not own her, I loved her presence. I wanted her to be my friend and not be so scared of me all the time.

"Okay, sir," she nodded, "I will do that." She looked a little excited for a moment, her eyes sparkling under the lights of the kitchen. She mellowed out again, "Thank you, my lord."

I went to my bed that night with a full belly after Anna Bee and I ate together in awkward silence. I laid in my now clean bedroom, my clothes cleaned and organized, my floor scrubbed, and my wall free of mold and dust. Even The light was cleaned as well, making it bask the same warm homey light as the dining room light. It made me wonder how she found the time to do all of this.

She must have cleaned it while I was working today, and I could not believe how it made the room so much more comfortable. I began to feel almost as spoiled in my own estate as I was at Nate's estate. I wished in my heart that Anna Bee would stay forever. I told myself I would build and sell robots to save up and buy a hundred more years of service out of my new loyal little friend if I had too. I would really like that.

I closed my eyes in my clean smelling sheets, and my pillows were even fluffed. Mandy never did that, but then again, Mandy's optical sensors were not capable of detecting the same impurities in a room as a human eye. She was not capable of cleaning like this, her eyes weren't as great as I wanted them to be. Since everything I had was at least a hundred years old, it made even simple repairs difficult, especially for a runaway learning from books and computer journal entries.

I really liked having Anna Bee here. I laid there wondering why she was so scared all the time, why she was so worried that she wasn't doing anything right. She always seemed scared of me like I was going to hit her. I wanted to find a way to show I appreciated her.

Soon I fell asleep with a smile thinking about her.

I sat up moments later, hearing a buzzing sound and I watched my light above me flicker on and off.

I rose to my feet, "Mandy? Anna Bee?"

I walked to the doorway, and there was a long trail of fresh potent blood along the hallway. The only real human in the estate beside me was Anna Bee. In a panic I spun in the doorway reaching for my sword and there it was. Walking down the hall, its teeth chattering, its claws tearing pieces of concrete and wooden splinters out of the hallway wall as it approached.

I caught motion out of the corner of my eye, and I spun to see the woman from Market Day in my room. Her long beautiful blond hair glowing in the flickering light as though it was a light source of its own, "Please my lord, it is only a dream. Please be at peace, it's not real." She gently took my hand and she smiled at me.

I loved holding her hand, it was warm and pleasant to the touch.

Her beautiful brown eyes flickered in the blurry light of the hallway light fixtures, and she gently squeezed my hand making my heart skip a beat, "None of it is real." She stepped from the doorway behind me, her soft hand placed in mine, "It is okay my lord."

I turned back briefly to see the monster was gone, and I looked down relieved to find the trail of blood was gone. The lights began shining steadily again instead of flickering.

I woke up, sitting up in bed with a yawn and a thorough stretch.

"My lord," Mandy was waiting in the doorway patiently, "I'm glad you are awake. Someone is here for you."

I rose to my feet in a panic, "Is it her? Is it the woman from a couple days ago? I am not ready, I have not practiced!"

"No sir, it is a very kind man. He came alone," Mandy nodded, "He is waiting in your living room."

"You let him in?" I asked.

"It was only one man. Anna Bee and I did not wish to wake you up," Mandy shrugged.

I quickly gathered my sword and shoes, and sure enough there was a muscular man in a long worn down armored trench coat. He had sandy blond hair and two big blue eyes, a sturdy broadsword at his hip, and long hand crafted recurve bow on his back with a quiver full of hand carved arrows.

He was drinking a cup of hot coffee talking to Anna Bee who was seated in a chair across from him with her hands behind her back politely as she always did.

When he saw me he nearly dropped the coffee cup, and Anna Bee rushed to it so it didn't spill looking irritated. He leapt to his feet and rushed to me, "You must be the Machine Lord, Lord Zander."

"That name is getting around?" I asked curiously, "I like it."

As I approached, he quickly dropped to one knee drawing his sword and Mandy quickly stepped between us, "My name is Danny Safely. My lord do you have a moment to listen to me?"

He did not attack me, he simply knelt on the floor presenting me the sword.

"Sure?" I asked raising an eyebrow, "What do you want?"

"I am a young strong man of twenty-two," he said proudly, "and I have mastered my bow and my sword. I am from a small village in Texas. I have traveled a long way here to the coast because I am in search of a chance to become a lord's knight. I tried Lord Wellington yesterday, and he told me that I was wasting his time, that he had too many knights. I tried Lord Osburn, who told me to come to you. He said you did not have any knights, and since I have arrived I see this is true. I beg of you my lord, accept me as your sword, and give me the chance to earn your trust and allegiance."

He offered me his sword holding it up flat against his palms, and he bowed his head.

"What do you mean by knight?" I asked, "Sorry, Danny. I am not quite sure I know exactly what you want from me. What does that mean?"

"He wants to serve you as a warrior, so that he may earn your trust. He is doing this so that you may give him the title of one of your knights, which is an honorable title," Anna Bee bowed, "Every lord has knights. They become knights by dutiful service to their lord, and are rewarded in return with the title of a Lords Knight."

"I am strong, I am brave. Let me serve you my lord; I wish to become a knight, and you are the only available lord in a hundred miles, Let me serve you. I am accurate with my bow, my sword skills are great. Allow me to prove it to you with my service," he went a little lower and held the sword up higher beginning to shake, "Please, I ask you to accept my blade."

"What happens if I accept?" I looked at Anna Bee who smiled, "He will stay and protect the Domain and serve you as a warrior, trying to earn your trust."

Nate's constant reminder that I needed a military came to my mind, followed by the flash of the terrifying bunny creature. Its claws rattling the fence, and its beady eyes watching me hungrily. If this man knew how to fight and he could help me protect my estate, then it was common sense to accept his service as my blade.

"I will accept you as my blade," I gently took the sword from his hands by its sturdy leather wrapped handle.

"I will prepare another room," Anna Bee smiled, "also, my lord, your breakfast is ready. I have prepared pancakes for you. Also you have to tell him to rise or he will stay on the floor forever."

"Rise," I said, and Danny rose to his feet, "Thank you, my lord."

I handed him his sword back and he sheathed it, "I will earn my keep around here. I swear."

"Okay," I shrugged and moved to the table, "Well, join me for pancakes I guess."

"As you wish, my lord. I thank you from the bottom of my heart. My horse, my beating heart, and everything I own now belong to you as your blade and servant. I hope to someday earn the title of your Knight," He bowed low and I shrugged, "You're welcome."

70

Suddenly an idea occurred to me, and I turned to him excited, "You said you've mastered the sword!"

He looked confused, "Yes my lord, I have mastered the sword type that I carry."

"Will you teach me to sword fight?" I asked eagerly.

"Of course my lord, your wish is my command," he nodded hesitantly, and then he stuttered staring frozen at the light bulb above the table, "w-wait a minute... you have *electricity*? Where do you get it?"

"Lord Zander has created a self-sustaining power turbine in a utility shed behind the main facility on the estate. We call it the generator shed," Mandy nodded informatively, "He also created me, and repaired the robots that you see working around the estate repairing the building or tending to the messy piles of old rusting metal lying around."

"That is awesome!" He grinned as he pulled out a chair and sat a couple seats away from me as Anna Bee put fresh churned butter and maple syrup on the table and began to load plates for us. They were little flat looking flour and sugar based cakes that I had never seen before. They smelled good though.

She then joined us at the table with her own plate and this confused Danny, "You eat with your maid?"

"I sure do," I nodded, "There's nothing wrong with that. I appreciate her."

"I just have not seen that before. Usually the maid eats after their lord has left, that's all. I mean no harm, my lord," he quickly swallowed and then he looked at the pancakes uneasily, "These look delicious!"

"Thank you," Anna Bee smiled a little smile and looked at me, "Are you sure you wish for me to stay, I told you I do not wish to embarrass you..."

"Yes," I said with an earnest look, "I am sure, Anna Bee."

She smiled and began to very neatly and politely cut her pancake and eat it. I noticed again she ate tiny servings and barely ever finished her whole plate. Once I learned you were supposed to put butter and syrup on the pancakes, I enjoyed them a lot more. They were delicious. I would have complimented her but I was busy stuffing my face full as we sat in silence.

After breakfast I finally was able to smile at her, "These were so delicious, Anna Bee thank you!"

"So shall we count on our time in your workshop being pushed to tomorrow?" She asked looking a little down. I nodded, "Yes, we will push it to tomorrow! I have a duel to prepare for that I completely forgot about last night! Sorry, Anna Bee."

How could I forget about the beautiful stranger at the market? Her long hair and the way it reflected the dim cloudy light around her made my heart skip a beat. She was *so* pretty. I was excited to see her again, and I was terrified at the same time.

I had to impress her. I could not make a fool of myself or I would never be able to live it down.

Danny and I headed to the front of the estate near the gate to begin lessons and practicing. He drew his sword, and I drew mine rolling my shoulders preparing to battle.

"Okay," he said looking me up and down, "In this battle we'll turn our swords to the side, so that we have air resistance to slow our blows and strengthen us. It makes it easier to swing it the right way when you need to. I always practice by swinging the flat side of the blade against the wind."

72

"That's a good idea," I agreed and Mandy joined us watching our sparring, and so did Anna Bee, who looked expressionless. She held her odd looking axe behind her back, watching Danny closely.

I realized that they must have been worried I was about to duel a stranger with razor sharp swords. That probably was not the smartest idea on my part.

He spent a couple hours teaching me some close forms, and taught me some alternative ways to block and attack. I soaked up what he taught me like a sponge growing more and more comfortable.

By the time he could not think of anything more to teach me it was midafternoon, and Mandy and Anna Bee were no longer worried.

"So, are you ready for a real spar then? I'll try to go easy on you, and adjust with you my lord, I'll grow harder as you learn. Though skill helps a lot, I should mention fights are won by passion and drive. The best way to become a skillful swordsman is experience." He nodded, "are you ready my lord?"

"Let's try this," I nodded excitedly, "you come at me, and I'll defend."

He charged me, and I swung my sword to block his blow, and before I knew it he knocked me on my rear, throwing my sword to the side, and nudging me to the ground with his shoulder.

"Oh wow," he blinked extending an arm and Mandy laughed at me, "That didn't take long."

"Are you okay my lord?" Anna Bee rushed to my side as I sat there in a daze.

Danny stood there, his hand extended out to me, "shall we try again?"

"Yeah, for sure, don't go easy on me, I want to learn!" I said accepting his strong hand and he pulled me up quickly, "Okay my lord, as you wish."

The second time, he charged me and knocked me on my back even harder, making me slide painfully through the muddy grass.

"My lord!" Anna Bee shrieked and rushed to me, and Danny approached, "I recommend we warm you up before I go all out sir. Start slow, however we will do it however you command."

Anna Bee helped pull me up and she whispered in my ear when he wasn't looking, "You are trying to block his blows. Try evading him and strike around him instead."

I glanced at her curiously for a moment and she gave a little curtsey pulling on her green maids dress. She headed away.

"Again," I ordered, "Let's try again."

He charged and I swiftly swung to the left and nearly dealt a blow to his side, and he swiftly deflected my sword and knocked me onto my back making me roll across the lawn.

"That was a little better," he said light hearted. I could see he was thinking pretty hard about the situation, and I gazed curiously at Anna Bee and her weapon as Danny pulled me up. After that she only cringed when I fell painfully to the grass over and over again.

There was no doubt that Danny was a dang good swordsman. I could not touch him. Hours went by and Anna Bee went in to prepare a light lunch for us as we dueled. I guess I shouldn't call it dueling because I was getting beat around like a punching bag. His sword leaving me bruises and welts on my arms, sides and legs.

I finally snapped and ordered him to slow down a little bit. Danny obeyed, but I still could not beat him. Mandy stood watching amused, "You're supposed to block Danny's blows, my lord."

Anna Bee came out shortly after with some light sandwiches she had cut into little triangles with the same fresh baked loaf that she had already made. I sat painfully on the lawn eating my sandwich. My body sore from the physical exercise as well as the physical repetition of the sword hitting me.

"You are getting a lot better my lord," Danny nodded after finishing a bite of sandwich, "You are learning quickly."

"Hopefully my opponent is not near as good, so I might stand a chance," I said swinging the sword around nonchalantly, "she is supposed to arrive any time today."

"She?" Danny asked curiously, "Your challenger is a woman?"

"Yes, a girl I met at the Market Day Fair. She rejected my attempt at talking to her by saying I was coward who did not know how to fight for what I wanted, so I challenged her to a sword fight. If I can beat her, she will tell me her name," I explained and I smiled dreamily, "She's really pretty."

"So, a girl rejected a *lord*?" He looked deep in thought, "and you are doing all of this still to learn her name?"

"Yes," I nodded.

"He didn't present himself very well, he needs another chance," Mandy shrugged, "That's all."

"Well," Danny shrugged a little concerned looking at me, "Whatever makes you happy my lord."

After lunch we continued, and soon I could see the dust of an oncoming carriage as it approached. My heart skipped a beat, "She came! She is here!"

Mandy followed me and I unlocked the gate and stood there eagerly. The carriage was a small one with an older gentleman at the driver's seat.

He hopped out of the driver's seat and walked around the carriage to the side facing me, and opened the door to let her out, "Please be careful miss."

She stepped out in a full set of smooth metal armor, a sword at each hip, and she bowed with a sigh, "My lord. I have come to accept your challenge." She smiled, "Let's make this quick, I am a very busy girl."

I stood there dreamily. She looked so good in her armor, the afternoon sunlight reflecting off the plate metal, her hair down and neatly flowing on the breeze behind her shoulders. She was so pretty, I could not believe it. I could never say it enough. I felt obsessed with her.

I bowed in return and she stepped onto my lawn, "So this is your estate?" She asked looking around curiously, "This is where, Zander, the machine Lord lives. Are your servants the only humans in your domain?" She asked amused, "You're not a very powerful lord are you."

I shook my head, "I never asked for the title of lord."

"Would you like to come inside for tea or a sandwich? Perhaps before you duel my master," Anna Bee bowed glancing at Danny and I as though trying to hint at something.

"How lovely," she smirked and looked at me, "I might have the time. Will you escort me to your estate, my lord?"

I turned facing the massive building, "Of course, right this way."

I lead her along the neat stone path I had created years ago to the front door. Mandy, Anna Bee, and Danny awkwardly all followed us and she stepped through the doorway, armor rattling with every step as she gracefully walked.

"It's awful empty," she frowned, "Do you have more machines and people somewhere else in the property?"

"No ma'am," I shook my head, "All I have is what you see."

"Great," she sighed with a gentle sarcastic tone, "A *really* powerful lord."

"He is a young lord, a new lord," Danny said quickly clearing his throat defending his master's honor, "Give him time. He will be a powerful lord."

I blinked, "I don't... sure. Right." Even though being a powerful ruling Lord had no beneficial or tempting trait to me, I wanted to impress her, "I am learning. I am beginning to recruit."

"Well," she admired the fireplace as she seated herself in one of my old rickety chairs, "You do not even have a couch?"

I shook my head, "There was one here a while ago, but it was thrown out because it was just a metal frame. I wish I had a couch... but I will get one. I am growing as a lord, I assure you." I quickly changed my tone and she gave me a humored look and then did a double take at the ceiling, "My lord... You have *electricity*?" She adjusted in her chair and then eagerly looked full of thought and wonder before she turned back to me, "My lord *where* do you get *electricity*?"

Anna Bee brought her a cup of steaming tea, "My lord has created a self-sustaining reactor that powers his entire domain. Every accessible room has a light that functions perfectly, and he has an electric stove... it's incredible."

"Is that so?" suddenly she was very interested and I was relieved that for a moment she seemed impressed, "Do any of the other lords know you have electricity?"

"Just my ally, lord Osburn," I said clearing my throat, "But we are trying to keep it a secret, so I would greatly appreciate it if it stays that way."

She raised an eyebrow, "so if I moved my home to your domain, you would give me power to my home?"

"O-of course," I said smiling. I had to force myself to stop staring at her. Her skin so clear and soft, her eyes so big and beautifully clear.

That would mean she would be closer to me, and that would mean I could talk to her more. The thought excited me and I repeated, "Of course I would."

"Or perhaps I could sell this information of your electricity to Wellington," she shrugged, "and watch him take your estate by force, and then I get power right where I live comfortably now." She leaned forward raising an eyebrow to study my reaction to what she said.

"What would it take to persuade you, *not* to do that?" I asked a little irritated for a moment, but all she had to do was lean back and smile that pretty smile and wave her hair as though she had been kidding, "I could b-build you a robot..." I offered.

"A robot," she ran a hand through her hair and smiled at me, "a robot huh? Just like your Mandy," she motioned to Mandy standing behind me, "That sounds like a fair trade, a robot, and in return I'll keep my mouth shut."

"Okay," I said sighed under my breath. I felt a little betrayed and hurt, but her beauty seemed to rekindle my fire and make me feel better. I just wanted to make her happy, and I wanted to impress her. Maybe I could get her to approach me as she did in my dreams, her words sweet and low. The thought of holding her hand for real drove me wild.

"Shall we cross blades, so I may learn the name of such a beautiful woman?" I asked clearing my throat to change the subject, my heart pumping, and smiling from head to foot. I was ready to fight.

She grinned and set down her tea gently, "Let's get to it then."

We headed outside, and Anna Bee stayed loyally at my side for reasons I did not understand, even closer now that this beautiful woman was here. So did Danny and Mandy as we walked out to the front lawn. He was standing so close to me on the opposite side it felt as though he was going to put his arm in mine.

"I will only draw one sword for this battle," the beautiful girl drew her sword with the sound of metal scraping against the sheath, "Shall we?"

I drew my own sword, and my servants took a couple steps back, and Anna Bee gently chimed, "Please, be careful my lord."

"You got this, my lord," Danny assured me.

"Words of encouragement," Mandy spat sarcastically which made most everyone crack a brief smile, especially Danny who nodded approvingly in her direction.

"I will defend," the blonde woman's armor rattled as she smiled twisting the sword skillfully on her palm, "Let's see what you've got, *Machine Lord*."

I stepped closer and swung at her as though I was testing her. She skillfully threw my sword out of my hand and smacked me down with the broad side of her sword, "That was cute, shall we spar for real now?"

I picked up my sword slowly cringing inside. I took a deep breath, "Right, that was just a taste of my humor. Now our battle begins in earnest."

Danny face palmed to my right and murmured under his breath, "Quite humorous actually."

I charged her again being faster and more careful. Again she knocked me onto my face and knees painfully dropping my sword as I spun. Her blade scratching my arm drawing a little bit of my blood.

She was more graceful than Danny, and she was faster. It felt as though she was even better than Danny was, and I tried again and again. She laughed at me knocking me down harder and harder every time I tried to advance. I grew close only once because she was laughing, and even then she deflected my blow and clobbered me in the chin, making me fall on my back.

She was so cool, so pretty, and so strong. Her sword skills were far greater than I thought which was very embarrassing. She knew I was trying my hardest, and she still let me keep trying. I just loved the way the sunlight reflected on her hair, the way she did not break a sweat as she knocked me back and fought me off.

I was almost scared to hurt her, but angry I could not best her at the same time.

I had to find a way to impress her... Or this whole mess I was in would just be a painful beating to my personal ego and physical body. I couldn't let her slip away, I wanted to at least learn name.

I stood there painfully ready to come try again and she sheathed her sword, "You just don't seem to know when to give up, so I will end our little sparring session now. Thank you for the tea. I shall return to get my robot in a couple days as we've negotiated."

She turned to head towards her carriage, night was beginning to creep over the sky above us.

"When I give you this robot," I said talking over my own battered breathing, "Will you tell me your name?" I asked desperately, my head hung low in embarrassment.

"Oh honey, you're persistent," she spun towards me with a smirk, "I'll tell you what. I'm not trying to be a mean person. I don't want you to think I'm blackmailing you for the robot, I just like what I want, and I go get it. I'll think about it. When I return for the robot, if it meets my expectations, I shall tell you my name."

"Okay," I smiled exhausted with a little relief wanting to collapse.

"Thanks again," she laughed at me, "You were a really entertaining part of my day. I'll see you around, Machine Lord."

The old man opened the carriage door and she stepped inside and then she waved through the window as I watched the carriage glide away down the gravel road.

"Are you sure you can design a robot that fast?" Mandy asked as her, Anna Bee and Danny approached behind me.

"Are you okay my lord? She was not very gentle with you," Anna Bee helped me to my feet, and gently let me lean on her. I could see the worry in her gentle blue eyes as I stood straight and stretched my sore muscles miserably. Anna Bee was stronger and more solid then she looked, she wasn't straining at all with my weight on her.

"I said I wanted to slap you..." Mandy said standing on the grass, "but I think I can accept what I just watched to satisfy me. You would never give me away, would you?"

"Of course not," I shook my head, "No one could replace you, Mandy."

"That's the girl you think is beautiful?" Danny asked and turned to me honestly, "Maybe on the outside my lord." He turned watching the carriage disappear into the trees with a cloud of dust in the evening light.

"Perhaps you should pick a different woman to go after. Someone who actually cares about you, and appreciates you. Someone who doesn't blackmail you like that," he said obviously. He had a skeptical look and his glance momentarily moved to Anna Bee and then immediately back to me.

I stood there dreamily zoned out and blindly staring at the carriages fleeing direction, "She's right that's all. I need to grow a lot stronger. She is just so beautiful? Especially her hair, did you see the way it shined in the sunlight?"

"Sorry my lord," Danny sighed and then he mumbled annoyed under his breath, "You really have spent your whole life alone in this estate. Perhaps I should have moved on to the next town."

6: Loves Blind Loyalty

I looked at him in a massive dreamy daze. The beautiful woman's eyes and smile replaying in my mind as though she was standing in Danny's place.

"S-she truly is very beautiful, I can see that she makes you happy," Anna Bee commented staring at the cloud of dust, "I am sorry she mistreats you so."

"Mistreats me?" I asked, "She just doesn't know me. The same way I don't know her."

"I am going to start supper," Anna Bee bowed and then headed inside, "I will hopefully see you all inside safe and sound. Zander, my lord, I shall come find you when it is ready."

"Thank you Anna Bee," I nodded to her and then turned back to Danny, "shall we continue practicing?" I said lifting my sword painfully.

Danny shrugged looking at me with a disbelieving look, "If that's what you want."

We practiced until Anna Bee had prepared tacos, and they were as delicious as anything else she cooked. Warm tortillas with ground beef and multiple other condiments. I loved it, I loved having a maid. She didn't speak very much the rest of the night, she just looked deep in thought.

After Dinner I limped painfully exhausted to my bed with a full belly, where I curled up and went to sleep.

———

Eight men were gathered around a pot of boiling and thickening beans over a crackling fire laughing and talking amongst themselves. They all wore armor with the painted crest of Wellington and had swords and various weapons on them, including assault rifles. One man even carried a wood and metal cross bow as well as a long razor sharp sword on his hip.

"It's easy," the man with the crossbow glanced at the chain link fence in the moonlight, "the orders are clear. The scheduled informant will tell us what little military resistance this guy has. After that, we will storm the estate, kill the idiot lord Z-something in his sleep, and take the robot called "Mandy". Wellington expects us back in the morning with a robot, so we can't screw this up." He lifted the crossbow to his shoulder confidently watching the fence line in the distance, "As Alder, his trusted knight, I will see to it that this happens."

"Do we know who the informant is?" One of the men asked.

"The boss said it would be a woman," he said, "That is all I know."

One man piped up, "I heard the fool lord does not have a single soldier in his entire estate. I even heard he does not own a sword."

"Speaking of rumors, did you hear the rumor about the monster bunny lurking around?" One man laughed, "One of Dave's men reported seeing one outside Wellington's estate. Can you believe that, "A monster bunny? It's going to come cuddle us to death."

There was a rustle in the bushes over towards the chain-link fence, and Alder pointed his crossbow and laughed as they all turned, "Here it comes. The monster bunny."

Anna Bee stepped from the bushes and brush, her arms full of firewood, on her back her sharp battle axe with a sword handle. She hesitated when she saw them all gathered around, and gently set down the firewood.

"Who are you? What is the password?" The men suddenly all stood up urgently, readying their weapons and Anna Bee glanced at them one at a time in nervous thought. It looked like she was planning, her eyes fearfully accepting the situation.

"Password?" She asked, "What are you doing on my master's estate?"

"It's the damn maid," one of the men growled, "She *can't* be the informant."

"Informant?" She asked, "W-what do you need to know?"

They gently walked around the fire approaching her with wicked and malicious smiles, "aren't you a pretty little thing..."

She took a step back, "I think I remember..." she said quickly, "I was supposed to be a spy and tell you how much military strength he had..." She said hanging her head shamefully stuttering nervously, "I think I r-remember now, so that I could tell you the b-best way to attack the estate quickly."

"Oh good," Alder grinned and sat back down on his log, "So it *is* you. Well then? Let her talk men, then you may have your way with her."

"Do you know what it's like to never be as good as everyone else?" She asked facing them, her knuckles growing white around the handle of the axe from squeezing it frustrated, "To never be good enough, not for your own parents. Not good enough for anyone to adopt you... not good enough at all."

She hid her eyes behind her bangs and a quiet tear fell from her cheek, silently falling to the grass glinting as a silver streak in the moonlight.

"What are you talking about, I guess I don't understand?" Alder's eyes narrowed impatiently, "What does that have to do with this idiot's forces."

"That's me..." She said, "Never good enough, never fast enough... I can't cook as well as the other maids..."

"Okay," he shrugged, "Whatever. Does he have any armed men? Tell us everything."

She clutched the axe standing there, another tear falling, looking just as silver as the first tear in the moonlight, "If you think I would ever betray the *one* person who tells me *I am good enough*..." she raised the axe quickly towards them shaking and aggressively, lifting her bangs so she could clearly see them, "P-please leave, I don't wish to hurt anyone."

Alder burst out laughing, "*You*, the maid? We're eight full grown experienced fighting men. We're soldiers of Wellington, and you're going to clean us all up? Take us out for wanting to hurt your master, is that your plan? I have to admit that's quite some loyalty to your master, especially to betray Wellington like that. Standing alone against impossible odds. You must be terrified."

Her eyes grew serious, her hands growing steady, "I will defend my master with my life. He gives me happiness, and I am his servant. It is my duty to defend him."

"Look at *this*. Remember those beware of dog signs?" One man asked leaning over, whiskey on his breath waving his sword, "He should hang up "beware of maid" signs on his fence."

The men all chuckled at the joke and lowered their guard. Some men even started heading back towards the logs to sit back down. Alder took a step forward, "Talk or I'll make you talk, *traitor*."

"The only person I would be betraying if I said a word, would be my lord. I will only warn you one more time, do not take another step," She growled.

"Get her," Alder leaned back on the log irritated.

An armored man moved towards her not drawing his sword, and the man with the assault rifle came forward grinning.

Anna Bee threw up the axe grabbing it by the handle with both hands steadily, "Please, forgive me for the mess, Zander."

She slid the long sheathed sword out of the bottom of her axe handle and spun her body skillfully launching the axe with a glint of steel in the moonlight. It tore through the man's armor and ribs who held the assault rifle and he choked on his own blood with a cry hitting the ground hard. The closest surprised man swung his sword at her with sudden urgency. She spun dodging it skillfully and twisted around him shoving her sword through the armor on his back. She ripped out the sword and rolled for her axe retrieving it and rolling back to her feet.

The rest of the men charging her angrily.

"Kill her!" Alder screamed loading his crossbow quickly standing up from his comfortable log surprised.

Another man charged and swung his mace and she ducked and slid his companion's body towards him with her foot knocking him off his feet. Anna Bee waited for the man to fall to her feet and she brought her axe down on the tripped man's skull. She ripped out the axe with a gruesome crunch and spun evading a man drawing pistol to fire at her. She twirled like a graceful ballerina and took off the man's hand with the pistol as he fired, forcing him to shoot the attacking man on the opposite side of her before the man's hand even hit the ground.

A man desperately swung with a knife and it nicked her arm, her blood shining through the moonlight making her whimper before she spun the sword around and cut him down with a grunt, and then she threw the axe. The razor sharp blade cut through the cold air and tore through Alder's wooden crossbow and cut into him.

The last two men besides Alder thrusted skillfully with their swords and she jumped back deflecting both jabs with one swing of her sword and spun around one of them quickly and efficiently, running her blade through his gut so skillfully it came out his back cutting him clean in half.

Alder drew his sword and blocked her blow as she charged him and he forced her back, foolishly sending her straight back towards her axe. She ripped it out of the ground, and for a moment she stood there, and Alder caught the last angry man by his arm as he charged her.

"Let me handle this one..." Alder growled raising his sword walking towards her, "What the hell kind of maid are you?"

"I'm Zander's maid," she said dual wielding the blade and axe, spinning them on her palms skillfully, "I will not let you pass me. You will not harm him."

"Do you know what I had to go through to gain the title of Wellington's Knight?" He growled stepping towards her angrily.

"Do you know what I had to go through, to find someone as soft hearted and as kind as Zander?" She asked looking at him through her bangs with serious angry eyes, her nervous and shy demeanor completely replaced, "You will leave now, or I will be sure you remain here forever."

"Well then, I'll kill you, and I'll return with an army to destroy whatever he has, and I'll slit his throat, "Alder growled swinging his sword through the air with a smirk.

Anna Bee's eyes relaxed and she closed them for a moment, and then they opened with an intense ferocity, "I won't let you hurt him!"

She drew back her weapons and charged lashing out at him with the axe and he stepped back and skillfully deflecting the bow, and then he spun the blade to block her sword with a glint of sparks in the dark. She dropped low swinging her axe, and he leapt over it striking downward with his sword.

She swung her sword blocking the sword above her head, and took her opening with his arms lowered. She drew the sword and axe from both sides exposing herself for an attack down the middle of her body.

Alder lunged with the sword seeing the opening, and Anna Bee's sword skillfully veered off course with terrifying speed trapping him and blocking his sword while her axe tore through his armor with a smear of blood that went as far as the crackling fire. She kicked him off her blade, and he slumped onto his back with a groan spitting up blood.

She threw the axe and spun it towards the last man and he trembled and cringed, the axe striking a tree with a heavy thud having missed his face by a mere terrifying inch. His master's blood stained his face and lips from the impact of the passing axe and he screamed shaking and collapsed falling against the tree.

"I need you to deliver a message to Wellington..." Anna Bee said to the lone standing man, "I need you to live."

"W-what are you?" the man asked shaking backing towards the nearest tree, "I'm sorry... I wasn't going to touch you... I'm not like the other guys. I swear!"

"Tell Wellington I never agreed to his task. I have no intention of spying. I will protect my master with my life, you understand that?" She turned to him with an angry glare.

Anna Bee collected her firewood back up into a neat pile. She retrieved her axe and wiped the bloody sword on her thick apron. The man cringed at the sound of sliding metal as she sheathed the sword into the bottom of the Axe Handle.

"He won't like that... he could kill me for returning empty handed..." the man choked and fell to his knees and pulled his hands together, "I beg for mercy, please. I cannot stand in front of him with nothing."

"I have given you something to tell him," Anna Bee brushed her bangs out of her face and sighed glancing at her bleeding arm, "If it's truly that bad then perhaps you should find a different lord. I'll kill you if you come near mine."

She gently took her firewood and headed back toward the chain link fence where she crossed through an old gate overgrown with weeds. She turned re-locking it with a fresh padlock she had found while cleaning around the various offices and workshops. The distant glow of the crackling fire deep within the trees in the distance.

In the estate Anna Bee changed into another green maids dress in her room, and put on another apron. Shortly after she finished changing, Mandy poked her head in after a gentle knock on the door.

"Anna Bee?" Mandy asked, "Are you awake."

"Yes," Anna Bee nodded washing out the cut on her arm, "C-can I help you, master?"

"Zander is having those nightmares again," Mandy commented, "Can you do the thing again, the thing that you did last night?"

"Of course," She tightly stitched up her arm quickly, her eyes bloodshot from the pain, and then she bandaged it and tied a thick piece of fabric around it and then followed her shyly to Zander's side.

"What happened to your arm," Mandy asked.

"It got cut," Anna Bee said innocently, "I was careless when I was out gathering firewood this evening."

"Please be careful," Mandy insisted, and they stood in Zander's doorway. He tossed and turned sweating fiercely in the night.

Anna Bee approached the bed and sat lightly beside him. She reached over taking his hand, "It is not real my Lord. It is going to be okay." She used her thumb, gently stroking his hand as she watched him calm down and lie peacefully, "It's going to be okay, my lord."

"I thank you," Mandy nodded standing in the doorway.

Anna Bee smiled and turned to him, her hand stroking his in the dark, "Zander's very handsome in his sleep. He looks peaceful and very weak, but when he is awake he is so strong..."

Danny poked his head in the doorway rubbing his sleepy eyes, "What is going on? Everything okay?"

Anna Bee gently pulled her hand away to preserve her master's reputation as Mandy spoke, "He has nightmares. We are just making sure he is okay. Anna Bee, you should probably get to bed."

She rose, "Yes master."

"What happened to your arm?" Danny asked her as she passed by.

"I was just cleaning up the estate," she smiled and headed off, "I'm so very clumsy..." and she waited until he was out of earshot and whispered hastily under her breath, "Or maybe I was doing *your* job."

7: A Taunting Attack and a Lying Lord

I woke up, and I was lying in the dark forest near the front fence of my estate. I was lying on my back in the mud and grass. It was hazy around me, and as I slowly sat up I could see the same trail of blood from my dream the night before going through my damaged and open front gate. The whole metal gate was hanging off a single bent hinge.

I quickly got to my feet in a panic, "H-hey! What the!?"

I drew my sword and leapt through the gate running toward the estate, and I felt my heart pound as I saw Mandy's damaged arm lying in the lobby doorway. The door to my own living room ripped off its hinges, lying in the center of the lobby, and I followed the trail of blood as quickly as I could. I crossed around the corner and I saw the beast.

It's back to me fresh blood dripping from its claws. It snapped around facing me as though it had heard me approach. Its teeth chattering, "You did nothing. You let them all die, I destroyed them... I killed them!" Its voice was low, and its scratchy evil snake like sound sent shivers up my spine as it raised its claws walking towards me.

"N-no," I stuttered, "This can't be real!"

The beast charged me, and I swung my sword to defend myself. It just knocked me around as the woman did earlier, "Look at how useless you are..." It hissed as it forced me to the ground with its claws, I will kill you..."

I heard the sudden rattle of armor, and I watched the flash of a sword tear through the monster. It melted into darkness fading away into the night. My heroine standing there in her beauty as she quickly sheathed her sword. Her blond hair and armor shining in the light of the estate lights along the hallway ceiling.

She took my hand and gently pulled me to my feet, the feeling of her hand in mine making my worries melt away. Her hand was soft and warm, "It is not real my Lord. It is going to be okay." She smiled sweetly, her thumb gently rubbing against the back of my hand in a very comforting way, "It's going to be okay, my lord."

Everything melted peacefully away around me, and I peacefully drifted into darkness.

I sat up in my bed blinking. Drool sticking to my cheek, my eyes slowly cracking open from the night. I felt myself up and down, and then waited for things to clarify so I knew I was awake for real this time.

"Another dream," I said flatly. I made sure I had really woken up this time, and I rose out of bed and wandered to the lounge just to make sure.

Anna Bee was cutting tiny shapes at the counter, her back to me. As she turned around I could see a bloody bandage tightly coiled around her arm. She noticed me with a sweet smile, "G-good morning my lord. Mandy told me you liked cereal, so I am trying to make it for you... but I have never done it before."

"What happened to your arm?" I asked hesitantly, the dream still stirring in my mind.

She blushed, "I'm sorry lord I was careless. I got cut by some trash on the estate. I assure you there is nothing to worry about."

"You promise?" I asked and cautiously approached her arm, "Jeez it looks like someone took a knife and hacked at you. Please be careful, I would never want to lose my Anna Bee."

She trembled and lowered her head quietly nearly dropping her knife she was working with, "W-what did you say, sir?"

I carefully took her hand confused and placed the knife on the counter so she did not drop it, "Are you okay? What I mean, is you are so much better than any robot, you do such a great job around here. I really would not want to lose you, that's all. I honestly keep trying to figure out how I can keep you when my two years are up," I explained, "That's all."

Her lip quivered and I watched a slow smile cross her lips as though it was cutting through her usually shy face. She began to shake, blushing and turned away from me quickly acting overwhelmed with emotion, "Do you really mean that my lord?"

I carefully removed my hand once the knife was in a safer position, "Yes... I don't get why you are behaving this way, are you ill from your wound?" I felt her fore head gently for traces of a fever.

"No my lord, I am fine... I just don't get why you say those things... I am just a maid, I am not as good as the others... I have never made cereal before..." She motioned to the little shapes she was cutting out turning to face the counter.

I noticed she had cut out little squares and circles, and among them I noticed a single heart and I laughed amused, "Why did you cut out all these different shapes, but only one heart?"

"Because..." She whispered staring at the small fragile dough heart, "Everybody has only one heart, my lord... My lord can I ask a strange request?"

I raised an eyebrow, "Of course, Anna Bee. What is it?"

"May I have a hug?" She asked and she looked down blushing, "I mean... It's weird I know..."

I awkwardly wrapped my arms around her, "Of course, Anna Bee. It's only a hug."

She sucked in her breath as though I was going to squeeze or hit her, but slowly let loose a comfortable sigh and hugged me back.

"Well..." I took a step back after a moment, "It doesn't matter if you mess up the cereal, because accidents happen. Everything you have done so far is awesome, so I don't think you will. Besides, today is the day we work in the workshop remember? I have to make a robot for *her.* I wish I knew her name, I have to be ready when her beautiful presence returns to me in a couple days, then I'll learn her name!"

I turned and headed for the lobby. Danny urgently exploded into the lobby as I entered, panic written all over his face, "My lord! I found bodies! Seven of them, a little ways away from the estate fence. They are really torn up..."

"W-what," I asked and I turned surprised, "what do you mean?"

"Lord Wellington's men, they had set up a camp. It looks like they were going to attack, but something killed them before they did. There was no other bodies, all the bodies had his mark, but none of their weapons matched their gruesome wounds. I am not sure who killed them..." Danny's voice trailed off.

"Or... what killed them..." I whispered remembering the beast that rattled the fence and my reoccurring nightmares of it.

"There was very small footsteps, and they looked human, but it was only one set..." he looked confused, "Either way Wellington plans on attacking you my lord, and clearly something or someone is watching out for you. That or Wellington's men were just in the wrong place at the wrong time..." he looked as though his mind was spinning in circles.

"Salvage what you can of their weapons and armor," I said rubbing my temples growing stressed, "take Buster with you, and take some of the service droids to bury the bodies I guess."

"Buster?" He asked curiously.

"Follow me," I said and headed out the door watching the fence line apprehensively. I almost wanted the thing to show up; attack if it was going to, just get it over with.

I began to weave through the scrap in the back of the estate. Danny followed me curiously, "So I assume Buster is a robot then?"

"Yes," I nodded, "an old G class construction robot. In good shape because they had do have thick armor to protect themselves from debris and falling buildings. It was one of the first robots I repaired since it was so well preserved. I swapped a couple wires and reset it..."

I approached the massive fifteen foot seamed cylinder and clapped twice, "Buster, wake up, I need you up."

The ground began to rumble as he warmed up, then the sides of the rusty cylinder shot out. The massive cylinder unfolded and untucked itself into the twenty foot armored robot.

Dust fell from its seams as it stood. The sound of metal scraping against metal and the noisy hiss of hydraulics that needed lubrication made the air tremble as he grew to his feet,

"Zander," His massive voice grumbled, "Are we starting a new project today?"

"I need you to bury some things for me. Danny here will show you where they are," I nodded motioning behind me to Danny who was looking terrified up at the massive armored robot, "Just follow him."

Buster's giant metal fingers clicked together and curved, his hand transforming into a massive digging bucket, "I will obey." His massive flat steps shook the ground, crushing and bending scrap steel with every step as it came towards us and it stooped low, "Nice to meet you Danny. Let us get to work."

The ground shook with Buster's steps as I watched them leave. Danny went through the gate, and Buster just stepped over the fence accidentally knocking a tree over with a loud crash as he stepped with a wide powerful gape.

Buster's raw awesome power never ceased to amaze me. He was a fantastic asset to my robotic team when I needed things moved that I could not move myself. I headed back to the lounge where Anna Bee met me at the door with her axe, "Is everything okay? I thought I could feel the ground shaking."

"Just Buster," Mandy interjected as she walked through the door behind me as I entered. She unloaded an armload of firewood to the growing pile beside the fireplace, "Everything is okay."

"Okay," Anna Bee smiled, "breakfast is ready my lord."

I headed to the lounge and took a seat as she poured me a bowl of fresh delicious cereal, and slid me some carefully toasted bread.

I ate slowly, thinking about everything that Danny had told me and I grumbled, "I wonder what happened? It must have been the monster rabbit... It must be real..."

Anna Bee shrugged, "What is important is the fact you are safe, my lord."

It was not as sweet or as crunchy as the cereal I had at Nate's but it was still delicious. It made me happy that I now had access to it, and Mandy stood at the end of the table her motors humming as though she was having a noisy epiphany.

"Mandy," I said briefly pausing from my breakfast, "I'm going to assign you a new task today while Anna Bee and I are working in my workshop. Danny should be returning with salvaged weapons and armor, so I want you to rearrange the old locker rooms into an armory, and I want you to find another lock to lock the door. Please clean it up, and use the lockers to store the weapons. Make sure you clean them out as well."

"Of course sir, a change in tasks is always pleasant," she nodded, "I shall set to work right away." She turned and headed down the hallway after an obedient bow.

"Sir?" Anna Bee asked standing there, her hands neatly behind her back politely and professionally as they almost always were unless she was using them... "May have permission to ask you a personal f-favor..." her voice trailed off, "N-never mind, my lord."

"No, no," I said quickly, "don't you dare do this to me. You've peaked my curiosity, what is it?"

"I just realized it was for my own gain..." she said almost hanging her head as though she was ashamed, "So it is irrelevant."

"Spill it, that's an order," I said as I lazily finished my bowl of cereal and I leaned back in my chair, "Thank you for the wonderful breakfast, Anna Bee."

"Your welcome my lord... I was just wondering if you would... like me to give you a haircut?" She asked almost as though she was trying to force it out. Her blue eyes were glancing at me hopefully, shining in the lobby lights.

I had not had a haircut in eight years, and I thought for a moment, "Umm, sure." I felt my long shoulder length hair, gently bouncing the tangled mess, "If you want to."

"I do," she said, "but the decision is up to you."

"Sure," I shrugged and she gently smiled, "Okay."

She gathered a pair of sharp scissors and a razor from her room. She then prepared a warm bowl of water from the kitchen faucet, and she set the bowl on the table to my left. She gathered a couple other things and creams from my room with a graceful speedy stride. Before I knew it she was prepared to begin standing there with a sweet grin.

"Why do you want to cut my hair?" I asked curiously, "That's a random request." She began working with the sound of snipping scissors behind me.

"As your maid and servant it is my responsibility to make sure you are always presentable when you receive guests, and I think you would look..." her voice trailed off for a moment, "...more professional if you have a haircut."

She began to snip away at my tangled hair with the scissors, "I appreciate you letting me do this my lord."

"I suppose I was about due for one," I shrugged, "It will be easier to clean this way."

"I have never actually taken a real shower until I got here under your service, they are truly wonderful," she said as she worked behind me, "I had heard that they were very refreshing, and it was one of my childhood dreams to take a shower. So I believe it is safe to say I truly enjoy the showers here. Electricity comes with more blessings that I could ever imagine. I do not have to boil water over a wood stove to do dishes and clean, I do not have to replace lamps or candles. I believe your electricity does the work of four or five servants, without the servants."

"I guess I never thought of that," I shrugged, "I just needed the electricity to repair the power cores that I found to power up and fix all my robots. The lights, plumbing, and water I fiddled with long after I had the power actually."

She gave a sudden sweet little giggle, and her eyes softened as she continued working. Then began gently shaving my face with the razor.

I looked confused, "What's so funny?"

"I'm sorry my lord, your hair just tickled my arm," she said quickly, "I won't do it again,"

I sighed, "Oh dear. You don't have to apologize, you have a cute giggle. I wonder what the woman from the fair's giggle is like." I envisioned the beautiful blond hair, the feel of her soft hands in my dreams. I bet she had a beautiful giggle. Though she had confused me the last time she was here, and literally beat me with a sword, I could not wait to see her again. I missed looking at her brown beautiful eyes, her neatly brushed blond hair.

"Please hurry," I smiled, "We have a lot to do."

"Yes, sir," she said behind me, "I am almost done. Thank you for allowing me this special request."

"No problem," I shrugged planning out my day, there was so much I wanted to do, and there was three robots in my construction cue. Not to mention I wanted to continue training with my sword. I still needed to design some kind of soldier droid A.I adaptable enough to attach to different models of processors so that I could create a lot of "soldiers" as quickly as possible. With the looming possibility of an attack from Wellington, and whatever was in the forest around my estate, I needed the military strength.

I wanted to protect Mandy, and I wanted to protect Anna Bee, as well as all of my creations, and in order to do that, I needed to get better at fighting myself. I told myself my nightmares would remain nightmares, and that I would learn to fight and protect my friends.

She handed me a mirror when I was done, and I looked much different than before. My blue eyes could be clearly seen now, and my head felt much lighter. It made me look much older, more respectable. It was amazing how much of a difference it made. I gently touched my soft shaven cheek.

I headed to the shower as Anna Bee was cleaning up all my fallen hair below the dining room table with a broom and dustpan. After I had finished my shower I headed to my room to get dressed and sheathe my sword to my belt. Once I was dressed I headed to my workshop to begin a day of hard work. Today was different though. I was more excited than usual because I knew I would have company and help.

Anna Bee was patiently waiting with a shy smile, looking at the torn up robot I had been working with. "So, what will we be doing today?" She asked. I pulled one of the damaged robots onto my workbench and then I turned briefly to the computer and began to type. I brought up Mandy's file, and studied it for a second before returning to the workbench.

"I think I can do it. I think I can manipulate Mandy's programing to create a new A.I with a new personality, if I can do this, all I have to do is reconstruct these service robots with a plastic casing. I should be able to do this in only a couple days," I said I began to pull the old robot apart.

She thoughtfully watched over my shoulder, "How did you do that?" She asked as I popped off a rusty metal casing by carefully twisting it off the internal frame. I showed her, pointing to the release, and I reattached the casing and showed her how to pull it back off.

Mandy poked her head into the room, "My lord, someone is at the gate to see you."

I turned a little frustrated, "Really? Who?"

"Lord Wellington," she nodded and I froze, "How many men did he bring?"

"The same amount as he did the last time he was here," she nodded, "He says he simply wants to talk that's all. He does not seem to pose a threat."

"I think I have learned enough to remove the rest of the armor like you have been doing," Anna Bee said, "If you wish me to continue working while you are away, I think I have learned enough and I could try and do it without you."

"Sure," I shrugged, "I'll be back shortly."

Mandy and I went through the large empty estate and eventually approached the gate where his wagon was pulled up. Wellington and his guards were already out of the carriage, impatiently waiting on the other side of the fence. Wellington had a single woman on his arm now, different from either of the other two women I had seen before, and he was wearing an expensive hand stitched suit as well.

"Zander," he said with a sly smile. He waved as I cautiously approached the gate, "I'm sorry to interrupt. I'm sure you're very busy."

"What is your intention?" I asked trying to hide my nerves, but I did not see that many guards around his carriage. I tried to hide that I was desperately and suspiciously watching them.

"You see it's quite embarrassing..." he said in awkward thought, "But I seem to have given you the wrong maid. I meant to give you a different one, and I was wondering if I could repay you two maids in return for your one. A fair trade I would say to correct my foolish mistake."

He gently pushed on the fence as though hinting he wanted to come through it.

"You want my maid?" I asked, "You want Anna Bee?"

"Yes," he said quickly and gave me a charming fake smile, "You see I accidentally gave you the wrong one and..."

"It did not seem like the wrong one at the time. Wouldn't you have noticed which maid it was? She walked right passed you." I said. My voice was defensive and suspicious as I watched Wellington and his guards cautiously through the fence.

I liked Anna Bee. I did not want to give her up. I was afraid to stand against him, but I was not going to let him take her. I saw how he treated her, and she didn't deserve that. At the same time I truly was terrified of this jerk and I did not know what to do.

He scratched his chin thinking, "You make an excellent point, please remember however she was very dirty, and I was distracted by your generous gift of the two robots, which are fantastic by the way. Hard loyal workers that don't complain about the conditions in which they are working."

I cringed trying not to imagine what he could be putting them through, and began to and carefully think of a way out of this situation.

"One of my men found the bodies of your men near my estate," I said, "Why did you have armed men so close to my home, I was under the impression we were friends. Were you planning on attacking me?"

He shifted in his leather shoes, "I heard the rumor of some, "Monster Bunny." They were there for your protection, and I was under the impression they were *still there*. Something has happened to them?"

"Why did you not tell me if you sent men to protect me?" I asked him skeptically.

"It slipped my mind," he said with a frustrated look, "Now, about the maid, Zander." He tried to change the subject and I cleared my throat loudly.

"We'll talk about it when your robot is complete," I said quickly, "I'm trying to sort things out, everything is changing around me, and it's hard to adapt."

"You see I need her sooner because she has a short contract..." he tried to explain.

"A short contract of two years?" I raised an eyebrow and he seemed frustrated and unamused closing his eyes as I spoke quickly, "We'll talk about it when we are negotiating what I get in exchange for the robot."

He began tapping his feet and gave me the same dirty look as before, and the ground gently began to shake. I turned to see Buster approaching, crushing metal and segments of untrimmed lawn as he approached and Danny was power walking ahead of him with arm loads of weapons and salvaged armor.

The ground shook with every step as they approached and Wellington's eyes grew huge at the sight of Buster and he took a step back.

"Wellington," Danny set down the load and cleaned his hands on a rag as he approached, "What do we owe the honor?"

Wellington uncomfortably stared at Buster in frustrated terror, "That's quite the machine you've got."

"It's very powerful," I nodded, "So, is it agreed we'll continue negotiations when you come for the robot."

He took a step back frustrated, "Keep the maid. I'll just accept the mistake that I have made and move on. Perhaps we could negotiate you making me one of those giant robots as well, when the time comes. I shall warn you in the future if I have men come guard you to avoid any miscommunications."

He loaded up looking tense into his carriage. The woman on his arm tried to say something to him to calm him once they were seated, and I watched him knock her off her seat with the back of his hand angrily. I stepped forward to say something but the carriage door slammed shut before I could.

The horses were whipped by the mounted guards, and the carriage turned around heading away. It flew down the gravel road at an alarming rate, nearly crashing into a much smaller second white carriage that was approaching.

Buster bent over with the hiss of his cooling systems, "Do you have any more projects for me lord? Or shall I head back to sleep?"

"Head back to sleep," I nodded, "Thank you for your service."

He transformed into a giant cylinder right there by the gate, and I could hear his systems and motors turning off slowly one by one.

"That has to be the coolest thing I've ever seen," Danny motioned to Buster, "and what did that jerk want?" He motioned to the leaving cloud of dust in the distance.

"He wanted my maid..." I said and I turned around to talk to his face, "I don't really know why, things are not adding up. Perhaps she knows something."

The smaller white carriage arrived behind me and I turned back towards the gate as the carriage door swung open.

A young man in jeans and a black hoody hopped out of the carriage with a briefcase and a rolled set of kitchen knives as he stood there awkwardly for a moment. He had a short black hair and bright thoughtful green eyes and an excited bounce in his step. His hair greasy from hair products and his hands muscular and callused.

"Lord Zander?" He asked through the gate.

"That's me," I nodded and he shrugged, "I'm Terry Loomer, you're new cook."

"Oh, I see," I unlocked the gate and let him in, and I immediately closed and locked it right behind him.

"I'm fairly new to being a cook. I'm good at it though, I assure you my lord," Terry bowed, "I cannot wait for you to sample my cuisine. I just graduated, and I sincerely aim to please!"

"Mandy, get him a room and give him a tour," I said relieved that he was friendly, "I'm going to return to my workshop to continue working. Terry, I am eager to sample your cuisine as well."

"Yes, my lord," Mandy nodded, "Right this way, Terry."

Mandy took his things and lead him in, "Here, let me help you carry these."

"Thank you!" He smiled. He seemed excited. He was only a couple years older than me like Danny, who was now walking by my side as I headed for my workshop, "Is there anything I can do for you, my lord?" Danny asked.

"Patrol the estate. I fear Wellington clearly intends to attack me soon," I nodded, "Please keep up your guard up, and stay prepared."

"Will do. No monster bunny will get passed me on my watch, my lord," he grumbled something under his breath and wandered away. I just ignored his attitude with an uneasy glance towards the fence, and muttered, "I hope so, Danny."

I headed back inside to continue working with Anna Bee, and when I found her, she was struggling to take the last piece of rusted armor off and her eyes lit up gently as she saw me enter. I crossed the room quickly to help her.

———

Danny had been walking along the chain link fence mumbling to himself focusing on the tree line for a couple hours since Zander had headed into the estate. He grumbled as he walked frustrated, "I just volunteered to serve a lord who is obsessed with some stuck up woman. He has one maid, now a cook, and nothing else. I bet if I snuck off he would not even care. I could find a lord who knows what he was doing and become a knight. I can't fight off Wellington's army by myself, that's suicide..." He walked along his hands in his armored jacket's pockets watching carefully for anything suspicious.

"What have I done...," He hung his head watching the grass as he walked, "I wanted to serve a real lord... oh man, this is not what I wanted...I'm so stupid." He looked up at the cloudy sky with a sigh, "But he accepted my blade... and he is a lord..."

The fence rattled behind him interrupting his thoughts, and he spun quickly drawing the bow, notching an arrow ready to fire by the time he had turned around.

There was nothing, and he gently released the tension on the bow confused, "Is there anyone there?"

His eyes narrowed watching the fence line. It sounded like someone clearly rattled the fence, and then his eyes suddenly caught movement deep beyond the tree line outside the fence.

He dropped low crouching, drawing back the arrow again carefully watching through the links in the fence, "Who is out there?"

He could see a vague outline of a figure through the brush, wearing a long white robe that covered his entire body, making him look like a ghostly phantom standing in the distance, wearing a plain white circular mask that had nothing but two curled horns above two eye holes.

"Who are you?" Danny yelled into the trees, and he took aim with the arrow but the figure backed up and eerily faded into shadow.

Danny released the arrow into the trees where the figure had been. He heard a blood curdling scream that made the hairs on the back of his neck stand straight up after he heard the solid "thwack" of his arrow striking something in the shadows.

The scream did not sound human at all, but sounded as though it was hundreds of different animals and humans screaming in desperate pain. It was nothing like he had ever heard before and it made him shiver. He swallowed terrified, watching the tree line frozen in place.

Danny saw a flash of mangled pink fur come through the trees so quickly it just looked like an oncoming blur. He watched the sparks of snapping metal as a terrifying and powerful pink creature slashed straight through the chain link fence with a swipe of long razor sharp bloody claws.

The freakishly thin bloody rabbit had a massive grin of rattling razor sharp teeth and a long pointed head with two angry beady black eyes that stared at Danny.

It stood on two feet like a human, with the smell of rotting flesh and blood drifting on the breeze moving towards Danny as the rabbit drew back its bloody claws and screamed again.

"What are you?" Danny choked reaching for an arrow in his quiver.

The rabbit charged him and slashed with the powerful claws forcing Danny to roll backwards. He desperately notched the arrow he had grabbed from his quiver as he recovered, but the creature was already swinging at him again with terrifying speed forcing him back again.

He blocked the rabbit's powerful strike with his bow, not having enough time to dodge the claws, and then the rabbit brought back the claws on its other hand and slashed again. He ducked quickly, and jumped back as far as he could keeping his balance out of breath, "It's too fast..."

It was already on him slashing and hacking at him with its wicked claws, forcing him to duck and weave around it without hope of retaliation. Amongst the assault he finally found an opening in the monsters attack pattern and struck the notched arrow square in the monster's chest.

The arrow tore into the monster, and there was a mist of black powdery blood that seemed to blow away and fade on the wind.

It screamed angrily, the arrow sticking out the front and the back of its body, and it flexed its thin decaying muscles in its arms making them squeal like old rubbing leather, and its claws grew an entire foot longer on each hand making an awful crunching and splattering sound as they seemed to force themselves out of its flesh as it slashed at him again.

It didn't even care, the arrow lodged in it like it had always been there.

Danny abandoned the bow and drew his sword quickly and swung it skillfully blocking the monster's gruesome claws and then he dove backwards barely dodged the next swing of its claws.

He countered with the sword getting back to his feet, and his blade cut through the creature's arm. The creature's arm exploded into a flash of dark powder, and the creature spun and leapt over the fence with a single bound, its arm growing back slowly as though the powdery blood flowing from it transformed back into the rest of its arm.

"Dammit... what was that?" Danny was out of breath staring into the trees watching the monster disappear into the shadows and he bravely yelled, "That's right! Don't mess with me! It will be more than just your arm next time!" His heart pounding adrenaline into his veins, his lungs sucking in needed oxygen.

The awful scream echoed in his ears, the monsters smell still lingered in his nostrils. He calmed himself down staring at the slashed hole in the chain link fence. He quickly went over to it and began to mend it. He used his bare hands to spin the metal wire on itself moving it into place, "What the freak was that?"

"What was what?" Mandy asked startling him and he spun wildly with his sword and grazed her plastic chest with the sound of crunching plastic.

"Oh, I'm so sorry!" He dropped his sword to the lawn, and then looked over his shoulder into the woods. He bent low facing the trees and picked up the sword when he thought he heard rattling leaves in the distant shadows.

"You look like you've seen a ghost. Your emotional levels are chaotic, are you okay?" Mandy asked curiously.

"I was just attacked by a..." his voice trailed off... "By a..."

"Monster bunny?" She asked, "Lord Zander saw one the other day I suppose. Perhaps you should report to him immediately. Also dinner is ready. Terry has prepared marinated and grilled chicken with a fresh salad vinaigrette for us this evening. "

"Well when you call it a bunny, it does not sound near as terrifying..." Danny said as he gazed briefly behind them into the trees, and then followed Mandy back to the estate.

"Isn't that what you called it?" Mandy asked turning to him, and he looked at her with understanding eyes, but remained silent.

8: Metal Soldiers and Invitations

Later that evening, Mandy came to get Anna Bee and I to inform us that dinner was ready. Anna Bee and I eagerly went to the dining room and sat at the table across from each other. As we sat down Mandy headed outside through the front door to inform Danny that dinner was ready as well.

"I have to say my lord," Terry grinned and bowed standing with his back straight at the table side, "This has to be the most incredible estate. I have to ask where you found a building with electricity... Where does it come from!?"

"I created the power core that fuels this building," I said proudly. Anna Bee smiled as she pulled out my chair for me, "Lord Zander is awesome like that. He created and repaired all the robots here as well. He also repaired all the appliances, including the water heater and the dishwasher."

"I tell you, I thought dishwashers were myths, and look at this fantastic..." He was squirming with excitement as he pointed to the white cleaning appliance behind him, "This is *so* incredible!"

His voice trailed off, his eyes growing huge, "...wait a moment... did you say water heater... running water... do you... do you have a *shower*?"

"Yes," I nodded, "You are more than welcome to use it."

"You are such a kind lord!" He bowed, "This is such a luxury! It is such an honor to serve you!"

After Anna Bee had cut my hair earlier today, it looked like she had a hard time looking at me. Every time she did happen to glance at me, her lip would quiver gently and she would distract herself and look away. I could not figure out why, so sitting there at the table I waited for her to glance at me.

Her lip trembled as I expected it to, and I carefully confronted her trying not to sound aggressive, "Why do you keep doing that?"

She blushed and looked down at her feet, "I just think you look very nice with short hair. That's all, my lord."

"Okay? You are the one who gave me the haircut," I shrugged, "I thank you for that."

She remained very quiet, "You're very welcome, my lord. It was truly my pleasure. Do you think we will be able to finish the robots in time for Lord Wellington and the madam from the fair?"

"If we work as hard as we did today, we should finish it by tomorrow evening..." I was interrupted by Mandy and Danny urgently entering the lounge.

"My lord," Danny dropped to his knee quickly and he seemed out of breath. He seemed almost shaken, his tone serious, "You say you saw a monster rabbit? I was just attacked by one a moment ago, it came straight through the chain link fence."

I spun in my chair shocked, "What? Did you kill it?"

"No, my lord," he swallowed lowering his head, "I regret to inform you it was too fast for me, and I only cut off its hand. Then it just left after that, *re-growing* the hand..." his voice trailed off in angry disbelief, "My lord, the freaking hand immediately regrew, *right* after I cut it off... I also saw someone with a white mask and cloak shortly before the monster attacked me..."

"You said monster bunny?" Terry burst out laughing, holding his sides, "Really? A monster Bunny?"

"Silence," I turned an angry finger towards Terry. He looked shocked clearing his throat, "I I-I'm sorry my lord."

"Are you okay?" I asked Danny, "Did it hurt you? Is the fence still damaged?"

"No my lord," he shook his head, "I repaired the fence, and I am okay. Just shaken, thank you for believing me."

"Where is it coming from?" I asked confused and frustrated gazing back to the table, "What are we supposed to do? Why does it keep bothering us?"

"My lord, please calm down," Anna Bee gently took my arm, "We'll figure it out. No monster bunny... I mean rabbit... could beat *all* of us. Right?"

I took a deep breath and glanced into her calming blue eyes, "You are right. We'll eventually figure this out."

I returned to my seat at the table with my mind spinning in circles, and Danny joined us.

Terry served us all looking a little uneasy, "I have created for *you* my lord, marinated and grilled chicken and a fresh tossed salad with vinaigrette. It's a combination of salty and sweet that I have perfected in my time at the academy."

It was very delicious. It had to be the best meal I had ever had in years, the chicken tender and moist, and the salad fresh and crisp. Anna Bee sat beside me eating, and Danny sat a couple seats down shaking as he ate. He slowly began to gather himself and recover as time ticked by.

I complimented Terry when I was done, and as I motioned for Anna Bee to follow me to the workshop. She spoke up, "My lord, I have yet to gather firewood this day. With your permission, I would like to make sure we have a proper amount of fire wood."

I shrugged, "Sure thing..." then my voice trailed off, "Danny, go with her and protect her. Together you can carry twice as much wood, and I would not wish to see harm to befall my Anna Bee."

She sucked in her breath and closed her eyes with a gentle smile, and for a moment she seemed to glow. Her face flushed with beautiful emotion as she tilted her head to cover her eyes with her bangs.

I didn't want to call her my maid, and I loved the way it made her act when I called her *my Anna Bee*, even though I was not sure why it made her so happy. I had noticed similar behavior when I had called her that before, and it warmed my heart to see such a shy sad girl smile.

"I will be careful my lord," She smiled, "I'm sure I'll be twice as safe with Danny coming with me."

Danny rose to his feet hesitantly, "Very well my lord. I hope we do not see the monster again. I shot it through the heart with an arrow and it did not even flinch... I've never seen anything like it..." His voice trailed off.

I shivered, the beast lingering in my thoughts as I rose from the table. Instead of heading to bed like I usually did after dinner, I headed for my workshop to continue working.

Instead of working on the robot frame for my unnamed crush, I continued the programming and testing of my new soldier droid platform. I wanted good soldiers, I wanted machines that could fight with a sword. I wanted combat with the accurate skillset of a well-oiled machine. I did not want something that just pointed and shot a weapon. I wanted a machine that could pick up and use different weapons, as well as get dirty without weapons in hand to hand combat.

Time ticked by as I typed at the computer on the dusty keyboard, and then slid over to the robot. I ran wires through its frame, and grinded the rust off of the robot's armor. Then I drilled holes into the frame so I could bolt on more armor.

My attention was slowly drawn to the fact that I needed to increase my own personal power. Sure brute strength was something I had, but I could not beat my opponents out of skill. Danny had beaten me left and right, and so did the girl I was trying to impress. I began designing an armor concept, and I worked until I comfortably fell asleep in my old dusty office chair.

I woke up Saturday morning, and I expected everything to be another dream, but I had clear unclouded vision, and I was still in the chair in my workshop. Morning sunlight was streaming in through the one window the room had. I noticed that it had been cleaned to a crystal clear transparency. As I looked around, I saw the dust on my keyboard was gone, the parts were sorted, and the walls and floor were scrubbed.

Anna Bee was sorting through some small bolts and scraps across the room on a bench she had cleaned up. She was actually making noise for once, humming a small high spirited tune that I did not recognize.

She turned with a bright smile when she heard me stir, "Good morning my lord. You really slept in. Luckily not much has happened. Danny has been patrolling the fence, walking all the way around nonstop. He keeps telling me he wants a rematch now that his nerves have settled."

I wiped the drool off my face and she giggled, "You were really out."

I shrugged and stretched looking at what I had done last night, so I could pick up where I left off. After a thoughtful calculation, going through my notes, and inspecting the assembly and adjustments I had made, I decided it was time to test out my new soldier droid A.I.

I crossed Mandy's learning and self-writing program skillfully with the program that was already in place as well as modifications to allow the A.I to make the decision to harm a human. After a moment, I was finally prepared to repair its core. By swapping the casing of the old humming core with a less damaged one, and then I sparked it with a jolt of electricity to re-activate the output of the small vibrating core.

As I slid it in I looked at Anna Bee, "Let's cross our fingers."

She nodded, "Please, be careful my lord."

I slid it in until it clicked, and then I turned the core locking it in place. I felt the electrical connection click and the robot came to life.

The eyes lit up as the machine came to life slowly. Dirt, rust, and rocks were blasted out of the robots cooling vents. It began sitting up and stepping off my bench looking around. Its eyes flickered a couple times as it worked out bugs, and it stumbled a little bit as it learned its surroundings.

The hum of motors and the soft high pitched whine of hydraulics sounded as it moved with every noisy step. The steps grew quieter as it learned what it was capable of, and grew more familiar with its mechanical body.

"Lord Zander," It said after a moment, "Facial recognition complete. Ready for duty, sir."

Its voice was a little harsh, and a little scratchy, but hey I was impressed so far for its functional success. It was working nearly perfectly, and It took me little to no time to make a couple quick minor adjustments.

"That is incredible," Anna Bee smiled, "Wow. You really did it!"

"There is an assault rifle in the armory, Go get it and meet me in the front of the estate. There is a map in your database so you shouldn't get lost," I said my eyes lighting up. "Let's see what you can do."

"Yes, sir," it nodded, and it turned and quickly left the room.

"Cool," I grinned, "Not too bad."

"It's incredible my lord," Anna Bee smiled, "*You* are incredible."

I scratched the back of my head smiling at the compliment, "I just enjoy it, that's all. I wouldn't call myself *incredible*." Then I motioned for her to follow and I headed for the front lawn of the estate.

The soldier droid was waiting patiently, debris spitting out in small amounts from the vents as it ran system cleaning cycles. The assault rifle in its hands was a well cleaned and maintained laser rifle with a solid power core and an electrical red dot sight.

"Okay," I said, "How to test you..."

I walked over and picked up a piece of metal and threw it up in the air as high as I could, "Shoot this!"

The assault rifle snapped to its shoulder and with the loud buzz of flashing light, it shot a smoldering hole in the metal before the metal fell smoking to the lawn.

"Nice," I grinned, "That was awesome. I would say it is a success. Wouldn't you?" I turned to Anna Bee who smiled, "Of course my lord."

"I want you to patrol the fence, and destroy anything that seems hostile," I said quickly to the machine, and it nodded, "Yes sir."

119

It then set out patrolling the fence line as instructed.

"I want to see it in action," I smiled, "I almost kind of want that beast to show up, or I want Wellington to come back…"

"I don't, sir," Anna Bee said, "I do not wish any situation to come to you where you might be in harm's way."

Mandy came striding across the lawn, "I see you finished your soldier droid prototype, my lord. Impressive. I can replicate the process now, if you want. It would be a pleasant break from sorting junk day and night."

"Yes, and I want you follow this guy a bit and make sure he is fully functional. Watch for glitches and processing errors, and once you've concluded that it is a success, I want you to abandon all your other tasks to duplicate the process and make more soldier droids. I left the exact modifications to the programming in my computer files, and your robot hands can do it faster than my slow human ones."

Her voice switched to a happy tone, "Heck yeah. Let's build an army."

"Buster!" I turned to the cylinder and clapped twice, "Wake up, I need you."

Anna Bee panicked a little bit, placing herself in between me and the cylinder as it hissed and groaned unfolding into the massive machine.

"Yes," it bent over to listen to me, "Are we starting a new project?"

"Yes," I grinned, "I realized I don't have a carriage. I want you to clear out the whole parking lot to the east, leaving only the most intact of the old delivery box trucks. I will fix one of them, since I do not have horses. It will be my carriage."

"Yes. I obey." Buster turned and stepped over us going across the lawn toward the sea of concrete in the distance that had been facility parking lot.

I walked back to the estate, and Anna Bee caught my sleeve gently, "Have you always had that?"

"Yes," I nodded, "His name is Buster. He is very useful, and very strong."

"Would you like me to go help him?" She asked, "Or would you like me to continue helping you?"

"Come on, Buster can handle himself," I nodded, "Let's head on in, we still have some more robots to finish, especially the one for the beautiful girl...man I wish I knew her name. She could arrive any day now, including today."

"Yes my lord," she smiled a forced smile, "let us continue where we left off."

We crossed back to the workshop and I began to cast new plastic parts for the machine, and before I knew it, Terry had prepared a light lunch of grilled cheese sandwiches with thinly sliced roasted turkey, and they were absolutely delicious. As Anna Bee ate she smiled at me before we continued working, "It's nice to not have to cook. He's a lot better at it than I am."

I shrugged, "Even if someone is better than you at something; that does not mean you have less value. You are great, don't you forget that."

Her eyes lit up but she remained quiet as she thoughtfully gazed towards the window.

When we were finished with our lunch, we worked on placing the external blue casing on the machine we had been working on. When that was finished, I carefully reseated the

Artificial intelligence in the robots head, and replaced the power core. I did a thorough double check as I downloaded the programming modifications into the AI, and finally once I was ready, I connected the core to power on the machine.

It turned on quickly and it was a man's voice this time, "Oh hello..." The machines eyes lit up and it looked at its blue plastic fingers and they rattled as it began to hum from the motors, "What is my name?"

"You do not have a name yet," I informed it, "I am not your master. Power down."

The machine's eyes gently turned off and then it fell backwards onto the floor, sitting with its back leaning against the workbench.

"There's another one done!" I said excited, "This one will be for her..." I said clearly referring to the woman set to come any moment now, but I was interrupted by Mandy who poked her head in the doorway, "My lord, a lone rider is waiting for you at the gate."

My eyes lit up, "It must be her!" I jumped out of my chair and eagerly ran to my front door and then I power walked to the gate. Anna Bee walking behind me easily keeping up with my speed.

He was a middle aged gentleman, with a rough unshaven beard and a scar above his left eye. He wore a thick set of worn leather armor. He stood at the gate with a rugged and tired smile, holding the reigns to his armored horse patiently.

He waved through the gate, "My lord. I have a letter, from my Lord, Ella Lovewind. May I please introduce myself? I am her knight, Ian Lavender."

I unlocked the gate slowly, Mandy and Anna Bee standing at my side, and Danny and the soldier droid came running up as well.

Ian extended his arm to shake my hand, and I shook it. Then he bowed and presented the letter, "Your letter, my lord."

I accepted the hand cut envelope made from thick recycled hand pressed paper. I opened it and pulled out the paper and read it.

"Lord Zander, the machine Lord,

Please! I Wish you to come to my Ball I am having this upcoming Saturday night, if you are not too busy. I wish to meet you, and I have heard that you have robots! I would be truly honored if you would bring one of your robots for me to see, but mostly my husband and I wish to meet *you*!

The ball will be held in the old church on my domain, and I have included a map to get there from the market if it is any help to you. Please present this invitation! It is your key to get in! I very much wish you to come!

Sincerely, Lord Ella Lovewind."

I lowered the letter, "An invitation to a ball?"

"A ball?" Anna Bee squeaked, and then she pursed her lips in depressed thought, "A real ball? I've always wanted to..."

"Well," the man gazed at her and she quickly stopped talking, "You may of course bring a guest, or you may come alone. My lord's best regards." He bowed, "Thank you for your time."

"No problem," I grinned, "thank you for the invitation! I already know who I will invite!"

He remounted his horse and gave a little wave, and turned the horse around and headed onwards towards the trees, "It was interesting to meet you. Take care, Machine lord."

"When she returns to get her robot, I will invite *her* to the ball, this un-named beauty. I just need to find a way to impress her, both times I have not been able to..." I said to myself and Danny caught up to us.

"Why would you need to impress her?" Anna Bee asked me, "I think you are very impressive... and perhaps she will just see how impressive you are in time," she looked at her sneakers and then she cleared her throat and faked a cough as though she was trying to cover something up and then straightened herself out with a forced smile, "She'll see in time, my lord."

"I don't know, with that lady," Danny shrugged, "Excuse me lord, but she kind of blackmailed you."

"It's just business. I'm sure I would do the same thing if I wanted something pretty bad, I get that functional robots are rare..." I said, "Either way, thank you Anna Bee. I hope you are right."

She smiled after a quick sigh, "Of course, my lord. You're welcome."

"Well," I nodded, "Let's get back to work. There is a lot to do."

Anna Bee followed me to the workshop, where we began working just as hard as before. She began to pull apart an old robot for me to convert into another plastic cased robot, and I made the last careful modifications to this new blue robot that I had recently put together.

We worked in silence for most of the day until Terry poked his head in, "Dinner time."

"Oh cool," I said surprised, "Wow, the day went by quickly."

Terry had made a pizza pie, and I loved it. It was probably my favorite thing I'd tried so far. I thought I had pizza once when I was younger, but I could not remember. Back before my parents threw vases and furniture at each other. I wondered if one of them had killed the other yet, or if they had made up and quit fighting.

Either way I did not care too much because I loved my estate, and my hobby of tinkering with robots all day. Whenever their eyes lit up from being repaired I felt like I was truly making a difference, like I had rescued someone.

After dinner as I got out of my chair, and the soldier approached the door, his assault rifle held at the ready but aimed downwards, "You have a guest, sir."

"This late?" Mandy asked, "Who could it be?" She stood and crossed to the front door and glanced out.

"A guest?" Terry asked, "I shall prepare another pizza."

"Who could it be?" I asked. I turned and headed out for the gate, "Danny." I motioned for him to follow, and he quickly took his bow off the table, "Coming, my Lord."

Anna Bee watched from the doorway, and I crossed the lawn to the gate. A lone rider was approaching through the darkness on a white healthy horse.

The horse came to a stop at the gate and the figure gracefully stepped off her horse with a beautiful sympathetic smile. Her blonde hair was shining beautifully in the moonlight and it made my heart skip a beat.

"You are just in time," I said unlocking the gate quickly, "I just finished your robot! Come in, it will be dark soon!"

"My name is Skylar," she said gently approaching. She was taking off a white pair of riding gloves as she walked, she was wearing a beautiful white gown. She had a crown of blue and yellow flowers in her hair and she bowed, "That's why I am here, Lord Zander. I want to talk to you about that."

I had never seen her behave this way. She was being kind, she was being gentle, and she was being sweet as she rounded the gate. As I opened it she leaned over kissing me on the cheek, "I owe you an apology my lord. It has been eating at me, you have been treating me so well, and I have been so rude."

I was frozen in place blushing. I was glad it was too dark to show how red my face was. I closed my eyes with a giant grin after she had kissed my cheek.

"You can give the robot to someone else, or keep it for yourself. I realized that I could simply come here to admire your robots. I do not really need one. It was merely a want. You are so sweet, for making me one, really you are. You look like a true handsome Lord now, just look at your hair."

She ran her hand up my cheek and stroked my hair, "Though I see a couple hairs out of place. It's not the best haircut I've ever seen; Nonetheless. You look very different. Very handsome."

"Thank you, Skylar," I smiled, "That means a lot to me."

"I'll head to patrol the fence, there seems to be no threat here," Danny sounded frustrated. "Come on," he motioned to the soldier droid and they headed away. I also turned to see Anna Bee was gone as well, having headed for the front door without saying anything. I wondered what was wrong, she never just walked

126

away without asking permission. She must have realized she had forgotten something.

"This is quite a turnaround," Mandy said her head humming as she thought, "This is quite a flip from your usual behavior, Lady Skylar."

"Yes, I apologize," Skylar gave a gentle curtsey, "I have not been on my best behavior. My move was long and hard. I wish to ask if there is a way for me to make up my past behavior towards you, my lord."

"There is a ball this upcoming Saturday, would you go with me?" I asked eagerly.

"A ball?" She smiled, "I would love to! My lord! What an honor? You are so sweet! Even after the way I have treated you so poorly, you still ask me something so generous."

I swallowed and smiled, nodding in the dark.

"I will give you my address, so you can pick me up on your way," she said and her hair shined in the moonlight as it caught on the breeze, "I would be a lucky girl. Going to a ball with a lord."

I could not believe how pretty she was, standing here so close to me in the moon light. I was at a loss for words as she smiled, "May I come in?"

"Of course? Come on in. My cook is preparing some pizza for you," I motioned for her to follow me.

"I'm okay," she bowed, "I've already eaten this evening. I will come inside though, I want to get to know you a little better, my lord. If that is okay."

"Well okay," I said nervously, "What would you like to know?"

"I see you have been creating soldier robots now?" she said, "That's awfully smart of you. Why are you only now building a military as a lord? How come you did not have a military before?"

"That day at the fair was my first day out of the estate in almost eight years. I ran away from home when I was twelve, and grew up tinkering with robots. It was not until a couple years ago Lord Osburn discovered me and my estate, and because of society, I was declared a lord..." I explained and she giggled. It was a gentle quiet giggle and she gently covered her mouth, "That explains a whole bunch, actually."

As I expected I liked her giggle, although it felt as though it wasn't what I was expecting.

"Yeah, I guess. I have just been interacting more as a lord with other people. I have been hearing that Wellington wishes to claim my robots and estate with military force. So I plan on building up as fast as I can. I've even been considering putting up some sentry turrets along the fence." I said, "I have never done anything like that before, and I don't know how much time I'll have but I am sure it will be easier than a robot."

"Impressive," she smiled, "It sounds like you are really growing from when I first met you."

We entered the estate and I closed the door after Mandy entered with us.

"I cannot stay too long," she said gently, "I just wished to stop by and say I'm sorry for the way I have behaved."

"That's okay," I smiled in happy disbelief that this was actually happening, "I accept your apology, but I insist Skylar. I want to know more about you."

"Well," she looked at her slippers as she sat down in my creaky old wooden chairs, "When I was a young girl I was obsessed with being an actress. So I became an actress in Las Vegas and I was quite popular. Later I found out that they just hired me because I was eye candy. All along, I thought it was my acting, but I suppose acting is not my strongest talent. I was so mad that they only wanted me for my looks that I quit. Some old friends got ahold of me and invited me to come out here, and I moved away to this little town of Wellington."

"Do you like it here?" I asked curiously.

She nodded, "I like the serenity of the trees. I like that there is a lot less people, for example, my peaceful ride through the trees towards your estate this evening was wonderful. I really like it. I can see why you would want to live in isolation, away from everyone else. I really truly get where you are coming from there. I tell myself I want to find a man and settle down in the country, away from the bright lights and especially all the busy, noisy, and stupid people."

"Exactly," I said happily, my mind spinning. My heart skipped a beat, "It's nice to know that there is someone that feels the same way."

"I really do... anyway, it looks as though I have talked my time away," she smiled pulling a pocket watch from her gown pocket to check the time, "I look forward to the ball, perhaps I may stop by and visit you again."

"I would really like that," I said quickly, "I truly enjoy your company."

"That's very sweet of you," she smiled, "I suppose you won't mind walking me to my horse. It can get spooky alone in the dark. Especially with these monster rumors. I feel fine once I'm on my horse, but walking alone gives me the chills."

"Of course," I nodded, "but as you know, I'm not much help if one does show up."

She laughed, "You're learning. I could tell you were trying."

I liked her gentle laugh. It was a very flirtatious and adorable kind of laugh that I did not expect.

I smiled as we rose from our seats and stepped from my home onto the lawn. We walked to the gate, and I got to hold her a hand for a moment as I helped her onto her horse. It felt different than it did in my dreams. In my dreams it was warm and comforting. In real life her hand was colder than I expected. It reassured myself that it must have been because we were outside.

I watched her hair sway in the breeze as she waved and wished me sweet dreams. She headed on her way, galloping away on her horse into the shadows of the trees on the moonlit gravel road.

"Something felt off about that," Mandy said standing beside me which startled me. I was so distracted that I had not noticed her follow us.

"I know, I'm not used to seeing her that nice. I quite enjoyed it," I said dreamily, "I told you she would come around. You heard her, she has just been through a long move."

"I wonder who the *friends* are she spoke of," Mandy said, "My lord, I mean it felt like she was up to something to me. She asked an awful lot of questions about your military power."

"She said she came to apologize," I said a little frustrated, "She was just curious, Mandy."

I thought of her smile, her sweet voice, and the way her hair shined in the moonlight. It was all so magical to me. It made my stomach fill with fluttering butterflies. I wanted to see her again so badly, I almost wanted to chase after her into the night.

"I think you are acting on blind emotion my lord. Perhaps you should examine some clear facts here," Mandy tried to approach me and I stopped her cold, "Please. Mandy, don't ruin the moment I had. That was the first time I had such a sweet experience with such a beautiful woman. If she was some form of spy, why would she tell me her name? Isn't the point of being a spy being sneaky?"

Mandy stared at me, "I'll withhold my next comment. Just be careful. I shall begin replicating the soldier droid conversions tomorrow. The prototype passed my careful inspection after I made a couple minor modifications. I shall begin making them as fast as I can tomorrow morning, until then Anna Bee has asked me to aid her in a project she has been working on this evening." Mandy bowed, "Please think about everything *thoroughly* my lord." She turned and headed around the estate, and I turned heading back inside grinning.

I could not stop thinking about her. The way she stood so close to me, the way she kissed my cheek, and the way her gentle voice sounded in the moonlight. It felt as though the feelings inside me would drive me mad over time if I did not get to see her again.

As I lay in my bed, I could see her smile, I could hear her giggle, and I eventually fell asleep thinking about Skylar's smile.

I woke up abruptly and I sat up in the blurry dark of my bedroom. I got out of bed and I moved in a blur toward the light switch. As I reached for it I could see the outline of the monster. Its teeth rattling and its eyes began to glow eerily red in the darkness.

I flipped on the light, ripping my sword from the sheath from where I had set it by the door and spinning to slash at the monster but the beast was gone. Skylar and her beautiful smile stood in its place

She giggled and crossed to me, "It's only me. I won't hurt you. Everything is going to be okay. It's not real my lord."

Her hand was warm as it touched mine and she rubbed her thumb comforting on the back of my hand, like she did in my dreams before, and I loved it. I wished I could just stand there with her forever, our hands gently touching.

9: The Broken Maid and the Spark of Insomnia

I woke up for real, smiling staring at the ceiling in my bedroom. As I sat up, I heard a loud clang come from the living room. It sounded like metal striking concrete, so I immediately drew my sword from its sheath, and leapt from my bed moving urgently to the living room.

"What's going on?" I shouted as I charged through the doorway, my sword ready to strike.

I was expecting trails of blood and a terrifying monster ready to pounce on me. Instead I found a tired looking Anna Bee setting down her side of a long comfortable red and white patterned couch with a second loud clang. Mandy stood opposite of her bent over as though she had set the other half down a moment ago.

"I'm sorry, I didn't mean to wake you up?" Anna Bee sighed, "That was too loud."

"A couch?" I asked excited.

Anna Bee smiled sweetly, "Yes my lord. I remembered you said there was an old frame in the back. So I bought fabric and cushioning so I could turn it into a couch again."

"She's been working hard. I had to do some carpentry work for her to increase the stability of the frame, but she insisted it be a surprise," Mandy said motioning to the couch.

"No way?" I asked, "This is that old bent rusty frame I pulled out of the estate years ago?" I approached excited, "This is so cool! Thank you Anna Bee!" I turned and sat down on the comfortable cushion, bouncing on the old couch springs a couple times, "Very comfortable."

"Your welcome my lord, I remembered you said you wanted one... So I thought that it would help make you more comfortable... since my job is to serve you..." Anna Bee smiled, and then she looked nervous, "I-is it comfortable enough?"

"Very," I leaned back against the cushions, "I love it!" I bounced again and then sat up, "Thank you, Anna Bee!"

"We stitched the whole thing by hand," Mandy said, "it took us all night to finish it. Now I'm off to replicate the soldier drones as promised." She turned and headed almost immediately out the door.

"Were you were up all night Anna Bee?" I asked. Her eyes had low tired shadows and her eyes were trying to close from her exhaustion.

"Yes. I'm sorry my lord..." she frowned looking at her shoes, but it's my job to serve you..."

"*Please*. Go get some sleep, that's an order," I pointed to the hall way, and I remembered I needed to talk to her about what Wellington had said to me. So I followed her down the hallway, and I closed the door gently behind us as we entered her room.

"Do you need something more of me before I head to sleep?" She asked watching me as I followed her in and I gazed around the room. She was very neat and organized. On the floor under her bed I noticed her awkward looking axe. It positioned so it was covering some eerie scrubbed and faded blood stains.

She stood there by her bed worried, "Is everything okay? Shall I start removing my clothes?" She choked looking at me fearfully.

"No! No! No! I would just like to talk to you for a moment, that's all," I said loudly, "Something happened a couple days ago and I forgot to talk to you about it."

I approached her bed and sat on the cushioned side, "I just have a couple questions. That's all." I smiled at her, "Honest."

She seemed incredibly nervous as she slowly moved closer to my side, "S-something that happened? D-did I do something wrong? W-what have I done my lord? For whatever it is... I'm sorry." She almost went into a state of panic.

"Relax Anna Bee," I laughed at her, "You're not in trouble. Lord Wellington stopped by. He said that he accidentally gave me the wrong maid. He said he wanted to trade me, you for some other maids. He really seemed like he wanted you, so I was wondering if you knew anything about that." I motioned for her to sit by me and she slowly sat down.

She swallowed looking scared, "D-did you agree to the trade?"

I knew just what to say to convince her I meant no harm. I just loved her reaction when I said it so I grinned, "*Of course not. You're my fantastic little Anna Bee.*" I was hoping it would cheer her up, like the way it usually made her smile warmly.

She sucked in her breath and looked down, color flushing her cheeks and she did not say anything. Her lip quivered and shifted into a heartfelt smile, her eyes closed tight as though she was trying to savor my words.

"So," I asked, "I won't bother you too long. Just tell me, do you know *why* he wanted *you* so badly?"

She swallowed and cleared her throat, "I don't know."

"Okay," I shrugged, "I trust you, and I believe you. If you don't know, you don't know."

"I don't understand at all..." she said glancing at the floor boards, "He did not even originally want my services when he approached the booth. *No one* did."

"What do you mean?" I asked, "You are a fantastic maid. Why would no one want your service?"

She smiled and a tear stung her cheek, "T-thank you, my lord. That means so much more to me than you could know."

"Well then explain," I shrugged, "Talk yourself to sleep if you need to," I teased her trying to lighten her defensive and nervous demeanor.

"My parents left me at an orphanage when I was less than a year old," Anna Bee said lowering her shoulders, "Because they did not want me. They said it was because I was mistake, and I was not the child they wanted. They wanted a strong son, and I was a small daughter."

"Okay, continue," I said confused because it had nothing to do with what I asked, "I'm listening," but of course she seemed upset, and I was still willing to listen to a friend in need.

She continued, "The orphanage where I lived had a rule, because it had so many admissions. By the age of twelve, if you were not adopted, then you would go to the Brix Academy for maids and servants. So many parents talked to me, so many people had interviews with me. They all said I was not what they were looking for, that I was not good enough... they all said they did not want me, and on my twelfth birthday I went to the academy. Just like all the other orphans and orphanage volunteers teased me and said I would.

Even in the academy, all the other maids were better than me... they could cook more delicious food, they could sew faster and straighter. They could even clean faster and more effectively then I could. I had trouble grasping concepts, so for four years I was the lowest one in the class... and when I graduated, all the other maids got hired for their services right away, and still, no one wanted me.

Just like the parents, they all turned their cheeks to me saying "I was not good enough", or "I was not what they were looking for." Henry, the man who was at my booth on Tuesday, is a sales representative of the maid academy. Henry offered me to Wellington as a *bundle*. Henry said he would throw me in because he wanted to get rid of me. Henry's offered deal was that if Wellington bought two other maid contracts from the academy, then he got my services for two years at half price.

On the ride to your estate Wellington made me undress in the carriage, and he said that "my breasts did not have the correct shape"..." Anna Bee's voice painfully trailed off for a moment, and then she continued, "Wellington then decided he would simply "dump me" on you when he visited you and then he made me ride on the back of the carriage... he called me an unwanted pet."

"I was never good enough for anyone... even Wellington said he did not want me, that is why it confuses me so greatly that you say he returned wanting me," she swallowed and I could see painful tears begin to burn her cheeks falling onto her maid's apron, "I-I am weird."

"That sounds like a horror story," I gently put my arm around her not knowing what else to do, "I'm so sorry nobody can see how awesome you are. What do you mean you are weird?"

She gently leaned her head against my chest, pulling herself closer. I looked down in disgusted thought at what Wellington did to Anna Bee, "He really made you undress?"

She nodded, "Yes, my lord." Her tears began to fall against my faded shirt and she shivered.

I gave her a small hug and began to rub her back trying to be comforting. I remembered once in a while my mother would do that to me when I was upset, and it worked for me.

"I- I am sorry, my lord. That was so unprofessional of me to do that..." she wiped the tears from her tired eyes and pulled away from me gently, "I am tired, that's all."

I could tell Anna Bee was in a lot of emotional pain. It looked like she was reliving a lot of bad memories. I pulled her back over with an even bigger hug. I cleared my throat, remembering a speech that my father had given me when I was very little, and put my own little spin on it. She braced her cheek against my chest comfortably sniffling. Her eyes gently closed and relaxed, but tears still fell against my chest.

It was comfortable, and I liked being so close to her. She was warm, and she was soft. I ran my hand through her neatly brushed hair trying to be comforting. I liked being this close to a girl, especially one that was counting me. I felt like she was trusting me a lot by telling me these things, and it felt good.

I thought for a moment before I began my small attempt at a speech, "Anna Bee, people have different awesomeness levels... You're awesomeness level is just so much higher than everybody else that they can't see it. I can see it, I don't care what everybody else and their tiny levels of awesome say. I mean think about it. Those other *boring* maids at the academy, so what they can sew a little faster... That must mean they are all boring to the point that all they do is sew. Anna Bee, you are super special! You are at least super special *to me!*"

Her tears began to fall harder as I said that, and a smile crossed her tired lips. Her eyes were still closed, and her cheeks transformed into shade of cherry red.

"I don't care what has happened to you, but I tell you what. You are *my* Anna Bee, and as long as you are here, I will do my best to tell you how awesome you are. Those other people are bland servants without personality. You are the coolest maid ever, like I said, *you are my Ann Bee...*" My voice trailed off as she squeezed my shirt fabric with her fingertips.

She buried her sad face into my chest. Her tears began soaking a different spot on my shirt, and I just put my arms around her, not knowing what else to do.

"I'm so s-sorry. This is not proper behavior... I'm a terrible maid..." she sobbed. I ran my hand through her hair, "If it's that big of a deal, then it can be our little secret. I think you are an amazing maid."

Her face grew very relaxed, and her eyes fluttered. After a peaceful moment she released the tension on my shirt, "T-thank you, my lord."

We sat there in silence as I tried to think of what to say. I was not very good at the whole pep-talk or motivational speech thing. Before I knew it, she slowly and fell asleep against my chest from exhaustion.

"I'm right here for you Anna Bee," I said, "You are more than enough for me. I wish I could make you see that." I sighed my arms still around her stroking her hair. I had never been this close to a girl before. I kind of liked it. She was warm, and her skin was soft and comfortable to the touch.

She looked so peaceful in her sleep, without that scared and worried look on her face. She looked like a sweet little angel in a maid's apron asleep against my shirt. I did not want to wake her up, so I slowly laid back on the old musty mattress stroking her hair gently, my head on her pillow.

I could tell she was serious. I felt really bad for her, never being told she was good enough. I told myself I would do my best to try and change that. I wondered about her curious reaction every time I called her "my Anna Bee." Whatever it was, it seemed to help her lighten up.

Danny poked his head into the doorway, "My lord..." He raised an eyebrow and did a double take caught off guard, "A-are you s-sleeping with your maid? I mean not in a sexual way... I mean like... Is she really asleep?"

I gently touched my index fingers to my lips, "Shhh... you'll wake her up."

"Lord Osburn is here. He has news for you pertaining to the monster rabbit," Danny said, lowering his voice.

I carefully shifted Anna Bee, and I laid her comfortably on her bed. I made sure she was truly asleep before I stood up doing my best to avoid disturbing her.

"C-can I ask what is happening here?" Danny asked confused, "Why were you snuggling with your maid, in her room? Why were you snuggling with Anna Bee?"

"Please. Let's get to Lord Osburn immediately, "We must not keep him waiting. I will explain it to you later... We were not *snuggling*... were we?"

He nodded and then he shrugged in disbelief, "You were, but whatever." He headed out of the room. I glanced back to make sure Anna Bee was okay, and then I followed him out.

Mandy was standing there, the key to the gate in her hand, and the gate was open to allow Lord Osburn onto the path to my estate. His guards stayed behind, and it was just Lord Osburn coming up the path.

"Greetings, Lord Zander," Nate gave a tired wave as I stepped out of the estate, "How are you?"

I felt embarrassed at what Danny had said and I briefly turned to him under my breath as I waved at Lord Osburn as he approached, "I would not quite call it snuggling, it's complicated." I turned to Lord Osburn, "I'm great. What do you have to report to me my friend?" I was hoping Lord Osburn would have not caught what I said to Danny, but by the look in his eyes, he clearly did.

"Are you sure? Is this a bad time? I would not want to interrupt snuggling? If you need alone time I can come back in a couple hours..." He sounded as though he was trying to lighten his own mood with the teasing. He looked like he had just been through hell.

"You were snuggling with Anna Bee?" Mandy asked and her tone turned to teasing as well, "If you wanted someone to snuggle with, my lord, you could have asked me."

I glared at Lord Osburn, "What have you discovered? What have you come to share with me?"

He dropped his jocular tone and grew serious, "Where to begin?"

"My men and I came across a camp with men in white robes and masks. The moment we found the camp, those things, the monster rabbits, they came out of nowhere..." his voice trailed off for a moment... "Those monsters are somehow connected to people in white robes and masks. We tried to fight through the wall of monsters to get at the masked men hiding behind them, but the cowards had weaseled away, abandoning their entire camp.

We searched the whole camp and found nothing. The bodies of the monsters just turned to black powdery dust, and just blew away on the breeze, I have never seen anything like it.

The only thing we found in the entire camp was some kind of handwritten nonsense about the darkness. Something about how "the darkness taunts it's victims before killing them...," he scratched his chin and he gazed at me with a weary sigh. He was wearing blood stained metal plate armor like Skylar had worn during our fight. It rattled when he moved, and it was heavier and had more dents and scratches than Skylar's new looking armor.

"I thought you would be glad to know you are not crazy. Now that my men and I have found and slayed several of those monster rabbits, I can see something is clearly going on in the woods around Wellington. I've sent word to the other lords with what I knew, but most of them responded with skepticism," Nate said a little frustrated. "I told them that the monsters are hard to kill, but they are killable. The monsters fall easier from blades and melee attacks than bullets. Cutting off their arms and legs does little to nothing. Even if they don't believe me, hopefully the information I gave them will help if they are attacked."

Nate looked at me in the eyes for his next sentence, "A lot of good men died in the battle yesterday. I can tell you it is only driving me and the rest of my men harder to find answers."

He shook his head clearing his throat and then lightened the mood, "Anyway, I'll make our visit short since it's apparently your scheduled snuggle time. I'll be on my way. I just thought I would stop by and let you know that you are not crazy. The threat is real, and I'm onto it. I'm hoping to have the problem resolved by the ball on Saturday so I can truly enjoy myself at the ball without worry. Lord Ella Lovewind throws wonderful parties. I even heard you were invited, so I hope to see you there."

"Thank you for keeping me up to date, I really appreciate it. Danny was attacked a couple days ago, so it's nice to know you are attacking the problem head on," I said honestly and he got to his feet, "Stay safe. Don't have too much fun." He winked and headed out of the room, "I will keep you up to date."

"Thank you," I said. Danny stayed standing there on the lawn. I could see the gears turning in his head as he turned to me, "I knew it had a tie to the white masked figure. I knew it. We uncover more clues to this nightmare every day. It's good, we'll put an end to this mess soon, and hopefully we never have to see one of those rabbits again."

"I am going to head to my workshop," I told him with a deep breath, "continue patrolling please. Keep an eye out."

"Yes, sir," he nodded, bowed, and then he headed towards the gate looking around as Mandy closed and locked it.

On my way back to my workshop, I poked my head into Anna Bee's room to check on her.

She was still sleeping peacefully on her back in the position I had left her in.

I stepped into her room watching her sleep, my mind racing in circles. What would happen if she was attacked by one of the monster rabbits? I could see now that as a lord, it was as equally my job to serve and protect them as they did to me. I liked everyone in my estate. Danny was brave, Mandy was my best friend, and Anna Bee was always going to be more than just a maid to me.

I also still wanted to find a way to empower myself, so I could fight when I needed to. I began revisiting the idea of some power armor on my way to my workshop. The concept of an external skeleton style suit had been preying on my mind for many years, so I could run faster, lift heavier things, and even having an assortment of built in tools. What If I designed this armor for something other than construction or repair? *War.*

I measured my body by holding long pieces of metal to my arms, sides, and legs. Marking them and then I began to work. Every once in a while my mind would wander and think about Anna Bee. The way she had been treated her whole life, and the way she had been so fragile a couple hours ago. She always seemed like a cracked hanging piece of glass that would just cut itself from the swaying string and shatter on the ground. I worried about her immensely.

Mandy came and went, gathering robotics parts. She was either making snappy teasing comments about how I was not snuggling with somebody, or asking how I was doing, which most of the time I was too distracted to answer. I welded hydraulics and bent plates of metal into carefully shaped armor. I worked all night until I felt incredibly tired, and when I passed Anna Bee's room I poked my head in to check on her.

She was gone, and so was her axe. I figured she must have returned to hard work as usual, gathering firewood or something. That was the only explanation I had for her having the axe. It looked as though the poor girl could barely hold it when she packed it around.

I sighed, and I gazed around her little room. The blood stain on the floor was from when she cut her arm, I knew that much. Her bed was neatly made, her whole room was very organized with what little she had. It reflected the cleanliness that she kept every other room in my estate.

"My lord," Terry caught me off guard making me jump, "Is everything okay? Is Anna Bee okay? What are you doing in her room?"

"She was asleep earlier," I said turning startled, "I just wanted to make sure she was okay. That's all."

Terry shrugged, "that's awful nice of you. She is only a maid if I am correct. Like me, simply a contracted servant, why would you care that much?"

I thought for a moment, "I care for you guys regardless of your purpose here. It is the lord's duty to take care of his servants."

"I suppose that's true," he shrugged, "Anyway I have prepared shepherd's pie for you this evening. It is ready."

"A what?" I asked curiously, "What's that?"

"Come on, I'll show you," Terry smiled eagerly, and I could see it was already dark outside as I passed through the living room. The door was left open to keep it from getting too warm from the almost constant flames of the fireplace.

Danny was sitting at the table looking hungry and excited, but Anna Bee was nowhere to be seen.

"Have you seen Anna Bee?" I asked.

"My lord, she informed me she had been looking at that old eyesore of a tree west of the Property near the chain link fence. Since the old oak is so dead and rotten, it threatens to fall and destroy the fence. Anna Bee plans on going and cutting the tree into firewood," Danny said as he scooped up a spoonful of mashed potatoes.

"You did not go with her?" I almost grew angry standing there at the table, "She's all alone?"

"No my lord, She took some soldier droids with her. Two of them," he said quickly nearly choking on his mashed potatoes from my outburst, "I offered to go with her, and she refused."

"Okay," I said relieved and I sat down, "I hope she is okay."

"I'm sure she is," Terry shrugged, "It's only gathering firewood, she's a smart girl."

Terry served me up a plate and Danny quickly commented, "I will go check on her right after dinner."

"Thank you, Danny," I nodded, "With those monsters around I would not want her to get attacked," I said it trying not to imagine something so awful. I distracted myself by the delicious food in front of me, and began to eat.

It was delicious. I thoroughly enjoyed the melted farm fresh cheese and the mashed potatoes, ground beef, and vegetables all over a steaming pile of mashed potatoes and gravy. I told Terry that he should make this again, and that he should make sure that when Anna Bee came back he would make sure that she got some as well.

Terry agreed, and then Danny talked me out of going to check on Anna Bee by insisting that he was going to. He told me he wanted to earn my trust so he could be my knight, and he could only do that if I gave him opportunities. With my approval he headed out the door when he was finished eating, and I cautiously headed to bed. It had been a long day of hard work, and I was exhausted.

I curled up in my bed my mind spinning in circles, and I eventually fell asleep.

10: Cattle Drawn to a Slaughter

Four neatly placed white tents were gathered around a makeshift fire pit where a camp fire had been previously placed before. The tents were symmetrically placed on opposite sides behind the crackling fire. The tents they were giant padded cloth tents. Each tent capable of housing four or five people comfortably.

There was twelve masked people gathered around a small low glowing and crackling campfire, wearing white plain masks. Each mask had different sized twin horns pointing upwards about an inch above the eye holes. The chain link fence of the machine lord's estate in the distance visible like a rusty wall in the moonlight.

"It appears we are not the only people who have camped this close to the estate. Our informant has told us, this gentleman has treated us with such a joyous blessing. He has little to *no* military. Which is why we will attack just before daybreak," the man with the longest horns on his mask squirmed as he squealed excited, "Such a treat, we will see his blood flow like love from his body, and with light, we can bring the true power of darkness to life!"

He howled and giggled with excitement, "Oh what a treat! They will destroy all, a cleansing wave of darkness, immortality in death! What a wonderful... *Scrumptious* Treat! So much blood, so much screaming, my heart trembles with joy at the thought!" The twisted man was clearly the leader of the gathered men. He sat by the fire on a sawn log with the rest of them gathered around him, the stitching in his robes darker than the rest.

"Lord Burning," another masked man bowed from a couple feet away and motioned to an approaching figure who emerged from the brush. There were more men scattered around the trees around the camp keeping watch, Scattered throughout the trees like coiled snakes ready to strike with daggers in the bushes.

One of the hidden lookouts came gliding through shadows, and crouched low his robe blowing in the breeze, the pure white glowing in the moonlight, "My master, the maid who was cutting down the old tree has begun heading back to the estate."

"Excellent! You may return to your post my good man. We will soon destroy this *Zander*, and claim his light. So the darkness can come forth!" Lord Burning squirmed leapt to his feet cheerfully, "All will burn! All will be destroyed! All of it! Immortality in death for all of mankind!"

"With taunting scouts around us, with the darkness at our fingertips, such demons, such blessings, such a treat for our eyes! Such a delicacy, I lick my lips with the taste of the blood of who all will perish!" His voice and maniacal laughter tore through the night, "Men! This is our moment of glory, we need to capture his blood, this light, and we will bring immortality through death!" He repeated with excitement, and the rest of them howled eagerly as though their humanity was beyond their reach, their eyes like those of a predator in a cage behind the thick eerie masks.

They all had short dagger like swords on their hips, and the thick heavy cloaks hid what they were wearing underneath. The fire at a low crackle, there had to be twenty-five men, some in the trees, and others in tents, and the rest sitting around the fire.

Lord Burning snapped his fingers and four of the closest men to him stood up quickly, and he rubbed his hands, "We will leave to return to our base as our plan here unfolds.

We will be back the next morning with scripture and the holy box, when the estate has been rid of the burdens that stand in our way!" He howled lifting his scarred arms in the moonlight praising the sky, and for a moment tears of joy could be seen behind the mask, "Come men, we are leaving!"

He spun and the four men followed him but a quiet voice drifted through the darkness from the opposite side of the clearing, "Where are you going?"

Two bodies in bloody white cloaks fell to the grass with a heavy thud and a groan, and a lone Anna Bee stood on the edge of the clearing. Her hidden sword in one hand, the axe in the other, "W-what are you doing on my lord's estate?"

Her eyes were scared as more men sprang urgently from the tents, and others snuck through the trees, revealing themselves in the clearing gathering around her in the small clearing. They all watched her with wicked inhuman eyes that lusted for blood.

Lord Burning turned his head to look at Anna Bee with a dark emotionless gaze from the eyes behind his mask, and the men assembled as he moved without words towards her, the four men following him.

Lord Burning spun his head around like an owl in creepy excitement, the sound of his joints popping and cracking as he stopped and nearly floated across the grass towards her. He bent low to stick his finger in the cold blood of one of the men slain at her feet, keeping his distance from the girl

"What a treat, what a treat, What a TREAT!?" He screamed and spun, "The Blood!? What a delicacy, what a morsel of insomnia! She killed them! They are now immortal! Their names cast in stone, their stories retold..." his voice grew terrifying as he shifted his face and mask towards Anna Bee, "but you... you will have only death."

Around them the monsters pulled themselves from shadows, their chattering teeth, their bloody claws, and their mangled pink fur sliding off their freakishly thin rotting bodies. The monster rabbits dragging their claws across tree trunks and bark.

There was ten of them, and they anxiously moved back and forth, swaying and growling as though impatiently waiting for permission to attack.

"Lord Osburn is a nuisance, such a treat! He granted more of my men immortality... but you... alone *scared* fragile young girl... the servant to the lord who we will *KILL* and take his *Light!*" Lord Burning spun and squirmed. His words were chalked full of mumbled insanity as though he was trying to scream for help as he spoke, his voice growing louder and more aggressive, "How many of my men will you grant immortality?"

"I cannot let you hurt my master..." Anna Bee shivered looking down to avoid gazing at the monsters as the small army of men and monsters gathered around her, "I will give my life before I let you touch him." She clutched the weapons raising them up shakily in the moonlight at the ready.

"What a treat!?" He screamed with laughter, "Such loyalty! Such Love! You would stand alone against the spark, you would sacrifice your life in a slaughter just to protect your *Lord!* You would stand against *taunting darkness* for your master?" He spun with a small twirl excited, "And you would do it alone? You do not run for help, you do not cry, you do not shake or tremble in fear? Such a delicious morsel, I wish to sample your flesh! I wish to see the color of your blood..." He growled and breathed heavily behind his mask.

He then began to hit himself on the back of the head, "But I cannot! There is scripture I must follow, I must grant immortality! I must fulfill what is destined... Men! I give you the *blessing* to taste her delicate flesh but first I must know why..." He spun suddenly around towards her, "I must know *why* you stand so brave?"

"I-I am very scared," she stuttered looking at her feet, "but I think for a moment..." she tilted her head so that her bangs dropped in front of her eyes to hide them, "The way his eyes light up so excited when he finishes a project... the way they soften and move when he is thinking... the way he smiles so warmly when I need it the most..." Her tone began growing from scared into an angry selfless drive.

"...The way his hand feels when I hold it and the way he looks when he is sleeping... so peaceful, so graceful..." the hair on the back of her neck stood up as her face flushed with emotion, "The way he believes in me, the way he cares for me!"

She began to growl as she spoke, her knuckles white on her weapons, "... the way he keeps trying, the way he is so strong... He's so Kind! He's so sweet to me!" She wildly pointed the axe at him; her eyes dead serious, and she nearly screamed it, "I won't let you touch him!"

He turned curiously back towards her, as though he was spinning in circles, "Could this be? You are his maid, his servant..."

She growled as she interrupted him, "No, *I am his Anna Bee.*"

"hmm..." he said and he shrugged, "I thank you for this sweet treat for my mind to consume," he turned his back to her and snapped his fingers and the four men closest to him snapped around to follow him as well, "I am leaving now. You all may kill her."

151

He quickly slid passed the gathered men and into the trees, followed by the four men, leaving twenty men and the chattering monsters as they all cornered Anna and she began to tear up scared, her chest heaving, and her heart beating desperate and angry, "I won't let you hurt him!"

One of the monsters charged her, and she ducked and weaved skillfully below the monsters outstretched claws

Her axe struck the back of its leg, her sword swinging around tearing through the monster's flesh and she spun on the same motion swinging the axe wildly. It cracked through the robes and ribs of one of the men sending him rolling through the dirt crying out in pain.

Another monster charged Anna Bee slashing and growling. She spun her body, her sword's blade blocking its claws off course and then cleanly cutting off its right leg with a mist of decaying blood sending the monster crumbling onto its side with a terrifying scream. Two more monsters charged her from her sides, and two of the robed men charged her as well with their daggers raised as well.

The monster to the left of her slashed from below, and the monster to her right lunged straight at her with a straight stabbing motion. She leapt up, her foot landing on it claws as it swung upwards.

She spun with her sword as she was launched upwards lobbing off the monster's head with messy black fading blood splashing outwards, the second monster's claws tearing into the headless one without Anna Bee in the way and she gracefully rolled to her feet ripping her axe from a fallen body as she rolled.

The blistering flashes of laser assault rifles came through the rattling fence in the distance as soldier droids knelt along the fence firing with terrifying accuracy. There was four of the droids arriving along the fence in total. Danny leapt over the fence beside them shouting urgently, "I'm coming Anna Bee!" As he fell he notched an arrow, drew it back, and released it silently through the air. He fired the arrow skillfully before his foot touched the thick mangled grass, and the arrow ripped a cloaked man off of his feet.

An angry screaming monster charged her and Anna Bee dove between its legs both weapons outstretched ripping off its legs with a smear of blood. She spun and blocked another attacking monster's blows and on the same skillful swing her blade went skillfully through a charging man with a burst of splattering blood.

Danny charged towards Anna Bee diving below a monster with his bow aimed upwards as it pounced towards him. He released the arrow as he slid between its legs and the arrow tore through the monster's chin and emerged out of the top of its head with a splattering sound. Danny returned to his feet behind the rabbit drawing his sword, and the monster fell onto its back behind him,

Danny spun and cut into a masked man has the man drew his bent dagger, and more white robed men surrounded Danny with their sharp daggers. Danny knew he could not take all of them at once and he also knew Anna Bee could not take this many enemies out... no matter how bad she was making him look right now. They needed a miracle, he needed a plan.

Anna Bee was being forced back, three of the monsters slashing and swinging at her, all from different angles, sending her bouncing backwards blocking them desperately with both of her bloody spinning blades trying to find an opening as they drove her towards the fence.

The three soldier droids concentrated on the three bunnies, the two with assault rifles firing at the rabbits buying

Anna Bee some time as the monsters slashed at her. With nearly every slash they growled and screamed, their breath rattling noisily as though their lungs were torn and not expanding.

The soldier droids along the fence line scanned and rattled away with the assault rifles into the men who surrounded Danny trying to help him as well. Their line of fire was quickly interrupted by Pink monsters that slipped through shadow to intercept the firing, and the monsters angrily charged the metal soldiers.

They tore through the fence knocking the robots over with the clang of claws striking metal with a burst of sparks in the moonlight. The robots quickly calculated their immediate recovery and drew sharpened daggers from within their armored casings and quickly overpowered the pink attacking monsters with their mechanical efficiency.

The moment the pink monsters fell, more pulled themselves from shadows to distract the skilled calculating mechanical soldiers.

The white masked men all dodged the blistering laser fire and surrounded Danny. Danny glanced at his surroundings trying to form a plan, then pointed desperately to his left, "Look! It's Lord Osburn!"

They all spun pointing their daggers following his finger and Danny slashed through one of the men on his right. He broke free from the surrounding circle, jumped over a set of swinging claws with a shout of excitement, and ran for the trees picking up his bow. He ducked rolling into the shadows yelling, "Okay, New Plan! I'll try assassin style! Come get me losers!"

The men turned looking into the trees, and an arrow came from the dark underbrush of the trees tearing through a man's chest sending him spinning with a grunt to the ground. The remaining men all scrambled into the trees charging angrily after Danny.

Another arrow came from the shadows clothes lining a man straight off his feet painfully with the crack of his ribs and he flipped onto his back.

"Come get me!" Danny howled from the shadows as he jumped and weaved trying to draw as many of the men as he could, "I have *plenty* of Arrows! One for all of you!"

Anna Bee took one beast down, then another, and then another. They seemed to endlessly appear around her, their claws were growing closer and closer to her with every swipe. Anna Bee's heart was pounding, and her vision growing cloudy from physical exhaustion. She was glad Danny showed up, but she was also furious and terrified. She did not want anyone to know that she was *weird*... What if Zander found out what she could do?

As she thought about Zander in that brief moment, his voice whispered into her ear as though he was standing right there behind her, his ghost hand extended to her shoulder as it had been before earlier that day... "You're my Anna Bee..."

Her fire rekindled and her vision cleared up. Her heart began to steady it's beat, burning with a powerful drive, her blades spinning in her hands as she screamed, "I won't let you hurt him!"

She tore through the monsters, and launched her axe at another charging, man. After a brief moment an arrow that came with a subtle whistle from the trees and struck the last man in the side as he charged at Anna Bee. The charging man fell with a painful grunt and rolled to her feet.

Danny probed out of the trees, watching the carnage around the blood covered maid to make sure that truly was the last of them.

"Well," he said, "At least I helped a little bit, I got four or five... maybe six or seven if I'm feeling generous..."

"Please Danny," Anna Bee said quickly cutting him off, "Please do not tell our master, Zander that it was me. You can take all of the credit, I don't wish him to know that I'm different... I'm supposed to be good at cooking and cleaning, not combat. I am *weird*... Please, I beg you."

"Weird..." Danny swallowed, "You are kind of *terrifying*... me take the credit? I don't think I made a dent in this battle... you slaughtered nearly all of them. It was like cattle drawn to a slaughter."

"Please Danny! Please don't tell him!" She began to shake, "He means so much to me! I don't know what I would do if he found out that I am so..."

Danny cautiously approached, and set his hand on her blood covered shoulder with a single leather glove, "I can see the way you look at Zander. I know you care a lot about him. I know you would *never* be a threat to him... but what happens if he finds out we have been keeping your... abilities...or in your eyes, your *weirdness*, as you call it a secret."

"Please, Danny," Anna Bee said pleading, "Please."

He sighed, "You faced those things without any fear. How did you do that? When I showed up you were tearing things up... You didn't look scared at all, there was *so* many of them, I could barely avoid one and you..." His voice trailed off, "How were you *not* scared?"

"I was terrified. You could say it was just the fear in my heart that put the fire in my eyes. I just think about something else..." she said, "Something to distract me from how scary they are."

"Like what?" Danny asked curiously. Anna Bee blushed and slowly built up the courage to say it, "How s-special Zander is to me."

Danny took a deep breath and opened his mouth to speak. He was interrupted before his words could be heard.

All around them the bodies began to explode into crackling odorless flames, the smoke turning into a dark powder that blew away on the breeze through the dark night. He watched the body's combust one by one, and he sighed, "We better go tell Zander something, at least."

"We should tell him in the morning," Anna Bee insisted, "As urgent the matter is, the situation is under control for now, and it is our duty to protect him. He needs his sleep."

"I'll tell him the moment he wakes up then..." Danny turned and watched as even the tents just randomly combusted. The fire spreading across the bodies, but did not spread to the forest, as though It was some form of paranormal curse spreading through the bodies. Even the Monsters still alive, trying to crawl at them with re-growing legs burst into flames and fell with gurgled raspy breath and terrifying inhuman screams.

"Looks like we won't have to clean up any of this. Weird, they must have had some kind of reactant chemical in them," Danny watched the flames crackle and leap between the bodies, "Anna Bee?" He turned and looked at her. She was staring into the flames, the fire reflecting off of her moonlit blue eyes.

"Yes?" She asked turning to him.

"He was worried about you, did you know that? That's why he sent me out here," Danny said almost jocular as though he was failing at telling a joke, "He was going to come out here himself to make sure you were okay, but I insisted that I go. We should have been worried for the monsters that arrived... you killed Wellington's men too, didn't you?"

"He was worried about me?" her eyes shined for a second in the firelight and then she shyly looked at her shoes ignoring his question, "He really was? Did he say that... that he was worried about me?"

"Yeah," Danny nodded, "It's a good thing he didn't come out though..."

She snapped up, "Yes this is true! They were after Zander. They said they wanted his blood and they also wanted his light."

"Light?" Danny asked thoughtfully, "As in his electricity?"

"I am not sure... Just please don't tell him what I did here tonight. He means *so* much to me, I don't want him to be scared of me," Anna Bee nearly begged falling to her knees in the fire light

There was a long awkward silence and Danny finally turned to Anna Bee with a sigh, "You know what?"

"What?" She asked watching him through the light of the crackling fire around them.

"Your secret is safe with me, if it really means that much to you," he turned his back to her to begin heading back to the building, "but something tells me Zander would not find you weird for being able to fight." He waved at her as he walked away, "He really is lucky to have you. Also, remind me *not* to piss you off."

"Get back to patrolling, stay alert in case they come back," Danny ordered the gathered soldier droids and they immediately split up, "Yes sir." Danny notched an arrow and began to patrol himself watching the fence line at the ready. Behind him, Anna Bee headed for the estate.

Mandy ran into Anna Bee as she was walking around the corner heading back into the estate, "Lord Zander was worried for you. Anna Bee, where have you been?"

"Just..." Anna Bee thought for a moment, "I was cutting up that old ugly tree on the fence line, and I got distracted by how pretty the moon was. I apologize."

"Well, that tree sure had a lot of blood in it," Mandy said looking Anna Bee up and down, "I heard a lot of screaming too, that poor tree. Whatever, I suppose. Zander's having the nightmares again."

"Okay," Anna Bee bowed, "Let's go to him then."

Anna Bee went straight to the restroom to clean up, and then followed Mandy straight to Zander's bed side. Anna Bee carefully sat beside him and gently took his hand. She waited for the sweat to clear his brow, and for his body to lie peacefully and not continue tossing and turning.

Anna Bee gently stroked his hand, her lips curling into a sweet and shy smile, "I could hold his hand forever, Mandy."

"Surely that is unnecessary," Mandy said quickly, "I am sure he would want both hands free to work when he wakes up. We are lucky that he is a heavy sleeper, or I'm sure all the screaming trees, and us doing this to him every night would wake him up."

"That is not what I mean," Anna Bee said thoughtfully. Then she spoke as though she was crossing into territory that she did not want to, "I-I have dreams too, in my sleep."

"You do?" Mandy asked, "Shall I begin holding your hand in your sleep?"

Anna Bee giggled, "No, they are good dreams." She immediately began to act as though she regretted saying anything and looked as though she wanted to change the subject, "How many soldier droids have you made today?"

"Explain," Mandy said curiously, "Good dreams about what?"

"I know it is ridiculous of me to say. Dreams where Zander is my husband, and I am his wife, and we have beautiful and strong children, living here in the estate... but I am only his maid. It is clear that I will always only be a maid. He does not ever look at me the way he looks at *her*..." Anna Bee's voice trailed off for a moment, "I greatly desire Zander to be happy, and so I am hoping things work out well with him and Skylar. I know that would make him happy."

Mandy listened, and nodded, "I see."

"Those wonderful seconds, those beautiful moments in my dreams, where I am good enough, where I am happy... they are all I need," she smiled showing her white teeth and separated her hand from his, "I know they are only dreams, but they still make me happy."

"You should probably clean all that blood off of your apron and dress," Mandy said, "I don't care that you lied to me, but Zander might. I know you have been protecting him."

"Y-you do?" Anna Bee asked scared. Her smile was replaced by terrified tension, "and you haven't told him?"

"Nope," Mandy shrugged, "I suppose it is up to you to tell him. You cannot marry someone unless they know who you *really* are… I do not know what you are scared of. That whole marriage concept could be worth a shot for both you and Zander. No one really likes Skylar anyway… well except him."

"I just… the way he held me today, the way he let me cry into his chest… the way I slept in his arms," her voice trailed off and she shivered, "I don't want to risk having moments like that taken away."

"Humans are weird," Mandy shrugged, "All of you are. Robot's rule. Get some sleep Anna Bee… after you clean up all that blood."

"Yes, master," Anna Bee rose and bowed.

"Anna Bee," Mandy hesitated gently and turning before she left, and Anna Bee stood there facing her, "Yes?"

"I know his sight is set on Skylar. If he means that much to you, don't ever give up on him, in any way," Mandy said raising her voice just a bit to enunciate clearly, "He is not used to his current situation in any way whatsoever, give him time. Things will land in place where they need to be. Good electrical circuits find their way around bad ones in the end. It's a lame robotics metaphor, but hey, *don't give up*. I don't understand humans, but I understand how happy you make Zander. He truly does want you around. I also know he always does the right thing in the end."

"Thank you, Mandy," Anna Bee smiled and raised her head for a moment, "That means a lot to me."

"Go to bed," Mandy said, "I don't know what it is going to be, but you have quite a story to tell him in the morning."

Anna Bee moved to her room and closed the door. She changed her outfits, addressed and cleaned the wound on her arm. Then she laid under the covers staring at the ceiling until she closed her eyes to rest.

———

I woke up with a yawn and a smile. I had dreamed again, the same style of dream, the rabbit showed up with the echo of screams and a battle in the distance, and then beautiful Skylar showed up to hold my hand to make it all go away. I was starting to enjoy my dreams. Every time I drew closer and closer to Skylar. It felt as though my dreams it were very real, like I really was holding her warm soft hand, and I was never *that* close to her in real life.

I sat up with a stretch and a smile thinking about Skylar, "Oh how beautiful she is."

I hopped out of bed and I headed lazily for my workshop. Danny noticed me heading down the hall from the dining room, "My lord!" He quickly leapt to his feet, "There were people in white masks here last night, and more of those bunny things! We intercepted their attack while you were asleep. The soldier droids, Anna Bee, and I were able to hold them off."

I spun quickly, snapping out of my dreamy state, "What?" I asked shocked, "We were attacked and you did not wake me up?"

"It happened really fast, we didn't have time," Danny nodded quickly, "Anna Bee was nearby with some Droids and they fired through the fence. I did my best to keep them distracted and fight them off. This was different, there was more than one rabbit, and they had attacking men with them in white masks."

162

"Where?" I asked quickly, "Show me," and I returned to my room and quickly slipped on my shoes and sheathed my sword to my belt.

He led me out of to the estate beyond the western side of the chain link fence. There was massive piles of scattered ashes stirring in the wind around scorched crumbling skeletons. There was even a campfire that still had hot coals

"This was where they were camped. They all burst into flames when the fight ended," Danny said quickly, "like I said, we were able to hold them off, but some of them got away."

I stood there, and I shivered in disbelief, "An actual attack?"

"They were planning on attacking. Danny ambushed them," Anna Bee approached from behind, "My lord, they were terrifying rabbits, and Danny was very brave. Danny was fighting them, and then the soldier droids and I took them completely by surprise when we started shooting them from the fence line."

"They were so close," I leaned my back against the gate backing up, looking at the distant ashes and fire pit, "How many of them were there? What happened?"

"Not too many," Danny lied shrugging, "They were not expecting us to be as armed and prepared as we were, but now that we know they are after us, next time we'll be even more prepared, my lord."

"Good," I said, "and Mandy should continue her creation of the soldier droids around the clock, "so we can defend ourselves." I gazed at Danny and the droids with a sigh of relief, "I am glad that the soldier droids are working as well as they are."

"You should not have gone to the Market Day Festival," Mandy approached from behind crossing the lawn to me, "More strangers. Someone is here to see you my lord, I have not seen her before."

"Great," I sighed, "and what timing, the morning after an attack."

"I'm right behind you my lord," Danny gave a quiet teasing glance at Anna Bee who shot him a dirty look as he spoke the next line, "You are safer than you think."

I wasn't quite sure what that was all about but I turned to Anna Bee, "Are you okay? The last time I saw you, you were... tired." I was worried about her, but she smiled and nodded.

"Okay," I said with an uneasy sigh, "Please be careful, okay?"

"I will my lord," she smiled and bowed gracefully.

We turned and the four of us headed for the gate, and I could hear scraping metal in the distance as Buster worked tirelessly moving old rusty trucks around the Eastern parking lot of the estate.

She was a young blond woman, maybe twenty-three. She held a brief case in one hand and the other was dragging a leopard print luggage case behind her with two white plastic wheels that were sunk into the gravel from its weight.

"Lord Zander?" She asked with a pleasant smile, "My name is Vanessa. I am wondering if I could be one of your maids, or a servant. Rumor is really going around that you don't have anything, and I would be honored if I could serve you. I only ask a place to stay, I do not require a monetary purchase. My home burnt down so I'm hoping for a fresh start somewhere new."

I blinked for a moment, "Yeah, Come on in." I unlocked the gate with a sigh, "Mandy give her a tour, and get her a room."

"Thank you, my lord," Vanessa smiled and headed in following Mandy. I closed and locked the gate and I got Anna Bee's attention and motioned her closer.

"Yes my lord?" she kept her voice low as the two walked away behind us.

"Keep an eye on her, make sure she is not a spy for Wellington or something. If you see anything fishy, get Danny right away," I said, "but don't let her catch you."

She bowed, "I'll do my best, my lord."

"Thank you Anna Bee," I said and I looked into her eyes and put a hand on her shoulder, "and please, be careful. No maid could ever replace you."

"Thank you," she smiled, "You don't have to worry about me. I am only a maid. C-can I give you a hug my lord?"

"A h-hug?" I raised an eyebrow, "That's random, and kind of odd. I guess you can." I opened my arms and she gave me a hug. She quickly separated, and her cheeks flushed as she bowed, "Thank you my lord... I'll get right on it. I won't let anything slip passed me, I promise."

She took off power walking as though she was embarrassed up the path to the estate.

I scratched my head confused. She was a sweet girl, she was. I enjoyed her company, but most of the time I simply could not comprehend her actions.

11: A Spy and a Birdy

The whinny of a horse behind me on the other side of the gate suddenly startled me.

I spun around my hand on my sword to see a head of long black hair that was watching me carefully with two concentrating blue eyes. It made me immediately wonder where she came from, and how she was so silent and hidden about her approach. It threw up all kinds of red flags, making me feel on edge and nervous.

The girl hopped off her horse wearing a black unzipped hoodie and underneath it a laced up almost maid like apron, but was wearing it like a detailed touch to her grey and black comfortable dress, "Yo. How's it going?"

"What is your intention?" I asked ready to draw my sword.

"Sorry to sneak up on you," she said standing at the gate watching me with a curious look, "You Lord Zander?" She had a tense look in her eye like she was just as suspicious of me, as I was of her.

"Yeah," I nodded, "What do you want? How did you sneak up on me like that? We were standing right here. We didn't see, or *hear* or a thing."

Danny uneasily lowered his bow and put a hand on an arrow in his quiver at the ready but she did not seem very phased by this standing there confidently, "Your lack of observation is not my problem. I'll get straight to the point. I heard you needed blades, and I want to be a knight."

Danny burst out laughing, "But you are a girl! Girls can't be knights."

"Well I'm not going to be a maid. I'm no good at that stuff, I'm good at *fighting*. That's what all the other lords said, that's why they all rejected me. I'm hoping you'll be different, since you're the last lord in fifty miles," she said flatly, "You're better than the other lords right? You'll allow a *girl* to be your humble servant, and the chance to earn the title knight? Won't you?"

"My lord, it is improper to have a woman knight…" Danny tried to talk, and I held up my hand for him to stop talking, "Danny, when have I honestly cared about what other people think of me?"

"See I like you already," the stranger said through the fence motioning to me, "The name is Robin, but people call me Birdy. What do you say boss, give a girl a chance?"

"My lord…" Danny swallowed, "I just don't advise… if Wellington finds out… if *Skylar* finds out you have a *woman* knight… you could be the joke of the town."

I scratched my chin, and she shrugged, "give me a chance. Let me show you what I can do, I'll earn the title fair and square as anyone else would."

I glanced into her serious blue eyes and I sighed, "I have a lot going on. I was just attacked by monster rabbits. What is your reaction to that? You going to make fun of me like everyone else?"

She looked serious for a moment, "I see, I've heard that rumor. I'm not sure what to think of it yet. I don't care what I fight, as long as I can kill it."

I raised an eyebrow, "Well, I guess…" I thought for a moment, and I glanced at Danny who shrugged, "You are in charge here, my lord. If it was me, I would preserve my reputation and not have a woman for a knight."

I unlocked and opened the gate, "well Birdy," I extended a hand to her, "Can I count on you when I *need* you? If I accept you as one of my blades?"

She removed a wicked curved dagger from inside her hoody spinning it in her palm with terrifying skill in a flash that made Danny raise the bow and flinch. She raised it above her head dropping to her knee as Danny had done before, "If you accept my blade then I'll protect you with my life. That is my oath."

I thought for a moment staring at her, "Sure. Just please don't make me regret this decision." I took the blade handle and I pulled her back up and handed her the razor sharp dagger.

She bowed low, "Sure thing. I'm worth your time, I promise."

"Give her a tour Danny, Keep an eye on her though, she could be one of Wellington's spies," I said it out loud and on purpose right in front of her to carefully watch her reaction.

She blew a massive amount of angry air out of her lungs, "That greedy, no good, perverted..." I could see the honest bitter anger in her eyes, "You know what the bastard said to me when I offered him my blade? He told me that he could maybe make another use for me and told me to take off my clothes... if you are in some kind of feud with the guy, I guarantee you just recruited the right girl! I'll go take him out right now if you want."

Her seriousness made me unnerved as she leaned closer, "I would never be his spy. Not in a thousand year, not for a million cents a day... not for a million dollars if those were still currency! not on the life of my first born child..." She growled leaning in even closer, "I'll let it slip you called me that because I like you, my lord. I'll ask you kindly once, lord or not, don't compare me to that bastard."

"I'm sorry," I swallowed a little nervous, but several soldier droids came up weapons at the ready at the sight of the intimidating scene and she caught sight of the machines and her eyes lit up.

She pulled back excited looking at the approaching robots, "Well then Danny boy! Give me a tour! If I would have known I might to get to kick Wellington's ass, I would have come here first. The *robots* make it cool too though."

Danny gave me a nervous look and I motioned for him to follow her. He turned and went after her scratching the back of his head in disbelief, "So Birdy, what kind of weapons do you have?"

I closed and locked the gate watching the fence line for anything out of the ordinary.

Something felt off. Two random girls in a row, right after an attack. It felt as though it could not possibly be a coincidence. One of them was more than likely a spy of some kind. As angry as Birdy got with the whole Wellington thing, I felt as though it could have been good acting, or *bad* acting because she reacted so boldly.

I would have to keep a very close eye on both of them, for sure.

After double checking to make sure there was no one else arriving, I headed straight for my work shop. Why would I make them do all the fighting? So what if I was the lord of the estate? I wanted to fight, I wanted to face my fears and go toe to toe with one of those monsters. I wanted to be strong, I wanted to be able to beat Skylar and earn her respect.

I went straight to working on the power armor again. Lining a frame of an old exoskeleton like suit with the bolted and bent armor. I had strength, not skill. So I was going to have to fight with brute force, like an armored tank. The skill would come over time, if I worked hard enough like Danny had told me.

Before it was dark, I caught Danny when he passed by in the hallway. I made him spar with me some more right there in my workshop

I was not as bad off as I remembered. Maybe I was just more prepared for it. He also noted that I was greatly improving and that he promised he was not just lying to make me feel good.

He then left to continue patrolling like he always did, and I set back to work with an eager new confidence. I still could not beat him, but at least there was improvement on my part.

The armor was a simple concept, but I still kept finding flaws in my design. I kept uncovering different ideas to tweak and adjust as I designed and began to build. There was a million and a half things to do to improve its functionality and effectiveness, I could see myself spending forever making new and different models.

I busily worked the entire day away. Eventually Anna Bee appeared in the door with a shy smile, "It's time for dinner, my lord."

I rose with a nod, "I could use a break. If I've really been working that long. Man time has flown by this evening."

Anna Bee smiled, "I agree my lord," and she led me to the table. Vanessa was standing with a beaming pleasant smile as well as Terry who stood there presenting himself in a professional fashion. Danny and Birdy sat around the table, patiently waiting for me.

"I made a chicken alfredo this evening," Terry said gently, "I do hope you enjoy it my lord."

I pulled out a chair and sat with a yawn, "I am sure it will be delicious."

"How long have you had electricity?" Birdy leaned over the table eagerly as Terry came from the counter with clean plates covered in steaming noodles, and Vanessa's eyes also lit up, "It is fantastic! I have never even seen a lit light bulb before. Let alone *working plumbing* and a *water heater*..."

"Oh yeah," I sighed, "You are both more than welcome to use the shower," I said almost emotionless. Everyone loved my electricity so much, it seemed to blow minds and fulfill childhood dreams to everyone else. To me, I just needed it to build stuff. I could understand the luxury it was now a days, but the way Birdy shivered made me laugh as she began staring at me intensely, *"You have a shower?"*

"Yep," I nodded, "and you may use it as long as you are in my service. Since I am receiving an increase of people in my estate I ask you limit to fifteen minutes per shower going forward. Beyond that limit to keep things easy on the hot water heater, you can shower every day if you want to."

"For a loner, you don't have it too bad out here," Birdy shrugged, "it's pretty cool. I hold no regrets accepting you as my lord."

"Thank you," I shrugged, "but I was not a loner? Has anyone seen Mandy?"

"She was out back working on some old robots, my lord," Anna Bee said politely, "Shall I go get her?"

171

"No, it's okay," I smiled, "Let her keep working. We could use the firepower around here. I'll have Danny check on her after dinner.

Danny nodded when he heard me, "Of course, My Lord."

Terry served us all noodles, chicken, and creamy white sauce and we all ate with the exception of the new maid who stood with a straight back at the table side watching in case we needed anything. She also kept watching Anna Bee with a confused look who sat across from Danny and ate as I ordered her too.

I invited Vanessa to join us, and she shook her head refusing bluntly.

"After dinner is there anything you require of us my lord?" Vanessa asked curiously.

"You," I pointed to Anna Bee, "need to get to sleep since you have been sleeping so poorly lately. Danny I expect you outside patrolling the fence after you check on Mandy and keep your eyes peeled in case we are attacked again, and I expect the same from you, Birdy."

"Sure thing," Birdy shrugged, "I'll help keep watch."

"What about me?" Vanessa asked curiously, "What shall you have me do?"

"I don't know," I shrugged, "Clean something? Maid stuff?"

Vanessa smiled, "Will do!"

"Speaking of which! Anna Bee, how has Vanessa been doing?" I asked.

"She is a lot better maid than me, she has passed my thorough inspection. I have been keeping in mind what we discussed earlier. She seems to like it here, and fit in nicely." Anna Bee bowed and I turned to Danny motioning to Birdy, "and the other new girl."

"I love it here," Birdy shrugged cutting off Danny, "Less people, pretty scenery, robots, electricity... it's a cool set up, I'm glad to be here to be honest. I'm pretty straight forward, if I had intentions to attack or something I would have done that already..." She pulled up a fork full of noodles and slurped them up, "Besides you needed someone with skills. I'm sorry you only have this guy over here..." she winked at Danny who turned red frustrated, "I can fight!"

I laughed and did a warm smiling sweep of my new friends around me. It felt good to not be so alone anymore. I did not know I missed other humans this much.

"My lord," Anna Bee spoke up, "I wish to stay awake this evening..." Her eyes looked at the floor, "there are things that I wish to do before I get to sleep."

"Like what? Are they things that Vanessa could do?" I asked quickly, "The last thing I need is you exhausted to the point you cannot work. I want you in bed, *asleep*."

"Yes my lord," she said and she curtsied, "I'll go straight to bed. Please, sleep well my lord." Then she dismissed herself.

"You as well Anna Bee," I rose from the table, "I am going to return to my workshop and continue working."

Vanessa cleaned up my dishes behind me humming to herself. Danny and Birdy slid their chairs noisily out from under the table and headed outside when they were finished eating.

173

Vanessa went around collecting their dishes and pushing in chairs cheerfully.

She seemed awfully happy for someone who just had their house burnt down, but I suppose a lot of people grew happy when they saw I had electricity.

I headed to my workshop where I began to continue working on the set of armor. Fitting it and tailoring it to my body as well as trying to maintain its functionality. It was a simple and effective design, and around 11:30 I reached a satisfying testing point. I felt as though it was complete enough, and I turned to head for my bedroom.

As I headed for the doorway all I saw was the lights quickly switch off, and a figure charge me with the glint of a kitchen blade. I quickly threw up crossing my arms in a reflex, the blade sliced painfully through my forearm with a sharp burning pain and the spread of my blood across my jacket and shirt.

"What the hell?" I croaked and stepped back as the attacking figure swung the knife at me again, my hand caught a piece of metal from the frame and I desperately threw it up and blocked the wildly swinging blade coming my direction. I could barely understand what was happening as I desperately defended myself from another jagged knife slash.

"I really need you to die. My lord, that is my purpose," Vanessa's voice said quickly and in the darkness, and she spun the blade skillfully, standing there for a moment in the dark.

I slid my arm into the gauntlet I had just barely been working on, and she swung at me again. This time there was a burst of sparks and the sound of metal striking metal as the blade bounced off my gauntlet and I spun quickly and tried to hit her with the gauntlet but she leapt back drawing another knife from under her apron skillfully twisting gracefully.

174

"It is only business my lord," she said, "I come from a long line of assassins. I come with *Wellington's* regards, but soon I will kill you. So it does not matter. Please don't take this personally, you seemed very nice. The money is really good. It's only business."

I stood there in a panic, my chest heaving, and the wound on my arm covered by an armored gauntlet, the straps pulled tight to keep pressure on it, my sword leaning against the doorway behind her.

I was defenseless. I could safely assume she planned it that way. I tightened the straps on my arm to an uncomfortable pressure as a tourniquet, "I should have known."

She charged me again in the dark and I could barely see her so I just went forward as hard and as fast as I could. I went between her crossing blades, and hit her with the gauntlet across the bridge of her nose with a crunch and shoved her back. She rolled backwards through the darkness and I reached for my sword where I found the hilt and pulled it from the sheath quickly.

She swung at me again, and I swung the sword upwards blocking her blade. I ducked back evading it, and she spun like a martial artist and kicked me with a painful kick that sent me crashing painfully through the door across the hall into another old dirty office, shattering the old wooden door.

The door fell in splinters around me and she came through the doorway and swung down at me wildly with the blades with a quiet growl under her breath, "there is no one to save you, you've sent them all away, and to sleep. You are nothing but an idiot who does not deserve the power you have…"

I swung the sword at her ankles and she leapt over it giving me the chance to roll away. I leapt to my feet and slid across the old desk and shoved the whole crumbling desk towards her. She leapt over it and swung at me wildly with the kitchen blades. All I did was evade her, swinging my sword wildly to block her attack, and I jumped around her.

I sprinted for the doorway, and painfully regretted that I needed to run for help. I bounded through the shattered doorway as fast as I could. I could hear her frantic breathing and lightning quick footsteps chasing me.

I heard the thud of the knives hitting with skillful thuds striking the wall behind my body as I rolled through the doorway into the hallway. I leapt to my feet, and I froze in my tracks in shocked disbelief to see Birdy standing there patiently with a colt 1911 well cleaned and maintained rust free pistol pointed in my direction.

"My lord," she bowed, and quickly spun the pistol in the air cocking it with one hand. Her black hair reflecting in the light of the hallway, "Well, it looks like you're having a rough night."

"You were both here to kill me?" I complained as Vanessa came around the corner behind me with a bloody nose and two swinging kitchen blades.

"Thanks for the service," Birdy sighed flatly and pulled the trigger. I saw the muzzle flash with a burst of flames three of four times, the echo of gunshots echoing in the hallway around me.

I stood frozen terrified, and then began to pat myself down for bullet holes shocked. She had missed me, yet she was so close...

I stared at her confused as she lowered the pistol with a subtle musical whistle, "I'm sorry my lord, did you say something? Something about, "both of us being here to kill you?"

I heard the slump and the collapse of the body behind me. Vanessa slid to the back of my feet slumped in a ball, her blood puddling below her on the clean wooden floor. The kitchen knives still in her lifeless hands, her blood splattered on the walls behind her from the bullets.

"I told you I wanted to be your knight. If I killed you that would *kind of* defeat the purpose, of being your knight, my lord," Birdy rolled her eyes and tucked the pistol inside her jacket, "It's a good thing Mandy told me to come check on you."

"My Lord!" Anna Bee exploded through her room door in a white night gown spinning the axe in her hand as she dropped to all fours and sprung up from her desperate turn through the hallway, "My lord! Are you okay?" Her eyes in a terrified panic, her chest heaving quickly.

"He's fine," Birdy sighed, and stepped aside to let her approach me.

Anna Bee saw the blood coming from below my incomplete gauntlet, and I saw her face grow pale, "My lord, you are hurt... what happened?"

She glanced down at the body and began to shake, "I think I can understand what happened... I am so sorry I did not come sooner, I am so sorry..." her tears began to fall from her cheeks to the floor, "I wasn't fast enough, what if she would have hurt you more seriously?" Her heart was pounding, her little chest almost hyperventilating. Her voice was flooding with desperate emotion.

"I'm fine," I took her shaking shoulders, "Anna Bee, it is okay. Calm down."

She dropped the axe to her feet and buried her face in my shoulder with a hug, "I was so worried my lord. I was so scared... I was awakened by gunshots... I thought maybe I had lost you... as a master of course..." she corrected herself loudly and panicked, "If

I lost of you as a master, then I would have failed as a maid! I'm so sorry, I was asleep like you told me..." Her voice trailed off. I was the one attacked, and she seemed more upset than I was.

She tore off a piece of her gown sleeve and tied it tightly onto my wound... "I will be better, I will... I will protect you my lord, I will," she said quickly, "This won't happen again..." She sounded like she was trying to convince herself more than she was trying to convince me.

"It was not your fault," I said gently. I cautiously wiped the tears from her tired panicked eyes, "Calm down, everyone is okay. Birdy showed up just in time to rescue me, and everything is okay."

Anna Bee began to calm down, and Birdy began to drag the body out by the hair. Anna Bee pulled me gently to the estate restroom where she cleaned, stitched up, and bandaged my arm. The whole time it looked like she was beating herself up inside, and I could tell she was very upset. I was the one attacked and even I was already breathing steadily again.

"We could not have known," I said, "Anna Bee, you are *still shaking*. It is okay."

"She spoke of a celebratory surprise this evening, since she was excited to be accepted by a new lord. When I tried to ask her what it was, she would not tell me... I did not think it was worth telling Danny like you told me... but still I had the suspicion, and I failed you my lord..." her voice was cold and flat, she hung her hair in front of her eyes in silence, her knuckles balled up, but she did not cry, "You told me to watch for suspicious behavior..."

"Anna Bee," I sighed, and I got an idea standing there in the clean bathroom, "Let's go; walk with me."

She hesitantly stood up, "W-where are we going?"

"Come on," I gently pulled her along as she did to me, by grabbing her arm as we walked through the dark hallway, "Anna Bee you did not fail *anybody*. There was *no way* you could have known, and I am okay. It's all over, it really is. *You* are okay. No one was seriously hurt, the attack was stopped..." I opened the door to her room and pulled her in, "Please Anna Bee, go back to sleep..."

"I cannot my lord," she said cringing, "Even if I tried. I wish to make sure that you remain safe for the rest of the night."

I pinched the bridge of my nose, and she spoke quickly, "It is my duty to protect and serve you... that is what I want to do."

"Anna Bee," I said lowering my tone gently, "I shall meet you in the middle. I will go to sleep, and you may pull your bed into my room. You may sleep in there with me for the rest of the night. Is that clear? I care about you, and I want you to get some sleep. I don't care where you do it, but you need to go to sleep so you we can figure out the entire situation with level minds tomorrow."

I placed the bloody gauntlet in my workshop, then I turned and headed back into my bedroom. I left my sword by the doorway and I laid down in my bed. My bedroom was right next to my workshop, the last office in the hallway before all of the offices ended and the workshops began.

12: A Maid's New Approach

Anna Bee poked her head in the doorway nervously, hiding her eyes behind her bangs, "My lord?"

"I thought I told you to go to bed, Anna Bee," I said growing a little frustrated. She grew very quiet, and came around the corner revealing she had her battle axe on top of a neatly folded pillow and blankets in her arms. She crossed the small room and set it down next to my bed and sat beside me and stuttered so quietly I could barely hear her, "M-my lord, you said you did not care w-where I slept, so I wish to sleep right here, with you."

I sat up with an amused and awkward laugh, "Like in the same bed?"

"I understand it is an odd request, but I wish to know you are truly safe. That is the only way I will be able to sleep my lord..." She looked at the floor with a cautious tone, "I do not mean to inconvenience you my lord. I know it is unusual behavior, and I am aware of how improper it is. I just wish to..."

I held up my hand to silence her, "It's fine. If that's what truly helps you, go right ahead... just do your best to not... make it awkward and it can't be a regular thing..."

"Thank you my lord," she said smiled. She placed the pillow so that it would separate us. Then she laid down and curled up in my bed facing away from me. She began pulling up the covers so that she could face the door and so that she was between myself and the door.

She was very quiet. If I had not already known she was there, I probably would have never noticed her presence. Out of how quiet she was, and how little space she took up on the edge of my bed with her little blanket, it was almost like she was not even in the room.

I took one of my pillows and put it under her head, "Do you only own one pillow?"

She nodded but remained facing away from me, "Yes, my lord. However, I do not wish to inconvenience you any further, so I cannot accept one of yours..."

"Take the pillow," I said blinking with a disbelieving tone in my voice, "Just take it."

She hesitantly took the pillow, her hand shaking and briefly fluffed it and placed her head on it, "I will do my best to protect you as long as I am in here. This way I know for sure that you are okay."

I sighed and I curled up in a ball facing away from her, "Good night, Anna Bee."

"G' Night, my lord," she said sweetly.

I closed my eyes to try and get some sleep. After getting used to the fact that there was someone else lying in my bed, I eventually drifted off to sleep.

I began to dream again, and I was standing in a long cloudy hallway. For a moment I did not recognize the hallway, but the doorways and shadows began to form around me and it slowly transformed into the hallway of my estate. As things developed, I could see the damaged pieces of Mandy's lower half hanging out of a doorway. This dream felt so different, so real. I approached the maroon pieces I could see the image clearly, oil and pieces of wiring scattered about as though she had been torn in half.

A torn piece of green fabric was pinned to the wall by Danny's sword. A blood trail leading from that spot to another doorway, and with the repetition of the dreams like this, I just walked up the hallway glancing left and right.

Danny came from a doorway and ripped his sword from the wall. His chest was heaving, his thick leather armor was covered in blood his voice in a creepy growl, "There is only one left to kill, which should be the easiest one," he spun the blade in his hand with a wild hiss, "Lord Wellington will be so pleased with me."

Usually by now Skylar would have arrived to tell me it was a dream, but she did not. Danny charged me with his sword and swung at me left and right. I drew my sword and began blocking quickly, "This is only a dream. A bizarre dream just like the others."

"I swung a defensive blow and he countered swinging his blade at me quickly. It met Skylar's blade with a burst of sparks as she appeared in a gentle puff of sweet floral aroma right on cue. The moment her blade struck Danny's, he disappeared.

"It's only a dream my lord," she sheathed her sword to her hip and leaned her head against my chest almost as though she was snuggling into it, "I wish you would not have these nightmares... they make me worry about you. I want you to be safe and happy, like the way you make me happy..."

"You worry about me?" I asked her, "I know this is only a dream, but I wonder if you really worry about me. Wherever you are. I wonder if you think of me, like I think of you."

She smiled and wrapped an arm around me gently, "I am right here, my lord..." She sounded nervous for a moment, "It is okay. Be at peace my lord."

I looked down at her arm around me. Her blond hair hiding her face that was leaning against my chest, "I wish you to be safe my lord... please be at peace. I wish to repay the happiness you provide to me... you are so special to me... I've been thinking a lot about it... no one has treated me with the kindness you have shown me..." She sweetly touched her forehead to mine.

"Forgive me lord this is so unprofessional... it's just that I could not do this if you were awake. My lord... I just... I- just..." Her forehead trembled against my own. It felt so good, so romantic to see Skylar like this. I loved being this close to her, my heart on a roller coaster ride all over the place. She was so close, smelling so sweetly.

I had never been this close to her before, I felt paralyzed. My heart was pounding out a musical beat and my mind was slowing as though it was trying to preserve the precious moment. Her voice grew very quiet, even as close as she was she stuttered, "I-I...I love you my lord. I won't let anything happen to you."

Her forehead parted from mine, her face a blur, and she kissed my forehead. I felt her tear strike my cheek, and she kissed my forehead a second time. She lifted my chin making me smile, and my cheeks turned a shade of bright crimson. My heartbeat picking up again.

"You are behaving as Anna Bee would," I said shyly, not knowing how to behave in this situation, "It's only me, Skylar."

Then just like that Skylar disappeared leaving me warmly alone in the hallway, and I faded back into peaceful sleep.

———

Birdy stood as quiet as a ghost in the doorway of Zander's room, her eye through the crack in the door. She had her hand on the door handle watching Anna Bee who was leaning over Zander, her forehead against his, a tear falling against his cheek. Birdy watched Anna Bee nervously kiss Zander's forehead, once, then twice, and Birdy sighed.

Mandy stood behind her, "What do you make of it? Anna Bee rests by his side, sacrificing her sleep to comfort him, every night these nightmares occur..."

"Talk about a heavy sleeper, seriously," Birdy said under her breath, and to her surprise Anna Bee heard her and her head snapped in their direction, and quickly and separated and leapt to her feet in a nervous panic, "I wasn't... I was... I just was..."

"Anna Bee," Birdy raised a hand and gently let herself in, "I get it sweetheart. I really do, I heard everything. I would usually find that super creepy, but I'm going to be honest with you. It's kind of cute."

Anna Bee looked at the floor, "I am sorry."

"Sorry for what?" Birdy smiled, "It's adorable. *Nowhere* does it say it's a bad thing to fall in love."

"It is inappropriate for a servant or maid to develop any kind of feelings; including love or hatred towards her lord or master because it affects the quality of service provided to their lord or master..." she said and her voice trailed off, "P-please don't tell him... please..."

Birdy fiddled with her hands thoughtfully and Mandy poked her head in, "No one has taken care of Zander better than you, Anna Bee. Not me, not anyone here..." Mandy spoke honestly, "I am jealous of your ability to make him happy ever since you showed up."

Anna Bee exhaled a long melancholy breath. She tilted her head to hide behind her bangs as she sat on the bed, "Please do not tell him what I have done tonight... it *will* not happen again. I am so embarrassed..."

Birdy shrugged, "Don't be. Your secret is safe with me sister. I see where you are coming from, but if you really love him *that much...*" Birdy motioned to his sleeping body, "Maybe you should do something about it. Tell him how you feel. Maybe it will wake him up, pun intended. I can see the way he looks at you, like he enjoys every second he's with you..."

"Well, I know he does... he just does not look at me the way he looks at *Skylar...*" Anna Bee said, "I dream as he does, but I dream he looks at me with those eyes, the way he looks at her..."

"Skylar?" Birdy asked, "Who is Skylar?"

"Skylar, a beautiful girl whom Zander met at the market fair. She behaves sporadically towards him. One second she is mean to him, the next she is kind. I fear she is plotting something against Zander, but Zander has spent a lot of time in isolation and is obsessed with her," Mandy said, "I would prefer he was obsessed with Anna Bee to be honest. She cares sincerely about him. Zander is the only one who does not see Anna Bee's obsession with him."

"It's not an obsession..." Anna Bee said, "It's not... Is it? Oh no... what have I done?"

"Well, I have an idea. Anna Bee, let's ditch the maid concept for a couple days. Think you could do that?" Birdy said her blue eyes gently studying Anna Bee, "Follow me. Let me try to help you out. Let's see what we can do."

———

I woke up and sat up with yawning the next morning. The heat from the fireplace comfortably drifting through the estate.

I blinked a couple times to make sure it wasn't another dream and smiled gently reaching up rubbing my forehead where Skylar had kissed me. I could not wait to see her again, especially if she was going to be sweet to me like she was last night... maybe she would kiss me for real, instead of on my cheek or forehead...

"Hey lazy," Birdy poked her head in, "Breakfast is ready."

"Thank you, Birdy, for the assist last night. You truly saved my life from that assassin," I bowed to her gratefully crawling out of bed.

"It's my job. You're welcome. Also, breakfast is ready, Terry made French toast, whatever that is," she said, "Please hurry my lord, I'm hungry."

I slipped on my shoes to prepare for the day and before I headed down the hallway, I realized Anna Bee was not in my room with me, "Is Anna Bee okay?"

"Of course, maids wake up early. She's been hard at work..." her voice trailed off as we entered the dining room, and it smelled like freshly baked bread and cinnamon. It was a delicious homey smell, and Anna Bee was patiently waiting with a big warm smile.

Her hair was carefully braided and tied into a pattern down the back of her head. A big green bow was tied in her hair holding it up, and her apron was gone, replaced by a smooth green dress that was tailored to fit her very well. She looked different from her bland head band, boring green dress, and maid's apron.

It caught me a little off guard. "Anna Bee, what is the special occasion? You look very pretty this morning. Have I forgotten something?"

Her eyes shined and she giggled, "No, my lord..." she glanced at Birdy then back at me, "I just wanted to look nice today, that's all."

"Well you do look very nice today," I smiled, "I approve."

She blushed sweetly and looked down, "T-thank you my lord."

"So," Terry grinned, "Take a seat, So you can eat it while it's hot," he motioned to the chair I usually sit in as he set maple syrup on the table, "I developed this recipe when I was very young, it's one of my favorites... it never gets old."

He passed out plates to Danny, Birdy, and I, but when I turned for Anna Bee to join us, she had snuck away while I sat down.

"Where did she go?" I asked curiously.

"Moments ago she spoke of an idea she had to remove the blood stains from the floor," Terry shrugged as he passed out napkins and silverware efficiently as he always did, "She was excited about it. She's a weird girl."

Danny choked on a bite as Terry said "She's a weird girl", and all heads snapped towards him and Danny blushed, "How embarrassing, I was eating too fast."

I picked up my knife to sample this new dish, it looked like bread that was fried in eggs, with powdered sugar and cinnamon blended together. I had never seen it before.

I carefully sampled some, and it was delicious.

Everyone seemed to be in a great mood this morning. Birdy told us a hilarious story of how a thief tried to steal a necklace she owned. The thief missed with his snatching hand and accidentally grabbed her breast. The thief felt so awkward and embarrassed that he gave her twenty cents, and apologized for trying to steal her necklace.

It was a funny story and spirits were lifted. I felt as comfortable in my own home as when I had been sitting in Nate's carefree living room, surrounded by smiling friendly faces. I wasn't used to my estate being this clean and comfortable, it almost made it feel like I was not home.

Being a Lord came with major advantages and disadvantages, the advantages were the fantastic people around me, the disadvantage was my responsibilities I felt for every single one of them. I wanted to protect them, I wanted to take care of them.

13: Accusations

"My lord," Mandy entered the dining room. She broke the happy moment and cut through it with a wave of tension I could not understand with her next words, "My lord, Lady Skylar is here to see you."

"Oh great! Let her in, she can join us!" I smiled, thinking about my dream. It was a perfect addition to make such a great morning even better. I was excited to see her after remembering such a sweet dream that replayed in my mind making my heart skip a beat every time.

"Who?" Birdy asked, "That name sounds familiar."

Danny shrugged in disbelief, then shoved his plate away, "Alright. Okay then."

Mandy nodded and quietly left, "I will retrieve her as you wish."

"Thank you," I nodded, and as I turned to everybody they all had lost their light hearted demeanors, replaced by frustration and disbelief.

"I know she treated me poorly for a while, but I am a man who believes in second chances," I grinned, "Let's give her a chance. I don't get why you all grow so angry when she arrives."

"That's the problem," Danny grumbled under his breath.

I raised an eyebrow, "What do you mean?" He opened his mouth to speak but was cut off as Skylar quickly entered the room wearing a long red and black tight fitting dress. Her hair tied up in a messy bun. She still looked beautiful to me, it was hard for me to see her as anything else.

She held a manila folder under her arm and she had a concerned look on her face as she bowed, "My lord."

"How are you this morning? Hello Danny, and Terry. My courtesy extends to you as well, though I do not know your name yet." She bowed to Birdy who gave a wave with her right hand studying Skylar.

"What do I owe such a visit?" I rose to my feet turning to face her smiling, "It's good to see you!"

"Well, actually I come bearing bad news," she said in motioning to the folder under her arm.

"Bad news?" Danny asked, "What sort? You cannot go with Zander to the ball?" For a moment he looked excited glancing at Birdy. She placed a hand on his leg secretly to silence him like he was an annoying younger brother, and he glanced at Birdy confused before he settled down.

"No, I can still go," she smiled sweetly at me, "I am honored to go with Lord Zander to the ball. What a lucky girl I will be, to go with a lord, The Machine Lord."

I shrugged, "Then what is your bad news."

She handed me the folder, "Take a look. This is Anna Bee's folder that was presented to people at the academy booth where her contract was purchased. I found it helping clean up from the fair day a little while ago, and I was going to give it to Lord Wellington, but it made me start thinking. I have decided to give it to *you* instead."

I opened it and began to read it, curiously thinking about what Skylar meant and read "Anna Bee Rishel." There was a small faded picture of a sad and scared looking Anna Bee, and below her name, the price of ten thousand cents for two years.

It had her skills presented carefully like a report card. It made me angry as I read it. I thought she was so much better than what I read:

"Sewing: Barely meets expectations

Cleaning: Barely meets expectations

Crafting and carpentry: Meets expectations

Loyalty: Meets expectations

Discipline and time management: Barely meets expectations

Cooking: Below expectations

Emotion Control: Meets Expectations

Combat: Exceeds Expectations

Notes: (scratched in by hand) *has never been contracted before, this gives a discount to the contract. Other Maids fear her for her ability to fight, this causes an additional discount to her service."*

"She has met every one of my expectations," I said angrily, "Why are you showing me this?"

"Well, my lord," she cleared her throat glancing at the folder, "Think about who gave her to you... I hear Wellington talk of wanting to attack and take your robots; those rumors have spread through the whole city, and things have only gotten strange for you ever since she arrived..."

"Excuse me?" Birdy leaned forward looking irritated, "What are you trying to play at here miss?"

I took a moment and glared at her in some serious thought, "You are saying Anna Bee is a spy?"

"Flip over the paper," Skylar said motioning to it. I flipped over the paper to see what she was talking about. I found a sloppily hand written note and it read, *"Take a platoon of eight men to his estate. The maid will meet you and inform you of his military strength, then plan accordingly and take him down that very evening.*

Your Lord. Jazz Wellington."

"Well... I..." I said and my heart began to beat painfully in my throat, "there is no way."

"Let me see it," Birdy rose to her feet and snatched the paper. She inspected it for a moment, "That's Wellington's handwriting alright. I recognize it."

"I'm sure she has found a way to earn your trust. I would be willing to bet she's made you all care for her, maybe she's been acting sad or shy... have you noticed bizarre behavior from her?" Skylar asked glancing around, "I mean, think about it my lord."

"You said eight men?" Danny asked sitting back at the table in desperation growing angry, "I found seven bodies, that doesn't add up."

"I heard that one man returned speaking of a monster rabbit," Skylar said quickly, "That it killed the men... slaughtered them all with long sharp claws."

"But was it a rabbit?" Danny leaned forward staring at Skylar with an accusing and suspicious tone, "Maybe there is just a single part of the equation that you wish to remove? It seems like there is something or *someone* in your way you need to get rid of for whatever you are planning. Anna Bee is no spy. Documents can be forged..."

"I just thought Lord Zander should be presented with the obvious facts here. She was ordered to be an informant at minimum. We know this for sure, the information is clear as day," she said motioning to the paper, "I'm only trying to help, what could I gain otherwise from giving this information to Zander?"

"Go get Anna Bee," I said to Birdy harshly, "Bring her here."

Birdy took a deep frustrated breath closing her eyes, "Right away, my lord." She crossed down the hallway, passing behind me, "Let's talk about this though… Don't do anything rash, until we sort things out."

"I don't know what she has told you. My lord I fear she could be a snake in your nest, I have been worried," Skylar said, "I hate to be the bearer of such awful news, I just figured you needed to know.

"Funny," Danny said, his eyes serious and angry as though he was desperately trying to think of something, "My lord, does it not strike you that a follower of *Wellington* has a file directly presented to him during the purchase of Anna Bee's service? Skylar lives in Wellington's domain, doesn't that mean she serves him?"

"Danny, we have physical evidence regardless. Anna Bee is not what she says she is," I said coldly.

"Something is not right here," Danny said quickly, "Birdy is right, let's examine things carefully."

"I'm sure she has everyone convinced by her act, whatever it is…" Skylar cleared her throat, "The evidence is right in front of us." She leaned back as Anna Bee entered the room followed by Birdy.

"What's going on? Are you okay, my lord?" Anna Bee looked worried glancing around the room, a bloody rag in her hands.

I slid the hand written note and the file across the table to her, "I have a couple questions for you."

She picked it up and glanced over it. Her eyes began filling with fear, and then they quickly shot a scared look to Skylar, and then back to me.

Anna Bee was frozen, and she closed her eyes starting to shake, "I-I..."

"You what," I said painfully rising to my feet my voice growing angry, "You what? Anna Bee, Tell me everything."

"I-I'm sorry my lord," she teared up tilting her head and hiding behind her bangs, "Lord Wellington told me to tell the men what military strength you had but I..." her voice trailed off scared, "My lord... I-I..."

"Anna Bee, I trusted you!" I ripped my sword from my sheath angrily.

Anna Bee whimpered and braced as though she expected me to ram the sword through her, and in my confused rage I was tempted, pointing the sharp at her blade aggressively.

"The best way to kill a snake is to remove the head," Skylar said quickly with a smug satisfied grin glancing at Anna Bee, "Prove you are a lord. End the corruption on your estate my lord, before it gets worse."

Anna Bee lowered her head, and I could feel the break in my heart as I spun the blade on my hand and pointed it at her heart, "What else do I need to know?"

Anna Bee stuttered as though she was desperately trying to force herself to say something... "I-I L-love..."

"You love?" I asked, "You love what?"

"My lord," Danny aggressively placed himself between Anna Bee and myself gently moving the sword, "The wounds dealt to the men I found was by an axe and a sword. The weapons carried by Anna Bee."

"A lone maid killing eight men?" Skylar raised an eyebrow, "Including one of Wellington's elite Knights?"

"How did you know there was a Knight present?" Danny desperately slid the folder back towards her trying desperately to shift the blame, "It doesn't say anything on this folder about a knight."

Skylar looked offended, "Rumors. Rumors spread like crazy, and he was one of the men who has disappeared around the time of the demon rabbit sightings."

Danny growled, and slammed his fist on the table angrily, "My lord she has to be lying! Anna Bee would never!"

"Believe me," I said gently setting my hand on his shoulder "It's hard for me to accept too." I glanced at Anna Bee who was standing still, her head hung low as it almost always was, but lower than usual. She was crying, her tears falling to the floor from behind her bangs.

"Anna Bee," Danny said, "You should tell him... tell him everything."

"Yes, yes you should," I said aggressively, "Spill it. Tell me everything. What else do I need to know?"

Anna Bee shivered fighting more tears, "I-I'm weird..."

I did not want to hurt Anna Bee, but I felt so angry. I felt so betrayed, and so embarrassed to be fooled so easily by her. The evidence was right in front of me, and I had to be strong to impress to Skylar.

"Birdy," I said, "Lock Anna Bee in her room. Get her out of my sight," I growled.

"My lord," Danny desperately turned to me eyeing Skylar, "Let us deal with this matter on our own accord, perhaps we should thank Skylar for her *information*, and escort her out. We don't wish to drag her into our problems."

I turned watching them leave as Birdy shoved Anna Bee through the doorway, "Come on traitor. Let's go."

"I appreciate you bringing me this information," I motioned to the folder, "I really do."

"You can't just lock her up, my lord, what if she escapes and returns to Wellington. Imagine the amount of information she knows about you... My lord, you need to order your men to kill the snake," she said quickly.

I could not find the guts to order or even think about such a thing... My heart pounding, so much emotion flowing through me and stress pushing down my shoulders.

"Surely you are man enough to do so, my lord. You are a lord, I know you have grown since we met at the fair that day," she said and I stared at her big beautiful eyes.

Was this what it was going to take to impress Skylar? I did not want to... but if this meant it drew me closer to the idea of my dreams becoming a reality... Anna Bee *was* only a maid, right? I could get another...

"Danny get me a pen and paper," I said thoughtfully.

He obeyed, and I scratched something onto it and I handed it to him, "This is how I want you to do it. Make it quick."

I could still envision the real tears Anna Bee cried, and even when confronted she did not behave as a cornered spy would. I knew in my heart something felt off, and I wanted to look into the situation further. Get more information from Anna Bee, but I did not want Skylar to think I was cowering and breaking.

Danny was angry as he snatched the paper up and read it. He looked massively relieved then he played along, "That's very humane my lord. Are you sure?"

"Just do it," I ordered.

He stared at me in admiration for a moment which confused me, and then headed off down the hall, "Consider it done."

"Well, I'm impressed," Skylar smiled, "Even quickly and humanely after everything she did to betray you. You are such a sweet guy. I want to ask, how did you have it done? Be-heading? Hanging? I must know, so I can tell my friends all about it."

I cleared my throat desperately trying to think of something, "Death by electrocution."

She turned with a sympathetic smile, "Spies like that weasel under your skin and make you hone feelings for them. I can tell you don't want to be around when it happens, so would you care to walk me to my horse?"

Birdy burst into the room stepping between us with well placed footing, "My lord, Anna Bee has been taken care of like you asked."

Birdy gave a Skylar a smile that looked a little twisted, "Let me walk Skylar out, My Lord. You have not finished your breakfast, and we face multiple threats. You need your full strength in case we are attacked! I insist, please allow me to walk madam Skylar out, so that you may sit and clear your head."

Birdy walked hopefully up to Skylar with a clever spark in her eye and turned to me, "I deeply insist, it's been a crazy day, Anna Bee being a spy and all. We're going to have to scrub all that blood off of her floor now that Danny has..."

Skylar glanced at her suspiciously as Birdy mentioned blood and I quickly interrupted her.

"That's enough," I said swallowing. I honestly did not want to think about her getting hurt, she meant a lot to me, and the thought of her being a spy was incredibly painful... Something just felt off with Skylar's story. I appreciated her trying to help, but it didn't sound right. The way Danny grew so angry in trying to defend Anna Bee, but it made absolute perfect sense.

"That's perfectly fine, Birdy. I look forward to our date Saturday. Zander," Skylar curtsied, and I could smell her chemically created perfume that smelled overly sweet, "I am glad I could help you this morning. I can see you truly are a powerful lord. A real man in the making"

"Thank you," I said wishing I was walking her out, but Birdy insisted as she pushed forward, "Shall we be off, Madam Skylar?"

Skylar gave a curtsey to me and an impressed smell. She then headed out, Birdy following her with a clever smirk that she hid from Skylar and myself.

"Take good care of her for me, Birdy," I nodded and Birdy smiled, "Of course, my lord." They headed out, and I spun on my heel and went angrily straight for Anna Bee's room.

Mandy who remained quiet the entire time caught me in the hallway, "Allow me to distract you for a moment my lord. I am having trouble freeing a robot body from a pile of sheet metal. It won't take any time at all.

I nodded and followed her, trying to avoid the confrontation with Anna Bee that would follow shortly.

———

Skylar and Birdy headed through the front door and walked in silence for a moment through the dark grass of the estate.

"When did lord Zander gain you as a servant? Aren't you a little out of dress code for a proper maid?" Skylar asked Birdy curiously as they walked.

"I'm no maid. I do clean up the dirty things in the estate though," Birdy said placing her hand into her jacket as though reaching for something, "I know Anna Bee is not a spy. She is terrified of what her *master* thinks of her for reasons I'm still piecing together. Zander means a hell of a lot more to *her* then he *ever* will to *you.* There is no way that girl is a spy, and I want to know what you are up to. I see why they all dislike you around here."

Skylar raised an eyebrow, "you saw the evidence. She must have all of you wrapped up in her little web of lies..."

"It is true, she was supposed to be an informant. She has told no one anything, she would never betray Zander. I can see the passion in the poor girl's eyes, she would defend him until her heart stops beating," Danny came angrily out onto the lawn, his bow placed at the ready in his hands, "She has done nothing wrong, and you... *you* are getting on my nerves."

Birdy stepped quickly away from them and unlocked the gate. She motioned for Skylar to leave with a nod. Birdy then motioned to Danny's angrily shaking hand as he notched an arrow, "I would hurry if I were you."

Skylar stood there with a wicked smirk, "I heard Zander order her death. So... you are all spies? Working together?" She raised an eyebrow, "Let us go get him..." She turned back toward the estate, and Danny aggressively stepped in front of her the tension on the bow string creaking, "I don't think so. How about, you never talk to our lord again."

"Insubordinate little fools," Skylar laughed fearlessly, "there are greater things at play here then your little acts of courage this evening. What happens when Zander discovers his maid is not dead? What happens when there is no *blood shed*? I bet you did not even kill the girl."

"There will be blood," Danny angrily drew an arrow without hesitation. Fire burning in his eyes, "If you don't leave here at once, and stay away from him. Because of *you*, I did what my lord ordered. I don't know what you had against Anna Bee, she did nothing wrong... What are you up to?"

Skylar thought for a moment and looked toward the moonlight, "So, I can fool Zander the idiot, but not his servants. Troublesome. In fact I would love to kill all of you right now, including him, but I need Zander alive for what is coming. Besides, he is my date to the ball. What happens when he discovers you crawl around like roaches behind his back?"

"What happens when he finds out you do?" Birdy shrugged, "Just some food for thought there."

Skylar scoffed, "This is far from over. You will find things are just warming up around here." She mounted her horse along

200

with a smile, "have a good day. You never know how many peaceful days we have left in today's society."

She kicked her heels into the side of the horse and took off down the road.

Birdy turned to Danny and giggled, "And you say I drive you nuts."

———

I entered Anna Bee's room minutes later, wiping sweat from my brow. Mandy entered the room behind me and closed the door. It had taken longer than I thought, at least a half an hour to move some sheet metal that had preserved a metal robotic body from the elements. The half an hour it took us gave me time to think and prepare what questions I would ask Anna Bee. It also gave me time to consider what I would do to explain to Skylar if she ever saw Anna Bee in my estate in the future.

Anna Bee was sitting on the bed, and Birdy and Danny both standing and watching her intensely as I entered with a tired and frustrated sigh. I took a deep breath, and I exhaled slowly to calm myself down, "So what happens now?"

"Tell him," Danny said motioning to me as I took in another deep breath watching Anna Bee carefully.

She whimpered and Danny leaned forward handing me the note I wrote to him earlier, "Thank you, my lord. You did the right thing."

I glanced over and read the note that I had given him, "*We'll deal with this mess when Skylar leaves… Something feels off*"

"You are not really a spy, *are you*?" I asked Anna Bee crinkling up the note in my palm, "There *was* evidence, but evidence can be faked."

"I was s-supposed to be," Anna Bee said pulling up her knees and wrapping her arms around them, "I was supposed to report your military strength to men in the trees on the third night, so they could attack your estate and take your robots. I did not. Y-you are the only person who has been nice to me...I just could not betray you. My lord Zander, my loyalty is *only* to you in more ways than you know. You are special to me, and because of that, I betrayed Wellington."

I scratched my chin, "All that you have told me, is any of that true? How he rejected you because of your... and your whole sad back story you told me," I asked, "Is it?"

"Yes," she said sadly, "the informant assignment was a last minute thing he added when he was talking to his Knight Tobias, only a couple minutes before we arrived at your estate. Wellington is a terrible man. He keeps women chained just for pleasure... he takes whatever he wants with no regard for other people..." Her voice trailed off as she took in a deep breath.

"I hate him. My lord, you are kind... you are nothing like him..." She gently lifted her bangs and I could see the tears in the corner of her eyes. The sincerity in her voice unwavering, "I fell asleep in your arms not because I was trying to fool you, but because you are the only person I have ever been able to talk to about anything... without you laughing or making fun of me..."

I sighed and I sat beside her on the bed, "Well thank you for your honesty." I said, "And thank you for your loyalty. Why didn't you tell me this sooner, if it is the truth?"

"She's scared you won't appreciate her as much," Danny said a little frustrated, "She's a troubled girl, that's for sure."

Anna Bee gazed down, and I lifted her chin looking her straight in the eyes, "You are fantastic. You are the greatest maid ever, you are my Anna Bee. Nothing will change that, as long as you are *honest* with me."

She began to take deep breaths closing her eyes as though she was hiding relief, "My lord. In the academy they teach us to fight, to protect our masters or Lords. I was better at fighting than all the other maids...I am good at fighting... I am *weird*... That is the truth, the sincere complete truth."

I gazed at her, "That's pretty cool. I told you they weren't as awesome as you," I scratched her back comforting myself more than her with the physical contact, "As long as you are honest with me, you will be my Anna Bee."

She smiled relieved wiping tears from her eyes, "T-thank you my lord. What would you like me to do today?"

"Well," I said, "I could use a new suit for the ball Saturday, perhaps you could make me one?"

She smiled eagerly, "I would love to my lord. I shall head into town to buy the fabric."

"Birdy," I ordered, "Go with her. Lay low, keep her safe, and keep an eye on her."

"Yes my lord," Birdy bowed, "I won't let her out of my sight."

They rose and Anna Bee gave me a shy smile, "My lord... Thank you for believing me and not Skylar... It means more than you could ever know...May I have a hug?"

I shrugged and gave her a comforting hug squeezing her tight before she left.

"Why was Skylar trying to frame Anna Bee?" Danny asked as they left, "My lord it is clear that Skylar is just as much a threat as Wellington or the monsters and masked men around us. I just can't figure out how she fits into our current situation."

"She was just trying to help," I said, "I would have done the same for one of my friends."

"I get that you think she is pretty, my lord, but think about her behavior. You are blinded by your petty crush," Danny said. I laughed, "Danny, I don't get why you hate her so much. She was just trying to help, and she has apologized for her bad behavior." I could remember the way she looked under the moonlight, the sweet smell of her perfume, the shine of her smile.

"Do you know where her loyalties lie?" Danny asked, "Do you even know which lord she serves?"

"Well she lives in Wellington's domain," I raised an eyebrow and then rolled my eyes slightly frustrated and walked passed him, "Danny, I have a lot to do."

I headed toward my workshop to continue working on my armor. Maybe they were right, maybe I was overlooking something. I just wanted Skylar. I just wanted to touch her hand, to kiss her for real, and not on the cheek. I was overwhelmed with emotions every time I thought of her.

The thought that Anna Bee could be a spy felt impossible, but at the same time it made perfect sense. I wanted to trust her, and I wanted to believe her so that is what I chose to do. With everything we had been through, it felt like she was being honest with me. I could see how genuine her tears were, the way she cried against my chest. If she was a spy, she was doing a *really* good job.

I could see no connection or reason why Skylar would want to frame Anna Bee.

That is why I knew Skylar was honestly just trying to help. My mind was spinning in circles trying to connect dots, as I worked on the power armor.

The next time I was with her I would pay closer attention to her behavior and the way she spoke, in case Skylar truly was working for Wellington, scouting out information for him. I was full of doubt that Skylar's sweet musical tone of a demeanor could possibly be anything other then what she said it was. I could not understand the tension between everyone and Skylar when she was here.

It was just more stress for me to simmer over, and more weight for my shoulders to bear. It was a lot to think about.

14: The Machine Lord's Carriage

Skylar was so beautiful, everything about her made my heart beat just a little faster. I was obsessed with her company and her smile. She was like a daydream I could not stop having as I worked steadily in my workshop on a hydraulic addition to the frame in my armor.

Before long Anna Bee entered the room to inform me that they had returned from town.

"My lord," she said, "I need to get your measurements."

"Oh," I said standing up, "Sure, what do you need me to do?"

She approached with a measuring device that looked like a string with colorful beads and marks on it, "Please put your arms straight out."

I obeyed and she ran the measuring tape along my arms, scribbled down notes on a little notebook, and then wrapped the bizarre measuring device around my chest.

"My lord," she said shyly as she measured me, "I am sorry that I was not honest with you."

"It's okay," I shrugged, "Just be honest with me from now on."

"Well…" She gazed at her toes as she rolled up the measuring device, "there is something I really want to ask you…"

"What is it, Anna Bee?" I asked curiously as she measured the back of my legs and just worked quickly around me.

"Well, I have never been to a ball before, and I…" She sounded like she was convincing herself to continue talking, "and I was wondering my lord, if I could accompany you and your date as your servant Saturday evening."

"What do you mean?" I asked her, "As my servant?"

"I could get the carriage doors, and I could carry your things..." she tried to explain but I laughed at her, "I'm sorry Anna Bee. It's not a date if there are three people there. That would be awkward or uncomfortable for you, you would be a third wheel."

"I don't mind... I just really want to go to a ball. I never have been to one. My lord it would truly mean a lot to me if I could go to just one," She said quickly, "Y-you said I could speak freely as long as I was in your estate, and I understand it is unprofessional for a maid to ask a favor of her lord, but It's been my dream since I was a little girl... only, my dream is to be a date..." She spoke very timidly as I would expect of her, but for a moment she had a flair of emotion in her voice that made it louder for a brief moment.

"What if we throw our own ball?" I asked thoughtfully, "after this one is over?" I also had to keep in mind the pesky fact that Skylar thought that Anna Bee was dead. I would be a lot more willing if it wasn't for that.

"You really wish to invite that many people to your estate?" Anna Bee asked, "they would all find out you had electricity."

I groaned, "I suppose that's true. Well we will think of something Anna Bee, I'm sorry. I am sure there will be another ball. Then I will take *you*, okay?"

She bowed sadly, "I understand, my lord," and she left the room.

I thought for a moment about our conversation, and then I had a sudden epiphany.

"I don't have a carriage to pick up Skylar," I said out loud standing alone in the workshop.

I immediately began gathering up my tools and placing them into my heavy rusty toolbox. Once I was ready I headed out of my workshop toolbox in hand, down the hall, through the lobby, and then immediately straight over to the giant parking lot.

It was cracked and faded, weeds growing up through the scratchy asphalt. It was actually open and empty for once since Buster had cleaned all the old cars and junk up. All that remained in the giant parking lot were three old fairly intact rusting trucks that were parked near the closest entrance to the building, and Buster in his massive cylindrical sleeping state beside them.

I approached the closest rusty box truck, and I began to tinker around with it.

I had never worked with a vehicle before. It was really exciting to me to learn a new mechanical concept. Using a grinder and an extension cord, I cut the rusted shut hood open to learn how it worked underneath.

Under the hood, the electric engine was mostly preserved. I grinded the passenger cab door open to dig through the big jockey box to find the owner's manual. The inside of the truck was dirty and musty, with mice nest burrowed into the cushioned seats. Beyond the damage from the rodents, things looked pretty intact inside the cab as well.

I worked on cleaning up in the cab and the under the hood until darkness crept across the sky, Mandy came to retrieve me for dinner. So I quickly cleaned up what I was working on and headed inside to eat.

Anna Bee seemed sad. When I say that, I mean more than she usually was. Moping around as she worked, sweeping up the lobby as Mandy and I walked by, and the kitchen while I ate. When I told her to join us she sincerely insisted she was not hungry and then went to sweep the hall, as though she was trying to avoid me.

That night I had no dreams for once. No nightmares, no Skylar, and when I woke up the next morning I just ate my breakfast of grits and toast Terry had prepared for me, and then I headed out to work on the old box truck again.

I started that morning by prying the back door of the box truck open. I wanted to look at the inside and see what I could do to make it seem more like a comfortable carriage interior. I did not expect to find anything in the back of the truck, but what I found surprised me.

There were twelve perfectly preserved service drones. Still in their plastic packaging and stacked in their wooden shipping boxes in the back of the truck. There was also a shipping manifest clipboard hanging on a hook inside the metal box of the large truck, it said that these robots were going to be sent to a store in Texas, and the date on the paper read, September 1st, 2043.

I immediately caught the closest patrolling soldier droid, and ordered it to go retrieve Mandy immediately. It chimed, "Yes, sir," and then it ran off as fast as its motors could allow it.

Mandy returned almost as quickly as the soldier droid had left, power walking across the parking lot, "You called for me, my lord?"

"Check this out," I grinned motioning to the inside of the truck, "All of this time, I never thought to look in the trucks all this time, because they were so rusted shut. It should be snap to download the new soldier programing into these, and then get them armed. Check the trucks that Buster moved to the scrap yard in the back too, there has to be more of these preserved robots."

"Of course my lord," Mandy said obediently, "This is amazing. They are in perfect condition like they're brand new. I will get straight to work!"

"Thank you Mandy," I said excited.

"What are you doing out here? I don't think I've ever seen you tinker with a vehicle before," Mandy had a curious tone in her voice looking around the empty parking lot.

"I am going to fix up this truck, and use it as a carriage to go pick up Skylar," I explained, "I've got a lot to do with this thing before it runs though. I don't think it will be too hard to figure out."

"Not at all for a smart guy like you," Mandy said shrugging, "May I ask you something?"

"You just did Mandy," I teased giving her a funny look but then I sighed when she purposely ignored my comment, "but I suppose you could ask me something else."

"Why do you like Skylar so much?" She asked me, "What qualities do you admire in her?"

"Well," I thought for a moment and smiled a great big smile the moment the beautiful girl was on my mind, "She's really pretty... I like how her hair looks in the moonlight. Do you remember the way it shined? She's tough, that's another thing I like about her, and she's confident. She beat me left and right, and I think that her ability to fight just makes her so much more attractive. I don't think I've ever seen a girl that can fight as well as she can."

Mandy muttered something and I did not hear her so I glanced at her, "What did you say?"

"Do you plan on making Skylar your wife my lord? I mean no disrespect but she seems to have never cleaned a floor before in her life, she may not be good at it," Mandy said it an odd way like she was trying to hint at something, but I could not decipher her message.

"That's fine. That's what maids like Anna Bee are for. Mandy, I dream about Skylar nearly every night. I dream that I am holding her hand, or that she rescues me away from the monsters. I think I want her to be my wife…" I thought about it for a moment and my mind wandered back to the truck so that I could impress Skylar.

"So hypothetical question, my lord. What if that hand in your dreams turned out to be somebody else's?" Mandy asked, "Someone else who actually wants to be there for you."

"Like who?" I asked confuse, "It was only a dream. No one was actually holding my hand."

 Mandy glanced at my toolbox lying on the asphalt behind the truck. "You know for a genius, you are really dumb." She said as though she was referencing something else, but then picked up the tool box and set it in the back of the truck for me, "What would you do without me? What if it started to rain? Your tools would be rusted or ruined."

"Thank you Mandy," I rolled my eyes then grinned at her, "You are a good friend. What did you mean by that though? That was a weird question. Who else would have been holding my hand in my dreams besides Skylar?"

"My lord, I better get to work. Do me a favor and think about it really hard. Process it for a little while, and if you can't figure it out I will tell you tomorrow, okay?" Mandy offered, "However, I kind of want you to figure this one out on your own."

"Oh, okay," I scratched my head in confusion trying to split my mind between my task at hand and Mandy's random questions.

So I was not in Mandy's way while she worked in the back of the truck I headed out and returned to inspecting the engine. I began studying the motor, and pulling it apart. The truck's driving system seemed simple, just a power core and a powerful electrical converter.

The converter changed and amplified the electric core into serious amounts of horsepower, and fueled the motors to turn the wheels. That was the basics, the rest was all kinds of cooling devices, and a rusted out temperature sensor, that I swapped out. I spent a lot of time pulling better parts from other trucks around the estate.

I searched the scrapyard behind my estate for tires that were in a lot better condition, swapping out the shredded ones currently on the truck by having Buster follow me and hold up the trucks I was working on.

After I found decent tires, I tried starting it. When it didn't start, I followed the wiring to the problem, and continued the process until I got the truck to start around 5:45 P.M. that evening. IT started right up shedding dust and it filled my heart with excitement.

Just like the robot's I enjoyed fixing up, it was like I had brought an old beast to life. Its motors shaking the ground around it gently, its dull head lights flickered on casting a light through the shadows of the cloudy overcast.

I kept working on the truck eagerly, cleaning off rust, and rolling around under the truck inspecting everything I could. I replaced everything that looked like it would not function, and by the time I poked out from under the truck it was dark.

When I felt confident enough I took it for a test drive, and the old truck ran like a dream.

Now I had my carriage. I just needed to make it more presentable, and more comfortable riding. I could install seats in the back, or I could make cushioned benches to place in the back. I had a bunch of ideas stirring in my mind as I bounced around the old roads.

When I returned from the test drive I climbed out and began to wipe all grease and rust off my hands.

A blur of motion in the moonlight caught my eye, and I flipped around rag in hand to see Lord Osburn's carriage coming up the road on the opposite side of the estate fence.

I smiled and waved at the carriage, relieved that it was a friendly face. I immediately moved to meet him at the gate, unlocking it and opening it as he stepped down from his carriage.

Nate looked exhausted, his eyes had sagging arches underneath them, his armor dented and blood stained. He had a slight limp in his gape, and his wrist was in a fabric sling.

His men also looked exhausted, their armor all as dented and bloody as Lord Osburn's, if not more. All of them looked like they had just returned from a bloody battle. Patches of rotting pink fur wedged in their armor.

"Lord Zander," he said with a relieved grin and then he put his hand on my shoulder in a friendly manner, "It's good to see a familiar face."

"How is everything?" I asked, "You look like you've been busy…"

He got straight to the point, with an exhausted sigh, "They are called the Spark of Insomnia, the people in the white masks. They are trying to awaken a demon army called The Darkness," Nate said urgently, "That's what those damn rabbits are. They are demon monsters called Taunts. They are *only the scouts* of an *unstoppable* army. I can easily see how it would have destroyed mankind the first time. Their leader is a man lost to insanity named Joseph Burning, he wants to help the demons destroy mankind for good this time. He believes mankind gets immortality through death."

I swallowed uneasily, "Lord Osburn, How did you learn this?"

"I sent one of my best men in as a spy. He reported to me with a radio every night, but he was caught last night. He was a good man, and who knows what they did to him. They have a massive base of operations, hundreds of men capable of summoning more of those damn pink monsters, but I don't know how…" He took in a deep breath, "Excuse my language. That was out of line as a lord."

"Would you and your men like to come in and rest for a while?" I asked looking at the weary men around him.

"I can't fight them alone anymore, Zander," Nate said stressed shaking his head, "They are getting stronger, and my army is weakened. My once brave army is now more like a handful of scared men who no longer wish to fight, but are willing too. I need your help, we need to find this damn cult's base, and wipe them out before they summon the rest of The Darkness. I know they need the light to awaken the monsters, whatever that means, that's what they are waiting for. That's all I know."

I turned to see Anna Bee standing beside me, and she pulled out her dress in a curtsey, "Hello, Lord Osburn."

"I don't have much to offer," I said glancing back to my empty estate, "I need a couple days."

"I also need to return to my domain. Rearm, re-organize and recruit more men to fight a threat only those who have seen believe in. Can I count on you to help me when I discover the location they have been operating from? Ella Lovewind has agreed to aid me as well, but between Ella's army and my own we are still not very strong. You are my only other ally and we all face a very serious threat," he said it glancing into space and shivering before returning his gaze to mine, "I need your help, lord Zander. I can see you are following my advice, he motioned to the patrolling soldiers, "and I see you are building an army."

"Of course you will have my help friend. Just give me a couple days, then you let me know when and where to attack, and I'll be there," I said confidently. I found myself clenching my fist eagerly. The words sounded so sweet I could nearly taste them, *No more monsters.*

"Bullets don't do much against them. Swords are much more efficient. Show up with blades, not rifles. I know this from experience and loss. In fact I bet that's why mankind was nearly annihilated, their armies relied heavily on projectiles. Anyway, make sure your robots can use those blades effectively. The Taunts are not a force to be taken lightly. Even though I have learned they are only scouts," he said with a shiver.

Physically I was not ready to go to war, but mentally I was. I loved the sound of mobilizing all my new and old soldier droids and going straight for the source of the problem. Ending this nightmare as quickly as possible. At least one of them, I still did not know what to expect from Wellington.

Nate closed his eyes, "It's good to know I can count on you, Zander. I fear a massive battle may be coming, so be ready. I will come for you when I need you. Thank you, my friend. Perhaps when this is behind us we can return to setting up a power grid for my people."

"Of course," I nodded, "I hope you understand that I have been concentrating on defense and not the self-sustaining turbine that I promised you."

"It's a smart choice," he nodded, "especially with everything heating up so quickly around here. Wellington's been sneaking around my estate with his men. I don't know why, I've always been civil towards him. He's getting anxious, I think he wants to start something."

I lowered my voice not wanting to relive the memory, "He tried to assassinate me. I don't know what he is up to either."

"He did?" Nate raised an eyebrow surprised, "How?"

"He sent an assassin in the guise of a maid and she attacked me in the middle of the night. It was Birdy who rescued me," I said motioning back to the estate.

"He really is trying to start something then. We should stay alert, no doubt, an assassin could come for me next," He shook his head closing his eyes, "I really hate that man."

I shrugged, "It doesn't look like he has very many friends."

"Well, I must get going," Nate said rolling his shoulder as though it was sore, "Please be careful. Take care of yourself."

"You as well, my friend," I politely bowed to show my appreciation, "Thank you for keeping me up to date."

He bowed and headed back for his carriage.

Anna Bee tugged on my sleeve as Nate walked away, "can I have you briefly try something on, my lord?"

I followed her to her little clean bedroom where she had me try on a black suit coat she was working on. It fit me very comfortably, and I liked it. She then had me remove it, then thanked me with a shy smile, and I headed back outside to inspect the truck.

I needed to make it feel more luxurious, more like a comfortable carriage and less like an old box truck.

I spent the rest of the evening just sitting and thinking more than anything else. I thought about the truck, about the armor, about Skylar, about Anna Bee, about Mandy and what she had spoken to me about, and especially about the fact that in a couple days I could be expected to go to war against an army of men and demons.

I just sat with my legs hanging out the back of the box truck thoughtfully watching the moon fade in and out of the clouds. I was trying to calm my mind down and take control of my rampant thoughts.

Anna Bee shuffled out from the estate building, and crossed through the parking lot. She adjusted her dress and apron and sat beside me on the truck with a smile, "Are you doing okay my lord? You have not been as busy as you usually are?"

"I am okay," I said, "You heard what Nathan said; I might have to go to war against the very monsters that dwell in my nightmares."

"Well certainly not you... just your followers. I would fight for you, my lord. Danny would, and so would Birdy. I like Birdy, she seems to be loyal. She just has a lot of sass I suppose. Let us do the fighting for you, so you can be safe."

"Then what if something happens to my Anna Bee?" I asked her, "What happens if I could have done something to help? You bet I will fight alongside you. Don't worry, my armor I am working on will make up for my lack of skill. I would never expect my friends to do anything that I would not do for *my* sake," I sighed, "I just wish it would all go away."

Anna Bee smiled sweetly in the moon light, "My lord. I would give my life to see that you are safe and happy. I am your loyal servant."

"Surely some coins are not worth your life," I raised an eyebrow, "Don't talk that nonsense, maids are not expected to fight. At least not under my roof."

"It's not about the money or the fact that I am your maid. I promise," Anna Bee gazed down at her worn sneakers, "You are just super special to me. You are always super nice to me, usually I would get in trouble for sitting next to my master like this. You are my friend and I..."

"You repay my kindness towards you with your every smile, Anna Bee. You work hard, that is why I'm nice to you, and you are my friend. No one has to give their life for anyone. I would be mad at you if you did that."

She lowered her voice covering her blushing cheeks, "My, Lord, do you really mean that?"

I nodded, "Of course Anna Bee, you are special to me as well."

Anna Bee looked at the asphalt sweetly, "Thank you, my lord."

"Call me Zander," I said, "by the way you looked very pretty yesterday."

218

"It was Birdy's idea," Anna Bee shrugged brushing the dirt off her white apron, "Just a fun little gimmick I suppose. I do not wish to think about yesterday."

"Do you hate Skylar?" I asked her curiously, "Everyone else seems too."

"Despite our differences, I could never hate her my lord. I see how happy she makes you," Anna Bee said, "I like it when you're happy."

"Thanks, Anna Bee," I said leaning back in the truck relaxed, and she carefully leaned her head on my shoulder and gave me a hug, "Your welcome, Z-zander."

"Oh!" She suddenly had a spark in her eye, "I forgot, Terry has prepared dinner for you. That is why I came out here in the first place. I apologize for not saying it sooner..." She separated and hopped off the back of the truck and stood with a straight back facing me.

She neatly placed her hands behind her lower back, "Shall we go in?"

Her white apron was glowing softly by reflecting the moonlight, and her hair and green bow had a unique shine in the moonlight that made her seem as though she was fragile. It almost made her appear as though she was just a figment of my imagination. Her blue eyes studying me cautiously.

She was a pretty girl. I couldn't deny that, and she was also the sweetest girl I had ever met. I felt lucky and sincerely grateful to have her in my presence, but in my heart I felt like there was more to the situation as I stared at her shy smile. The freckles on her cheeks were hard to see because of the moonlight on her soft skin.

I gently reached out and touched her soft cheek making her close her eyes and she reached up and put her hand on my own nervously, "What are you doing, my lord?"

I shrugged, "I don't know. I'm sorry, I just felt like it. I was not trying to be awkward."

"No," She said it a little loudly, "Really, it's okay. I liked it my lord…" She grew embarrassed and tried to correct herself, "I mean you did not hit me, which I greatly appreciate…" her voice nervously trailed off, "I'm talking too much aren't I?"

I smiled and laughed at her, "I don't get you Anna Bee. I really don't. You are almost as weird as me."

She smiled, "You think we are both weird?"

"In different ways I suppose…" I was interrupted by my stomach growling, "Shall we go get some dinner?"

"Yes!" She smiled, and I hopped off and she followed me into the estate.

"What have you two been up to?" Danny asked us curiously as we walked in. He was sitting patiently at the table next to Birdy who turned and waved. Birdy gave Anna Bee an excited look, and then spun her whole body to face us.

Anna Bee was blushing at Danny's question, and I glanced at Anna Bee while I spoke, "She just came out to get me and talked for a while. What do you mean what have we been up to?"

Danny shrugged, "I was just starting conversation my lord."

Mandy entered the room with a handful of wires heading towards the front door and she stopped when she saw me, "Is it time for dinner already? Oh, wait… I'm a robot."

"Are you ever going to let me live that down?" I asked sighing and she shrugged, "Maybe."

"Will you please join us regardless?" I asked her and she shrugged, "Sure."

Terry had prepared grilled chicken breast and mashed potatoes and gravy. He eagerly served everyone as I pulled out my seat and I sat down. Anna Bee sat across the table from me, and then Terry served her as well. It was delicious and well prepared, and everyone seemed to have a happy attitude the rest of the evening.

After Dinner Mandy reported to me that she broke into the other trucks, and we had over fifty functioning soldier droids steadily patrolling the estate. Though they all had different amounts of armor, they were all functioning and running the AI program I had modified. My estate was so big even fifty patrolling robots still seemed kind of sparse to me. Mandy assured me she was not done, and that she would continue working. Even if she finished activating all the preserved droids in the truck there was plenty of fixer-uppers lying around.

After ordering Anna Bee to go to bed, I headed to bed. That night I had no dreams as well, and the following morning I went straight to work.

I installed some old comfortable cushioned seats from deep within the facility by bolting them inside the box truck along both sides along the bare metal walls. Once I was done I took some old chunky blue paint to the old truck inside and out after buffing out the rust. Painting the truck and cleaning and bolting chairs took almost the entire day, working alone in the cloudy daylight.

After the truck was more presentable and clean looking, I continued working the entire day away excited with the results. I worked until the moon once again replaced the sun, and Anna Bee came out to the truck.

Something about seeing her in the moonlight as she approached stirred emotions in me I could not understand. She looked fragile, and I was scared that she could collapse in on herself, like a small withered flower.

"I have finished your suit, my lord," She looked down, "Sorry... I meant *Zander*."

I shrugged, "It's okay. Thank you Anna Bee, When I saw it yesterday it was looking great. You always do a great job. Thanks again, Anna Bee, for everything you do for me."

"I just wanted you to look as handsome as possible for your date," she smiled sweetly, "You are very welcome my lord. I enjoy serving you more than you know."

"Well," I gazed at her confused, "Did you come out here just to tell me that you finished my suit?"

"Oh!" She suddenly breathed a sigh of disbelief, "Also, Terry told me to come get you because dinner is ready."

I laughed, "Already? My entire day just kind of flashed by, before I know it, it is time for dinner. Twenty minutes ago it was time for lunch." I grinned in disbelief wiping down my tools and setting them down. "What do you think of my new *carriage*?" I asked her curiously.

"Considering it's an old box truck, and it works. That is already impressive by itself, I would say you have done a fantastic job. It looks very comfortable. I hope to ride in it someday..."

I scratched my chin, "Really? You do?"

"It would be awesome to ride in a real working truck," she smiled, "I am sure I will get to eventually..."

I grabbed her hand with a playful smile, "Anna Bee, Come here for a minute..." I led her to the passenger door and swung it open, and motioned for her to get in, "Come on, we'll take her for a test drive, just you and I, Anna Bee."

Her eyes grew massive, "it's t-time for dinner... I can't... we're supposed to..." I gently picked her up. She was heavier than I expected, like she was held together by strong wiry muscles and I set her in the seat, "Shhh. It's a secret."

I had never seen her so happy, the shine in her eyes, the way I could see all of her teeth in a warm sweeping grin as I climbed into the driver's seat after closing the box door.

"A-are you sure my lord?" She asked stuttered, "B-but dinner is ready..."

I turned on the truck giving her a smile, "Last time I checked, I was in charge around here, and I want you to accompany me for an evening drive."

She froze with beaming excitement, and I pushed the gas. We smashed through the parking lot gate with a burst of sparks breaking the old rusty chain. We went around on the old dirt and concrete roads around the estate. I could see Anna Bee was excited, too happy to speak, holding on tight looking out the window as we rolled down the bumpy un-kept roads.

I had never actually seen Anna Bee actually squeal with excitement before as we bounced around the roads going at least fifty miles an hour. We eventually returned to the estate half an hour later, and everyone was patiently waiting in the dining room.

Anna Bee was so happy she was zoned out and did not talk very much unless spoken too. Even with her happy silence I still appreciated every second of her presence. Especially since she looked dreamy and happy in her own little world for the rest of the night.

I loved the new life that I had. When we returned the food was great, and I was surrounded by friends. I found myself thinking this was one of the best nights of my life.

Even Mandy noticed Anna Bee was much more happy than normal. She asked why she was so happy and Anna Bee excitedly told them all about our truck ride while we all ate.

"So you got an old truck working?" Mandy asked me after Anna Bee finished her story, "I'm impressed Zander. My creator has no limit to his engineering abilities."

"It was incredible!" Anna Bee smiled, "Just like in one of my dreams Mandy!"

I gazed at Anna Bee a little confused, "What do you mean by that?"

Anna Bee froze dead in her tracks staring in horror as though she had suddenly said something she instantly regretted.

"Just like she has always wanted to go to a ball, she has always wanted to ride in a vehicle," Mandy's right eye flashed, as though she was winking at Anna Bee who took a deep breath and shyly smiled.

I was not sure why Mandy winked at Anna Bee, but I did not think about it too much.

Before long we all parted from the table to head to sleep for the night. I followed Anna Bee to her room to make sure she climbed under the covers to go to sleep, and then I headed to bed myself. I slept well that night with no nightmares, it was just peaceful satisfying rest.

15: A Declaration of War

I was ripped awake by the thunder of angry gunfire echoing through my estate, and Anna Bee was leaning against the door, her shoulders braced against it with a panicked and scared look in her eyes. At first it felt like a dream, but things began to clarify around me slowly.

I rose, sitting up, "What's going on? What's all that racket?"

I heard the repetitive rattle of an assault rifle, and the scream of pain immediately followed by thundering gunshots. I immediately recognized the gun shots as Birdy's pistol from when I had heard them before.

"Wellington's men are attacking, my lord," Anna Bee said quickly, "Please stay in your room for safety … There are at least thirty of his men, they thought you were dead, and they broke through the gate attacking the compound… they just weren't counting on the robots to fight back I suppose…"

I leapt to my feet quickly, "Surely you're joking…" I pinched myself, "This has to be a dream."

"The moment I heard the gun shots I came in here to protect you! I was scared that I was not able to react in time…" Anna Bee looked panicked and she took a deep breath turning to me, "Please! Stay in here with me, my lord! I will protect you with my life."

"Absolutely not," I growled, and I drew my sword from the sheath, "If you want to protect me, get me to my workshop!"

"Yes my lord. If that's really what you want, but I advise against it strongly," she nodded hesitantly and unlocked the door.

"Anna Bee," I said urgently, "Come on let's go."

She swung open the door revealing Birdy crouched in the doorway braced with her pistol, "Sorry to wake you up, my lord," Birdy said nonchalantly.

A man in leather armor reinforced with segments of stitched thick metal scraps came around the corner swinging a long razor sharp katana, "I see Lord Zander! He's alive! He's over…" He turned his head back into the lobby shouting and trying to alert the other men, but Birdy shot him two times. He spun around crying out and painfully fell to the ground.

Birdy pulled a second pistol from her jacket and spun it on her finger skillfully before shooting two more men with different weapons as they came at us from the opposite side. Birdy's bullets drilling them with bone chilling accuracy, their blood splattering into the air and coating the wall like a can of spray paint before they fell to the ground.

"Quickly my lord!" Anna Bee pulled my sleeve leading me down the hallway to my workshop, and Birdy followed us skillfully shooting anyone who came around the corners after us. Birdy stayed hot on our heels protectively as Anna Bee led me to my workshop.

I nearly kicked down the door as I entered my workshop, and I quickly inspected the scattered pieces of power armor.

I motioned for Anna Bee's help and began to hook up the power armor as quickly as I could, "I hope it's ready!"

I could not believe what was happening, the confusion, the screams, and the thunder of gunfire echoing through the estate. It was no dream, but it was total bedlam, and Birdy was cutting down men with those pistols like they were blades of grass as they came running down the hallways trying to gain a flanking advantage on us.

Some men even tried to match her with gunfire spinning around the corner using it as cover, but it was a brief gun fight with Birdy quickly coming out on top with terrifying lightning fast accuracy, Anna Bee standing in the workshop doorway with the axe In case they got passed Birdy, but that didn't seem likely.

"Where's Danny?" I asked Anna Bee as I stepped forward towards the hallway drawing my sword. Only my head exposed from the strapped on metal armor. Every other inch of me was covered in plated armor and the hum of motors and hydraulics.

"He was near the front door outside the estate when we were attacked," Anna Bee said quickly slinking in the doorway and slamming the door, "Wellington's men are using the trees as cover, shooting up the estate..."

"Is Wellington here?" I asked angrily and Birdy shook her head, "He showed up originally and then left right after he ordered the attack. The soldier droids are doing a great job holding them back. The problem is a dozen made it through the fence before the droids could respond, Birdy and I immediately came to your defense. Danny got separated from us by the door like I said..."

Anna Bee caught my arm hesitantly, "Believe me, I admire your bravery. Please... don't put yourself in harm's way... stay here with Birdy and I, Danny and the soldier droids are doing a great job of fighting them off..."

"I told you, I will not let you guys do everything. I would not expose you guys to anything I would not expose myself too..." I said adrenaline beginning to fuel my veins, and I swung open the door and stepped out quickly. I charged down the hallway on sheer adrenaline, the armor warming up.

As I got to the end of the hallway a man came around the corner with a cleverly planned ambush, swinging a long sharp sword in his hands at me. I spun my sword deflecting his blow, and I lifted my powerful armored foot kicking the attacking man in the chest.

I could hear his ribs crack and he spat blood with a cry of pain, and then was thrown across my living room hitting the wall above the couch, the katana falling to the floor with a clang.

Another man came around the corner with an assault rifle, and I caught the rifle in my hand shoving it into the wall as it went off. The bullets tore up the wall showering me in pieces of wood and sheetrock as I swung my other fist. My fist connected with the man's cheek and he dropped the rifle as he flew several feet backwards and slid across the floor.

The fallen man desperately drew a pistol and fired at me. The smell of gun smoke, and the clang of the bullets ricocheting off my armor clouded my senses as I ran towards him, and I drew back my foot and kicked him in the chin.

I heard the crack of his bone and he cried out falling back to the floor. I picked up his body by the collar of his leather armor with one hand and threw it across the room into the lobby wall with the power of the functioning armor, the systems humming, the motors growing louder every time there was pressure on the hydraulics.

Birdy ran down the hallway behind me both her pistols drawn, but there was no living men left in the building. All that was left was just a bunch of bodies, and groaning injured men rolling around full of bullets and bleeding on my floor.

A lone man entered the lobby with a massive hardened shield, wearing a full set of thick and heavy plate armor. A fiberglass tinted visor and helmet covering his face and head. A long metal spiked mace in his hand with robotic oil dripping off of it like fresh blood.

The mark of Wellington was painted across his thick armored chest plate. "I'm impressed," He growled, "You truly are the machine lord. That was a lot of robots, and look at this, the Machine Lord himself hides inside a fancy set of armor."

Birdy raised her pistols in the blink of an eye pointing them at him, "That's quite a set of armor you're wearing, buddy. Look who's talking? You must be one of Wellington's knights."

The hydraulics hummed as I raised my left arm and reached over lowering her arms and pistols, "Birdy, find Danny and clean this mess up. Don't be nice about it. I'll handle this guy."

"The lord challenges me to a fight," the knight chuckled, swung the mace skillfully on his palm, and rolled his neck, "What a treat. Wellington will be pleased when I bring him your head on your own sword."

"My lord," Anna Bee said quickly, "That's Wellington's second best knight, Tobias."

"Thanks for the recognition, maid," the armored man said with a smirk in his voice, "but this fool has dug his own grave by challenging *me*."

Anna Bee swung up her axe at the ready, "I am right here with you my lord. I will help you fight him."

"No Anna Bee," I said quickly, "I don't want you getting hurt. Besides... I really want to see what I can do."

I rolled my armored fingers glancing down at my complex armor, already dented and scratched from bullets.

It wasn't finished. I wanted a helmet, and I felt slow and bulky. My mind wandered briefly over improvements that needed to be made, but it was holding up great. So far there was only minor malfunctions like hydraulic glitches and motors timing a little off. Still, it was enough to protect me from that mace.

I took a step forward, "Well, I'm having a really bad morning. Come here for a moment," I tossed my sword aside angrily, "I need to vent."

Tobias laughed at me, "Did you just drop your weapon? How insulting."

I charged him lowering my shoulders for momentum, the motors kicking in and pushing me faster and faster with the hydraulic power. He threw up the shield as I swung my fist angrily. The mace struck my armor with a clang and a burst of sparks as it bounced off.

The impact did not hit him, and his shield did not break, but the force of the blow dented his shield. The force of the armor's hydraulic power pushed him back, sliding backwards on the souls of his feet. I spun again knocking the shield out of the way and I lifted my foot as he wildly swung his mace.

My foot struck his chest and launched him back with a groan into the face of the fireplace. His armor taking chunks off the masonry, causing dust to fill the lobby from the crumbling mortar.

The dent on my armor where the mace had hit was big, but it still did not break through to my skin. I was a lot faster in this armor, it almost made things easy. The armor was working fantastically with a few glitches here and there.

Tobias stumbled to get to his feet, and I charged forward and kicked him in the jaw.

His helmet flew across the room, and he swung the mace into my chest with a burst of sparks knocking me onto my back. He leapt up over me, his face rugged and scarred. He had a buzz cut of cherry red hair, which had been protected from my blow by the helmet.

"Gotcha!" He growled and swung the mace downwards at my face. I lifted my feet and defensively kicked him in the gut as hard as I could, the mace falling short striking my chest instead of my head with a noisy clang.

The kick sent him through the concrete and wood wall shaking the building and sending up a cloud of dust and debris that scattered across the room. I got up and charged after him through the hole his body had made in my lobby wall.

He got up quickly protected by his armor, and I ripped the shield out of his hands and I brought the broad side of his own shield against the side of his temple with the noisy cracking sound of his skull. After spinning with a dazed look, he fell unconscious to the lawn.

I threw down the shield onto the lawn, and I looked around the yard to get an idea on what was going on.

It had calmed down, the gunfire had stopped, and Wellington's remaining men went on full retreat into the trees at the sight of Tobias falling.

"That was incredible my lord!" Anna Bee ran up behind me, "You did it! You sure beat him!"

I looked down at my armored fingers and my dented armor, "I had help..." My voice trailed off when I caught a glimpse of broken maroon colored robotics over by the fence, and my heart immediately sank, "N-no. It can't be."

I fell to my knees in silence, my eyes locked on Mandy's shattered body. She was in pieces, my best friend for eight years, scattered all over the lawn as though she was struck with a grenade when she was opening the gate for the "guests".

"That seems to be all of them," Danny limped towards me, blood from a gunshot wound in his chest seeping through his coat, his bloody sword in his hand, "They've retreated. Victory is ours..."

They all gathered around me their eyes following mine as I angrily stared at Mandy's plastic and metal body parts.

I could see the Artificial intelligence board scattered across the lawn in unrepairable pieces. That one piece alone was what made her who she was, that was the only piece that could not be repaired. I could have made her a new body... but she was gone. Her memories, her data, her knowledge, all completely destroyed.

My fist clenched tightly, and I closed my eyes. Anna Bee quickly wrapped her hands around me in a hug, "I'm so sorry my lord!"

"Every battle has casualties," Birdy said, and set her hand on my trembling shoulder, "There was nothing any of us could have done. The bastards cheap-shot us, right in the eye."

I remained silent staring at the scattered body. All the times she helped me, all the times she cheered me up, she was as close to human as a robot could get, and I made her that way by accident. My finest and most sophisticated machine, and my best friend *gone*.

Tobias stirred behind me with a grunt, and he got back to his feet slowly.

"I am not done with you, you cowardly bastard. A real man does not need a set of armor like that..." He growled gathering his weapons painfully, his blood staining the right side of his face where I struck him with his own shield.

"Like Wellington has ever had a sense of honor," I said snapping to my feet and turning to face him.

My face was red with rage, my fist still shaking, "Like Wellington and you thugs understand what bravery is. Like you are one to talk, the assassination attempt, the back door attacks..." I walked towards him and he spun the mace in his hand preparing for battle.

He spun the mace fast and accurately, but I simply stopped moving forward so that he missed and then I threw up my fist with an explosion of power, and I swung as hard as I could.

It shattered his chest plate, punching a hole straight through it, and ripped him off his feet falling face first and sliding backwards through the grass.

He coughed up blood from the broken ribs and probably a ruptured lung. He crawled onto his knees as I approached reaching for his mace and I kicked it away, "You go back to Wellington and deliver a message for me." I picked him back up by his hair, "You tell him that he has declared war against the machine Lord, and I'm coming for *him* now. He's going to pay for everything he's done. I'm going to put him down like the dirty little beast he is."

I spun and threw him angrily towards the gate grabbing him with both hands, and he rolled head over heels towards the gate leaving a small trail of blood in the grass from his wounds.

I stood there as he pulled himself to his feet painfully coughing up his own blood, "You're making a huge mistake, he has a massive army... he'll come for you."

"I hope he does," I growled and turned to painfully face Mandy's body, "Danny, please get that wound taken care of and get some rest. Birdy get this mess cleaned up. Anna Bee, please help her."

"Yes my lord," Danny said swallowing, "My lord, Are you okay?"

I didn't say a word, my eyes returning to the robot pieces all over my lawn. Words could never describe how badly it hurt to see my friend's body. Robot or not she was my best friend, and now I could never talk to her again. I could not believe it was really happening, my heart filling with angry and dark feelings. I was not going to wake up from this one.

In the distance a white horse came towards the gate at full gallop. Skylar's blonde beautiful hair and brown eyes became recognizable in the distance.

The moment I realized it was Skylar I sent Anna Bee quickly to hide in the estate so Skylar would not see her. I watched Skylar approach, hoping she did not notice Anna Bee.

Skylar had both of her swords at her sides and was wearing her plate armor. It rattled noisily as she rode through the hole in the fence where the gate used to be, "My lord is everything okay?" She hopped off her horse, "the whole city could hear gunshots... what happened?"

"Wellington attacked me," I said still staring angrily at Mandy's body.

Skylar followed my gaze, "Oh no, my lord! Not your robot!"

She cautiously approached me, "Are you okay my lord?" She opened her arms and slowly wrapped me in a well needed hug. I hugged her back wrapping my arms around her, my tears stung my cheeks and fell onto Skylar's neck and armor.

"She was my best friend," I cried on her shoulder, the pain growing harder and harder to bare.

"Wellington did it? He actually attacked you?" Skylar asked surprised, "I thought they were only rumors!" It felt good to be held in Skylar's arms, but the moment was ruined by the knowledge that I would never again hear Mandy's comforting voice when I needed it.

Skylar separated when the thunder of armor and hooves could be heard, a cloud of dust appearing in the distance.

I could see the dust of a line of cavalry approaching and shaking the ground as they thundered up the road towards my estate.

"Mandy!" I shouted, "Get me my sword!" I choked on my own words painfully and nearly dropped to my knees again.

She was not going to get me my sword. She was gone.

Birdy who had been standing there with a disgusted look took off towards the estate, "I'll get it for you!" She came sprinting out of the estate shortly after and handed it to me with a sympathetic look that made me want to continue crying, though I was trying to stop.

I swung the sword angrily, "I'll kill all of them. Every damn man with the mark of Wellington."

Skylar drew her swords skillfully spinning them on her palms in unison, "More of Wellington's men? I thought I was too late, but I suppose I arrived just in time."

16: The Machine Lord's Army

To my relief, it was Lord Osburn's heavily armored knights galloping along the fence line, crushing the bodies of Wellington's men under their hooves. They all assembled in a uniform line along the gate respectfully without entering.

The knight in the middle came forward and hopped off his horse removing his helmet tucking it under his arm revealing the rugged and unshaven handsome face of Lord Osburn, "Lord Zander! Are you okay!" He had blended right in with the knights, like he was born to ride into a bloody fight just as they were.

"Yes," I said sheathing my sword, "I appreciate your concern, my friend. I suppose we have successfully defended against this attack, but surely I must prepare for another. A much larger battle."

"It would be my honor to leave a couple of my Knights to help protect your estate, they will obey your orders. They're good men, great in a fight," Nate said breathing out a sigh of relief, "are you okay with that?"

"I appreciate the offer," I said politely, "but my friend, you need your men just as much as I need mine. Keep them, however I *could* use a horse..."

"You may have mine," Danny and Birdy snapped in loud unison stepping forward.

A desperate idea dawned on me. I felt dumb for forgetting that Danny and Birdy had both brought horses with them when they came to my estate. I turned to Danny gratefully.

He stood there, his chest still bleeding with his right arm keeping pressure on the wound. He had been shot, but yet he stood here still willing to help.

"Danny," I said quickly, "There is a change of plans. I want you to ride into town, get treatment for your wounds, and recruit some men. As many as you can who are willing to serve and fight for the Machine Lord. Offer them electricity to their homes and families. This game is over, we're going to burn Wellington to the ground."

"Yes my lord," Danny nodded and Nate saddled up in front to lead the armored horsemen away from my estate, "I will come to your aid much faster if this happens again. I apologize for my delay."

"I thank you for showing up at all," I said honestly, "It's nice to know I've got friends who will come help me," I nodded and glanced over at Skylar who was pulling a dagger off a body of Wellington's soldiers. She looked up at me, "Surely you shouldn't openly tell the whole city you've got electricity... Word really gets around... Lord Alysha Collinder can be just as wicked as Lord Wellington... She could form an alliance with him to attack you..."

"Your concern means more to me then you would know, Skylar," I said briefly, "but I have a lot to do. It's almost as though I *want* to go to war, I'm quite angry right now.

With that being said, I do sincerely look forward to our date to the ball tomorrow evening. I will pick you up at seven before the ball starts, I have recently created a means to do so," I politely bowed towards Skylar holding back painful tears.

"Look at you," Skylar smiled, "So brave, a true lord preparing for war. You're not as much of a sissy as I thought you were after all." She leaned in and kissed me gently on the cheek and whispered, "I also look forward to our date tomorrow evening."

She then bowed and headed back to her horse. She waved with a sweet smile as she mounted the strong white steed and rode away watching everyone around me as they grew as tense as they always did.

"Well Anna Bee," Birdy said gazing towards the estate as Anna Bee came quickly out to check on me, "We have a big mess to clean up."

We set straight to work. I started helping drag bloody bodies and piling them harshly in the scrapyard to burn. We stripped usable equipment, armor, and weapons, and I made several trips to the armory in the cloudy daylight.

The afternoon sky began to gray, and it began to rain. Rain forced me inside my estate to take off my armor to avoid sinking into the mud from my weight. Once the armor was off, I got distracted modifying quick changes I had noted when I was using it, and I began to repair it.

Danny had headed off for the town before it started raining. The rain seemed to help wash all the bloody mess off the grass of the estate, changing the lawn from crimson red to the naturally earthy green it was supposed to be. Birdy worked with Anna Bee, stripping the weapons and intact armor off of the bodies, and then taking the weapons and gear to the armory in my estate. Once the bodies were free of useful equipment, they dragged them out of the hallway and lobby back to the burn pile.

Flashes of gunfire danced on the inside of my eyelids, the screams of pain around me, the clashing of swords. All I could do was work to distract myself. I worked the entire day away improving the armor and repairing the damaged rusty droids from the battle in my noisy workshop.

"My lord," Anna Bee poked her head in a little later, "Lord Wellington is here, unarmed. He would like to talk to you." She seemed cautious watching me as I turned with a look of disbelief. "Him?" I growled, "He showed up *himself?*"

"Yes, my lord," she said, "I don't like it either, but he is unarmed."

"Well," I said tying my sword to my belt angrily, "This should be interesting."

"Of course my lord," she agreed, "I'll be right there with you. No matter what."

I stepped out of the front door of my estate. There was more than forty armed soldier droids at the ready, even if they just had sharpened pieces of scrap metal. Some of them surrounded me in a V-shaped defensive position around me as I walked along the path towards the massive hole in my fence that used to be the gate.

Lord Wellington stood there standing outside the hole in the fence, a woman on his arm that I did not recognize in a tight blue dress covered in white and black feathers. Two unarmed knights that hid behind helmets and bared his mark on their armored chests were standing to his left and right. The big luxurious carriage behind them seemed empty except for a driver.

"I received your message," Wellington nodded as I approached, "I get that you are probably mad at me. I would be mad in your shoes as well, Zander. My plan was, the assassin would take care of you, and then there would be no resistance when I arrived to collect your assets... but I have made a terrible, awful mistake of underestimating you and making you my enemy. My greed has been blinding me. I was closer to receiving your assets when we were friends and we were talking honest trade..."

"We were never friends," I said shortly.

He cleared his throat, "Well, I was hoping we could put things behind us. I've lost a lot of men, and you have lost nothing, I have lost our little struggle thus far..."

I glared at him fiercely, "Our *little* struggle? You attacked me."

"Word it how you will," he sighed, "I have made careless mistakes. I am here before you trying to stop more bloodshed. I am officially announcing that I will leave you alone from now on. No assassins, no attacks, nothing. If I was ever a man of my word, I would make it here and now. It's honestly just embarrassing really, everything I've tried to do has failed."

"If we can drop it, and let this be water under the bridge, on my honor, I will never start anything again," he separated from the woman to bow, "I am here with sincere apologies and good will..."

"I am not an idiot," I growled, "I will never forgive what you have done to me, and my friends. You sent a spy, you sent an assassin, and you sent an army..."

"That was hardly an army," he shrugged, "I could show you an army, Zander. That little spy betrayed me, your maid slaughtered my men in cold blood before they did *anything*. I've lost so many men trying to scheme against you. I simply don't want any more bloodshed.

This is a promise that I am going to leave you and your estate alone. I hope we can start over. I have simply underestimated you over and over. We could be powerful allies."

"What about the men that died in your name today? That was all in vein? You make no effort to collect bodies, at all," I said motioning to the blood trails on my lawn, "Why would I want to be allies with someone who does not care for his men? I can't even understand their reasoning for serving a man like you."

"Those men failed me, and they are only men. The promise of power and sweet words will bring any man to your service. Men are an abundant resource, soldiers are almost unlimited and my many wives and sons will always serve their father. If not they receive nothing, no food, no chance at power, and they do not receive the honor of becoming my knight…"

"Leave," I said angrily interrupting him, "Or remain as a body. I will consider your offer."

I was tired of listening to his words. They sounded like corrupted lies and nonsense, and I just wanted to plunge my sword through his heart. He just admitted to manipulating everyone around him.

"I will see you in good faith without arms at the ball tomorrow evening. I hope you will have reached a conclusion to accept my generosity…" he bowed and turned to his carriage, "My sincerest and deepest apologies. Sorry about your robot." He motioned to the scattered pieces of wire around me, "I am sorry that I destroyed her."

My fist balled up tightly as his knights climbed into the carriage behind Wellington, and his driver who was watching him with angry eyes turned back to the road and steered the carriage away.

"We're still going to kick his ass, right?" Birdy asked, appearing beside me on the opposite side of Anna Bee as the carriage clattered away along the gravel road.

"Absolutely," I said spitting in the grass angrily, "That changed nothing."

"Has Danny returned yet?" I asked.

"No my lord," Anna Bee shook her head standing beside me, "and Birdy and I have cleaned up most of the mess. I am planning to start repairing the hole in the lobby wall..."

"Wake up some of the service drones. Make them do it," I said, "You've done a great job, get some rest."

"Yes my lord," Anna Bee bowed and she headed off towards the lobby door.

"A-are you okay my lord?" Anna Bee asked looking at me with her big sympathetic blue eyes.

"How's Terry?" I asked ignoring her question, simply because I did not know how to answer it.

"He's fine. He was in town gathering ingredients when the attack happened. He was shocked to find bodies everywhere when he returned while you were working in your shop..." Birdy said and her voice trailed off, "Everyone's okay... Except..." She cleared her throat cautiously.

It was a painful feeling that Mandy was not around anymore. I could still hear her approaching me from behind to ask for orders, but when I turned around she was not there.

I began to collect the pieces. I knew she was just a robot, but it still hurt. I was angry and upset as I carried her piece by piece to my workshop and began to repair and reassemble her. I knew it was in vain. The body could be repaired, her personality could not. Even if I reinstalled the A.I I built it would be starting over, like I reset her. She would not remember anything, she would have to learn her own name all over again.

Anna Bee entered with her hands behind her back as I worked busily and she carefully approached, "I really liked Mandy. She gave me a lot of good advice. I think we are all going to miss her. Do you think you could fix her? I see you working..."

242

"No," I said harshly, "Well not exactly... I could, but it would not be the same... it would be a different Mandy. The old Mandy is gone."

"It's amazing that you were capable of creating something like that, smart enough and charming enough for someone to grow attached too. Perhaps you could make a new one, to honor her...." Anna Bee's voice trailed off, "Am I talking too much?"

"No," I sighed and I gazed at her, "I'm glad you are here. I can always count on you to come make sure I'm okay. I really appreciate that."

She smiled adjusting her dress and she pushed aside some robotic wires so that she could sit down on my bench, "That's my job."

"Yeah, yeah," I sighed and looked into her eyes, "You know something? I'm not saying it doesn't hurt, because it does... but I think this loss would have hit me a lot harder if I did not have you, Danny, or Birdy.

I've always hated interacting with other people, but I think over the years I must have outgrown that for the most part. Crowds still make me incredibly anxious, but I really enjoy all three of your guys' company. I think I'd be a lot more upset if it was one of you guys... I mean, you are alive, Mandy was only a machine..."

"Regardless of what we she was, she was your friend," Anna Bee said and leaned over and put her head on my shoulder, "She was my friend too, but if you can't fix her, you'll always have us."

"Not always, I only have your service for two years, Anna Bee," I said bluntly and gently pushed her away, "remember that little piece of information? You have to leave in two years."

243

She set her hand on mine gently looking into my eyes with a smile. Her hand was soft and comforting, and it almost felt like the hand in my dreams from all the times before, "You are my friend. When the time comes... if you ask me too. I will stay," She smiled at me.

I smiled, and it felt as though my heart melted with relief, "Thank you Anna Bee. You are a great friend, I would really like that." I wrapped my arms around her and gave her a hug. My hug took her by surprise and she made a small surprised whimper like noise.

She wrapped her arms around me, "O-of course my lord." She smelled like gentle floral perfume, and besides the perfume she smelled like dirt and iron from dragging around bodies. Skylar's chemically created perfume almost felt like it choked me with its potency, but Anna Bee's was a perfect little hint of flowers that always lingered around her.

We separated and I gazed at the maroon body parts along the workbench. I honestly felt a lot better. Anna Bee's comforting smile seemed to have that effect on me. The way her eyes could not look into mine for too long before she had to blush and look away. There was something about her, something about my own feelings that confused me, something I could not understand.

When she interacted with anyone else, it was like she was a different person. She always seemed anxious or shy if I was around. I thought at first it was because I was the lord of the estate, but it started to feel like more than just a fear of me. I just couldn't comprehend the way she behaved around me.

"Do you still want to come to the ball tomorrow night?" I asked her, "With Skylar and I?"

Her eyes lit up for a moment and then darkened, "when you told me that you did not want me too, I made plans to do something else… I would drop those plans in a heartbeat, but I wanted to surprise you, my lord. I have to decline so I can continue your surprise." She smiled, "I hope that you're going to like it, and I sincerely hope it will make you happy."

I smiled and ran a hand through her hair, "*You* make me happy Anna Bee. You *may* come if *you* want too. Think about it."

She smiled and a single tear of joy slid down her cheek as she lit up inside, "You are the best master a maid could ask for. You're nothing like the monstrosities that contracted the other maids."

"Well then…" I said and I was interrupted by Birdy poking her head in, "You two doing okay after this morning?"

"Yeah," I said and then I let loose a loud yawn. Anna Bee nodded politely, "Of course, ma'am."

"Well, Dinner is ready, and Danny is back with some people. This day really flew by, and you have a big day tomorrow," Birdy pointed at me, "Anna Bee and I are going to have you looking stunning for your date."

"You bet!" Anna Bee smiled and Birdy loudly commented, "I don't appreciate your date though. *At all*."

We headed for the lobby and I quickly forgot about Birdy's comment at what I discovered in my own living room. As I entered there had to be at least fifty men filling up my entire lobby, with more coming and going out my front door. Some were wearing armor, and most of them carried all kinds of different weapons of every shape and size.

I had never seen this many people before in my estate, and I hated it and loved it at the same time. I had just told Anna Bee that I hated crowds, but here I was with a growing army around me.

Danny pushed his way through the crowd coming towards me when he noticed me. For the first time I could see his bare skin, and he had a bandage strapped across his chest.

"My lord, All I had to say was *electricity,* or take down Wellington, and... BAM! Over a hundred experienced fighters in one day. Some of them even left Wellington's army. Most of them are asking to build homes in the forest near your estate so that they can be in your domain," Danny said glancing left and right, "They will serve and fight for you, In return for electricity." When they heard Danny say that and caught sight of me, all of the men quickly quieted down and dropped to a knee displaying loyalty.

"If you fight for me, you can build a home for you and your families wherever you want," I said awkwardly. Then I pretended to be busy to escape the crowd by turning to go find Terry, and Danny got caught answering questions that a man had as he walked in.

Terry was incredibly busy stirring in a massive pot, but when he saw me he still had a smile motioning for me to approach.

I approached and he grinned, "My lord! Quite a day it seems! I made a delicate sirloin and carrot stew for you. This is the third pot I'm having to whip up for the new recruits here at the estate, I mean most of them have their own food, but still, some of 'em forgot!"

"Thank you, Terry," I said pulling up a chair at my table after several men bowed and moved so I could sit down. I nodded to them as well, "Thanks."

They just bowed and graciously headed for the door with the crowd moving around them.

I ate quickly then I poked my head out to see collecting tents and improvised shelters set up around my estate on both sides of the fence with hundreds of armed men different sizes and ages around them busily working or chatting with each other.

After my approval spread, people began clearing out trees outside on the opposite side of the road to build small homes for their families. Which I was okay with, because I knew they would be in their homes and not crowded in my living room like this.

Now, I felt like a real Lord. It wasn't what I wanted at all, the crowd was driving me partially crazy. At the same time, I felt much more secure watching men ride in by horse or march in along the gravel road, some men with their families.

Danny re-approached me from behind me, "Can you believe this? I said you were wanting good fighting men in return for electricity to their homes, and the word has spread fast. We could have over five hundred men by tomorrow morning at this rate. I think that's almost the size of Wellington's army, but I am not sure how many men you have."

"I hope you are prepared, because you are now the lord of hundreds of people that are switching their loyalty to you." Danny pulled up a chair beside me, "Do you really plan on going to war against Wellington?"

"Somebody has to put him in his place. He has hurt two of my friends..." I pointed to his wound and corrected myself, "three."

"Even after his apology earlier? Wellington said he planned on leaving you alone," Danny said and I laughed, "Right. I wouldn't trust him as far as I could throw him, besides we need the men for this whole, Demon cult army problem we have as well."

"They have been passing around notebooks, not sure where they ended up. I told them that if their name wasn't in it they were not getting power, and if their name was in it they had to fight for you. They are all here to give their loved ones and family a better life," Danny looked out over all the men around us, "I told them you have electricity. That can easily give their families a better life. I hope you're prepared to honor that."

"If I wasn't I would not have offered," I shrugged giving Danny an intense look, "I'm no idiot."

"You *are* in some ways," Danny poked with a playful shrug and I raised a curious eyebrow, "What ways? What do you mean?"

"Her name rhymes with banana tree," he said with a funny look on his face. Before he could say any more that that several men approached him with questions about where the electricity would come from.

He explained to them that I was going to build a bigger self-sustaining turbine then the one that powered my estate and I thought about what he said for a moment, "Anna Bee? Danny, What about her?"

He just winked at me and led the men away to answer some more of their questions leaving me confused, but I just shrugged it off and headed for my room.

After flicking off the lights, I collapsed on my bed staring at the ceiling. Not even bothering to undress or take off my sword and shoes, I fell asleep a couple moments later from sheer exhaustion.

I woke up to the hazy bedlam of battle outside of my room. I leapt up onto my feet and charged for the doorway of my room, drawing my sword, "Attacked again!? This is two days in a row!"

My bedroom doorway transformed blurrily before my very eyes into the lobby doorway looking out into the forest. The trees were all cleared away revealing the downhill slope towards the distant city, screams and gunshots echoed off the hill side coming from the city below.

Massive columns of angry smoke filled the sky blocking out the morning sun above me, and the ground trembled below my feet.

I was standing alone in the doorway, the lobby empty, and the lawn free of patrolling soldier droids, the massive gathered army of men gone. The ground slowly beginning to shake harder and harder, and as I walked to the intact gate I could see a massive army marching up the hill covering the entire hillside, Wellington's flag flying high above them displayed proudly. Snarling pink monsters with their pointy ears and chattering bloody teeth were among their ranks. The whole army at full charge, jumping over fallen burning trees and stumps with their weapons drawn roaring with the thunder of a thousand voices.

"That's a lot of them..." Skylar appeared beside me as she always did when I needed her. She had a serious tone, her hand on her sword, "We certainly can't win this one, Zander."

"It *is* just a dream, whatever you're dreaming about," her tone and entire demeanor changed and her hand reached over and held my own. Her hand was warm, soft, and comforting. I had felt it before somewhere else, besides just in my dreams. Despite her presence, I was still terrified and overwhelmed at the men and monsters thundering up the hill.

"I promise I won't let anything hurt you," Skylar smiled at me and drew her sword.

She swung the sharp blade through the air wildly, and it generated a burst of gentle wind that transformed into a gentle morning breeze. The breeze left her blade and blew gently and peacefully down the hillside. It disrupted and blew the army away as though the massive force was transformed into little leaves.

Skylar was standing by my side, and she leaned in and put her head on my shoulder, "See, it's okay now."

Then I drifted away from her. I reached for her because I wanted to continue touching her hand, and she did not reach in for me in return. She just adjusted her head and gazed down the hills with a giggle. I drifted backwards into darkness, and then in my dreaming I could hear Anna Bee's voice whisper as I faded back to peaceful sleep, "I'm right here my lord. I won't leave your side until you're at peace."

I woke up to Anna Bee standing over me, "Please! Wake up my lord, you're going to sleep the day away!"

I sat up lazily feeling my head and I reached out grabbing her arm, "Are you real? Am I still dreaming?"

She looked confused, "Yes?"

I sighed, "Okay, so I really did wake up this time. I had another bad dream last night."

"I know," she said with a shy smile, "Anyway, I'm going to give you a haircut and a shave today. Then we will make sure your suit fits perfectly... we don't have *too* much time."

"Too much time? What time is it?" I asked and she pulled a small brass pocket watch from her apron pocket, "almost noon."

"Almost Noon?" I groaned, "Are you serious?"

"Usually we wake you up earlier if you haven't already woken yourself up, but we figured you needed the rest," she smiled and took me by the arm, "Let's get you cleaned up for your date."

She eagerly dragged me to the lobby. Most of the men had cleared out as we entered. In fact it almost felt like they weren't even here though I knew they were all gathering outside building homes, and cutting down trees.

Danny sat at the table going through a beat up old notebook, "the incoming recruits picked up a little bit this morning, I honestly lost track of trying to figure out how many people were here. It feels like half the city is up here."

"Hmm..." I was still groggy as Terry smiled and poured me a bowl of cereal for brunch.

Birdy came strolling through the front door with a smile, "Your electricity gives you a lot of power, pun intended," she winked, "Good to see your up. Good morning my lord, it's a big day."

I nodded, "It's nice to have a little fun, you know, relax a little more before another battle happens. I don't know who it will be, those damn cultists, or Wellington and his army."

"Well take it easy, with all the men here, it's never been this safe before. You can rest easy today, and that's what I recommend you do," Birdy nodded, "You deserve it, it's been hectic around here."

When I was done eating, Anna Bee brought me to the living room and sat me in one of the old rickety chairs. She pulled out a straight razor and leaned me back in the chair, "please relax my lord. Are you excited for your date?"

"Yes," I grinned from ear to ear, "and I am terrified. What will I talk to her about?"

"Just be yourself, you are very likeable," Anna Bee smiled, "It's good to see you smile, Birdy is right, it's been crazy lately. You were so angry and serious yesterday. It was scary."

The pain was still there because Mandy was gone, but it was hidden in a massive cloud of denial, and the excitement of the upcoming date.

"What do you plan on doing for security for your date?" Birdy asked, "You cannot, I repeat, you absolutely cannot go alone, not with that woman, not with all the enemies and dangers you face, and especially not with that woman..." She repeated and it made Anna Bee smile.

"Anna Bee," I said quickly, "Anna Bee can come."

Birdy snorted out a rude laugh, "Right, she may be good in a fight, but she is your maid. It's not proper etiquette to bring your maid. I've already picked out Danny's dress. With your permission, Danny and I would love to accompany you."

Anna Bee smiled, "Thank you my lord, but I will be okay. I have a surprise planned, don't you remember?"

"I don't know what this *surprise* is, but she seems awfully excited," Birdy shrugged motioning to Anna Bee's smiling face, "So you are stuck with Danny and I."

"Is Danny well enough to go?" I asked concerned, "How is he doing?"

Anna Bee's careful hands ran a razor down my chin, and then rubbed scented oil on my cheeks after every swipe.

"He's fine. He's held together pretty well," Birdy shrugged, "even if he wasn't he would demand to go."

I closed my eyes relaxing, "Really?"

"Oh yeah," Birdy nodded, "truly, the guy is stubborn. Sometimes I think he wants to be a knight as much as I do." Her teasing comment made Anna Bee giggle behind me.

"You both have done enough for me already. I wish I knew how to knight you," I wasn't sure how Birdy was going to react to that.

"Well," Birdy looked excited for a moment, "You tell us to go down on one knee, like we're going to propose to you, and then you take our blade and tap it on both of our shoulders. You say whatever you want at that point, as long as you include, "Rise as one of my trusted knights. Then we stand up happy as a clam, as one of your knights."

"That's it?" I asked curiously, "It's that easy?"

"Yes, but a knight is someone who would do anything for you and has proved it many times. A knight is someone who means a lot to you, and you feel they deserve the title for their hard work and dedication.

It's kind of a really big deal. Knight is the biggest title in our society below Lord, so don't take it lightly. Only knight someone if you absolutely, one hundred percent trust them with the lives of your people, as well as your own life. A knight represents you and your domain, kind of like a mascot *and* a trusted advisor and experienced warrior," I could tell by the way her eyes lit up as she spoke, that Birdy dreamed of the title she spoke of. I found myself smiling at her.

"Well can I trust you, Birdy?" I asked her, "I don't have any knights, I could use one."

She hung her head low, "That is your discretion, my lord. However I can say one thing. If Danny asks, you already knew how to knight people. You already knew all of that. Okay?"

I told myself I wanted to get to know Birdy just a little more, and then I would make her my Knight. I did trust her, and I trusted Danny.

Chapter 17: The Machine Lord's Date

After I had a clean shave and a haircut I headed for the shower. Once I was dressed in a light shirt and jeans, I met Anna Bee for the fancy black suit she had tailored for me. I met her in her room, the floor scrubbed where the blood used to be, and her axe was leaning against the old wooden door frame.

The suit fit me perfectly and it was very comfortable, and she would not look at me for long periods of time while I was in it. She would mainly stare at the floor with a sweet smile and her cheeks flushed repeatedly while I had it on. I was sincerely hoping perhaps I was handsome enough to get the same red faced reaction from Skylar, and I groaned in frustration as something occurred to me.

"What is it?" Anna Bee urgently looked at me, "Sir you suddenly seem upset... I'm sorry? Did I get you with a needle?"

"No..." I said thoughtfully, "Anna Bee I just realized I'm going to a ball."

"So?" She asked confused, "I don't understand..."

"I don't know how to dance... or how to act on date..." I said nervously gazing at the wall, "Why am I so awkward?"

"That's okay..." She cleared her throat, "I could teach you a couple of good solid dances... but only if you want me too... I mean... I am your servant so it is my responsibility to make sure you are comfortable..."

I interrupted her, "You know how!? Oh perfect, Oh please, teach me, Anna Bee."

She smiled as she continued working, "I would love to teach you, my lord. Just let me finish up these few stitches on your suit jacket and I can teach you."

"You're a lifesaver. You are truly bailing me out... but I just... how do I impress her?" I exhaled to catch my breath, "I *really* want to impress her."

"My lord," She said, "all you have to do is be yourself, don't try to be something you're not, it gives the wrong impression and then it messes up everything when they find out. Trust me. I know from experience."

I smiled and it turned to a sad frown, "I'm sorry I yelled at you. I knew in my heart you could not be a spy."

"Never, my love," she said and then she froze, her face turning ghostly white, "I meant Lord! I meant Lord! Silly me, whoops..." she let out a quick embarrassed laugh and briefly covered her mouth taking a deep breath, "Sorry my lord. Slip of the tongue."

"It happens," I raised an eyebrow and laughed at her, "It's no big deal. You always overreact to things like that."

She smiled closing her eyes tightly, "I could never be a spy. You treat me too well, Zander."

"I just try to repay you for how well you take care of me," I said and I teased her, "I can't compete with a "professionally trained maid" like *you* who went to a fancy academy though."

She finished up a couple touches on the back of the jacket and I asked her, "Is the academy where you learned how to dance?"

"Yes. I am not the best at it," She nodded, "but at least I could teach you some basics so you are not totally helpless. Like this..." She swallowed, "You put your hand on her side like so..."

She took my hand and put it on her side and turned as red as a cherry, "She puts her hand on your shoulder like so, and then you take your hands out to the side like so..." She shyly led me and then... she thought for a moment.

"We'll start with the waltz... so you want to imagine you are trying to draw a square with your feet at first and then you slowly expand it out and turn it into a circle. See, follow me, we will start slow," She smiled at me and then looked down at our feet, and I cautiously tried to follow her accidentally stepping on her toes, but she only giggled assuring me that I would get it.

Before long we were waltzing effectively around her room, and she became as happy as she was in the truck a couple nights before. We laughed together because as we swept around the room I kept tripping over my own feet. I eventually caught on, and it became easy, even in my newly tailored suit.

She gently set her head against my chest as we moved with a beaming smile, "See it's not that hard, you're catching on."

"Thank you, Anna Bee," I said honestly, "You are saving me a lot of embarrassment later," I grinned relieved. She closed her eyes smiling, "Believe me, it's truly my pleasure. It may not have been at the ball, but at least I got to dance with you..."

She pulled her head away embarrassed again, "I mean... at least I got to teach you how to dance. Before you got there, you know... you're right that would have been uncomfortable... If you knew nothing."

"So?" I asked, "What do I do when I pick her up?"

"Well," she cleared her throat, "You could bring her flowers; I would love it if someone brought me flowers. I really like flowers, and you have to open the doors for her, the doors Danny and Birdy don't get for the both of you. Take her arm like a gentleman when you're not dancing."

"These are all great ideas, keep going," I insisted. She thought for a moment, "Make sure you compliment her…" she said. I nodded, "Easy, she is always beautiful, that's an easy one, what else…"

"You could try hitting her with a shovel," Danny smiled from the doorway. I glared at him turning and Anna Bee quickly separated from me as though she had been caught doing something she wasn't supposed to.

"Chick's dig that stuff," Danny winked and air swung an invisible shovel through the air, "Oh yeah… Wa-pow! Down she goes! True romance at its finest."

I laughed and Anna Bee cracked a smile.

"What is it Danny?" I asked.

"Sorry for the intrusion," he said it as though he was teasingly directing the comment towards Anna Bee and then turned to me, "My lord, some of the men believe you are just a rumor. So I was thinking you could give a speech, or at least introduce yourself to your new loyal subjects, like a good lord."

"A speech?" I asked giving Danny a scared look, "I'm no good with speeches…"

"I'll even introduce you," Danny motioned for me to follow, "I've cleaned off the old second story balcony so it can be your grand stage! Just wing it, most of the men have not seen the man they are supposed to be serving. They think it's me and I'm

258

making up some deity called "the machine lord." Come on, you'll do great."

I carefully removed the suit, "Thanks for everything Anna Bee. Really, this has been fun."

"Your welcome my lord," she smiled, and moved to the suit folding it and finishing some last second touches.

I followed Danny up a set of stairs I honestly did not know existed and then through a doorway into the warm and comforting sunlight. I was now looking over hundreds of men and women gathered below the balcony, stretching clear back beyond the fence line. It looked like an entire subdivision was being built around my estate.

From the balcony I could see passed the thick forest and down the hillside into the ocean of concrete that was Wellington below. There was no smoke or screaming like in my dream. Just the peaceful sound of birds fluttering through the trees and the low rumble of the voices down below the balcony.

Danny stepped out onto the balcony and turned to me, "Just explain what's going on... that's all they really want," then he faced the crowd, "Ladies and gentlemen! Please Quiet Down! Quiet Down!"

The crowd's subtle roar turned to a gentle echo of whispers off the building below me and Danny extended his arm motioning to me, "I present to you! The machine Lord Zander..." he turned to me, "What's your last name?"

"Harmony," I informed him, and he turned back to the Crowd, "Your lord, Zander Harmony, the machine Lord! The only one in miles who can give you electricity to your homes!"

Then Danny grabbed me by my sleeve and pulled me up against the rusty rail and they all applauded eagerly as my hands clamped down onto the balcony rail scared.

"Thank you!" I yelled shaking, wanting to turn and hit Danny as hard as I could. I was terrified, doing my best not freeze in place. My stomach was tying itself in knots as they slowly calmed and quieted, "Thank you!" I repeated loudly.

Then there was silence and I stood there uncomfortably, "I am Zander!"

There was a couple laughs and chuckles and people glanced at each other down below swapping smiles and funny looks.

"That's great, I think they knew that much," Danny whispered behind me.

I swallowed and I shouted loudly, "I have stage fright!"

They all laughed and chuckled again which made me feel a little more comfortable.

I heard a voice down below laugh, "At least the kids got a sense of humor."

"No, he's got stage freight," another laughed and I cleared my throat for them to calm down.

"I..." I carefully planned my words trying not to panic, "I invited you all here because I sincerely need your help."

"There is two massive threats that are at my door. A demon army called the darkness, as well as Wellington and his greed. He is going to try and attempt to take what I have spent most of my life creating!"

They all shuffled looking at each other and I continued, "A battle is coming soon! I need all of you to stay on your guard, and protect the electricity that I have promised you! When it is all settled you will see the comfortable and homey glow of a lightbulb in your very own home. You will feel the luxury of an electric water heater... But it will not come without the sacrifice of defending it from the people who wish to take it from us."

They all cheered and threw their weapons into the air with their thundering war cries. I waited for them to calm down and I yelled, "I will share with *you,* what *we* are all protecting together! I need the help of every one of you, every man, and every woman!"

I could not think of anything else to say so I just swallowed and awkwardly bowed, "Thank you!"

They applauded and I quickly disappeared off the balcony and Danny gave me a pat on the back, "Good enough."

I headed back down the stairs towards Anna Bee's room to continue my dance lessons, and Danny was waiting for me leaning up against the wall, "So, do you want to teach me how to drive the box tru- I mean carriage? Neither Birdy or I know how to drive it."

I nodded, "I suppose." With time ticking away it was growing closer and closer to the time to leave for the ball, we headed for the truck.

I showed him the brake, and the gas. I showed him how to the open the back door and how to latch it. He did a couple a practice latches standing there in the sunlight, and I looked him up and down thoughtfully thinking about what Birdy had told me.

"Danny," I said hesitantly, "I want to do something."

He gave me a skeptical look, "Should I be worried my lord? You have never sounded like that before, especially when addressing me."

"I want you to get down on one knee like you are proposing to me, and give me your sword," I said nervously.

He looked really confused as he obeyed, "You know I'm not into men, right? Is this an execution? Have I done something wrong?"

His sword was a lot heavier and a lot longer than mine as I held it above his right shoulder.

"Danny, things are getting complicated and hectic very quickly. I need someone I can count on through the chaos. I need someone as my trusted knight by my side through this mess. You have done nothing but prove to me your loyalty in this week..." He lowered his head realizing what was happening, and he began to shake. I even noticed him happily begin to tear up a little bit.

I touched the sword to his armored shoulder, and then I lifted it over his head to his other shoulder, "We have not known each other for more than a week, so I extend this offer to you in good faith. Danny, I want you to rise as my loyal knight."

He rose to his feet proudly, his chest pushed out, his face beaming with excitement and pride.

I spun the sword to hand it to him, "What do you have to say?"

He choked, "My lord, I *will not* let you down. You just made my dreams come true. I will gladly accept the title of your knight. My blade is yours."

He sheathed his sword proudly bowing to me, "I won't abuse this, and I still plan on earning it."

I noticed behind him how dark it was in the dark box truck. It was going to pitch black inside the truck when I went to pick up Skylar. I had to give it some form of light source, and I did not have much time.

"Danny," I said, "start carefully practicing with the truck, I've still got work to do in it."

"Yes, sir," he nodded and made his way around the truck to the driver's seat.

I grabbed a grinder as quickly as I could and cut windows into the box sides. Men gathered around amazed as the truck started up at Danny's hand and rolled around the parking lot slowly with me working inside it.

Time flew by far too quickly and I wished it would slow down. I was terrified for the night ahead. I was almost as scared as I felt when the army charged up the hill at me in my dreams, if not a little more.

It was a different kind of fear though, and my stomach was feeling upset as the sun was slowly beginning to set.

Before I knew It, I was putting on the hand tailored suit and digging around my workshop for the invitation and Skylar's address.

Birdy was dressed up in a long black and blue dress, her hair tied up in a neat ponytail and braided down behind her ears, two pistols holstered on both sides of her dress, the very dagger she presented to me in her belt. She looked pretty, but she still had a slightly mysterious and intimidating demeanor.

Danny wore an old faded suit jacket around his thick bandages and hardened leather armor underneath it. He had suit pants on, and his long sword at his hip. He had the design from my flag painted across his armor proudly in white wet paint, and he did not have his bow on him as usual which surprised me.

They were both standing beside the truck and Danny winked at me, "You ready? Let's get this over with."

"Awe, look at you," Birdy pinched my cheeks, "My little lord growing up so fast! Make sure you take her hand and help her into the back of your tru- I mean carriage." She raised an eyebrow, "Are you ready?"

"As I'll ever be," I took a deep breath, and they helped me into the back where I climbed in and they closed the door behind me. I sat on the cushioned seat, looking nervously at things I should have done to improve the quality of the truck.

I noted that I should have cut a hole between the cab and the box, so I could communicate with whomever was driving. I thought for a moment that I should have brought my sword, but with Danny and Birdy with me, I changed my mind feeling as though I would not need it.

Birdy was good with her pistols, terrifyingly accurate and fast. While Danny from what I knew fought off the majority of an attack from those monsters by himself. I would be safe with them, I did not need my own sword. Not that I was any use without my armor anyway.

Before I knew it I could see the city of Wellington out of the windows cut into the side of the truck. We began rolling down the old cracked streets and the truck we rode in turned several heads. Children stopped playing and pointed in surprise, "Look! Mom! No horses, look! It's a real truck!"

"That's the machine lord," I heard a woman say with an impressed tone, and she picked up her child as the truck rolled by.

In most cases the adults seemed just as excited as the children watching my big truck roll by.

I just smiled and waved as people "oohed" and "awed" like I was a fast moving parade.

We arrived a lot faster then I expected, and I could soon see her luxurious home out of the truck window, just as described in the note she had given me.

Skylar's home was a two story home near the center of the city, on the edge of Wellington's domain. A massive newly built home with columns of stone holding up the second floor of the home that beautifully overlapped the first floor on the front of the building. It was clean, and it was well maintained.

Danny stopped the truck, leaving it running, and came around and opened the door to let me out. I could see the home was well maintained and cleaned. The lawn was mowed, and the windows were spotless. It looked *nothing* like most of my estate.

As I nervously knocked on the door, a younger man in a butler's uniform opened it, "Lord Zander. Right on time. Please come in, Lady Skylar is just finishing up."

I entered hesitantly and the man cleared his throat, "I heard you have working robots... is that true? That's so cool... and you rolled up in a *truck*? I'm jealous, wish I could ride in a truck..."

He looked maybe six or seven years older than me and he looked at me kind of confused and lowered his voice, "So why did you ask Lady Skylar? I mean she's pretty, but... you should see how she treats her servants..."

"What do you mean?" I asked and I began to glance around the inside of her home curiously.

"Some of her servants go without eating a couple days in a row if they have done something wrong, and she hits us with the blunt end of her sword... I mean no offense, but she is not very nice to us. Is she nice to you?" He asked.

"Recently she has been," I said looking at the comfortable couch, and the neatly wood stained coffee table that looked regularly polished.

Her home was well decorated with paintings and potted plants scattered about. As I looked around the home, something on the kitchen table caught my eye.

It was a plain white mask with two long horns that curled upwards placed above the eye holes.

I approached it and picked it up off the table shaking. My mind began to wander in scared thought, was she one of them? Was she attacked? Why did she have it?

The servant followed me, "Oh that? It was given to her by one of her friends that I never get to meet. I mean seriously dude, you are like one of the only people I have seen in months... I'm not allowed to leave the estate..."

"What do you mean one of her friends gave it to her?" I asked suspiciously. Maybe she knew who was behind the attacks. I told myself that if I had a moment later I would try and bring it up.

"Lord Zander!" Skylar's voice chimed down interrupting us, and she came down the stairs, "I have been surely looking forward to our date!"

She hesitated when she saw what I held in my hands and nervously pulled on her dress, "Spooky isn't it. One of Wellington's knights offered it to me when he asked me to company him to the ball this evening, but I told him I already had a date. I don't know where he got it, but he said I could have it."

"One of wellington's men?" I asked thoughtfully and set it back down onto the table, "Are you ready to go, Lady Skylar?"

I studied her pink and white dress, and one of her maids was standing behind her. The shy woman gave me a smile and a wave from behind Skylar as though she did not want Skylar to see.

"My, you look very handsome," Skylar smiled, her eyes looking me over, her hair like silky smooth cloth hanging in beautiful curls at the side of her head. The beautiful strapless and luxurious dress made me smile at how beautiful she was. I could not believe my luck.

"You look... incredible," I smiled, "I simply cannot wait to show you off."

"You don't mind if I bring a servant do you, Zander? This dress is *so* hard to move around in. If I did not have someone to help with my dress or hold my drinks for me I would not be able to dance with you."

"Not at all," I said forcing a smile. For a moment I thought of Anna Bee, and how she asked if she could come.

Suddenly, I wished I would have told her she could the first time. I knew she wanted to come pretty badly, and it would have not made any kind of difference if I would have known Skylar was bringing a servant as well.

"Well," Skylar adorably curtseyed, "Shall we be off?"

"Of course," Skylar smiled and the young man grabbed the door.

I took her arm as Anna Bee had told me to do, and we headed out the door towards the truck.

She felt colder than Anna Bee, and she walked faster than me. She was nearly dragging me along to the back of the truck where I extended my hand to help Skylar in, and with Anna Bee on my mind I realized I had forgotten to get flowers for Skylar.

Her young emotionless servant followed her in, and then Danny helped me in and nodded, "Just hit the wall when you are settled and ready to go, my lord."

"Will do," I nodded and he closed the door behind me. I seated myself across from my date, "I apologize for the discomfort. I did not have much time to get this old truck ready..."

"Please," she laughed, "It may be ugly, but it's an incredible opportunity to ride in a working car. I believe that is what this is called? Am I correct?"

"This is technically called a box truck," I corrected her with a shy smile, "It was used to transport goods around the old United States. It specifically moved robots from the facility where I live, when it was in operation."

"Fascinating," she smiled, "Look at you, like a historian, how did you know that?"

"There was a manual in the front of the truck," I said gazing up at the moon, "And there was robots in the back still in their packages.

The dark spots on the moon began to remind me of Anna Bee's freckles on her cheeks, and I began to miss her. I did not know why she was suddenly on my mind so much, I just could not stop thinking about her. I did not like how far away she was, and I really wished I would have told her she could come.

"Are you okay, my lord?" Skylar asked me curiously, "You seem off this evening. Are you nervous? Lost in thought maybe?"

"I'm fine," I nodded with a forced smile, "I am trying to savor the moment, that's all. I am riding with a young woman as beautiful as you." I smiled at her and I took a deep breath.

This is what I wanted, Just me and Skylar on a date. Alone together, why was I thinking about Anna Bee so much, when I sat across from the girl of my dreams?

"That's very sweet of you Zander," Skylar smiled, "I would like to say I'm very impressed with how far you have come. An awkward dork who could not tell me his name, turned into a brave lord who has fought off Wellington's attack. I'm sure it was terrifying, what was the battle like? How many men did you kill?"

I felt uncomfortable with that question and adjusted my small green bowtie, "You know, I did what I needed to do protect my estate. I hope I did not kill anyone. A lot of people died that day. I mostly... threw people through walls."

"Threw them through walls?" She asked impressed her eyes lighting up, "Wow you must be very strong!"

"I know I am lacking in skill so I created a set of armor to make me faster and stronger. It helped a lot during the battle," I nodded.

I remembered that I was supposed to start monitoring what I was going to tell her just in case, so I did not say anything beyond that with a shy smile.

"That's interesting," she said thoughtfully, "I noticed you had way more of those soldier droids, how many do you have now?"

"I'm not sure exactly, a lot were damaged during the battle," I said vaguely, "but I still have quite a few, and the army gathering around my estate makes me feel a little safer."

"I also heard you are recruiting. Nearly the whole town knows that you have electricity now," she smiled and sounded as though she was teasing, "and I wasn't paid to tell anyone at all. That was pretty brave, every lord in a hundred miles is going to find out you have electricity."

"That's what the army is for," I shrugged and she smiled, "smart man. I'm impressed, you really are coming along as a lord."

We traveled in silence for a moment and then the truck came to a rolling stop.

"What do you know?" She smiled, "Here we are!"

"Yeah," I smiled, "we are."

Danny opened the door and I took Skylar's gloved hand and helped her out.

We were at a massive well maintained old stone Chapel with a tall tower that penetrated up into the cloudy night sky, casting a long through the city in the cloudy moonlight.

Torches and candles lit up the inside of the large beautiful building as I presented my invitation to the well-dressed door greeter who bowed, "Welcome Lord Zander. Please enjoy your stay."

There was a talented live band playing upbeat music that made me tap my foot and bob my head if I wasn't concentrating on resisting. Streamers were stretching across the walls, and many people were gathered dancing to the music laughing and bantering.

"What a lame ball?" Skylar sighed, "I've seen much better in Las Vegas," she said disappointed. I glared at her for a moment, "I've never been to a ball, and I think everything is quite nice..."

"They had lots of colorful flashing lights at the balls in Vegas, and they did not need bands. They had what was called a D.J." Skylar said smiling, "They were so much fun, and they had lots of free champagne."

"Lord Zander!" An older woman in a red dress and a smiling man in a matching red suit and tie approached me from across the massive Chapple, "what do you think?" I recognized them as Lord Ella Lovewind and her husband. I had heard they were sweet and very kind, and I could see the rumors were true by their smiling faces.

"It's lovely," I smiled, "Thank you for the invitation."

"Did you bring any robots?" She asked eagerly, "My name is Ella and this is my husband Jacob Lovewind." She motioned to him, "Thank you so much for coming!"

"Unfortunately the robot I planned on bringing was damaged beyond repair," I said trying not to think about Mandy, "My apologies."

"Don't you worry," Ella set a sturdy hand on my shoulder, "My domain has a lot of mundane dirty work that needs done. Our greenhouses and farms produce most of the food here in Wellington, so I would love to be business partners someday! I would love some robots of my own, our capacity to grow food here in Wellington would double if I had some! Not tonight though, tonight is about having fun, and what a lovely date you have!"

She bowed to Skylar and Skylar bowed with a beautiful smile in return, "Thank you."

"You look so handsome!" Ella smiled turned back to me, "I heard you looked like a wild man, with crazy hair, and a crazy beard, and here in front of me, is a young handsome lord!"

"I have a fantastic maid that takes good care of me," I said smiling, "I used to be a bit crazy. I probably still am, but hey I lived alone in a robotics facility for eight years."

"Goodness!" She smiled, "Well please do enjoy yourself, have fun! Let us know if we can do anything for you! Anything at all."

"What nice people," I said waving as they disappeared into the crowd.

"They're old," Skylar said it as though she was telling a joke, "They'll keel over anytime now, and Wellington and Collinder will go to war over the domain for control of the food. That's a scary thought, one of *them* controlling the City's food."

I just smiled a dry smile and the band came to a stop and there was a mild and polite applause before they began to play a slow song.

"Well," I said nervously holding up my hands, "shall we dance?"

"Well certainly," she said and gently took my hand, and my shoulder and I took her side and I cleared my throat, "Shall we waltz?"

"A man who knows how to dance?" Skylar seemed impressed with a smile as she took off her gloves, "You are full of surprises. Where did you learn to dance?"

I sighed staring up at the torches as we danced, "I had a great teacher." I was so weighed down, so angry. I just was not having fun, this isn't what I thought it would be. My heart was pounding as though it was trying to tell me something. I looked around at the decorations and torch light, and I listened to the slow beautiful music.

It all felt so magical to me, and all I could think about was Anna Bee.

Skylar's hands felt cold. They felt nothing like the hands that had comforted me in my dreams. Her hands were smooth but they were harsh and forceful. I had touched a hand that felt like the ones in my dreams before, a hand that matched the hands in my recurring dreams perfectly.

In that moment I had an obvious epiphany I should have had a long time ago, staring at Skylar with a blank look. My heart began sinking and my mind became full of frustrated emotion. I closed my eyes in angry thought as my feet quit moving on the dance floor.

A single tear slid down my cheek and I whispered to myself, "How could I be so stupid? It was always *her*... It wasn't just a dream... Anna Bee was always by my side... It was her... through all of the nightmares..."

"What?" Skylar looked confused and separated from me, "Your maid? You are confusing me, Zander. Didn't you order her execution?"

I looked at the inside of my palm in painful silence. Her beautiful shy blue eyes smiling at me when I closed my eyes. The way she grew embarrassed, and the way she lit up when I called her my Anna Bee. It all made sense, my feelings for her materializing and solidifying inside me with the music flowing around us.

"Hello?" Skylar asked looking uneasy, "Zander, are you in there?"

"You really did blackmail me..." I said cocking my head to the side studying her, and she sighed, "I said I was sorry, sweet heart. That was the old me, I was upset, troubled." She leaned in and kissed me on my cheek, "Are you really upset about that?"

"No," I shook my head, "You look truly beautiful, a woman any man would be lucky to dance with but I'm afraid I've made a massive mistake. I've asked the wrong girl to the ball."

She looked confused, "Wait... what are you saying?" She began to grow angry and gathered her dress, then smiled, "Surely you're joking!"

"It should not take you very long to find a new date. Sorry, Skylar, this was lovely," I bowed and turned and began to work through the crowd, leaving her standing alone on the dance floor in a speechless fit of rage behind me.

I pushed through the crowd and I was stopped by Lord Osburn's friendly hand, "Hey Zander, you made it!"

"Yeah," I smiled, "I'm going to grab my date, and I will be back shortly."

"Stay safe," Nate smiled, "I'll be here if you need me."

I smiled and moved back through the crowd and out of the building. As I was approaching the truck, Birdy and Danny were finished locking up the truck. They were standing together with Birdy in Danny's arm as they were walking away.

They stopped walking when they saw me, and Danny looked surprised as I approached the truck without my date.

Birdy raised an eyebrow, "We didn't even have the chance to walk in yet. Was it was that bad?"

I looked Danny straight in the eyes, "Take me back. You were right. I am the world's biggest idiot, I took the wrong girl."

"Did you just leave Skylar alone at the ball?" Birdy jumped up excited, "Dude!" She threw up her hand for a high five.

I high fived her and cleared my throat, "Danny we need to stop and get some flowers, but I order you to take me to Anna Bee."

"Don't be so dramatic," Danny rolled his eyes, "Hop in." He unlocked and opened the box door with a proud smile and an approving nod. I climbed in, "There was some flowers near the fence back at the estate, plenty of length and color combinations, Make sure you stop so I can get some."

It felt good, like the night was clearer than it was before. Every thought I had was of Anna Bee and it made me close my eyes smiling and thinking about her. Who cares if she was my maid? She made me happy, and she was there for me when I needed her. She cared for me even throughout my blindness to her love and loyalty.

The truck started up and the ride back lasted a lifetime. The moment it stopped I went on a hunt through the trees and along the fence for the most beautiful flowers I could find in the moonlight. I bundled them together as neatly and I did my honest best to make the most beautiful bouquet I could.

When I had finished I headed through the tents and gathered men and then through the building's front doors, sweeping left and right searching for her brown hair and shy blue eyes. My heart skipping a beat, tears stinging my cheeks as though my body could not contain the emotions surging through me, "Anna Bee! Are you in here?"

I was so excited to see her. I wanted to take her back to the dance and have her teach me more dances. I wanted to be with her so badly, and the more I thought about her the harder I searched.

I entered her room in my search to see her bed was neatly made, her axe gone, and a handwritten note sitting on her pillow.

I hesitantly picked it up, my heart beginning to pound in my ears, "What? What is this? It must be part of this surprise she promised me..." and as I read, my fists grew white with rage, more tears beginning to burn my cheeks, this time from terrified fear.

"Anna Bee..." I shook, "Anna Bee, No."

Zander, my lord,

It is my job to serve you, and to make sure you are safe and happy.

You are so very special to me, and I meant what I said. I would sacrifice my beating heart to make sure you can feel the same happiness and peace that you have given me. I will do my best to try and eliminate one of the problems that pesters you so.

You spoke to me the other night that you wished that some of your problems would go away, and I told you I would give my life for you if I needed to.

Please do not worry about me my lord, I've gone rabbit hunting.

Love, Your Anna Bee

I held the note with a death grip. I could feel my heart breaking in my chest, my hands balling up in frustration, and I let lose a frustrated yell throwing the note at the wall as hard as I could. Painfully watching it crinkle up and float back onto her pillow through my blurry vision, *"Dammit! No!"*

Birdy poked her head in, "whoa, dude what the heck is going on?"

Birdy quickly entered the room urgently looking around rushing to my side and repeating, "Zander, talk to me. What's going down?"

Danny entered shortly as well with a concerned look, "Hey have you found her yet... My lord? What's wrong?"

18: The Machine Lord's Blade

The moonlight shined through the trees casting different shapes and glistening the blood on the axe blade as Anna Bee walked quietly through the shadows and underbrush. A body of a man in a white gown lying on the ground behind her as she walked forward through the trees.

A man in a white mask and a white robe pushed his way through the brush and Anna Bee disappeared into shadows to avoid him, "Hey! Your time's up as lookout brother, trade off..." He saw the white cloak and mask lying on the ground blood soaking through the bark and grass underneath him.

"What the...?" He crouched over the body, and Anna Bee's bloody axe blade tore through his white robe with a sickening crunch smashing into his back. The axe came through the trees out of the darkness as though it was the darkness itself that threw it.

Anna Bee stepped out of the shadows and ripped the axe from his back, the sweet image of dancing with zander playing on her mind. She had never been happier in those moments, going in circles around with him. Her lord, the one who cared about her, and the one who thought she *was* good enough.

She would repay the favor, she would make him happy. She would make him *safe*.

Another man came out of the trees, "Hey you two quit slacking and hurry..." He came face to face with Anna Bee as she spun around to face him, and he drew his dagger, "Hey! What are you..."

She spun gracefully, the axe glinting through the moonlight for a fresh coat of blood tearing through the man's chest. He screamed loudly into the night spitting blood as he fell into the brush, and Anna Bee approached and ripped the axe from his chest.

The bushes rattled and a pink rabbit exploded screaming out of the bushes snarling and slashing wildly with its razor sharp claws. Anna Bee shot forward off of her left foot swinging the axe and pushed deeper into the bushes disappearing behind the rabbit. The rabbit spun on its heels to pursue her, and half of the rabbit fell with a splatter to the ground. Shortly behind it, the second half, its raspy breathing growing short before the monster burst into flames.

"We're under attack!" Someone yelled from beyond the trees, and bullets blistered the trees around Anna Bee as she zipped behind a tree. Shards of wood flew like debris and shrapnel from the laser bursts and bullets that came through the air humming and whizzing around her.

She waited until the firing stopped, and she could see another man searching through the trees with a readied dagger. She spun around the trunk of a tree on a wild ambush and tore into him with the axe, his body jerking like a meat shield to stop bullets as she dove behind another tree. The man's blood was dripping off her apron and green maid's dress as she weaved evasively through the trees towards the clearing ahead where the men were gathered.

"Go! Into the trees!" Someone screamed, "Find the assailants!"

Another taunt came screaming through the trees and Anna Bee skillfully ran up the side of a tree and flipped spinning her body upwards clotheslining the monster with the blade of the axe, its head and its body toppling to the forest floor separately. More bullets screamed passed her before her feet touched the ground again, and two men charged through the darkness trying to find her.

"She's over here! It's the maid our master spoke of!" One swung at Anna Bee with his dagger and the other lunged. She leapt back drawing the sword from the bottom of the axe, and in a split second she took both the men down with one bloody motion forcing them to the ground. She ripped her weapons from their bodies, and then re-sheathed the sword, hiding behind a tree.

A man with a pistol and a dagger leapt into Anna Bee's view searching for her, and he lifted and fired the pistol as Anna Bee leapt towards him. The bullet piercing through her shoulder with a splatter of blood striking the tree behind her making her cry out in pain.

Anna Bee rolled forward barely evading the next shot swinging the axe at his feet ripping him off his feet. Then she brought the axe down on his chest, forcing his body to the forest floor faster and harder with a crunch.

Another screaming rabbit came at Anna Bee slashing at her with its claws. She spun skillfully swinging the axe and it entered the monster's body on its left collarbone. The axe slid through the rest of its body tearing out the bottom of the monsters right side.

She rolled through the last set of bushes and entered a clearing, the two halves of the monster falling behind her.

There was an old two story forest ranger station in the center of the clearing with a wraparound balcony on the second floor. The building was fixed up, and there was men all wearing white lining the balcony and watching for her to emerge. Like spotters they were all carefully following the commotion with assault rifles and scoped rifles.

The grass was thick and uncut around the ranger station. It was up to the men's knees in some places as they all turned towards her when she was spotted. Then masked men and women flooded out of the station or rushed over from standing around it and surrounded Anna Bee.

There were hundreds of men in the clearing all of them chanting something in eerie unison. The massive pink monsters were appearing everywhere with rattling teeth like a predators smelling blood. The monsters all leapt and pushed passed the men and surrounded Anna Bee as well preparing to attack, lowering their stances to pounce.

All of the heads around her whether monster or man watched her furiously. Two more men and three more rabbits charged her. She cut them down mercilessly spinning around them with the axe blade as though it was not a weapon, but a graceful prop for a bloody ballet.

They all sprang into action, surrounding her. She drew her sword from the axe taking a deep breath and slashed through them, pieces of man and rabbit falling to the grass in the clearing. Anna Bee fought as hard as she could, the screams of men and monsters echoing the cloudy night sky.

As she fought, a rabbit claw struck her back and her blood glinted like metal through the moon light. Moments later a claw nicked her side making her scream in pain. She slashed harder and faster, spinning through the charging bodies. She counted them as they fell, twenty, thirty, and then forty...

Swinging and slashing trying defend herself she kept fighting, wanting her love to be safe and happy... no matter the cost. Every one of these monsters she took with her was one that could not hurt him.

"Wait! Wait! Wait!" a man came charging out of the ranger station, "What a treat! Stop the slaughter! What a treat! WHAT A TREAT!" The massive surrounding wall of men and monsters pulled back their weapons and parted so a familiar mask she had seen before could approach. The horns on his mask long and curled, his eyes shining with the stars of insanity.

Anna Bee could recognize him from before, watching him angrily through her own bloody scratched up face, her chest heaving. She pointed her axe towards him, "Are you the leader?"

"All these men, their names cast in immortality," he licked his lips behind his mask motioning to the bodies lying about, "Thanks to you... look at this, more than fifty of my men and demon blessings... Slaughtered so beautifully at your hand! Cut into little Teeny-weeny bloody pieces!" He howled and spun in a loud excited song.

Anna Bee charged him, but several taunts appeared like a wall and forced her back with outstretched claws, then they stood guarding him, but stood parted enough so he could see her.

"You come to us on such a night, such a beautiful *BLOODY* night! You come alone! Such a drive! My heart sings with admiration, so precious! Your drive! Why woman? Why do you fight! All alone! No one can find us, there is *no way out for you*! Why? Why do you fight? You cannot kill us *all*..."

He screamed with excitement into the night, the hundreds of men gathered around her regrouping, maybe more than three hundred gathering men, and more and more taunts came chittering from the darkness rattling and screaming like predators held back by chains.

A sea of white and bloody pink surrounding a single bloody dot of green and white kneeling with unsteady breathing in the grass in the clearing. Anna Bee had the tree line behind her for retreat, but she had no intention to do so. Her blue eye's angrily set on the insane man as he rambled.

"Why?" Anna Bee asked softly, "I only have one reason. His name is Zander."

The man howled and spun eagerly clapping in applause spinning and moving like an excited child.

Behind him a white horse came urgently galloping along the road toward the ranger station. The small sea of men and monsters parted for the lone rider in a pink and white dress as she rode through the army of men and monsters slowing down, and approaching the grizzly spectacle. Skylar's hair shined in the moonlight from behind the white horned mask that covered her face.

"Joseph," Skylar stepped off her horse as she made it to the clearing. She ripped off the flashy dress with a smile revealing a long white cloak that matched all of the cloaks around her. The dress had perfectly hidden her two swords sheathed to her hips. She turned to Anna Bee her smile growing wicked, "What do we have here? My master?"

Skylar looked through the carnage at Anna Bee. Anna Bee rose to her feet standing bravely, wiping blood from her chin, "You," Anna Bee growled under her breathe, "Aren't you supposed to be at a ball?"

Skylar threw up her head and laughed, "How precious. The maid, the *unappreciated* maid who loves her master *so* much. I thought you were dead? You are a long way from home darling. And look, you're bleeding, what a *tough* little maid."

"She has blessed us with immortality, she gifts us with her blood!" Burning howled, "Skylar what a treat for you to return to!"

"I would kill myself too," Skylar laughed at her, "If the man I loved never gave me a second glance, obsessing over a much prettier, more perfect trophy of a girl. He'll never love you, you are the maid! What are you trying to accomplish tonight, besides your own death."

"If I can take as many of you with me as I can," she coughed painfully spinning the sword and axe in her hands, "My love will be safer. His challenge easier, his burden lightened."

"Why? Why? Why?" The crazy man licked his lips behind Skylar twisting his body into unnatural positions, "Such love, and such loyalty!"

Anna Bee growled, "You are right, I may never have his heart, but I will die being his *blade*."

"How cute," Skylar drew both of her swords spinning them on her palms, "You know I can't let you live little maid. You've discovered our little hideout," she turned to the crazy man, "My master, allow me to kill this girl."

"Skylar!" Burning howled, "Such loyalty you've given me! Your wish is granted!"

Skylar smirked walking closer to Anna Bee, "So, do you want me to make it quick? End your pitiful misery, and put you down like the lost puppy you are?"

"I want to kill you..." Anna Be said raising her blades to attack, "for so many reasons..." Anna Bee swung her weapons and skillfully lunged at Skylar.

Skylar blocked her attack and they became locked in battle. Their weapons causing sparks as they slashed at each other. They moved around each other attacking and defending under the light of the moon.

"Not bad for a maid," Skylar found an opening as Anna Bee began to grow weak from her injuries. She kicked Anna Bee in the stomach sending her back rolling painfully through the grass.

Anna Bee leapt to her feet shaking, "I'm not done yet, witch!" She growled and swung and their blades caught again in a shower of sparks.

Anna Bee ran up Skylar's front with a barrage of quick and powerful kicks and the last kick was a harsh blow to Skylar's chin knocking off her mask. Skylar swung her swords desperately as she fell onto her back, the blades dicing the back of Anna Bee's legs.

Anna Bee landed on her feet with a cry of pain and collapsed. Anna Bee's blood spreading across the wild uncut grass through the night.

Skylar leapt to her feet and licked her own blood form her lips, "You're losing a lot of blood princess," Skylar frowned stepping towards her, "You had better stay down."

Anna Bee tried to get up, but Skylar shoved Anna Bee to the ground and put her shoe on Anna Bee's collar painfully pinning her down. Skylar spun her sword upwards preparing to swing at Anna Bee's dirty neck, "Thanks for making things fun, maid. Any last words from the defeated, useless maid?"

Skylar hesitated for a moment and her eyes moved to the tree line as though she heard something. For a moment there was silence and then she shrugged and turned back to Anna Bee, "I wish Zander could see you now, so useless, lying in your own blood... He *would not even care* now would he? You are just a stupid little maid..." She rose her blade her lips curling wickedly, "Now you die, maid."

Again Skylar thought she heard something, and after a moment of staring into the dark trees she readied the blade again, "I better hurry then," and she swung the sword downward, "Good night, maid."

Skylar saw a blur of rattling metal and armor explode wildly from the foliage with terrifying speed. Charging straight at her with an outstretched metal armored fist, the figure blocked Skylar's sword with a bright flash of sparks in the night.

—

I grit my teeth and without drawing my sword I lifted my fists as the sword bounced off of my gauntlet, "DON'T...TOUCH...MY...ANNA ...BEE!" I roared the words between my every blow, swinging my right and left fist tearing into Skylar as hard as I could. The blows took her by surprise knocking her around and sent Skylar flying several feet away from Anna Bee like Skylar was fired out of a cannon.

She rolled through the grass cursing and moaning before lying unconscious.

19: Destroying Insomnia

My chest was heaving from so much running, my veins burning with adrenaline. The monsters and men in white surrounding us slowly started moving inwards towards us readying their weapons.

There was so many of them. The terrifying masks, and the monsters from my nightmares with chattering teeth were completely surrounding us except for the tree line behind me, and even then I could hear the chattering teeth approaching from behind us as well.

I didn't care. My heart beating in my chest, every tear burning a line down my cheek more painful than the one before it. Anna Bee's body lying still and she adjusted moving her arm to look painfully up at me, tears in her eyes, "Z-zander? I'm sorry... I failed you."

"No Anna Bee," I said softly, "I failed you! I'm going to get you out of here."

"What a treat!" the masked man with the longest horns stepped forward his eyes lighting up, "What a delectable little morsel for my eyes to feed on! The lord of the maid, come alone to rescue his maiden!"

I dropped to my knees, feeling the ground begin to rumble beneath my feet, and I ripped the chest plate off and pulled off the armor on my arms, so I could feel the fragile girl against my body. Tears burning my cheeks and falling onto Anna Bee as she laid in my arms. A shy fading frown on her lips, "I'm s-sorry my lord... I just wanted you to be safe..."

"So you wish to stay and die with your maid?" a true story of romance," Burning grinned and spun, "Look at them, standing completely alone against an army of demons..."

"Who in the hell said I came alone?" I asked, a smile curling my lips. It was not a happy smile, in fact it was a wicked and vengeful smile because I knew what was coming. My sword sheathed to my hip to be drawn at any second.

The eyes in the mask looked confused as the ground began shaking harder and harder.

A massive wall of men to my left exploded from the tree line roaring for war, the flag of Osburn flying high in the moonlight. Taking the standing men and monsters completely by surprise, they all spun with their weapons, and I watched the charging Calvary tear through them like a lawn mower before the surprised foes could mount resistance.

To my right Danny and Birdy came smashing through the trees into clearing in full charge right after Nate's men. Danny held the hand stitched flag of a single gear and broken wires that Anna Bee had made for me days ago in one hand, and his sword in the other leading the men that had gathered at my estate. The crest with the gear and wires painted proudly across Danny's armored chest.

Birdy had her long curved dagger in one hand one of her pistols in the other, a wicked smile of deviant glee spread across her lips. She fired into the men making the already surprised men flip back around. My recruited army of mounted men charged out of the trees behind Danny and Birdy, weapons drawn, soldier droids and men hoping off the back of horses to charge on foot as they collided violently with the men and monsters.

I lowered my teary gaze to the pale girl in my arms and I took in a deep breath, "Hold on," I insisted, "I'm going to get you out of here."

"How did you find me?" Anna Bee asked, lying there with a fading smile, her face growing peaceful.

"I followed the flaming bodies and screams like bread crumbs …" I said and I began to cry like a baby, my tears washing the dirt and blood off her soft cheeks as they fell down her face. I touched my forehead to hers, "I'm going to get you out of here. I promise, you're going to be okay. There's a doctor waiting back at my estate…"

"Fat chance!" Skylar limped painfully through the chaos and leapt through a gap in fighting men. She swung her sword at Anna Bee and I, "You leave me at the ball? You expect me to just be okay with that? I was going to kill you later, but now I'm upset…"

I quickly spun my body around, setting Anna Bee down gently and kicked my legs against the ground so my back smashed into Skylar's legs knocking her painfully over me with a flip onto her back.

I leapt to my feet drawing my sword and standing in between her and Anna Bee, "I should have known, you are one of the demons!"

"Yeah," she smirked and nodded getting back to her feet, "You should have."

She swung at me and I blocked her first blow, but her second struck the armored section of my arm with a shower of bright sparks.

I just lunged forward with my whole body shoving her off her feet and her body back into the dirt. She rolled skillfully getting back to her feet, and she worked around me as I charged her.

She tripped me, and I fell rolling to avoid Skylar's wickedly fast blades. I was just doing my best to draw her attention away from Anna Bee. I could not beat Skylar and I knew it, but with Anna Bee's life on the line, it was my life or Skylar's. I had to get Anna Bee to medical help at my estate, and I had no time to run out of.

I pushed away with my legs and got to my feet and I grabbed her wrist as Skylar swung a sword at me, and I twisted and swung her body with her own momentum. I felt her shoulder pop with a crunch pulling out of its socket.

Skylar's face went painfully pale and she spun. I threw up my foot sacrificing my own balance to kick her square in the back as hard as I could. She rolled painfully into the mud, and I fell onto my back.

I tried to get up, but Skylar had already jumped up. Her foot came up kicking my chin knocking me painfully onto my back. She leapt up dodging my desperate kick to keep her off and she landed on my unarmored chest with her foot. She pulled back her sword pointing the bloody tip at my heart, "This was fun." She hissed. Then she lunged the bloody sword straight at my chest, "Now you die, *Machine Lord.*"

I closed my eyes and waited for the sword to puncture my heart. At least if this was how it ended, I would die beside Anna Bee.

Things slowed down for a terrifying moment. I heard only the sound of a sword cutting through flesh and I could feel the warmth of blood soaking through my suit as it splattering against my chest.

My eyes cracked open to get a glimpse and see where the sword had pierced through me.

There was no sword in my chest. There was fresh blood pooling across my chest, and Anna Bee was knelt over me, her bangs hiding her eyes as she shielded me, the sword through her back instead of my chest.

Time was completely frozen for a moment as I stared in horror. Anna Bee held her sword backwards in her wrist, the blade pointed upwards and through the center of Skylar's chest.

Anna Bee's body fell against mine, her bloody brown hair fell against me and she coughed blood painfully. The sword was completely through Anna Bee's chest, and she twisted her body as she fell so that Skylar's sword did not hurt me.

Skylar choked and spat blood for a moment stumbling back. She grabbed onto the hilt of Anna Bee's sword in her chest in shock, "Y-you damn maid! You useless..." she fell to her knees screaming angrily and then she fell onto her back after pulling the sword out of her own chest with the splatter of her blood through the grass.

I wrapped my arms around Anna Bee and I reached up to pull the sword out of her.

She flinched as I pulled it out with both of my hands, and then she laid still. Her head lying against my chest with a bloody smile on her lips, "You said I could speak freely..." she adjusted her head to comfortably to look at me.

"What? Anything Anna Bee, just hold on," I asked beginning to look around for a path out of the violent chaos around us.

"I love you, my lord," She whispered.

I didn't know what to say. I sat up and covered my crying eyes with my hand, her blood smearing across my brow as I sat there. I just stared at her with my heart shattered in my chest, not knowing what to do. Not knowing how to comfort her...

Her eyes gently closed, and I rose to my feet with one powerful lift of my legs carefully holding her in my arms, my skin crawling with emotion.

I spotted a white saddled horse nearby, and I recognized it as Skylar's horse. I stumbled for a moment in the blood and mud, but quickly regained my balance moving towards the horse that was jumping around in the chaos alone. I ducked between a taunt and soldier as they charged one another, and I slid through the mud and grabbed onto the white horse.

I grabbed the reins and the horse quickly settled down. I lifted myself onto its back with one hand. I placed Anna Bee in front of me with my other hand, and leaned her back against my chest taking control of the horse. I kicked the horse's sides steering toward my estate and away from the violence, "Go! As fast as you can!"

The horse took off through the trees jumping over bodies that burst into the unusual black flames and dust, its breath shining in the moonlight, and its breath cutting through the air like steam.

The sound of clashing steel and screams of pain began fading behind me as I rode on into the night, going back the direction I had come from.

I was grateful that I had found, her, but I was so angry. So fiercely frustrated for being such an idiot, for not realizing what I had right in front of me all along. I could not stop crying from the painful guilt, tearing through the trees with my ankles repeatedly kicking the horse's rump yelling for it to go faster.

Anna Bee was breathing, but she was growing weaker every second, her blood staining the suit she had made me. She rested against me on the horse with a peaceful serenity on her face that I loved and hated at the same time. The horse's hooves thundered through the night. I was running out of time, as I kicked the horse holding my fragile Anna Bee tightly, "Go! Go! Faster! Please!"

I arrived at the estate, and steered the horse through the hole where the gate once was. The remaining people at my estate literally dove and shoved each other out of the way of the horse as it galloped for the estate door.

The doctor was waiting patiently with his assistants near the front door right where I told him to be. He was an older handsome man with a pot belly and was wearing a white lab coat who had arrived the night before and asked if I had use for him in my domain.

I slid her gently into his arms, and he transferred her into her own bed which was conveniently already an infirmary bed with wheels. The doctor wheeled the bed away and his several young nurses followed him inside carefully walking around Anna Bee pushing her into the lobby and down the hallway.

"Quickly," I said dismounting the panting horse with a limp from my brief fight, "Please, you have to save her!" I fell to my knees in the door way exhausted. A young man ran over to help me up, "Come on my lord. I'll get you to her." I didn't even look at his face, but gratefully accepted his help as he led me in.

They worked to the best of their ability around Anna Bee efficiently, sticking her with a needle to slow the bleeding. They began tearing off her bloody clothes down to her underwear, cleaning her off with warm soapy water and a rag.

I stood scared in the doorway leaning against the man without even looking at his face, staring terrified at the serene face of Anna Bee lying on the bloody bed.

The mysterious man helped me get into a chair and scooted me to her side before dismissing himself. I sat by her side, and I took Anna Bee's cold white hand as they tended to her. My head hung over her, my tears falling gently onto her hand. I refused to let go, for all the times she held my hand... I was going to stay here for her, like she was there for me all those times.

Anna Bee's memories danced across my mind. The way she smiled, the way she blushed when I knew she was okay, the way she always loyally stood by me. Everything about her was stirring my heart and mind.

Chapter 20: The Near Loss of a Maid

Her warmth was leaving her hand slowly, as I sat there terrified holding it. I could feel the heart beat in her wrist growing weaker as the doctor and nurses stitched, cleaned and kept pressure.

When she accidentally called me her love… when she cut out the single cereal heart… It all made painful sense as I pieced everything together with her hand in mine…

The heart beat in her hand faded away, and the doctor noticed and quickly shouted, "We're losing her!" and he began CPR on her as I sat there frozen holding her hand as it moved around.

I felt that I had lost her. I could see her becoming a memory in my mind as Mandy was. Her hand was cold when it was once warm, her eyes closed peacefully. I sobbed over her, and all I could chant was, "I'm so sorry. I'm so sorry…"

When I had lost my hope, and in my darkest moment. The doctor kept doing compressions and trying his hardest, but somehow I knew. Somehow I expected the heart beat to once again come back, and after a long and intense moment, it did.

The doctor stopped the CPR, and then slowly, Anna Bee's heart beat became steady once more. Then her condition became weak but stable as they worked.

The doctor gently caught my shoulder startling me, "My lord, we've done what we can for now. It's really a miracle she's still alive, and the cuts on her legs are really bad," he said wiping blood from his hands on his sleeves as the women rolled in an IV, while others wrapped blankets around Anna Bee's unconscious body tightly to try and keep her warm.

"Luckily," the Doctor turned and sat on the bed so he could somewhat face me, his hand lifting off my shoulder, "The sword through her chest has missed everything vital. We're very lucky for that, but she has lost *a lot* of blood. To be perfectly honest, she should be dead several times over for multiple reasons... it doesn't look very great..."I reached for my sword handle taking a step towards him.

He raised his hands quickly clearing his throat, "but the body is a *miraculous* thing I suppose. She's tough, and she's fighting."

"It's up to her now. I'll check on her in the morning," he said bravely.

"Thank you, doctor," I whispered and I let go of my sword.

"I honestly don't know what could happen. My lord... I've seen a lot less trauma and they died twice as fast. It's not very promising... the cuts on her major nerves in the back of her legs are pretty serious, she probably won't walk ever again..." he said nervously and I growled, "Leave us."

He bowed, "Yes my lord," and he hesitantly left the room after doing a double take towards Anna Bee. When the women were done setting up the IV I told them to close the door behind them as they left. My hands separated only once from Anna Bee's, only long enough to pull up the blanket and make sure she was comfortable.

"I'm sorry Ann Bee," I said sobbing in the darkness sitting at her bedside, "I am so sorry."

Leaning forward in the chair, I fell asleep from exhaustion my head on the side of the bed.

The next morning I awoke almost as equally tired as I had been the night before. The doctor and his assistants were all waiting around the room with sad looking faces. Some of the assistants were checking Anna Bee's machinery carefully, and the Doctor was looking over everything as I woke up.

I sat up clearing my throat, looking at the doctor as he crossed around the bed seeing that I had awakened. He felt her pulse and then felt her forehead as though he was double checking something, his assistants following him.

I also felt Anna Bee's pulse to make sure she was alive, and it was there but it was weak.

Danny, Birdy, and Lord Osburn entered the room, all of them were looking tired and sore. They all had dark circles under their eyes, blood staining their clothing, and Danny's armor was nearly coated in brown crusted blood and the dark black ashes from the monsters. Birdy looked fairly clean compared to the other two, but she still looked like it had been a long night.

"I'm sorry, everyone, I left you all to battle without me…" I tried to explain.

Birdy set a hand on my shoulder, "Easy big guy. We sent those white masked freaks running with their tail between their legs. It was honestly kind of satisfying, how badly we beat them. They're long gone."

She patted me on the shoulder and stepped away as the doctor nervously cleared his throat to give me a report.

"Well she is still alive, that's promising," the doctor said, "However, she is running a pretty high fever this morning. She is going to need antibiotics. I'm sorry my lord, antibiotics are not a very common thing nowadays…" I gave him a fierce look and interrupted him, "can we make some?"

"It would take weeks, and I don't have the correct equipment," he said with a sigh, "Without them, her struggle is going to be a lot harder. Her situation is steady, but still not very good. She's a real fighter, like I said, I've seen strong healthy men die from a lot less than what she's been through. If she does survive, she won't be able to walk form the damage to her legs, but we can't dismiss the fact that she is probably not going to survive this..."

I jumped angrily to my feet picking him up by his collar pulling the man clear over the foot of Anna Bee's bed with my arms outstretched, and I spun slamming him against the wall, "Where can I find the medicine she needs?"

"My lord," Danny immediately rushed and tried to pry me off, "He's only trying to help!"

"Don't kill the only doctor who can help her," Birdy warned, "That's a bad idea." She put her hand on my shoulder, "Calm down my lord."

I glanced around at his terrified assistants. Even Lord Osburn was looking uneasy, his hand on his sword. I didn't care, I needed to save Anna Bee.

"I get that you're upset," The doctor squirmed, "Please, put me down, my lord."

"Where can I find some antibiotics?" I asked again flatly. He swallowed, "There is some in the hospital in Las Vegas, but that's days away and even in your truck...," I growled and pressed him against the wall a little harder.

He choked, "Wellington may have some left from when he got an infection a couple years ago. He had his scientists make some penicillin. If he does have some, it would be locked away guarded in his personal estate... Please put me down, perhaps you could go talk to him..."

I dropped the doctor to the floor, and he rubbed his neck as he picked himself up, "You are freakishly strong my lord."

I spun to Danny with a deep breath, "Then we shall pay Lord Wellington a visit. How did the battle go? Are the monster's gone? Please tell me more."

"We really ripped them a new one," Lord Osburn nodded, "We took them completely by surprise. You had them so distracted my lord, they did not even resist at first. You're a brave guy."

"I told you we got them," Birdy said with a wink, "We got them good."

"Unfortunately some of them got away. The crazy guy with the big horns got away with a handful of them. I couldn't find Skylar's body so I think she got away with them. We tried to pursue, but they started spawning more of those damn Taunts which slowed us down. They have some ancient scroll and chant that spawns them..." Birdy said looking distant for a moment, "It was a win, but we lost a lot of people, and we've got a lot more injured. It looks like the most important ones got away though, classic right?"

I sighed, "We will find them. But for now..."

"My lord, I think remember hearing something about that actually," Danny spoke up, his hand on his chin, "I remember something about wellington getting sick. I bet he does have some."

Danny handed me the missing pieces of my armor recovered from the clearing the night before, and I reattached them carefully.

"What's the plan?" he asked loyally.

"Wellington has what I need," I said coldly, "I'm going to take it from him."

"Wellington's compound is heavily guarded by well-trained knights and hundreds of men. Not to mention if we tried to march our army through the city he could rally a much bigger army then we have. We would have no element of surprise," Danny explained, "Maybe we should just ask him. He offered peace to you. This could be a chance for him to prove it."

"Danny, you are supposed to be my brave knight," I shrugged, "Birdy, don't you still want to earn the title of my Knight?"

"Well... duh. I was not the one complaining, let's go get him," she said.

I picked up my sword from the bed side, and I gently separated my hand from Anna Bee's, "Birdy, now's a good time to earn that title."

Danny nodded encouragingly and Birdy leaned in, "I would sincerely enjoy kicking Wellington around a little bit. If the chance comes along."

"Then let's go," I said, "Every second is wasted, Danny gather the able bodied men and droids on your way to the truck. But not too many though, ask for volunteers. I have a plan."

"Yes my lord," Danny and Birdy followed me out of the room, "What is our plan of attack my lord?"

"I have a big surprise," I said as we walked through the lobby, "a big calculating, armored, heavy, and efficient surprise," I grinned.

Danny and Birdy followed me across the lawn through all the tents of ready and injured soldiers. As we walked, the soldiers that could bow in respect to me did so, and even most the injured ones at least waved. All of the men and women injured or not looked tired, some of them a little scarred at what they had seen last night staring off into space.

There was no way I was going to demand another immediate battle from these people. I had a much bigger and more powerful asset I had been failing to put to use.

We stepped onto the cracked parking lot where my carriage was parked, and I approached the massive resting construction bot, "Hey big guy!" I clapped my hands together, "We've got a new *deconstruction* project."

Buster transformed with the sound of hissing hydraulics, his eyes lit up, "Yes, my lord."

"The next time I activate you, I want you to demolish the closest building, can you handle that?" I asked Buster who bent over to look at me and nodded, "Yes, Sir."

I immediately ordered him back to sleep, and with the help of several men and droids we loaded him into the back of the truck, leaning him over and sliding him in on the left side.

He nearly took up the entire back of the truck. There was only room for six people on the right side of the truck to sit in the seats, not counting the driver or passenger. We quickly loaded up into the truck and it was me, four armed and brave volunteers, and a handpicked armored soldier droid that I caught on my way to the truck.

Danny was driving the truck, and Birdy was riding shotgun. I felt the truck start up with its low ground shaking rumble, and it struggled to get going because of Buster's weight. No time was wasted, as I closed the back door we began to drive towards the gate to leave the parking lot.

"So what is this urgent mission?" A man turned to me with nervous green eyes and a thin moustache, a sword on his hip and an assault rifle across his lap. I immediately recognized his voice as the man who had helped me get to Anna Bee's side the night before, and I turned to him with my full grateful attention.

"We're attacking Wellington's estate," I said eagerly, and he laughed, "Right, just us. What are we really doing?"

I stood up without a word and opened the heavily armored programming door on the massive robot, "You know what this is?" I asked hitting the side of the giant swaying cylinder as the truck moved, and I reached in yanking out a small fuse carefully with a burst of sparks.

"A bomb? I'm sorry my lord. I heard you were looking for volunteers, and I had nothing better to do. By the time I got here it was already in the back of the truck," he shrugged.

"This is a massive giant with sheer awesome hydraulic power. A construction machine design to lift sections of entire buildings and hold them in place. It's designed to survive if a building falls on it. They would even shoot these machines with high velocity cannons to test their armor. They're expensive and rare pieces of machinery, great for destroying old abandoned structures," I explained staring at him and he looked confused, "I don't get it."

"Do you know what this is?" I slammed the programming door shut and handed him the fuse I had jerked out. I sat back down beside him, and he shook his head looking at me, "No sir."

"That's what altered the programming to keep it from hurting human beings while it deconstructs property. You see it was not programed to *stop* destroying things if there was *life* in the structure it was destroying. That fuse was a last minute fix to keep people safe..." he smiled as he realized what I was saying, "Wow, You're going to tear apart his estate?"

I winked, "While people are flying through the air, distracted by this indestructible beast. We walk in, kill whoever is in our way, and we find penicillin. Simple enough? I know we can't take Wellington's army on, but we can distract it. Robots are programed to defend themselves from humans as long as they don't hurt the humans..." I touched my head with a hinting spark in my eyes and I pointed at the fuse in his hand, "That's why they quit making these models, they have a loop hole."

He smiled, "Awesome."

"Yup," I nodded petting the side of the massive metal cylinder "Buster's going to hurt a lot of people... Listen," I changed the subject, "Thank you for your help last night."

"No problem. Everybody needs help once in a while," He shrugged, "Besides, I've been thinking about becoming a blade so I could be a knight..."

The truck suddenly rolled to a stop, and I heard some brief shouting outside. I braced against the cylinder clearing my throat with a growl, "Alright, let's get ready!" I got ready to clap my hands and wake up Buster as the doors swung open.

The door swung open and Ella Lovewind stood there beside Danny, a glass corked Vial in her hands and a brown paper bag. We were nowhere near Wellington's estate, we were just barely out of my estate. In fact I could see the fence in the distance. I shot Danny an angry and confused look, and he motioned to Lord Ella.

"Lord Zander," she said kindly, "You were looking for Antibiotics?" She extended the brown paper bag and the vial of murky white and grey liquid to me, "We've been developing antibiotics in secret for a couple months now using some old medical journals. This should do the trick just fine."

I carefully accepted the bag, "Thank you... how did you know?"

"Rumor went around that you had an injured servant dear to you. My husband and I want to help you..." She leaned forward and whispered under her breath, "And you're not the only one who wants to make Wellington pay. One day, you, my husband and myself, and Lord Osburn could all collectively come together and finish him off once and for all." She pulled away with a smile, "The medication is simply an act of good faith, and we hope that your injured servant recovers."

"I heard the servant girl means a lot to you, and it is no trouble at all to my husband and me... Please just keep us in mind. We may not be military driven, but we wish to help with the downfall of that maniacal tyrant Jazz Wellington."

I cleared my throat shaking, "Lord Ella... I sincerely appreciate this..." My voice cracked tears welling up in my eyes.

"Hurry up and get back to her!" She smiled. She mounted onto the beautiful brown horse that she had ridden, and she waved kindly, "We'll talk when she's better, okay? We'll get Wellington when everyone is ready."

"Turn the truck around Danny," I said holding the medication, "We'll punch Wellington in the face another day." I was a little disappointed. I wanted to watch the man burn, but my Anna Bee was far more important.

"What about tomorrow?" Birdy poked her head around the corner into the box truck, "Can we do it tomorrow? I am free tomorrow."

I reached up taking the box truck door to close it, "Get us home Danny."

Birdy frowned, wiggled her nose at me, and headed for the passenger seat.

I closed the door, the truck turned around on the gravel road, and we headed back towards the estate. It did not take us very long at all to return.

I moved as quickly as I could to Anna Bee's side, handing the medication straight to the doctor who looked impressed

"Wow. How'd you get it so fast?" He worked quickly setting up the antibiotics to go into the IV carefully calculating, scratching numbers and notes on a dirty memo pad while he worked.

"I found some before I reached, Wellington's estate. I was lucky," I shrugged.

The doctor nodded, "I suppose. We did our best to clean her wounds, but germs are of course invisible to the naked eye. This medication is going to really help, especially with all the dirt that had been in her wounds and the risk of infection being so darn high... But now we can effectively clean the germs out too."

Anna Bee looked peaceful, quiet, and pale. Her skin was clammy from a high fever that I could feel it as I sat beside her feeling her forehead. As she laid there I gently felt her heartbeat as well, just to make sure it was still there, by placing my fingers gently against her neck. It was weak, but it was still beating.

"I wish I would have realized it sooner," I said staring at her, "I really do."

"Realized what? My lord?" The doctor asked curiously as he worked.

I gazed at him with a sigh, "What I had right in front of me."

"Well, if she ever comes around..." the doctor said shrugging and I looked up correcting him harshly, *"When she comes around*. When that happens, I'm going to ask her to stay with me, and we are going to have a ball every month, just for her..."

The doctor smiled an apologetic smile, "Of course, *when* she wakes up, you go ahead and do that."

Danny urgently burst into the room, "My lord, we have a massive problem"

21. The fall of The Machine Lord

"I guess Wellington found out you went to war against the demons last night. He's mobilizing his army as we speak to "reclaim his honor.""

Danny pulled up a chair, dragging it through the doorway, "He's planning a full blown attack on your estate. He's been preparing since last night. Just what we need, another battle. He's already organizing his entire army to march against you. They are probably already starting to move. I heard he has over fifteen hundred men. After last night's battle we have a little over three hundred, two hundred of them already tired from the battle last night, but still willing to fight. A lot of them injured as well."

"That is just what I would expect from him," I growled, "I'm not even surprised. Looks like I get to fight him after all."

"We're right here with you my lord. I'm ready to fight," Danny put his hand on his heart, which was right were the painted gear was placed.

"I don't deserve any of you," I said it staring into Danny's eyes, "Not one of you. You all have my permission to leave and avoid this coming battle. It does not sound like we have any other options besides surrender. If anybody wants to leave, and not stand against Wellington. I can't make them stay. Like I said, I don't deserve any of you."

Danny looked amused and sat back, "Do you really want me to tell everyone that?"

"I've already asked too much," I lowered my head, "Everyone has already helped me save the one thing that matters to me. Because of *my* stupidity men have died."

"No lord does deserve his servants," Danny said bluntly, "I agree with you one hundred percent. My lord, those men died to *protect* their families from an army of Demon bunnies, and you gave them the *opportunity* to do that."

"No single man deserves that much power, no matter how kind or mentally collected the guy is. The men who truly deserve to be a lord usually don't want the title at all."

"I wanted to be a knight, it's my dream. I don't want to be a lord, I don't want to be anything else, I just want to be a knight, and you are a lord. You helped me get to where I wanted to be, and I'm going to keep fighting to keep what you've given me, the title of knight. I'm going to stand and draw my blade when they show up whether you want me too or not. So is Birdy, I guarantee it. Mostly because she just really wants to watch Wellington burn, and he's leading the massive army himself."

I leaned back in my chair. My mind tactically beginning to prepare for an attack on my estate. I had no idea what to do, I could not defend the estate from that many men. I had already lost, and I knew it.

"Whoever wants to leave may protect themselves and their family and return to the city," I said looking at him, "spread the word. Nobody has to die because of me."

"I'm on it," Danny said reluctantly, "I'll return once I've done that, and keep you informed of what's going on." He bowed and left the room.

"What about Anna Bee?" The doctor asked, "She is in no condition to protect herself, it would be nearly impossible for you to protect her if the building is attacked. Wellington's men will come storming the hallways, hundreds of them..."

"I am thinking, Doctor," I said quickly raising my hand, "I lose no matter what... I lose my estate, I lose the electricity..." I said an idea dawning, "The electricity."

"What about it?" He asked and I grinned changing the subject, "Can we make this setup mobile, can I count on your continued support to help her?" I motioned to the wires and pumps around her.

"Well of course," he nodded, "I came just like every other man, wanting to give my family electricity to better their lives, and I will serve you as long as you can offer that to my family."

"Of course," I said, "We can transform the inside of that truck into a make shift hospital room. We can route the power from the trucks core to power the equipment keeping her alive. That would be enough power right?"

"It would be risky to transfer her off the equipment even for a couple minutes," the doctor said, "She's very weak."

A plan began to develop in my mind, a tactical strategy that would give me a wicked underhanded advantage against Wellington, but it would cost me everything.

Danny returned, "I spread the message, and we lost about fifty injured men only because they were injured. Most everyone is deciding to stay. They all want electricity for their homes and families. They are willing to fight for that. Like your little speech you gave, they want to protect what you've offered them... and a lot of them hate Wellington."

"Well okay," I said with a deep breath, "Here's the plan then."

He listened as I explained it to him, and once I was done explaining he sighed nervously, "I'll bring the truck around, and I'll gather some men. I'll go with Anna Bee to personally protect her and to tell lord Osburn everything."

He headed out of the room, and I took up Anna Bee's hand, "I'm going to protect you with *my* life this time okay..." Thinking about it made tears run down my cheeks, "I just need you to be strong okay; don't leave me. Please. Anna Bee. Please don't leave me, I need my Anna Bee."

Birdy stepped in a moment later, "Sup bro. That's quite a plan Danny told me, you truly are kind of a genius," she bowed, "I'm impressed, especially with the whole "*ka-boom*" plot twist. What do you want me to do? I have been tending to the wounded, but it seems I've run out of people wanting to be treated since they are either getting up to fight or running away."

"I need you to run to Lord Lovewind," I said, "Let her know if she really wants in on kicking Wellington's ass, now's a good time. This is going to be the final battle, I'm tired of the ignorant jerk," I growled, "Wellington dies, or I do."

"Right," Birdy nodded, "I'll be off as fast as I can. I should be back within the hour, and I hope it's the second one of those two options for everyone's sake..."

"Okay," I nodded, and I set to work carefully helping the doctor preparing everything. I helped him slide the bed down the hallway with all the equipment never leaving her side, and holding her hand.

When the time came, I routed the power and wiring from the box truck through the floor so we could immediately power on the machines. The doctor began to work strapping the bed down and making sure she was stable with the help of his assistants.

He checked on her vitals because of the risky move and gave me a nervous thumbs up, "Alright, she looks good. We'll head to Lord Osburn's estate." I stepped off the truck clearing my throat. I pulled the box truck door shut, and I watched the truck drive away down the gravel road throwing up dust and rocks.

Armed men gathered around me awaiting orders. It was a combination of men, tired and sore, some of them still injured standing on two bandaged legs. There was kids younger than me, and men almost three times my age that still had a straight back and an angry will to fight. They encircled me armed to the teeth awaiting orders at the ready.

The man with dark colored moustache who had helped me get to Anna Bee the night before approached pushing through the men, "I never told you my name," He extended a rough muscular hand and I shook it, "The name is Alek, and if it's alright with you, I do want to be your blade."

"Well, Alek," I said, "We have a lot of work to do, and not much time. Let's skip the tradition, I declare you my blade."

He shrugged, "Good enough for me."

We were all preparing mentally and physically for a battle. I ordered men off of the estate into carefully placed positions behind and around my estate along the tree line.

We reinforced the entire chain-link fence along the front of the estate, and we rolled Buster towards the middle standing him up with ropes and pulleys where the old fence gate used to be.

Before long it was only fifty men plus me on the estate working quickly to fortify positions to stand our ground to buy some time. We sweated away turning sections of the estate into bunkers positioning sheet metal and cutting holes in the building itself.

As the day went on every hammer I swung, every time I shoved heavy slabs of concrete into position Anna Bee's smile flashed behind my eyelids, driving me harder and faster so that I could see her again.

Terry had packed up his things and as much food as he could then headed for Nate's estate galloping away on a horse at my request. We worked hard and the day faded away quickly turning into early evening, sweat beating my brow as we prepared the best we could.

Around seven-thirty I was standing near the front door of the estate fixing up an assault rifle, and I was startled by a man who ran over and caught my shoulder, "My lord! Wellington is here!"

Three horsemen were moving at full gallop on a narrow path beyond the tree line. Two of them were heavily armored knights. They held massive flags that were decorated with Wellington's mark. The three horses' armor rattled as they came to a stop outside of the hole in the fence.

The third horseman was Wellington himself. He confidently steered his horse through the fence and came straight up to me. The horse was unsettled and moved around as he spoke to me trying to get it to hold still, "You said once that wanted my army, Zander, well here it is. I'm done messing around. Surrender your estate and your machines to me, or you will die," He said loudly, "Our treaty is off, I changed my mind. I will accomplish what I wanted from the very beginning, and if you try to stand in my way, you will *die*!"

I blew air out my mouth with a disbelieving laugh and then I spit at the horse's feet. He growled at me shifting on his horse, "My army is marching up the hill as we speak! Only I can stop them! Surrender now, and your people will live."

"Stay at the bottom of the hill," I angrily drew my sword and aimed the blade at him aggressively, "And *your* men will live."

I was terrified. How did he get here so fast? Danny and Birdy weren't back yet, and we were not ready at all. I was expecting his army much later, there was so much left to do. I expected his army to arrive maybe tomorrow. I could work with what I had, and I was ready for a fight. In fact I wanted to fight. I wanted to fight for Mandy, and I wanted to fight for Anna Bee.

Wellington swore at me with a rude look on his face, "Very well, you will all die."

His over decorated horse rose up on its hind legs with a noisy whinny before it went back down and Wellington steered it away. His knights turned waiting for him to get a distance away and then followed him. The three of them disappeared into the trees the same way they came.

I stood there frozen for a moment, "This can't be happening."

"How are they here already?" Alek asked shouting from across the lawn urgently, "My Lord, we're not ready!" He glanced around the estate panic lacing his words. Men and women scattered around the estate spreading the word, things began to heat up and grow tense quickly.

"Everyone to their battle stations," I yelled re-sheathing my sword, "We can work with this! Stick to the plan! It will work out! I'll get the reactor ready!"

"Right!" Alek bravely gave me thumbs up, and then he ran through the estate yelling, "Here they come! Everybody get ready for a fight!"

Men, women, and droids dawned bows and assault rifles taking carefully chosen cover around the estate. Most my men and droids were waiting around the outside of the estate beyond the tree line, having been placed there earlier in preperation. Everyone still in the estate scrambled around settling down behind cover.

I headed straight for the noisy utility shed that housed the massive core powering my estate. I grabbed up my tool kit tripping over myself in a hurry as I rushed. People were still getting to their places, lining the roof of the estate, diving behind leaning concrete, and digging small trenches as quickly as they could. The ground below us began to tremble from Wellington's army marching up the hill with battle drums filling the trees with powerful driving rhythm.

The ground shook as the ocean of men came marching through the trees side by side towards the front of my estate. I could see them from the utility shed door, my hand on the door handle. I found myself momentarily staring in horror at all the marching men with weapons like an armored wall of metal and flesh. They were coming out of the trees steadily marching at a fast pace, preparing to charge beating their weapons against their armor rallying their courage.

I watched the army release a volley of grenades and explosives at the fence, shredding it and tearing it to pieces. Throwing pieces of shrapnel and fence like bullets through my estate. The moment the fence was gone and the fence was clear they began to march again.

I counted to ten putting on my old faded rubber gloves, closing my eyes as the ground shook. I threw the utility door open and moved in to work. I could hear the cackle of gunfire as my small hidden guerrilla groups lit up the marching army with assault rifles and bows. A volley of arrows fired three at a time came from the estate roof as the positioned soldier droids along the roof sprang up. They were right on cue, just as we planned, waiting for the men to cross the line that used to be the fence.

I watched the smear of blood and I heard the screams of pain as the marching men went down. The arrows smashing through their armor, and their blood spreading across the grass. They began to fall from the onslaught of ammunition and arrows that came at them like a storm from every direction.

The wave of soldiers all charged storming over the bodies of their falling comrades. It was as though my petty defense did little to nothing, men falling dead only to be trampled by an endless amount of charging boots behind them. The tide of assailants flooding from the tree line and sweeping through the grass and estate towards me.

They tore down tents and shelters as they charged, trampling belongings and bags. I wished I had a gun. I wished I could turn and fire into them as well, my heart filling with anger. It was all happening so fast, the massive army marching against me, just like in my dream.

They were already drawing closer to some of the positioned men who leapt up as Lord Wellington's army grew near in tactical retreat ducking and weaving running toward the trees on the opposite side of the estate.

I hurried into the shed, where I began to quickly put on the power armor which I had set there in advance.

Once the armor was on, I opened the reactor door quickly desperately abandoning my original plan. I drew my sword and slashed at the fragile wires with the blade. I did not have time to do it in a fancy way anymore, I just inflicted as much damage as I could. The reactor beginning to thunder and the lights flickered around me in the shed as it began to spit angry amounts of sparks out of the very hole I slashed into. The sword began pulsating in my hands from the electrical current running through it and going back into the sensitive wires.

"You want my core?" I screamed hacking angrily, "Wellington you Fiend! You can have it!"

The core finally began to trip over itself, and began to melt down. It was beginning to emit the high pitch buzz of uncontrollable electricity shooting and firing in different directions.

I ran out of the shed with a mighty leap slamming the door behind me and charged for the trees my armor still humming with the whine of hydraulics with every step.

Alek who was the closest to the charging oncoming enemy leapt out of cover, less than ten feet behind Buster as the army flooded around him unaware of what he was. Alek clapped twice, "Buster! Time to break things!"

The machine unfolded startling the men around it spinning and spitting steam. The men all ducked and rolled away starting to concentrate on him. Buster's earth shaking power was the perfect distraction for Alek and everyone else scattered about my estate to leap from their cover and begin their tactical retreat to the tree line.

Buster sent thirty men flying backwards into the ranks of endless charging men with a low sweep of his armored arm trying to defend himself as they began to desperately swing their swords at him and fire at him with their assault rifles.

I threw up my arms, "Let's go! Full retreat!"

We could have stayed, and we could have kept fighting, but I knew what was happening. The turbine was going to explode, the electrical current was going to go every direction. I didn't want the risk of the explosion hurting my army. I only wanted it to hurt Wellingtons.

I sprinted passed the utility shed lowering my shoulders, sparks spewing out from below the door behind me. The people around the estate abandoned their positions as they leapt out of their hiding places and ran back towards the tree line.

I used my armor and sword to jump up and take down an entire section of the back chain link fence so they could get through, the massive army in close pursuit behind us.

My scattered forces all ran through and over the fence in full desperate sprinting retreat. The army of men taking over every foot of my entire estate charging behind us sweeping around the now empty building. Some men went into the facility to search it, and my skin crawled hoping it really was empty. After one last glance, I dove into the cover of the tall trees.

I turned and watched the utility shed roof blast off with a thundering crack and a burst of angry dark smoke and sparks. "There goes the safe guard! Get down!" I screamed it desperately covering my ears tucked behind a tree to watch what was happening. My men all dove to cover behind trees protecting their heads and necks with their hands.

The blinding explosion was far beyong what I expected, and it ripped through Wellington's army.

The shockwave ripped through the trees around us launching us several feet backwards. It picked me off my feet and slammed me into the base of another tree painfully.

Debris, smoke, and body parts went in every direction from the wicked blast raining down around us. Some debris were fired through the trees around us like projectiles getting wedged into tree trunks and ripping off branches that fell around us.

The entire robotics facility walls collapsed acting as debris tearing through the army of men like aimed projectiles. Entire chunks of concrete from the facility walls blasted outward, crushing the tightly spaced men chaotically.

I watched everything incinerate in front of my eyes, the entire estate, even the scrap metal in piles behind it tearing into and through trees around us. The majority of my army safely away or in the cover of the trees, but Wellington's army surrounding the base of the explosion were hit like fish in a barrel.

The sea was reduced to ash and blood with one wicked deafening flash. I sat there my ears ringing braced against a tree coughing through the dust and smoke.

I waited for the dust and debris to settle, and then when it was clear enough I poked my head around the tree to look at the damage, "I was expecting an explosion," I swallowed as my men got to their feet carefully, "but damn."

My men pulled themselves from the ashes and debris eagerly, some of them had blood trailing from their ears from the explosion shockwave.

I could see Buster still was still intact swinging at the men attacking him as they regrouped at the tree line. For all I knew I had cut Wellington's army clean in half, but to my frustration, there was still so many of them coming through the trees. They were rolling around Buster firing up at him and desperately throwing grenades and small arms at his weakest points.

For a moment that simply because Buster was nearly indestructible I had already won. Buster had their full attention and it was awesome to watch him fight, but Buster's eyes flickered, and Buster unexplainably fell onto this back in the distance and powered down.

318

I was honestly surprised to see him fall, and he was too far away to see what damage did him in. He had taken hundreds of men with him trying to defend himself. The army all celebrated Buster falling with roars of victory, and I realized that they had thought they had won.

It looked like we retreated and counted on Buster to do the fighting, but that was not my intention

"I'm sorry big guy," I said, "I promise that was not in vain."

A lone rider rode ahead of the regrouping soldiers. I tried to focus on it, and I could see it was Wellington's horse as he rode through the smoke and blood towards us and keeping his distance. If I had a gun I would have shot him, but before I could order someone else to, he opened his mouth yelling into the trees.

"That was your plan machine Lord?" He yelled, "Your plan was to destroy your only advantage to try and take out my army with that? Pathetic! Pitiful! Look at you! Hiding in the trees! Don't you worry! We'll come flush you out! You can't win, Machine Lord!"

He drew and aimed his sword towards the trees, "Search the trees! Kill them all!" The men once again began to charge, sweeping around him as he rode away towards the rear of his army.

"Alright!" I roared, "They're coming to us! Alert the rest of the army! Use the metal and trees to our advantage! It's time! Anna Bee! This is for you! It's all for you!"

We readied in the trees, my heart pounding as I watched the army come charging through the flattened estate towards us. I could finally see the end to Wellington's infantry pouring from the tree line. When I saw this I shouted, "If you have ranged weapons! Fire!"

The first line of the charging men drew closer and closer, my smaller army rallying around me coming through the trees. A little over three hundred men waiting in the trees as Wellington's army charged towards us.

I heard the shuffle of people around me, the stress of bow strings, and the click of assault rifles. Then my men began firing into the army from the tree line. I watched men twist and fall as they were struck my lasers, bullets, and arrows but the more armored men came forward from within the ranks.

The armor could stop the bows and the lasers, which suddenly gave the army another advantage as they charged toward the tree line.

The rest of the men like me with melee weapons watched them draw closer, and we crept towards the tree line behind the firing men and women, getting ready to charge into the oncoming army head on.

"Now!" I threw up my sword signaling my readied forces to attack.

We all sprang from the trees on my order. My army jumping out firing off what they could without hurting friendly scattered forces as we emerged from the trees. I grit my teeth as I charged with my sword ready towards them. The ground shook from the army following behind me, and the army in front of me.

Bullets bounced off of my armor and whizzed past my head as I leapt from the tree line with my shoulder down. I went straight into the oncoming soldiers, running through the clearing until I could finally cut into them with my blade.

I tore through them throwing men around and smashing through their armor with my hydraulic power. As they surrounded me, I was forced to rely on my power armor to stop their bullets and blades as I swung, screaming and smashing in a blur of rage and adrenaline, "I'll kill you all!"

A blade nicked an unprotected section of my arm, and my arm began to feel wet inside my armor. I couldn't feel any pain. I was numb with rage slashing and tearing into the armor of Wellington's men, the bodies piling up around me as I slashed and hacked.

My men formed a scattered wall a ways behind me, and charged in unison to meet the oncoming forces head on. Just as Wellington's army had been, my army was pouring out of the trees. I could see casualties for both sides, but the flags of Wellington's army fell as their carriers fell into their own blood lying on the flags below them.

With the angry bedlam around me I just swung and charged, hurting as many people as I could. A bullet tore through my shoulder through a weak spot in the armor, and an endless stream of blades nicked my flesh. . I was ignoring my wounds with no regard. I was too enraged, all of my frustration and pent up stress from the crazy days in the past going into every stroke of blood as my blade swung using raw force to smash through every mark of Wellington I saw.

I knew we could not win, and my wounds kept increasing as men snuck in desperate slashes and shots at my weak spots. My armor was wearing out slowly from the constant abuse and hits against it. I told myself I didn't care, if I died it was because I was a fool and lost the one person who took care of me. The one person that mattered to me the most.

I slashed and smashed, dropping my sword as it eventually shattered and broke. I changed to my fists punching and tearing men off their feet throwing them around. The bodies were countlessly piling around me like I was laying down sandbags.

I picked up another sword, and as I bent over the armor malfunctioned and locked up as a sword cut a power line in my back. I ripped off the armor piece by piece throwing it at the surrounding men keeping them at bay slowly growing desperate. Without my armor I was nothing.

I was cornered, running out of armor pieces to throw, and on perfect timing an armored horse came charging through the men around me knocking most of them to the ground. A hand swept me up onto the back of the horse, and I realized my savior was Danny. He let go of me to take the reins, and his other hand was swinging skillfully with his sword as he rode. The single slash tore through three men as the horse charged, "You started without me, my lord? How rude!"

What was left of Nate's cavalry had arrived in the distance along the dirt road, his colorful banners and men on horseback spreading out and colliding into the enemy from the rear.

Danny and I rode through the chaos, the horse's hooves thundering below us, knocking men off their feet as Danny deflected their blows taking me back to regroup with my battling men near the tree line.

With Nate's cavalry arriving, tearing into them, it seemed like we had the advantage. However my hope for an advantage didn't last long, for Wellington gave an order and his powerful cavalry came thundering through the trees. The line of armored men on horses running over and knocking down their own allied foot soldiers as they charged, hundreds of men on horseback at the rear of the massive army.

"Danny," I growled, "Turn around! Let's get through that line as fast as we can. Let's find Wellington and end this!"

We got to a momentarily safe position surrounded by allied soldiers, "It looks like I got here just in time my lord!"

He pulled hard on the reins turning around the excited and edgy horse, "Sounds Crazy! Let's go *towards* the oncoming army of Cavalry!" He spun the horse around and we galloped through the men once again. When the men around us turned to enemy, we were blocking their desperate attempts at hitting Danny's horse with their various weapons. They desperately tried to knock us down, but the horse's armor also creating a damage threshold that truly helped now that it mattered.

"Did you see Birdy?" I asked loudly, "Is she almost here?"

Danny shook his head, "No! Ella's estate is on the other side of the city, I don't think we can count on their help any time soon. I don't think they can get here in time. Lord Osburn was ready to go at a moment's notice. The reason it took us so long was there was a complication with Anna Bee's equipment. We got it figured out, she is okay my lord."

"As for Ella, she will have to organize things to get rolling. Even if she was ready like lord Osburn it would take three hours to march her army through the town just to get here, where it takes half an hour for Lord Osburn. He has his entire army coming, the Calvary just got here first, with me leading them!"

Danny's attention quickly transferred to the oncoming line of cavalry approaching us.

We went passed the first wave of horses squeezing between two armored riders narrowly, and Danny swung his sword, clothes lining one of the men off his horse. The man fell off the back of his horse with a scream of pain, and before he even hit the ground we were colliding with the second line of cavalry going between the galloping men and stopping their blades.

I could see the end of Wellington's massive army as it came through the trees, and right behind the army, I could see the rat himself. Wellington was sitting on his horse at the rear watching the battle with a smug grin; a wall of his knights on horseback in front protecting him.

"There!" I pointed, "That's him Danny, Wellington is over there! Let's go! Let's cut off the head of the snake!"

Danny kicked the horse's sides, and we began galloping full speed through a brief clearing of rubble. Danny's horse jumped off a still smoking section of concrete wall and bloody mangled bodies, and came down in the bloody grass.

It truly looked like a war zone, the bodies of hundreds of men lying around what used to be my estate, buried under debris, or lying screaming for help in the smoking grass around us. It was so scarring and terrible that I kept my full attention on Wellington.

Wellington did not care. Hundreds of his men were slaughtered and he was smiling. His smile did however fade away as he noticed Danny and I charging through the chaos straight at him.

He motioned to his knights and pointed at us and the men tightened up forming a wall drawing their weapons. Some of them drew pistols, some drew swords, and some even drew long sharpened spears.

We rammed into the knights without any hesitation or slowing down. Danny blocked a spear with his sword, and my ears rung from the close range pistols firing around us.

I leapt off the back of Danny's armored horse through the opening Danny had gave me. The momentum sent me flying with arms outstretched towards Wellington himself. He swung his sharp sword at me, missing me by striking too fast in his haste, and I slammed into him knocking him off his horse and we rolled through the grass.

He was well trained, shoving me off and leaping to his feet, "Lord Zander, you fool!"

He smirked lowering his gaze, "Have you come to admit defeat?" his knights stayed back from charging me as Wellington held out his hand to them confidently.

With their full attention on me, Danny slinked away from their line trying to flank Wellington. Two of the knights noticed this, and spun taking off to engage Danny, tying him up in combat.

Lord Wellington circled me with a grin, "You have no estate, and your army is getting destroyed. In fact you've helped me destroy two enemies this day! Osburn's estate will fall *next* for this declaration of war against me!"

"No," I shook my head reaching into my suit pocket, "I came to give you this." I pulled Mandy's power core from my faded and bloody pocket. I had kept the warm power core for memory's sake, and it had been in my suit pocket all along. It was the only weapon I had, and I thought it suited the situation pretty well.

"What?" He seemed confused, "Is this an act of peace? A present given as a surrender?"

"No," I shook my head and ripped off the casing with angry strength and ripped out sparking wires, throwing it at him as hard as I could, "It's called *revenge*."

It rolled to his feet and he smirked at me, "What was that supposed to be."

The core exploded with a blinding flash smashing shrapnel against his armor and ripping him off his feet and sending him flying backwards through the brush.

Then the knights in a panic lunged at me on their horses, digging their heels into their restless horse's sides charging at me.

I dove to the ground desperately. Their hooves shook the ground around me narrowly missing me as I rolled left and right desperately trying to avoid the razor sharp hooves.

Another lone rider came from the trees behind me with a long black and blue hood. Like she had been waiting for a cue, Birdy came bounding through the tree line. She was holding her two rust free colt 1911 pistols, their barrels smoking. Birdy cut a path through the knights, bullets ripping through their armor and knocking them off their horses.

In the blink of an eye she swung off the side of her saddle and hooked me with her elbow. She pulled me onto the back of her horse, and she threw up the pistols skillfully reloading them in midair. She began blasting accurately at the cavalry's backs in the distance as we rode towards them. Danny was freed by the speed and accuracy of Birdy's pistols as well, and rode behind us drawing his bow off his back notching an arrow from his quiver as we rode towards the rear of the enemy cavalry.

"Sup, my lord. Ella's on her way, I rode ahead," Birdy told me turning back to me, "We just need to last long enough for her to get here! It looks like I was a bit too late though, I was *really* hoping to get Wellington! I saw him limping away into the trees, but I decided you needed a pick me up."

I began to lose my strength, blood dripping steadily off my fingers to the grass.

"Sorry," I said faintly, "I know you wanted him..." I looked down for a moment to see how beat up I was as my vision blurred. I could not believe the damage, I looked even worse than Anna Bee, covered in blood and bullet holes as well as sword nicks and cuts, and then losing my strength I fell off the back of horse. I watched Birdy pull hard on her horse's reigns, and behind me Danny hopped off his horse yelling something.

As things faded, I took one last look at the bodies and chaos around me, and slowly, it went black.

I sat up feeling weak, my body lying bandaged on a comfortable cushion. I was in the back of the box truck lying in an infirmary bed next to Anna Bee. My hand was out reached towards Anna Bee's bed and was on Anna Bee's hand. It looked like I had subconsciously reached for her while I was out.

The doctor turned from looking at his clipboard as I stirred, "You are awake, my lord!"

"Take it easy," he said coming towards me, and he called out, "He's pulled through! Everyone, he's awake!"

The seats had been unbolted to make room for me. My body was hooked up to the same machines as Anna Bee beside me, our hands still touching.

I used what little strength I had to re-grip her hand to make sure I didn't let go. I turned and asked as multiple familiar faces climbed into the back of the truck, "W-what happened?"

"Well if it wasn't for this electricity, you would be dead," the doctor said with a grin motioning to the truck.

"We won the battle," Birdy said, her arm was in a sling. Danny bowed and nodded.

"My forces arrived faster than I expected, we were *really* trying to hurry. When we arrived I found a handful of people defending a body from what was left of Wellington's army," Ella Lovewind poked her head into the truck and motioned to Lord Osburn and his bandaged knights who knelt before me. Lord Osburn bowed to me, then she motioned to Birdy and Danny and smiled at me, "You were the body lying on the ground."

"We won," I asked? "Wellington got away? What happened?"

Birdy winked at me with a smile and a thumbs up, "I found him hiding in the trees like he was waiting for his men to come rescue him. What I did to him isn't really important details, but I assure you, I... he's not a problem anymore."

"Yours and Lord Osburn's forces really had Wellington's army on the ropes. I don't know how you did it, but when I arrived, I felt more like a clean-up crew. Sure there was a couple left, but they surrendered as we surrounded them. Meanwhile, Lord Osburn and those who defended you brought you to Lord Osburn's domain. We thought you would die. You've been out for a couple days, and you were in pretty grim shape, so we figured you would want to pass away by her side... *if* you did die of course," She sweetly motioned to Anna Bee.

"Anna Bee," I said my body weak, "How long has it been, is Anna Bee okay?" I turned my head and my heart was immediately warmed as I saw her awake and hiding behind her bangs.

"At least three or four days," Lord Osburn said scratching his head in, "You can build another turbine-reactor thing like that right? You know since you blew yours up? You still are going to help me bring my people power right?"

Anna Bee smiled at me with an exhausted gaze, "Y-you're okay?"

All I could see was Anna Bee. All I could hear in that moment was her quiet steady breathing. I had never appreciated such a simple sound so much, "Yeah, and I'm glad you are."

"I missed fireworks?" Anna Bee frowned and then it slowly turned into a smile, "There was an explosion? What happened?"

"Fireworks?" Danny asked, "Everything is gone. The estate the, the couch..." His voice trailed off, "...I kind of hoped I would get to see the explosion too. I only heard it."

"Anna Bee," I said, "I'm so glad you are okay."

I just stared. My hand in hers, tears of joy stinging my cheeks staring in complete shaken disbelief.

Her blue eyes smiled, staring at me, "You don't have to ask me, I was never going to leave, my lord... and if we are going to throw balls every month... can we have a disco ball?"

-Six Months later-

The live music was loud, the disco ball spinning on the ceiling streaming colorful light all over the ballroom of Harmony Castle. There was hundreds of guests in fine clothing swirling around me to the music. Ella Lovewind and her husband laughed and danced within my line of sight, and Lord Osburn danced with his newly wedded wife Sarah only a few steps away from them.

Danny was walking through the crowds in a hand sewn tuxedo he purchased just for the event his eyes carefully sweeping left and right. On his back was a flowing cape with the insignia of the Machine Lord that he wore proudly as my knight, and he loyally patrolled watching for security threats.

He was especially on alert because the men and women in white robes had been once again been spotted yesterday near Ella's estate, and I had forces lead by Alek investigating the matter. I tried not to put too much thought into it, but they still had not returned. I told myself they had only been gone one day, and I told myself they would be back any moment to let me know what was going on.

I stood there with a glass of cherry punch created by Terry a couple hours ago in preparation for the celebratory ball. It was a ball to celebrate, and I was happy with everything around me. My new towering castle was under construction by service and soldier drones, being built almost twenty-four seven. Even Buster was out there helping. I could feel the ground shake every once in a while, which meant he was walking by outside the massive ballroom.

I thought that I had lost Buster, but to my surprise he was repairable. His armor had been so thick, that it was an electrical malfunction that brought him down, not the grenades thrown at his joints. After some new wiring and a new core, Buster sprang right back up. He was the one who lifted up the disco ball a couple weeks ago. The disco ball was Anna Bee's idea, my idea was to actually make it light up.

Anna Bee sat beside me in her wheel chair. She was wearing a flowery green dress she had made herself for the event. She looked beautiful, and the live music and magical lights around us made her cling to my arm with excitement as she looked around. It took me six months, but I had gotten used to the wheel chair, and even though it limited her abilities she still tried her hardest.

I was just happy she was alive, this castle, this ball, and everything I did was for her.

The ball was supposed to be for the celebration of the unification of three domains, and the electricity flowing to the entire city of wellington. With Jazz Wellington gone, I absorbed his domain and his servants, who all fell in love with my estate and my ways.

Lord Osburn gave up his title of Lord, and his domain was also added to my own. He sacrificed his title for more power, becoming my trusted advisor and commanding general of the combined army of all three domains.

Wellington was in a state of peace. The other Lords were either in debt to me for the electricity, or just plain my friend. Ella Lovewind made the best pies, and she always brought one when she visited. Lord Alysha Collinder was a clever woman who feared my power, but I still watched her carefully anyway.

"As you requested, My Lord," Tony pushed through the crowd with my sword and handed to me.

"Thank you, Tony," I smiled, "Now retrieve Birdy for me, Would you?"

"Of course," he bowed and headed off, "We'll be back shortly."

Tony was the blue robot that I had created for Skylar, and I activated him when I pulled him from the wreckage. He was as smart lipped and as fun as Mandy was. I figured it was because he was a modified version of Mandy's AI, and in my heart he felt like the reincarnation of her because of it.

In the last six months, Tony slowly weaseled his way into everyone's hearts. My servants regularly invited him to aid them in their projects, and he always happily tagged along. He could never be Mandy, but he was the perfect fitting patch for the hole in all of our hearts.

"Are you ready?" Anna Bee asked nervously, "She has no idea this is happening."

"Birdy deserves it," I nodded, "She really does it, and I should have done it sooner."

"It's perfect," Anna Bee leaned up and kissed me on the cheek, "Really, it is. She would want it to be a big spectacle."

"Are you having fun?" I asked Anna Bee who lit up brighter than the disco ball for a moment.

"It is better than I could have imagined," she smiled, "It is truly a celebration worth remembering."

"Would you like to know the real reason I threw this ball?" I asked her and she looked a bit confused, "It's not to celebrate the finished power grid?"

"No," I smiled, "It's for you."

She pursed her lips and a happy tear stung her cheek, "Really?"

I touched my finger to my lips, "Don't tell anybody though. It's our little secret."

"Secret's don't make friends," Birdy stood there with an interjecting smile, "You wanted me Zander? What did I do this time?"

Tony walked up behind her, his hands behind his back. Tony had learned to do that by following Anna Bees example, and he has done it ever since.

I motioned to my sword, "Go down on one knee, Birdy."

Birdy looked confused, "Dude you are freaking me out... Is this an execution?"

I motioned for her to go down and I motioned for the band to stop.

She went down, and the crowd all turned to face us with smiling and content faces.

"Birdy," I said proudly, "You have fought for me when I needed you. You have showed up in the nick of time to bale me out. Because of you, I do not fear the monsters I once did," I drew my sword from the sheath like I rehearsed with Anna Bee a hundred times.

Birdy's eyes lit up "Like for real? This is happening?"

I extended the dull end of the blade to her left shoulder, and then her right.

"Birdy, I did not know what to expect when I accepted you as my blade. You have proven yourself time and time again, and now you will rise as my knight. This time I will know what to expect from a loyal knight. Birdy will you rise and accept the title I offer you?" I asked proudly, and because of the happy tears in her eyes I began to shed a tear or two as well.

"I will!" Birdy rose to her feet, and then the crowd around us all exploded into applause.

"I am so honored... I will never wrong you Zander," Birdy shook, her fist on her heart and she bowed low, "Thank you, Zander." She then did something I had never expected out of Birdy. She took a step forward and gave me a hug.

I hugged her back and the crowd laughed happily. Birdy quickly looked at Anna Bee and took a step back surprised.

There was a sudden gasp and urgency among the crowd, and my eyes cut through the crowd to find the source. Was it an attack? An assassination?

A blur to my left caught my attention, and I turned to see Anna Bee carefully getting out of her wheel chair.

"Hey! Careful," I rushed to put her back in and she smiled, "It's okay. I wanted to surprise you."

"With what?" I asked cautiously, "Please Anna Bee. Be careful."

"Birdy said that you would be too much of a sissy to do it," Anna Bee blushed and grew nervous, but then gently pushed me away and stood on her feet.

The audience exploded with celebration, and Anna Bee dropped onto one knee.

"Anna Bee..." I was in shock at what I was seeing, "The doctor said you would never walk again... Anna Bee what are you doing? I can't make you my knight..."

Birdy slapped me on the back of the head, "No stupid. She has a question for you."

Anna Bee produced a hand forged Silver ring from her dress and looked up at me scared, "My lord... Will you marry me?"

My heart skipped a beat, and a single tear fell from my cheek to the ballroom floor, "Of course, Anna Bee."

The End

74037955R00185

Made in the USA
Columbia, SC
23 July 2017